New and Selected Stories, 1959–1989

Other books by Charles Edward Eaton

Poetry
The Bright Plain
The Shadow of the Swimmer
The Greenhouse in the Garden
Countermoves
On the Edge of the Knife
The Man in the Green Chair
Colophon of the Rover
The Thing King
The Work of the Wrench
New and Selected Poems, 1942–1987

Short Stories
Write Me from Rio
The Girl from Ipanema
The Case of the Missing Photographs

Critical Biography
Karl Knaths: Five Decades of Painting

New and Selected Stories, 1959–1989

Charles Edward Eaton

Cornwall Books
New York • London • Toronto

Cornwall Books
440 Forsgate Drive
Cranbury, NJ 08512

Cornwall Books
25 Sicilian Avenue
London WC1A 2QH, England

Cornwall Books
P.O. Box 488, Port Credit
Mississauga, Ontario
Canada L5G 4M2

The paper used in this publication meets the requirements of the American National Standard for Permanence of Paper for Printed Library Materials Z39.48-1984.

Library of Congress Cataloging-in-Publication Data

Eaton, Charles Edward, 1916–
    New and selected stories, 1959–1989.

    I. Title.
PS3509.A818N43   1989   813'.54   88-47807
ISBN 0-8453-4821-3 (alk. paper)

To Isabel

Contents

8 CONTENTS

Acknowledgments

Arizona Quarterly: "Death Is Sometimes a Lover."

Epoch (Cornell University): "The Motion of Forgetfulness is Slow" and "A Chariot of Fire."

Folio: "Boat with an Eye of Glass."

Kansas Quarterly: "Daughter of a Poet" and "The Caryatid."

The Malahat Review (Canada): "The Faun."

The Northern Review (Canada): "The White Queen."

Pembroke Magazine: "The Rival."

Prairie Schooner: "A Passion for Emeralds."

Quarterly Review of Literature: "The Leech in the Chinese Rain Hat."

Sewanee Review: "The Case of the Missing Photographs."

Southwest Review: "The Ugly Duckling," "The Edge of the Fountain," "Skunk in the Skimmer," "The Lady in the Lavender House," "The Secret of Aaron Blood," "The Naked Swimmer," "The Hidalgo," "Saint Cecilia's Son," "A Prince in His Time."

University of Kansas City Review: "The Girl from Ipanema."

Works: "Connecticut Cowboy."

Also, "The Motion of Forgetfulness is Slow" was reprinted in *Best American Short Stories of 1952,* edited by Martha Foley (Houghton Mifflin). It was subsequently translated into Swedish and appeared in *Darmernas Varld* (Stockholm), into Portuguese and published in *Senhor* (Brazil). It was included in *Stories from Epoch: The First Fifty Issues (1947–1964)* (Cornell University Press, 1966).

"The Case of the Missing Photographs" was included in *Prize Stories 1972: The O. Henry Awards* (Doubleday).

"The Caryatid" won a *Kansas City Quarterly* Award for the short story in 1987.

New and Selected Stories,
1959–1989

I. From *Write Me from Rio* (1959)
and
The Girl from Ipanema (1972)

Death Is Sometimes a Lover

Winter weather in Rio is mild and flawless. The days of June, July, and August follow each other in unbroken clarity. The sun at noon, too harsh in summer, is just right for swimming or lying on the beach, and the nights cool to a pleasant dry chill. Otherwise, there is no winter. Flowers are everywhere, and the night winds bring into the bedroom their scent, lush and poignant, mingled with the smell of the undergrowth that lies sealed in the morning calm. Along the *avenidas,* the *gran fina* women, gay and over-dressed, looking themselves like flowers, carry eternal summer in their flamboyant hats. Walking through the windy corridor of a fashionable apartment house on the beach, one catches a glimpse of the opulent blue water through the front entrance, and it is neither summer nor winter, but forever.

On a morning of such weather, Alan Ferrell was finishing a leisurely breakfast of orange-fleshed papaya, crisp white rolls, and strong coffee. From the terrace of the hotel where he sat, he watched the thick color of the waves thin to aquamarine and break gold as they caught the sun at the shore line. In an hour or so the beach would be noisy with the voices of swimmers, but now he heard only the inhuman cry of the gulls, no more distracting than the sound of the waves. His physical sensations, like the morning, were smooth and serene, and there was not a mote of unrest in his carefully controlled good humor.

The reasons for his satisfaction and sense of well-being were many. At thirty he was one of the most promising young diplomats in the Embassy, good-looking, fine-mannered, perfectly tailored. The Ambassador, a clever veteran of thirty years service, had taken a liking to him, admiring, perhaps, the reflection of his own ambitious youth. Moreover, he lived at the best hotel on the Copacabana and was well appreciated there for his position of importance in the Embassy and his air of confident elegance. There was no doubt that he was cut out for what he was doing. If he could have held a mirror up to his ruddy face with the blue eyes and dark brown hair, he would have caught himself smiling at his good fortune. Though it was an early hour of the morning for philosophizing, he had cultivated a rather elaborate manner of communing with himself and a remark attributed to Talleyrand passed through his mind: "Fate cannot touch me. I have dined." That, along with "So far, so good," expressed two of his favorite attitudes, for he liked to remind himself that he had shared generously in the good things of the world. Nothing was better for the body, if not for the soul, than an amiable pat on the back of the only pretender to the throne of one's well-being.

As he finished his coffee, he thought over the affairs of the day in an orderly and untroubled manner: some business at the Foreign Office in the morning, lunch with the French Vice Consul, a lazy afternoon in his office, tea with Dona Gina, dinner and dancing at a nightclub. He would ask Livia to go with him to the club. She was an excellent samba dancer and always attracted attention with her blonde hair, white skin, and blue eyes, her gown of a striking color, blue, flame, or gold, and the long dramatic evening cape. She was from an old Carioca family, and it was important to be seen with her. But, more than that, she was one of the pleasantest things in his life now, swinging in his hand as easily as a censer with which he perfumed the atmosphere. She was never difficult, she never brought him any displeasure, not even what the French called *"un mauvais quart d'heure."*

The waiter was solicitous as usual, ready to pour more coffee, but, waving him away, Ferrell was preparing to leave when he heard a scream, quick and sharp, near at hand, followed by a sickening, thumping noise like the dropping of a huge melon to the ground. He paused in irritation. It was similar to the sensation he would have felt if the waiter, whose dexterity and deference were faultless, had dropped a dish in front of him.

There were other cries, high and feminine, and when he turned toward the *avenida* that skirted the side of the hotel, he saw people moving from several directions in quick jerky strings, drawn to a central knot. No one screamed again, but an excited murmur arose, louder in proportion to the steadily increasing crowd.

The waiter, who had gone to the far end of the terrace, listened a moment and returned with a smile, deprecatory, almost contemptuous.

"Nada, Senhor," he said. "Absolutely *nada. Não importa.* A crazy *empregada* jumped from a balcony. Nothing but a lunatic, *com certeza.* Good riddance."

Empregada, Ferrell thought, probably a maid from one of the swank apartment houses along the *avenida.* He saw many of them in the streets every day, Negroes and mestizos for the most part, usually balancing a bundle of clothes or a basket of fruit and vegetables on their heads. In their loosely fitting dresses they walked with soft undulance, and, in contrast to the flowerlike society women, made one think of limber, swaying trees. They met the eyes of passersby with the timid apprehensiveness of those to whom uncertainty is constant. He had sometimes wondered in a disinterested way how they managed to live on the ten dollars a month they were generally paid.

As he went down the terrace toward the garage where his car was kept, he noticed that the tight circle of the crowd had broken at one end into a narrow irregular opening. Crossing the street, he saw a squat, heavy-featured, dark-haired woman pushing her way to the center. She wore a soiled, expensive-looking, pink morning robe, and her eyes, puffy with sleep, blinked crossly and belligerently. She seemed resentful of the crowd, as though only her right to be there were indisputable, and Ferrell guessed that she was the mistress of the servant girl.

Before the gap made by her bulky form began to close, he looked through a focus of crowding flesh into the heart of the circle. A Negro girl lay on the smooth mosaic of the tiled walk. Someone had turned her over, and she was stretched on her back, arms flung out, in the shape of a cross. Her eyes were closed, and the eyelids, where the light fell, were faintly luminous in contrast to the broad planes of the cheeks, giving her face a look of sleeping softness. Her lips were loosely parted, and their fullness looked rumpled and bruised, the only part of her body suggesting violence. The formless, faded blue dress, bulging slightly at the breasts, just covered her knees and stressed essential nakedness.

Everyone wanted to take a look, and they crowded around Ferrell, the women nudging him with their damp, puffy arms, now and then the angular thrust of a man's elbow like a secret, bony, little bludgeon, clearing the way for another mass of soft, feminine, cheaply scented flesh. The stuff of human life was around him very rankly. He had never liked the herding instinct; there had always been something unpleasant about animal-flow loaded heavily as it was with impulses of stampede. Though the earth gave a feeling of spaciousness, the outlets of society were ultimately small, and someone was inevitably trampled under. But so far, into the swelling estuary of the street, the human stream was feeding itself as though sure of the tumid capacity of its interest.

Ferrell had seen the dead only at funerals where every effort at disguise had been made. The rigid, painted features, the stiff attitude of the body were dehumanized, impersonal, and, to the distantly concerned, unconvincing. But mobility was not entirely spent from the face of the *empregada,* and it was in the shock of death where life lingered faintly, not quite jolted from the body, that terror lay. Ferrell felt like shuddering.

And yet what rot all of this was, how intellectually unacceptable. He must have had too much to drink last night to be so balmy. Ever since the death of his mother to whom he had been passionately attached he had hated any sentimentalization about death. Whenever he remembered T. S. Eliot's little jingle: "That's all the facts when you come to brass tacks: birth, copulation, and death," he always thought the first two "facts" were right to the point, especially the second. Actually what he liked most about making love was that it distended him with the here and now. He could never understand why some of his girls whimpered and cried at the moment of climax. And one of them, now that he thought of it, one of the nicest, had said that "love was a little death," and she had always taken him into her arms as if he were some dark avenging angel who had come to overpower her. Sometimes after they had rested and he wanted to make love again, she would not let him and would not even touch him as if some destructive emanation arose from his flesh. Well, women could be such fools anyway. And the good girls, the nicest ones, were sometimes the worst. They did not know that you simply had to go as far as you could with life, avoid entanglements, fatal conclusions, and handle things with an imperial hand. Half of the troubles that were supposed to have piled out of Pandora's box could be cured by good grooming, and this, as he understood it, was a mental as well as a physical concept meaning fastidious care in every detail of living. He agreed entirely with the judge who sentenced a group of juvenile delinquents to a haircut, a bath, and some clean clothes.

Moreover, he had been able to put this figure of himself across among his friends and acquaintances, this image of a white knight in a spotless, linen suit, except now and then of late, as just now, he had been aware of a kind of emotional seepage. That was the trouble with the emotions in the end. They threatened you with recalcitrance. You wanted to feel like a prince and you ended up feeling like a tramp. Or you found yourself for no good reason leaving the terrace of the Copacabana Palace to stand in a noose of filthy strangers and gawk at a dead servant girl.

All around him he could still feel the human kneading process which he had always so disliked. He did not wish to be pressed or stirred into anything against his will, and yet the crowd, rough and gentle, continued to push in, swaying and rippling the uneven circle. But there was a distance beyond which none of them would go, stepping back when shoved from behind as though the space around the body were a perilous element. The rough ones, some young and brightly arrogant, others old and bitter of expression, looked on unmoved but with curious, all-seeing eyes. A few young girls were weeping and repeating in a kind of chanting bewilderment, "*Coitada, coitada,* poor thing, poor thing." One of them stopped crying long enough to take out a mirror and adjust her make-up, frowning a little at the streaks of dissolution the tears had left on her cheeks.

The raucous voice of the disheveled woman in the pink morning robe rose above the jumble of excitement and murmuring. "*Sim, Senhor,* that's my *empregada.* That's my Maria." Her tone was almost surly. "These *empregadas. Meu Deus, meu Deus.*"

A boy slipped unnoticed as a small animal through the crowd, tunneling haphazardly between the men and women. When he saw the pink morning robe, without looking up, he clutched at it in recognition. Leaning his thin frame against the heavy corpulence of his mother, he curled his hand, fragile and leaflike, into a fold of the robe. He must have been about seven years old, but his moist dark eyes and large feminine mouth, hectic with a sensuousness his delicate body seemed unable to support, made him look older.

"Look, *Mamãe,* Maria's sleeping." He spoke gently as though he had come across a lazy pet lying on the sidewalk. A tangle of people drew in closer, jutting around and above him like the mouth of a cave from which he was emerging.

"Hush, Antonio, hush," the mother said angrily. "Go upstairs." With a motion of her hip she shoved him from her side. Ferrell was conscious of a brushing against his legs, and, looking down, saw the boy recoil with apprehension and uncertainty and fumble past like a child in a forest. He was soon lost in the mingling folds of the shifting crowd.

"Here comes the police," a flashy little man carrying a briefcase said. Momentarily, the crowd drew quieter, awaiting the intruder. An officer uniformed in olive drab and wearing a white sun helmet came briskly up. The circle of eyes, uneasily and furtively or with cool unconcern, looked toward Antonio's mother who lost her composure and glanced nervously around. The policeman went directly toward her, and there was something pompous and ceremonious in the way he began to question her, as though death had invested his function with gravity and somber power.

Ferrell listened carefully, conscious of a feeling of pride that his Portuguese was so good that nothing could escape him. If this then was Eliot's final "fact," perhaps, for once, it would do no harm to take a good long look and get it over with. *See life steadily, and see it whole.* Perhaps the college prof had hit it right. The thought made him feel confident and superior again. His education had always served him thus.

But was it, in fact, only the knowledge of death that attracted? Wasn't it also that this was the end-product of something else? This poor primitive woman had risen to what for her was an enormous height of some sort or other in contradiction to everything she was otherwise: weak, retarded, half-civilized. He thought of Livia, exquisite girl who was so easy to take. Thank God, she would never be capable of anything like this. There never would be anything anyone could do which would dislodge her from the summit on which she was born. She had almost an eternal quality in the world of change. There was something comforting about that. It relieved one of any future neccessity for feeling sorry.

The eyes of Antonio's mother, a Senhora Natal, glinted with excitement now, and she gesticulated rapidly, the querulous sleepiness driven from her face. If someone tied her hands behind her, Ferrell thought, she wouldn't be able to talk at all. Under the shadow of the helmet, the sharp Indian features of the policeman were impassive. He was thin and wiry, and his rigid manner was like a blade leaning into her loose coherence.

"*Sim, Senhor,* there, there," she said, pointing to the balcony of one of the apartments. "From the tenth floor. *Imagina.* Foolish girl, foolish girl. And on my Antonio's birthday too." Anger flickered across her face again.

Out of the copious flow of words that circled back upon themselves, Ferrell extracted the facts: *Age nineteen. Home, Villa Rica in the provinces. Father and mother dead. Worked two years in Rio. In love? Yes, of course, in love. What else? That was it. Jilted. A big idler named Henrique. Foolish girl. Foolish girl.* Somehow the tone remained, and the words reverberating in his mind had the sound of Senhora Natal's voice, shrill and tense, and not like his own at all, a resonance that was faintly disturbing.

He looked down at the body of Maria, the corpse now having taken on a name. All maids, he reflected, seemed to be Maria this or Maria that. An ambulance had been called, but the service was

slow. It might not arrive for an hour. At home the ambulance
would have come in a white rush as though nothing were more
important to conceal than death. The attendants working rapidly
and deftly would remove the body, and the ambulance would
shoot through the channel of stopped traffic, out of sight in an
instant, leaving hardly a superficial incision in the emotions of the
crowd. But here there was no hurry about death. They let it sink
slowly into consciousness. Even the brutal and unfeeling knew it
was there.

This was a scene he would like for some of his friends back in
the States to see. It might cure them of the notion that Brazil was
just a sunny land where Carmen Mirandas went around wriggling
their bottoms. As a matter of fact, there was a heavy, viscous
melancholy in these people which manifested itself in a morbid
preoccupation with the dead. There was even a national holiday
called *Dia dos Mortos*—Day of the Dead—when the whole family
spent the good part of a day at the cemetery in an absolute orgy of
doleful thoughts. It was a sort of unacknowledged holiday at the
Embassy too since little could be accomplished, and when he
drove by the cemetery on his way home he had wished for a
modern Goya to do justice to it. In the first place, a dark race
should never wear black and that, coupled with the veils the
women wore, would have made the Via Dolorosa look like a street
during Carnival. It was about then, he supposed, he had really
begun to dislike the masses of Brazilians. When he got home, he
went out on the town and had himself a good lay.

Well, he could always try that palliative again, he thought. No
one around him made a move to leave, as though it were felt in the
queer emptiness of finality that something might be missed if the
back were turned. The more restless wandered from place to
place, jostling against him. Several delivery men edged to the
inner circle. They had coarse features, and their thick, black,
greasy hair, large hands, and wide, bare feet made them seem
burdened with their own animality. Anyone of them might have
been Maria's.

*A big loafer named Henrique. Always coming up the back way. Always
taking money. Always quarreling. Maria weeping in the morning, dragging around half-dead. Foolish girl, foolish girl.* The words kept coming back. Ferrell looked at Senhora Natal and was almost startled
to see that she had stopped talking. She was moving, the first to
leave, and as she passed, he saw that the look of disgruntled
intrusion was still on her face. The policeman swung his stick and
the heavy solidarity of the crowd wavered.

Ferrell glanced at his watch. It was nearly ten o'clock. The Old Man would be expecting him at the Embassy soon. He always went in for a talk before going to his own desk. Never openly, but tacitly, the Ambassador demanded it. It was one of the many little attentions that were the price of his favor. But Ferrell did not really object, liking to think that this compliance insured the strength of numerous secret bonds, forming a kind of subtle conspiracy between them. The Old Man was all right even if he could be a bit grumpy and fussy on off days. The Department regarded him as a diplomat of the old school, one of their smoothest trouble shooters. He never slipped up, never bungled. Ferrell liked to think of him as secure and enduring in the hard hermetic power of his life.

Everyone was dry-eyed and coolly observant, he noticed, except a huddle of three *empregadas* who were still whimpering. They might have been friends or merely members of a common station of life, but, in any case, they would not be cheated of the chance for a releasing flow of tears. They would stay there, he thought, until the merely curious had left, tending the body with a kind of ritual sorrow.

He looked away from the circle of people down the street to the white curve of the beach, the tranquil dark blue of the sea and the cloudless paler blue of the sky. There was the other side of feeling. There was the unhurt, unblemished richness of the earth. He would be driving along the beach in a moment, he told himself, out of this strangely slowed down, stretched out action of time into the invulnerability and confident quick pace of other concerns.

He was rather ashamed that he had loitered in the crowd at all. He had been acting like a native. A light sweat had formed on his brow, and there was a sense of physical straining in him as if his blood were having a hard time pumping itself up from a greater depth than he had ever imagined his body had. The heat had begun to make him feel a little sick and reminded him again how encroaching and disintegrating the climate was, even at this time of year, if you stood around too long in the sun.

The hell of it was too that now he would be late for work and miss the Old Man's blessing. He desperately wanted to expunge the entire morning from his mind, and yet here he was peeling off emotionally as though his white suit concealed a leper. For one foolish moment he thought he would simply start crying without knowing why. He felt strangely dark in the light, as if one of the tawdry girls had approached him and he had responded, but, for some utterly irrational reason, had been repulsed. He might have been a large figure of black wax set in the sun to melt. With a great effort of will he rescued this darkness and inclosed it in himself as if against all further exhumation.

Why, in fact, should a violent incident on a street in Rio be any more "real" than what he had believed all his life? The modern world was morbidly attached to extreme situations and suggested that no other kind of experience was authentic. And yet, today, the moment he asked these pertinent questions and summoned these comforting theories he felt like a statue keeping in a vast, chaotic untidiness by main force, or, if he let himself go for a moment, out tumbled the images of darkness as if something were determined there should be two idols in the sun. This wretched girl who had dropped like an overripe fruit literally within earshot had shaken him unduly. If he had believed in omens, this might have been one, as though the tree of life, reminding him that he still walked underneath its boughs, let fall an unexpected charge, smiting its concussion into his abstract blood.

As he looked toward the circle again, one of the *empregadas* lit some small candles bought in a store nearby and encircled the body's cruciform. In the brilliant glare of the morning the tiny lights were dim and ghostly. The yellow reflections on the black flesh flickered, lucent and pliant, over the face, hands, and legs, as if those limbs, alone, might feel their heat.

When he could finally bring himself to leave, he did manage to make the meeting with the Old Man and got through the day somehow, remembering that Livia would be waiting for him that evening, tall and luminous. And when he met her in the penumbral hall of her ornate house, this is exactly what she reminded him of, a lamp in the form of a beautiful woman. Not many Brazilian women are naturally blonde, so perhaps those who are glow against one's unconscious sense of a race's composite darkness. Also, Livia was so totally, one might almost say *naturally,* artificial that one could not help thinking of her as an artifact of the most intricate design and expensive materials. Escorting her always had in it a trace of making a getaway with a treasure, for the whole world she lived in was like a carefully guarded museum.

She was dressed for dancing in yellow silk and a long white cape, but, for the first time, Ferrell did not fall into the comfortable acceptance of their elegant routine. He abruptly suggested that they take a ride along the *avenida* instead. She was surprised, glanced at him as if she were looking at another person, and readily accepted the idea.

It was a night for lovers, the kiss of the sea air clinging to one's lips, tinged with indefinable sadness. Around them the modern buildings loomed white and ironically old like the tombstones of the indiscretion and sorrow of a race that had tried to measure up to the landscape and failed. Along the curve of the bay where the streetlights glimmered, it seemed that some giant goddess, stricken in splendor, lay with only her necklace still shining, face down in a sea of passionate grief.

Ferrell took them in a roundabout way through a good part of the Copacabana, scrupulously avoiding the place where the servant girl had fallen. His gray Cadillac cruised through the liquid darkness like a shark in a tank as if he were hoping to find some outlet the city did not offer. Livia sat beside him, still the most luminous thing the night held, but now like a baroque lamp that was coming to life, for she talked in a more natural manner than he had ever known her to do. She seemed excited by the way he was prowling through the nocturnal secrets of Rio, and he realized that she was reacting rapidly to the fact that for once he had done something unpredictable.

He parked by the ocean and kissed her, putting a force into it he had never displayed before, but it wasn't enough. Suddenly he wanted to go all the way, not out of simple lust, but because he wanted to see what kind of an effect he would have on a girl like her. He asked her to go to his hotel, and, again looking at him as if he were laid bare of yet another layer of himself, she agreed.

When they got to his room, they undressed rapidly, and she never suggested by any arrogance in her behavior that girls of her class did not do this sort of thing as a rule. It was he who felt embarrassed and, in self-defense, relied upon his old techniques. With less preliminary than he would formerly have spent on getting her to kiss him, he began to make love violently without any allowances for her inexperience. If she were going to be surprised, he thought, he would surprise her all the way.

She did not resist him, and this both angered and excited him further, and the thrust of his hips became like a knife going in and out of her body. They were both exhausted when it was over, and she rolled away from him crying just like one of his ordinary girls, and he thought: This is all it is, this is all it is with anyone.

Since he did not want a hysterical female on his hands, he finally asked, "Are you all right?"

"Yes," she said quietly. "Now I am. But isn't that what I should say to you?"

"What do you mean?' he asked wearily, shifting his body which had always been so vigorously male but now seemed to have drained its seed into an infinite pool of darkness that surrounded them.

"I mean I had the feeling that you weren't here at all, that you had sent someone to make love in your stead. Someone you didn't even like."

"What a curious statement," he said and tried to stroke her again, feeling toward the little tawny shield of hair which he had been assaulting so roughly, but she pulled away and wrapped herself securely in the sheets.

"What is it that you are demanding of yourself?" she asked, and her voice softened.

"Would you believe it if I said I did not know?" he answered, and he felt like the oldest of gladiators who would be glad to unbuckle his sword forever. "I thought it was you. I have thought all along it was someone like you."

"Would you believe me if I said that I had hoped all along it was?"

"Why, why?" he asked as if it were the generalized question of his life.

"I am afraid no one can answer that but yourself." She spoke without a trace of rancor, dressed, and went down to get a taxi alone, and there was no more light in the room at all and no balustrade which would carry him up through the darkness to some landing to which she had returned like an illuminated figure.

All that remained was the immediacy of darkness, and the restless gestures of his naked body seemed merely to stir up its effluvia. Almost until dawn he watched the shadows which writhed and entwined like the bodies of men and women doing their *Totentanz* along the ceiling.

After dozing off fitfully, he awoke with the one thought that he would never see Livia again. A special door into the world of beauty and pleasure which he had always thought of as his stronghold was closed forever, and it made him wonder if all the entrances into his Brazilian paradise that had seemed gloriously open had not been fictively so. Life now seemed to be unequally divided between a *tableau vivant* which contained the enigmatic, the beautifully inert, and the immediate, violent, unreflective world where people dashed themselves into the streets below. And he was one of those "who walk between." Was that the truly condemning thing Livia had tried to imply? Had she been ready to step into any number of his private worlds if he could have persuaded her any one of them existed with some viable impulse?

He got up and put on his white linen like a suit of asbestos. It was another day full of altogether too much sunshine, and the white knight in him creaked and clanked. He went down to the terrace, ate his papaya, rolls, and coffee, and accepted the deference of the waiter who was like a dark shoehorn which might ease him into his usual life. As he smoked a cigarette, the gears almost began to mesh again, but not quite, so he got up to leave for the Embassy. At least the Old Idol would be sitting in his office, waiting to see him, and it would be up to him to animate those wily features into a parody of life.

It almost worked and would have if he had not mopped his face with last night's handkerchief, which had the little tribal marks of Livia's lipstick upon it and her lingering perfume. Instead of getting his car, he went irresistibly across the street to the place where the servant girl had lain. He looked for a stain where her body had been stretched out, but there was none, and there was not a trace of anything that had happened the day before. People were passing incuriously along the sidewalk until several took a slight interest in him since he seemed to be searching for something or someone, the look of an only survivor on his face. But appearances notwithstanding, the scene had not been eradicated. It was an ineluctable place. He had returned to a country within a country where he was also the only stranger. As he turned away, as it seemed to him now he had always been doing, a light wind stirred, and he heard the harsh dry sound of the clashing palms braided in jagged antiphony with the soft crying of girls. He looked up where the green fronds swirled near the wall of the apartment house. For a moment, the air around him swayed, and he felt that he was falling, not as in an elevator out of control, irresponsible and lost through impersonal mechanical destruction, but as the willful body, alone, can fall, unencased and sprawling in the air.

A Passion for Emeralds

"Mais um," the blonde young woman said loudly, shoving her beer mug toward a white-coated boy.

The little café on the first floor of the Metropole steamed with odors of *comida brasileira,* and it was incongruous to see almost nothing but Americans shouting bad Portuguese to the volatile waiters who skittered by. The food was poor but the beer excellent, and one didn't have to walk out into the summer sun since the Embassy annex was on the floors above.

It was certainly as far as Jim Walker wanted to go with the blonde who looked as though she would lard the streets of Rio if he risked taking her through the heat to one of the better restaurants. The Old Goat had asked him to invite her to lunch since this was her first morning in the office, and he had had to comply. He looked at her aloofly, with barely concealed distaste. What in the hell was she doing in Rio anyway? She was all that he loathed in a woman, big, boisterous, pugnacious-looking. At least five feet nine, she could have run interference on a football team, her shoulders humped high in a padding of fat. The arms were particularly repulsive, hanging down large and meaty from the short sleeves of her summer dress like etiolated hams.

But it was not only her size that repelled. She was otherwise outlandish-looking with her hair in bangs like a wig that concealed a balding head and pressed against her ears in weird, flat braids. Even more annoying was the fact that she was not all of a piece. He couldn't classify her as one more blowzy female on the loose and let it go at that, for there were touches in her dress, moments of decorum in her manner, a kind of glaze of superiority which suggested the lady. Her long, straight nose and short upper lip were patrician, and the blue eyes were those of a Hedda Gabler, arrogant even in laughter. But of one thing there could be no doubt. She was very much *there,* mythically American, conceived in the ponderous image of the Statue of Liberty.

Her prevalence was particularly discomforting, for Walker hated to be conspicuous, the object of even momentary ridicule, and he knew that they were quite a pair together. He was a formalist by nature, and this little scene promised to have all the disorder of "life itself," as people were so fond of saying. At thirty-four he had never married, but his very aloofness, his decontaminated quality, had brought a number of women his way. Lean, trim, and dark, wearing glasses over brown eyes, he was ascetically handsome, without the rich saturation in himself which good-looking men often possess. He and the blonde—incredibly enough, her name was Anna Covington Parker—were the "bones and flesh" of life, and it was the way she swelled dangerously near him and, by projection, around him, that he resented most. There she was on her third beer and the fruit cup not even finished! She must store it in her arms, he thought gruesomely.

When the boy set down her mug, she looked at it glowing in the sun like a chalice of her pleasure and said with obnoxious good spirits, "Well, this is the life, eh what, Mr. Walker? We couldn't do this back home, could we? Take an hour and a half and get looping at lunch. That's what I like about the tropics, the abandon. Nobody gives a damn."

"Really," he said dourly. Yes, she *was* going to be a trial. No wonder they had tossed her into Agriculture. He had heard by the grapevine that she had made them all sigh frostily over in Chancellery, and they had not quite known what to do with her. Someone had been requested for Cultural Relations, but who would have thought that State, hard up as it was for wartime personnel, would have sent down a Carnival queen. But she was to be kept in Rio rather than exiled to the provinces along with the other "accidents" the Department had made. In her case, there were connections. He remembered the piecemeal rumors now: two parents in *Who's Who,* a prominent Washington family, auras of the horsey crowd, a country place in Virginia. And she *was* a *cum laude* from Smith. That he knew from her papers.

"Yes," she went on, raising her mug, jangling a bracelet of heavy costume gold and green stones. "I simply decided it had to be Rio, and here I am. *Saúde!*" The toast came out like a burp, and Walker cringed, but she continued with opulent fluency. "I wish you'd tell me something about our work before we go back upstairs. You know, I don't know a damn thing about Agriculture. I came down for Cultural Relations, but there was a mix-up in my orders, I believe. I suppose you know I'm Administrative Assistant to Mr. Brown. Tell me, what's he like? Is he hard to get along with?"

This was incredible, Walker thought; she was already treating him like a confederate, an equal. It took the strong memory of the fact that he was Third Secretary and Vice-Consul and that she was only an aberration in the disordered soul of the Department to keep him in balance. Anyway, he could leave her to the Old Goat who was an intruder too, one of the Department's wartime collection, for it always took one to kill one. It would be fun to watch the fireworks, and, in answer to her question, he cleverly laid stepping stones that led straight into a bog, taking care that she would never be able to remember how she was sent astray. He made it sound like a honeymoon for a young lady who was not afraid to speak her mind, and she bubbled gratefully, calling for another beer, "a little sedative for the afternoon."

When lunch was over she had tossed her life to him in large chunks, and he was left not quite buried alive, grunting an occasional "Yes. No. Is that so?" It seemed that preparations for her job had been on an invasive scale. She had gone to see everybody who was anybody in Washington for briefing on the intricacies of diplomacy, and had enrolled in the Harvard Summer School for an intensive course in Portuguese until she could spit it out like glass in the mouth.

"If they think I'm going to be just a little ole secretary down here, they're crazy. You know, I can't even type, so I'll just have to work on policy and administration, won't I?" She winked wickedly. "Get it? Play dumb and let someone else push the wagon."

The rest of the afternoon was spent on Anna's settling in. Back in his office, Walker felt her presence throbbing against the walls portentously, and it appalled him that perhaps they would never seem strong enough again. And yet he could not resist opening the door to catch glimpses of her poking around into everything, "casing the joint." The secretary, Sally Montgomery, who had never been known to speak above a whisper, was letting out loose, nervous, little plumes of laughter, regaled with a retelling of the "story." But an imperial flourish came at the end when Anna laid down her rights.

"I see we're missing a secretary, Sally." She glanced at the vacant desk. "We'll simply have to get someone else. You know I'm not an office girl, and you won't be able to handle my work as well as Brown's and Walker's. You see, I'm Brown's new assistant. I suppose I really should have a desk in his office." She looked around as though various ideas about the furniture had occurred to her.

Walker listened with a mounting, heady mixture of anger and pleasure, for he knew the break would come soon. He experienced a real catharsis when the Old Goat trotted out, scowling truculently, fanning the smell of stale beer from his nose. Sixtyish, dumpy, not over five feet three, brown as an earth-clod, he had a sour face which said that everything insulted him. Vindictive little animal eyes peered through steel-rimmed glasses, and his white moustache over curling lips gave him a goatish look. Walker hated the "old shoe," his lack of class, his soul of a mean little bully, but, for the moment, felt a perverse glow of warmth for him.

"Miss Montgomery," he said curtly. "Come into my office please. I want you to take some dictation." He looked at Anna without a trace of courtesy. "And, Miss Parker, you might spend the afternoon going over the files getting acquainted with our work. Come in first thing in the morning, and I'll tell you what your duties are. We start at nine o'clock sharp, you know."

Walker could see them eying each other, the terrible pygmy and the tawny Amazon. Anna took a deep breath as though she could blow him out of the world if she would and said, "Yes, sir," but her submission was ominous, the pause of a hand above a crawling fly.

Next morning, Walker had already conferred with Brown about the work of the day, taking occasion to prod him in just the right places about the new arrival, when Anna stalked in fifteen minutes late grumbling about "the damn Brazilian buses. You'd think they were taking you on a tour of the city." On his way out, he smiled darkly at her. "He's all yours, Miss Parker."

"Oh, come on, wish me luck, Walker. Anybody would think you're scared of him," she whispered impudently as she surged past, crowding him against the wall.

He would have liked to slap her face, for the morning already had a pleasant sadistic tingle about it. And he would have given a month's salary to be in on the showdown. It was downright disheartening that there was no shouting, no hunks of hair or a few stray false teeth heaved through the door. But when Anna returned, "full" was the word for her, frazzled but grander than ever, a consort for Lucifer. She sat down at the other secretarial desk, tucked her voluminous handbag carefully into a drawer as though it contained dynamite, folded her arms and peered down at the blotter like an empty map whose strategy would be staked out with human heads.

One afternoon six months later, Walker sat alone in his office, given over to the inertia of the languorous day, waiting for Miss Parker to come in and arouse him with some unexpected irritation. Yes, she had become a sort of drug; he needed her to get the day started. Sally was no good, she never did anything wrong, and the Old Goat was tiresomely predictable. But Anna's capacity for taking issue was endless without becoming repetitious. She had become the great golden gadfly of his Southern slumber.

Why didn't she come in, he wondered, so that he could toss her out and settle down to an active tranquillity? Though the door to the reception room was closed, he could hear the muted torrent of her life tumbling through the morning air. Giddy girandoles of laughter rose above the grand current of her voice—that would be some of the retainers, of course. She was holding court and getting away with it as usual.

Looking back over the past months, Walker realized that he had been contending with a way of life subversive to his own. Though forced to act as secretary, Anna had made this the chief function of the office. Her desk was inlet and outlet for the tides of their activity. The files had been completely reorganized according to a system understood best by her but apparently representing a terrific new aspect of efficiency. No one could get in to see him or Mr. Brown without preliminary screening, for she believed in the presenting of credentials. There was no such thing any more as a personal letter or private phone call. Correspondence with a distinctly unofficial look somehow got "opened by mistake," and anyone who telephoned was asked to state his business. But, in spite of the valvular control, a spring freshet of work poured out of the office. Anna discovered a miraculous ability to type at a rapid speed, and Agricultural reports that had lain festering for months were made ready. Though she was intermittently an enormous lounger, when the mood was right she could pound the typewriter mercilessly as though it were the only enemy.

The Old Goat had long since capitulated, only trotting out occasionally to look around as if escape might one day be possible, grunting some command which would be carried out according to Anna's whim as to whether "it was the right thing to do." Of late, she had taken more and more to going over his head, asking Walker to initial the dispatches when she came back to discuss "policy" with him, intimating that if he were half a man, he would have had the Old Goat's job a long time ago.

For she loved nothing better, Walker had learned, than invading his privacy, taking every occasion to barge in unexpectedly until he felt rather like the adolescent boy whose mother twitched the covers off when he lay too long abed. She knew if she made him mad enough, he would think up something really "super" for her to do, and that would start another disputatious round. There was a quality in his scorn, Walker concluded, which fascinated her. He overheard her tell a crony, "That Walker's a real s.o.b. But I'm wearing him down. He's my little insoluble. Maybe someday I'll give up and toss him in the rock crusher." And she made a grinding noise with her teeth.

But the greatest change Anna had brought about was not in others but in herself, as though so definite a type had to be crossed with its opposite, longing for ascendancy. Physically she looked so different that she almost should have had a new name. The blonde hair now fell to her shoulders sinuously, only the bangs remaining, forming an airy, yellow cowl around her stark white face which was marked with deep circles under the eyes like smudges made by heavy, black fingers. A rigid diet had left nothing but the gaunt framework of her energy and still she continued to lose weight with a discipline almost sensual. Though the days of stale beer on the breath were gone, the boundlessness in her temperament was transformed, not dead. She boasted loudly about her gambling sprees at the casino, sometimes flashing a role of *cruzeiros* like a withered corsage of her winnings. Her eyes rolled in the manner of blue disks in a celluloid toy when she bragged about her prowess with the samba, and Walker shuddered at the thought of her large skeleton aloft, bumping and rattling around as though it needed the remembered ballast of obesity.

Nothing but "love" could have brought on a reformation so dolefully buoyant, Walker reflected, to whom the cause and the effect seemed of doubtful rational cohesion. The lover-boy was a young Navy lieutenant, Payson Chandler, something of a pansy Walker had always thought, whom Anna hung over her arm as easily as a scarf the first time she saw him despite her vociferous hostility to this species of male, having often hinted balefully that the Embassy was nothing but a "house"—"You know what I mean, Mr. Walker. A real *house*. It's a disgrace. They should know about it back home. Take that Mr. Hall. He ought to be named Radclyffe. Have you ever seen the way he walks—if you can call it that? And that Peterson ghoul. If he ever came out from behind those dark glasses and took a look at the world, he'd faint."

But Payson when he was off duty could wear neckties as gaudy as a peasant skirt and Anna staunchly defended his manhood like a possession he had given her to keep. Of course, she was making a fool of herself. But let her. One day he would find a way of taking the top of her head off, and she wouldn't know it until later when she felt the draft in her brains.

If he had believed in Nemesis, Walker would have recollected later how violently the seasoned bitterness of his thoughts was broken off while he sat there chewing his cud of "Annarisms." As he described it later, he was enveloped in a loud explosion, went "up and then down" like a man shot through a cannon, dropping without transition in a parachute to fall and stop with a jolt, held fast in the harness at the end of the rope which in the rapid synaesthesia of the moment melded and solidified and "became" his swivel chair.

Anna ran in as though drawn by the suction of his fall.

"Oh, Mr. Walker, did you call?" she said, and even at that moment of dispersal Walker was delighted with the supreme fatuousness of her remark.

"Yes, Miss Parker. I *think* I did," he gasped. "I'm over here. *Not* on the ceiling. You can come over. I'm not radioactive." He lay quietly in the uncomfortable peril of the chair, now become a wooden crotch, his feet dangling, his head hung back in decapitated limpness, for he wanted her to see him *in situ*.

"Dear me, Mr. Walker—the chair—it exploded, didn't it?"

"Yes, I believe it did, Miss Parker. Everything I am tells me that it is so." He looked up as though an eye, an arm, a soul, might still fall in place and complete his recognition.

The Old Goat ran down the hall, puffing from trying to get there in time.

"Walker, are you all right? What the hell's going on down here anyway? You weren't doing *jiu jitsu* with Miss Parker, I hope." He leered wickedly and grabbed at the end of his moustache as though he pulled the bell-rope of his vindictive good humor.

Anna moved quickly toward him, using her body like a door.

"It's nothing at all, Mr. Brown. There's been a little accident. Mr. Walker's had a shock, and I think we'd better not crowd him. I'll see to it. You don't need to worry." She had the air now of one experienced with earthquakes and the Old Goat stepped back heavily onto the foot of Sally who loomed anxiously near, and, when she squealed, there was a siphon in the confusion which left Anna alone with the "victim."

As the door closed, Anna breathed deeply of command and came toward Walker in whom curiosity and indignation violently contended, but he lay there waiting. She bent over him for a moment and there was the strength of the curve of the sky in her back, and he realized that it was the only still moment that had ever existed between them. There was a curious nuance of grief in it, the shadow of the capaciousness which her body had lost came back like a memory of what use it had longed to put itself, and he could have sworn she wanted to kiss him. Then bringing back motion, she fluttered like a great, golden bird ready to take him to the Elysian fields, a superior world, a substitute existence.

Anger rose in him, but fell back weakly, a geyser diminishing into itself. That moment which stretched to the far corners of their acquaintance and blotted out all of the rest, returning to the center like spreading circles in a playback of reality, had seen him "broken." He felt as though one of his most important personal traits had been sundered, his courage or reserve, and the fluid of sarcasm drained slowly from his veins. Above this ruin an atmosphere of mammoth tenderness hovered which threatened to suffocate him, and he was thankful when Anna, like a ventriloquist casting the old familiar voice into a body which had now become strange to him, spoke out brashly and cheerily as she helped him out of the tilted chair.

"Never say die, say damn, Mr. Walker." She picked up his glasses, which were broken at the bridge, and pretended to dust and straighten his suit.

"That God-damned chair!" he complied at last, breaking the trance. "I thought a terrorist had gotten me." Gutty feelings flooded back, feeding his dry surprise like a red river. "Are you sure you didn't come in the dark of night and tamper with that mainspring, Miss Parker?" Something about the way she had touched him just now had snapped him out of it. He recalled the other meaning of that moment of the hovering kiss, and it now seemed gustatory, as though she had come upon the only forbidden morsel in an edible world.

"I sure did, Mr. Walker. I'd work nights for a month just to see you bend in the middle," she said.

"You probably would, Miss Parker. You probably would." His nearsighted eyes strained in the haze to form a cutting edge.

"You sure were a pretty sight. Lucky you didn't bump your head. Some people are never the same afterwards."

"Do you speak from experience?" he asked demurely.

"Oh, no, Mr. Walker. I'm just the way God made me. Never had an accident or a sickness in my life."

"You mean you're one of those who just kept growing merrily along?"

"That's right. Papa says when I was a little girl he used to wonder if I'd ever wake up tired."

"Did your father die a long time ago?"

She looked at him and laughed raucously. "Why, Mr. Walker, you do say the funniest things. You know, you're getting to be downright witty. It must have been that jolt. I told you you'd never be the same." She picked up something from the table. "I feel so good I think I'll knock off and fix your glasses. You didn't know I was a mechanic at heart, did you?"

"No, that hadn't come to me yet."

"Well, I am. I just hate to type. Give me a machine shop any day. I can fix anything in a jiffy. Did you ever hear that song, 'I'm just a Kitchen Mechanic,' dum de dum, dum, dum?" She rolled her eyes and thumped the desk.

The dwindling afternoon was spent on patching his glasses with adhesive tape and attempting to repair the swivel chair which Anna picked up like a toy, reattaching, to her own satisfaction, the broken spring, though Walker advised her to tack on a sign, "Explosive, Handle With Care." He had never seen her in better spirits. She hummed, buzzed, and wisecracked while he thumbed at his dispatches blindly, feeling her life shimmying the room like a generator. In the old-fashioned phrase, she seemed to be happiest "doing" for him, and the whole thing had a steamy domestic atmosphere like a laundry or a nursery after the baby's bath. But Parker didn't really like him, he knew; she merely wanted to catch him "naked"—she was after the primordial child. It was merely another way of destroying the male at the bare, postfetal stage of it all.

At least that was still as positive as he could be about that sulphurous miasma which she called a soul, for, in spite of all her sharp, particular, apparently characteristic acts, she was still diffuse to him. He had a habit privately of thinking of people in terms of animals or things—Mr. Brown could be dismissed as the Old Goat and Sally conceived of caressively as a dear little rabbit. But Anna was amorphous—a golden cloud, a blonde pervasiveness darkening at times to threat of storm. She was one of those people who seem to want to remind one of something, somewhere else. Now he realized that he had been taking in great draughts of her for months, his nostrils wide open, as through scent we gather together memory into a form, some aroma of personality that promises to belong to memory. If he had liked her better, he would have said that perhaps she reminded him of home, impregnating the foreign air with American allusiveness, streaking it with the rich currents of another climate.

After the "debacle of the chair," as Walker privately referred to it, Anna's personality began to pile up before him in a precarious, nearly zigzag heap like boxes set sloppily one on the other, and the hand, from a generalized human desire to see a fall, longed to give it a shove. As the work in the office settled down into humdrum routine, she compensated with her most extravagant behavior, giving herself a "bounce" by blowing most of her salary on jewelry at Hugo's. She had already acquired a large aquamarine, a topaz, an amethyst, and "several little trinkets" from Payson. No man was a sport who saved his money, and Walker decided her tropic proliferation was complete when she discussed what he called her "gemcrack" phase with him.

"You know, Walker, jewels have a life all their own. Take a guy that doesn't know that, a real tightwad, I mean. Well, you'll find he doesn't know anything else worth knowing either."

But it was to Dr. Edgar Babcock that she philosophized most precisely on this subject. Babcock, an agronomy expert from the University of Missouri lent to the Brazilian Government for consultation, had fallen willingly into her toils when he first entered the office. A bachelor of fifty, a prissy but pleasant man, good-hearted and intelligent, he was thoroughly susceptible to the "great girl" such as she. He adored her, and she had his life in Rio organized for him almost the day he arrived. But he liked Walker too, thought him a decent fellow, brainier than the average career man, and they had become rather clubbily intimate. Anna, determined not to be excluded, played one against the other mercilessly. Babcock found her vastly amusing, gave up sightseeing time in order to loaf around her in the office, and she knew her man, assaulting his dignity in just the places he secretly wanted it to be piqued until he was always in a pleasurable dither. With Walker and Sally she called him "Babzinho," her own version of the Portuguese diminutive of his name, and once on a sleepy afternoon did a "female" impersonation of him singing "Violate me in violet time in the vilest way that you know," which was riotous and yet made him somehow more endearing.

A few days before Babcock returned to the States, Anna was advising him on what to take back. "Jewels, Dr. Babcock, I assure you, jewels. There's nothing else worth while. There's no art down here, I suppose you know that. Not an author you'd ever want to read when you got back home. But jewels, yes, they do have jewels."

Mr. Brown called Walker into his office, but he felt like crowing with delight for he knew the two sides of that discussion would converge toward him in the end. A half hour later he was sitting complacently in his chair waiting when Babcock entered, looking somewhat drained as by some heroic action but chuckling pleasantly.

"Jim, I suppose you heard. Anna's been after me about the jewels."

"Yes, I know. I hope you sent her packing."

"Well, no, not exactly. She wanted me to buy an aquamarine for my sister. I told her that wasn't quite good enough. I thought I'd get an emerald."

"What!"

"Yes, I know that sounds crazy. But it just popped into my head like the natural thing to say. I think it gave her quite a shock."

"Well, I'm sure it did. I'm surprised she didn't sprout a dozen arms and strangle you with love."

"She did get red in the face. Sort of like somebody had opened up a big furnace door."

"You're not going through with it, of course—just because that big blonde bully made you say something foolish. Emeralds, my God, man!"

"No." Dr. Babcock squirmed uneasily. "I haven't got that kind of money. But I can't say I'm sorry," he continued reflectively. "I think it did give her quite a thrill."

"Naturally, but that's beside the point. You don't know what you're in for. She'll track you down. She'll make you *show* the bill of sale and what's more the emerald."

"No, I got around that. I told her I was picking it up just before I left. And, you know, the funny thing is, she believed me."

"But why did you do it at all? In heaven's name why?"

"I don't know. I just suddenly said it. I knew she would like it. And it seemed like a good thing to say." He looked up almost pleadingly. "I suppose you think I'm an awful fool."

"Well, Babcock, I can't say this is the most brilliant move you ever made," Walker said, trying hard to keep from laughing.

"I guess I was thinking about Anna, the way she takes things. Maybe I can explain it this way—did you ever run across that tale about Mount Kâf, the mountain grounded in emerald which Mohammedans believe encircles the earth? Well, Anna is sort of like that. She wants to think the whole world is built on a jewel. Let her believe that, Walker, and she'll let you alone. She knows most of us think it's all basalt. That's why she's after us." He paused, and his eyes looked dim as gray stones under water. "I suppose it's hard to try to be happy, maybe harder than being . . . well . . . like us."

Walker would have answered—there was surely a slope on the other side which could lead them down into their usual rapport, but Babcock forgot for once to level off. He merely stepped abruptly through the door's precipitous edge as if a fall would do him good. There was hardly time for the little slamming concussion to stop reverberating like an after-crash when Anna came through the side entrance.

"Walker," she said. "Hold me up. I need help. Don't refuse me just this once." She leaned against the desk and her smile was nearly iridescent with mingling feelings. "The old boy's gone and done it. He's shot the works. Isn't he the most adorable man you've ever known?"

"Parker," he said, forgetting the *Miss* for the first time. "Control yourself. What on earth are you carrying on about?"

"Babzinho—" Suddenly her confidence had never been more radiant. "Of course. I had forgotten. Naturally, he wouldn't tell you first. He wanted me to do that." She leaned forward with a great, luscious air of conspiracy that threatened to encircle Walker like a golden arm.

"What makes you so sure?" he asked, feeling a throbbing fist of venom in his mind.

"You could never guess. He would never tell, I see that now," she went on devotedly, though Walker sat as impassive as an idol. "I had to worm it out of him myself. He's so shy, you know, such a darling. But it's true. He's simply doing a grand thing. He's buying an emerald for his sister, a big one. She's an old maid, you know. They live together."

She tossed her hair back and gave him a long, arching look like a curve of her world let down behind him. "Walker, I'd give a thousand dollars to be that woman when he gives her that gorgeous green rock."

Walker felt it coming now, and he could have wished that some great hand would stanch his mouth, for all the realm of counter-possibility, full of beckoning, luminous shapes, bulged against the membrane of the moment.

"You don't believe he will do it, do you?" he asked tonelessly as though it were better to sound like someone else.

"What do you mean? Of course, I do. After all, I'm the one who put him up to it. And all the time I thought he was a cheapskate."

Then she began to notice his face, the one, he thought to himself, she couldn't control.

"You haven't talked to him, have you? You didn't persuade him not to do it? It's not a trick. It's on the level, isn't it?" Her face flickered with a tinge of Plutonian darkness, and Walker glanced down at his desk.

"Don't be absurd, Anna. Really, old girl, why don't you grow up?"

When he did not hear her familiar, raucous laughter, he looked up with his most sardonic smile, certain that it would bring on a swift reprisal. But she waited there gauntly, almost as though listening for echoes of her old flamboyance to prompt her, gripped with the obsession in his face that she should rise to the occasion. As he stood up at last in the overpowering quiet, he felt harder and taller than ever before, a dark pillar to whom the only person alive had somehow tied herself. But still she didn't move, very white now, the gold and green bracelet hung sprawling on her arm like bruises from a twisting chain. There was a quality of lost music about it all, and the walls of the room wanted to yield and melt to a film of gauze beyond which shimmered the reversal of pillar and suppliant. It was she who looked like a columnar statue, glorious in a green world of spring, with him in attendance, and the depth of his life seemed yearningly close.

The Motion of Forgetfulness Is Slow

They met at the Atlantico, one of Rio's most popular nightclubs. They knew from the beginning why they were sitting next to each other, and this enabled them to dispense with the stiff and tedious preliminaries of conversation and be almost immediately easy and informal. Their hostess, Jacqueline Laurent, was a garrulous, masculine, French woman of forty-five, a refugee, somewhat bitter about life, but still a great arranger of romance, an authority on the principles of love, although she had no lover at the moment, and it was doubtful whether she would ever have one again. Some said she was a lesbian, but that was probably untrue since it would have been too easy and almost natural for her, and she was a woman who enjoyed what was most difficult for her to do. Her preoccupation with love had made her widely and ardently social, and she was a familiar figure of café society. Though people feared her, knowing that she could be vicious or benevolent according to whim, they were always glad to be entertained by her because she was never dull. With her penchant for intrigue, she never gave a party that did not have its implications of the destruction or arousal of a liaison between at least one of the couples present.

She had chosen the proper time for this particular conspiracy. A few weeks later, and it might never have happened. But, tonight, success was probable. She knew it, they knew it, and, as a consequence, the surface of the evening moved rapidly. Since she liked them both so well, she had gone to some trouble to inform and prepare them carefully beforehand so that nothing would go amiss. Ingrid Lombard was an old friend from the prewar days in Paris, and Robert Atherton, a young journalist with the Office of the Coordinator of Inter-American Affairs, had won her sympathy not only through his personal charm but because he was a type which she liked, very blondly and brightly American, evoking sentimental memories of her life in the United States when she toured the country on the old Keith vaudeville circuit singing French songs.

Jacqueline knew, and she was satisfied now that they knew, what she called the "circumstances." A week before, Ingrid's husband, Charles Lombard, had left for Paris, recently occupied by the American army, and it was understood that he would not return. Monsieur Lombard was a handsome man of fifty, a painter of minor talent but much ego, possessed of the aloofness and confidence that are often so attractive to women. Ingrid had met him ten years before when she came from Sweden to study art in France. Out of her respect and need for love she had made of him something he was not, but something she could admire, and they lived rather happily together until his selfish possession of her was sated. Now at thirty-nine it was hard for her to lose him, and for the moment she had almost ceased to exist since she realized that the world of her invention, of which he was the center, had really never had any validity at all. There is nothing lonelier than living among the ruins of belief, and because she could not bear this loneliness she had come to Jacqueline's party.

Robert Atherton had not known much about love when he came to Brazil. Like many young Americans of thirty, he had slept with a girl or two, but the relationship had always been of short duration, rather frantically and hectically physical—the kind of experience that later enabled him to understand what a Brazilian friend meant when he said that love in America was usually a matter of athletics. The girls he had known at the University had been wholesome, usual in opinion and attitude, pretty but sexually rather dull, and he had lost interest in them quickly. Not long after his arrival in Brazil, he met Yvonne Vautier, who had come to Rio to visit friends and had been stranded there by the outbreak of war. She was urban in manner and outlook, small, unathletic, but firm and trim of figure, and she had a very intense color of red-gold hair and brilliant blue eyes. She was two years older than he, had been married once and in love several times. She liked Robert, understood him quickly, and became his mistress after six weeks. They had a *garçonnière* together, and Robert went through a complete experience of love, beyond the merely sensual, beyond the spirit of youthful adventure, and knew for the first time what Europeans meant by falling in love mentally as well as physically. Jacqueline, who was a close friend of Yvonne, had enjoyed every stage of the affair, thinking it a perfect union of the Old World—New World. She foresaw what would happen to Robert when Yvonne found it necessary to return to her family in Paris, was ready with comfort after the departure and, finally, the party and the meeting with Ingrid.

They knew, and yet they had come, were staying, and were

going through with it. They knew it was one of Jacqueline's little amusements, and that it might be desperate for them, but there was a chance it might not be, and nothing was worse than shutting the door completely and admitting it was over, that one had been loved and now was not loved and might not love again since love was miraculous and even haphazard and accidental and not to be expected more than once in a lifetime. No, it was better to pretend that the door was still open in a place where self-deception was possible, where there were people, music, and motion—pretend, at least for tonight, that circumstances were still fluid, that it should and would happen again, that it might happen more beautifully than before.

The party of six couples, all foreigners, was masterfully engineered by Jacqueline, although she was not really interested in any of them except Ingrid and Robert who were the nerves in the body of the group. It was their presence alone that excited and stimulated her and enabled her to play with skill the part of the gracious hostess, knowing that the whole elaborate social texture of eating and drinking, gestures and small talk, had a purpose and a center of intensity, a covert drama which was of her own instigation. As they talked, they were conscious of the fact that through the sound and actions of others present, in intrusions and withdrawals, the unpredictable pattern and direction of reciprocal speech, the sudden close-knit vocal unanimity, Jacqueline was listening to them with a focus of attention, central and direct beneath its superficial digressiveness.

They knew that they were being used, and they did not care. They knew that Jacqueline was increasing the sense of her own power by finding them, for the moment at least, pliant in her hands. If things worked out as she intended, she would never let them forget. No, she would never let go of them. But sometimes it is better to be used than to remain inert since movement is life, and in both of them there had been a great and sudden slowing down, so that memory receded into the past hardly at all and the present was stagnant as if the means of extending feeling had been shut off within the blood, leaving in the heart neither the possibility of death nor birth. Jacqueline promised to unlock this rigidity. So being used was moving and better than being still at the point where one could not move voluntarily, the point where someone outside had to play Fate and free the congealing of circumstance.

Inside where there were music and light, and whisky had loosened the tightness of thought, it was possible to feel the surface of life moving, not quickly yet, but mobile again and moving toward the old rapidity. It was possible to believe this even more securely, knowing that Jacqueline was helping it happen. Jacqueline, too, from the outside believed, and it is the viewpoint beyond the personal which supports confidence. Yes, she was very sure. When they left at midnight, their sense of identity, which had been hard and stopped, was fluid again, lightened and diluted in the hazy but swirling suspension which alcohol makes in the mind. The past did not weigh as much as it had, so that they felt they could move through it or around it and that it was not any more oneself lying in a closed small place. And Jacqueline was standing there, telling them good-bye, sure of it, smiling and solicitous like an accomplice. The last thing they saw was her mouth with the thick, coarse lips, smiling and obscene in the foreground, and if it had not been for the whisky they would have been embarrassed.

Then in the cab they were not so sure of motion, although the physical movement was there in the rolling of the wheels along the Avenida Atlantica, down the damp curve of the beach in the phantom-dim light. Through the open windows the rawness of the sea came in. The apartment houses were all dark and like a huge cliff on one side, and there was a heaviness again everywhere. By contrast, the sea was loose and flatulent, having no thrust and incisiveness where it struck the ponderous earth, pouring on the sand a white spray without power. They said nothing and sat apart, strange and stiff, on either side of the seat. It was not a long drive, but it felt long and stretched out as though the pace of the moments had shifted again and was going slower and might stop altogether. The driver sat at the wheel, rigid, tense, noncommunicative, strangely so for a member of his trade, and seemed to lean with intensity on the accelerator like a man who kept his feelings distended in order that they might remain fluent at all in a night of thickening dross.

Ingrid had an apartment in the hills above the city. Most of the foreigners lived there because of the long open view of the sea, the lighter air, and the feeling of being above the tropic languor of the beaches. But tonight the fog and sea-mist were reaching up into the higher air and were curdling around the tops of the hills, and it was hard to imagine that morning would ever open the sky again and that the harbor would lie there below in a rippling scarf of blue, fluid with outward-going ships and racing light.

When the car stopped at the top of the hill before the entrance to the apartment, laboriously and massively as though the func-

tions of the engine had finally been choked with night, Ingrid said
to Robert quietly, "Come in. Come in and have a drink."

"All right," he said, and they went into the dark entrance without looking to see whether the cab moved on.

Inside it was better, with the rawness of the damp air leaving
their skin and the warm interior light, and they could forget a
little the strange solidification of the drive up the hills away from
the music and movement of the nightclub and Jacqueline, glowing, triumphant, transmitting impulse and impulse as though her
body were the channel for the current. But now it was better
again, although the house was not cheerful. It was furnished as a
foreigner might furnish a house, thinking of home. There were
things that recalled Sweden and Paris, and they looked dead and
rootless here, as they would have in any of the fashionable apartments of the city where one always sensed beneath the structure
of modernity the jungle earth, unreceptive to anything that was
superimposed and not of its own. But more than this, the living
room where they were sitting was cheerless because of the things
that were missing, little things that had indicated that two were
living there, closely and intimately, and whose absence now said
one, and one alone, one, now and perhaps forever, alone.

She had nothing in the house but gin, and it was bad to mix it
with the whisky, but there had to be something to start from and
this was not like the nightclub at all but a sliding backward to a
point where the emotions were once more constricted, and they
would not have been able to start again without something to
drink. But as the gin awakened the ebbing, warm radiance in their
bodies, they wanted to talk and to knit the nightclub feelings and
the feeling of now together. And he began to see her for the first
time through his own eyes, not remembering very much of what
Jacqueline had told him to think, and he wondered whether she
were seeing him similarly.

The reddish hair and the blue eyes, he was thinking. *Like Yvonne, and
yet not like her, not like her at all. The red hair and blue eyes of Sweden.
Not Paris. No, not from Paris. Not delicate and very slender-compact. Not
small of shoulder and breast. Not the small mouth and the blue eyes with a
film of the sea across them. But very kind and generous like her body,
filling the sofa with abundance and the wish to give it and the feeling that
her abundance lies fallow and unclaimed.*

And now, perhaps she was thinking—still remembering partly
what Jacqueline had said, not being able to forget the other one
wholly—*he is thinking of her. And is needing not to think of her, not to
remember because it hurts, but to touch and be touched, finding the under-*

depth and the inner, healing, pain-forgetting heart of touch. Wanting to forget, being young, and not yet all-despairing. Remembering and not wanting to remember how love suffers. But remembering and still remembering. Being young, uncynical, and what I would have wanted of love.

Then they were speaking aloud, but it was difficult, for Jacqueline was not there, transmitting impulse and impulse, joining their diffidence through the force and confidence of her personality. It was difficult because there was a feeling of guilt beneath their being together. A feeling of betrayal and shame at trying to forget too soon, and yet, undyingly, the wanting and willingness to love, the furtive hope of filling the image in the heart with another image, of blending form, gesture, and word upon the memory of another form, other gestures, words that were now a consummation and a death, inert and final, forcing upon the mind the recognition of not-love, the fear, hardest to bear, that love lies in a compartment of the soul severed from current consciousness, suspended and immobile in the enslavement of memory.

The music of the samba came in through the open window, primitive, simply melodic, without rhythmic sophistication, unabashedly and unashamedly sensual. In the night that had seemed to be going solid and weighted, it was a cry that said the darkness had not died, that the body of the night had heart-life still.

"That's a *batuque*," she said, singing the refrain. *"Quero chorar, não tenho lágrimas.* I want to cry, but I have no tears."

"That's Brazil," he said. "More deeply Brazil than anything else I know."

"Yes," she said. "I'll miss it when I leave. I won't miss much else—not any longer. There was a time when I would have, but not now. How I hate the *gran finos* and their silly floating-flower lives, the false front of the Copacabana, like a stage setting imported from Europe. And how I hate myself for ever thinking I wanted it all." She paused and listened to the music once more. "But I want to remember that crying. I don't ever want to forget that."

"They laugh so much here," he said. "No wonder in their music they want to cry and don't have any tears."

The women's voices carried the words, soaring and quivering, seeming to fall back into the deep and resonant under-boom of the men. The sound was like a rocking arm beneath them both, cradling their weariness, and they sat back for a while without talking, wanting merely to listen.

"When Charles and I first arrived, I liked it better here than any place I had ever known," she said finally. "Somewhere in the back of the mind all of us dream of a country that is love's. Perhaps it is because in the fairy stories we read when we are children love makes everything beautiful. The witch is really only a princess in disguise, the Beast a Prince Charming. And, of course, where they live happily ever after is the most beautiful country on earth. We will always remember this country. It is the one place we can never forget. I suppose I thought I had found it once and for all when we came to Brazil. The mountains, the sea, the clear blue of the sky, were fabulous, the perfect background to what I was feeling. Finally, the landscape was not background but part of the feeling itself as though there were nothing antipathetic in the world and I could reach out and touch a rock, a flower, a tree, and know it to be love's. Now I don't feel that any more, and I can't really see Brazil at all. I suppose that is why I want to leave it. I don't like hospitality, and I want to see again."

She spoke now without pausing, without even waiting for the conventional linking sentences that he might have inserted. It was not a monologue of self-absorption or indifference but of intense awareness of his presence, of an urgent sense of the need for fluency between them which she, being on the surface at least less constricted and diffident than he, must supply. Consequently, she talked steadily, intimately, and inclusively lest a silence occur, as in the car on the way to the apartment, and an intangible thickness coagulate and make communication slow to a laborious stop.

"When Charles told me four months ago that he wanted to go back to Paris, I knew he would not take me with him," she said. "He did not say so then, but I knew that he would expect me to understand in time, and that I would not go. He was French all the way through, very passionate, very complete in love, and very sure when it was over. My use was a thing of time, neatly measured so as not to last one day beyond boredom.

"To be the lover who does not lose, it takes precision in judging others, and the incapacity for regret, and Charles always saw things with a terrible precise clearness. He was afraid of growing old, and I had begun to remind him of the fact that he would. No man wants to live in a museum of what he was. He can go back there in memory but not live there. Charles saw the future clearly. It was my fault that I kept it vague and undefined."

He was glad that she was talking, since he himself was not ready to talk, being closer to memory, and he knew that she would come, as she had, to that point in the past where the rupture was, the point from which they must, if ever, proceed. He was thankful for the flow of her words. The ample talkativeness of women, he thought, is often a thing to be thankful for. In a moment of tension, it will do its best to push remembering forward into not-remembering or spread it horizontal and thin like water on a dry field to be sucked up and lost from sight. Silence is the cause of much of our suffering, the keeping of grief within us, acute, perpendicular, unreleased, and women, he felt, knew this better than men.

But, though he had not spoken, he knew that she was aware of the intensity of his response. It was she, ostensibly, who was moving them toward a starting point, but the tempo and extension of her conversation would not have been possible without his sympathy. Her words were the surface motion, but a hidden current, intuitive and deep, like a belt under a revolving tableau of figures and scenes, was moving them into conjunction.

When she paused at last for breath, they were once again, for a moment, silent, but the silence was not empty or formal but quivering with the reverberations of her words. She sat loosely against the sofa, her figure nowhere strict or taut, not fat but well-rounded, the body of a woman who, without fear of falling into excess, could stretch the sweetness of her senses a little beyond denial.

There are no rough edges in her, he thought. *She is gentle and hurt. Hurt and not able to hurt in return. The muscle of her heart is rich and strong but tired from loving, enduring, and not wanting to hurt. Now she is missing, needing the serenity of affection. Can I open in her the sealed-up power to touch again? Can I kiss her, touch her, taking the darkness of sensation into another darkness until there is warmth and the denial of darkness? To do this, to need to, to want to love again, to try in a passionate wanting.*

He moved very close to her, and put his arms around her. He did not look into her eyes because of his embarrassment and because he was ashamed of his desperation, of a desire to commit so soon a betrayal, of his wish to flood his loneliness with sensuous oblivion. Suddenly he was hearing, "Slowly Robert. Not so fast. Wait a little." Said gently, tenderly resistive, at the same time that she rose and went into the other room.

Before they lay down, she lit a candle and placed it on the table beside the bed. At first, he was shy about the light, but then he was not, for it left them visible to each other and yet indistinct, hardly familiar at all, more like dream-figures, even strange to themselves, and perhaps this was better and easier for not remembering. The candle had been used before and was encrusted with its own wax flesh and relic-weeping, and he thought that everywhere you looked in the world, at any hour, there was something broken, torn, crying, or frozen in an attitude where the crying had stopped. It was right that she had lit the candle, alive again now and liquid with fresh tear-form drippings, gleaming through all its cylindrical shape, dully so at the base, tipped with a tiny, molten, self-destroying crater where the flame, like an element antipathetic to the entombing wax, was almost disembodied from the wick. Without this light and its straining it would have been impossible, at first, to stay in the room. The night would have been too dense and they would not have been able to endure the muffling darkness without the wavering, shadow-shimmering flare of the candle whose almost incorporeal lucency moved, probing and pliantly caressive over the walls, bed, table, over them where they lay, as though to enter once more the thingness, the body, that it would, but finally, death-fearing, could not leave.

She did not undress entirely but lay there partially hidden from the candle glow like one who knew light and the absence of light, not calculating the risks, being incapable of doing so, but not rushing toward them either, knowing the pitiless price one pays for wanting to possess the beautiful whose possession always quivers with not-possession, bringing the final soulless wish not to have possessed at all.

As he looked at her, very quiet and waiting, with the light on her reddish hair, everywhere on the broad surface of her face except the recesses of her eyes which were dark and closed, he knew that he would always remember her saying, "Slowly, Robert. Not so fast. Wait a little." Not harshly spoken, but gently admonitive, as those who have suffered will admonish others who have also suffered but not so greatly as they.

Then she put out the light, and there was a moment of strange waiting and perilous equipoise in the darkness. And when he touched her, the touch of another was there. And when he kissed her, it was illusive and unreal since he could not kiss through memory, since he could not touch her really at all, suddenly in the darkness remembering, not being able to forget, feeling that forgetting, in a lifetime, would hardly move fast enough or far enough to leave behind in silence one word of all that remembering.

And where his hand, his physical hand, reached—but without feeling—to accomplish the touch, he could imagine that she, too, would put her hand into another hand, and that their past lives were locked in a trance out of which they looked, as from imprisoned sleep, into the outrageous, shame-haunted, pent-eruptive world of dreams to see the fictive motions of their present lives.

It was then that he remembered—as memory will always make you remember a clear indestructible moment of the past just when the present struggles toward freedom—the departure and final passage of the boat seen from the windows of his hotel, the boat, white, compact, poised like a bird on the water. The realization and shock-vision that within the boat was the other form, the other face, the absolute evidence of love. Within that boat moving, at first, slowly, almost laboriously and reluctantly, then quicker, more quickly, quicker, more quickly, quickly, quickly, quickly, until the sky at the far end of the harbor cracked open and, in a moment and forever, the boat drained out of consciousness.

Afterwards it was very quiet in the room. They lay there silently, unstirringly, as though in the darkness they were being watched hostilely from above. It was a long time before he dressed, and he began to wonder why she said nothing. But then he knew that her quietness was not anger, not silent reproach, not exclusiveness, not indifference, but deep patient waiting, the acceptance of not-possessing, the recognition of the vastness between one life and another.

At the door, she kissed him softly, without passion, and he wanted to cry out and shake his body for its obtuseness and his heart for its backward looking, but he did not. He could not. The sidewalk toward the city was steep and damp, and he had to walk down through the thick fog slowly, very slowly, to keep from falling.

The White Queen

I was new at the Gloria. The first secretary in charge of housing the officers told me it was the only good hotel near the Embassy and that I had better stay there in the interests of my work. I took his advice since I was anxious to do the right thing, but I soon found out that most of the young, unmarried men lived at the swankier Copacabana, a long, languid drive from the Embassy, and I wondered if he had sensed in me a difference as though, perhaps, I should be closer to the center of indoctrination.

In any case, it was a happy choice for me. Apart from the comfort and beauty of the hotel—it was done in the grand manner with capacious salons and rooms throughout, giving the sense of old fertilities still potent in its structure, nowhere suggestive of the white sterility of so many modern interiors—it suited my temperament. There had been a longing in me to live in the European way and, apparently, now I was to have the chance even though it were once removed from the ancient source. Nothing in my background, which had been totally American, could account for this longing. It was simply there, as though some stray seed from the Old World had drifted among the flesh of my people. Perhaps it was this desire to return to what I did not really know, a sort of wanderlust full of nostalgia but vague in the images of experience, that had been a motive in my entering the Foreign Service. I suppose I thought it would offer me various ways to attach my allegiance and embodiments of certain things which I wanted to believe important.

I was a little surprised at the deference with which I was treated at the Gloria. Used to the brisk, brusque treatment I had often had in the hotels at home, increasing an inherent feeling of insubstantiality, of not having been seen, I was delighted to indulge in the impression of "being somebody." I told myself that it was because I was good-looking, that I looked the part of the young, affluent, American careerist (for, you see, that part of me had always been certain—I had evidently been born with mirrors around me like a portable setting, and these pleasing reflections were the only solid conception I had). In any event, every attention was paid me until I felt that I had entered a new world of manners where people swept through life, bowing and being bowed to, and I didn't care to go into the subject of motive too deeply at the moment, partly, perhaps, because of the obscurity of my own possible reactions.

The *maître d'hôtel,* a handsome, ceremonious sort who did as much for my ego as anyone there, gave me a table to myself off the main dining *salon,* in a favored nook which was protected and yet had a generous view of what went on among the diners. The fact that during the first few weeks I often had to dine alone did not bother me at all for there was the exciting spectacle of the people. I was glad there were several Americans among the new faces for they would become the necessary contrast to the world I hoped to adopt. As a matter of fact, it occurred to me, they would provide me with a way of looking back, of cautiously considering the figures of an antipathetic past while I moved forward into a future defining itself more as I had dreamed. Consequently my position in the smaller dining room became one of privileged observation, an elegant echo of a fantasy I used to enjoy as a boy when I sat in the car waiting for my mother to return from shopping and watched faces, giving them names, characters, and destinies. To be able to continue this form of exploratory appraisal among people whom I might yet get to know gave me perhaps some sense of progress, which was one of the things I was worried about.

It was, I believe, the second day at lunch, when my focus on my surroundings was clearer and more particular, that I first noticed the old lady whom, reverting to the habit of long ago, I immediately called "the White Queen" because of her striking lordliness, the imperial manner in which she swept into the *salon,* took in everything at a glance, noting all changes, and sat down promptly in her nook within a nook, an extreme corner of the room where several ornate columns cloistered her regally without obstructing her panorama. You could see that she was an old-timer at the hotel—if there had been deference for me, there was something sacrosanct in the manner in which she was treated by the *maître d'hôtel* and the waiter. She was obviously an American, one of the whitest and oldest looking individuals I had ever seen, and it fascinated me to consider how and where all this age and powder-whiteness had come upon her and whether the secret of national senescence might not be concentrated in her, distilled, as it were, in the alembic of the tropics. Her body, surprisingly slender and springy, was not congruent with her head, giving her the look of having once been decapitated and physically refurbished with an older countenance. Her face was bound in a network of wrinkles stretching even across the nose to the ears, up to the roots of the hair, and disappearing into her dress, not particularly noticeable on her arms and hands, as though some tremendous will had stanched their further progression.

I noticed how she watched the movements of the waiter, sometimes smiling at something that pleased her. Her eyes were bright, unaged, and of as indeterminate color as those of a bird. There was a kind of dry, white effulgence emanating from her, and the lithe, dark waiter seemed a sensuous and encroaching shadow which she alternately wooed and repulsed. I saw him spill a little sugar on the table, and immediately a shrill barrage of heavily accented Portuguese came chattering out of her mouth while she began to fidget and flutter, and I characterized her as a *rara avis*, a very old, white bird of a woman sacred to herself and apparently to others. But this image did not last, for I was to see her, as I did not then know, in innumerable changes and avatars, an elusive, chameleon-form of memory and imagination. The slender shadow of the waiter bent over her, as obsequiously pliant as an overhanging tree, and the anger drained from her face, leaving it more supple with life. Then she smiled, and I could have sworn that she looked twenty years younger, so positive she was in regaining her manner and composure, looking around the room with cool arrogance like someone who had been accustomed to please. I was used to the inconstancy of the human face, my own included, a factor in the sensation of the illusory character of things I sometimes experienced (that was why, I suppose, I had become an unobtrusive starer), but I was not prepared for such variability in an old face, for, after all, I told myself, it at least should be "set."

I knew that she had been immediately aware of my presence—such eyes as hers sharpen themselves upon the minute perception of the world around them, growing keener with age—and I was certain that she glanced my way from time to time. It seemed that she looked more histrionic, more assuredly the *grande dame* at intervals during lunch, and I had a notion that it was when she was aware of my furtive scrutiny. When our eyes met first, a fleeting trace of a smile, like the condescension of royalty, passed over her face, but the second time her glance paused longer, and I felt myself completely enveloped in her concentration which broke into a freer smile, brushed with a nuance of coquettishness. She was inviting me to admire her! That I could see. The impish little albino monkey (for now that was the momentary image) was trying to radiate its force across the room in a travesty of seductiveness, commanding the blandishment of my attention. And, strangely, there was something hypnotic about her smile, charged with an old, tireless, inexhaustible habit of allurement. She believed that her beauty endured, and there was a force of memory and confidence that had never given up its transmittal. She looked younger, yes, she did, her features stimulated with intent, and it was an easy thing, in the trance of a new impression, to see the face rebuild itself, like slow-motion played backwards, until she was to me something more of what her own conception might have been. It highlighted a conflict of mine to see that the way a person thought of himself, if it were dynamic enough, might partly produce the aura he walked in for others.

II

Several weeks had passed, and I had come to know the White Queen, although my understanding of her, it seemed, had scarcely begun. From my first awareness of her, I had been fascinated. She was surely one of those who had "lived"—she had something to teach me if only I could know her. There must have been a "secret" and a "struggle" in her life—her face said that—and with my old desire for penetration into human character I was determined to find out. If I discovered what her great moments had been, her crises, defeats, and victories, it might indicate to me how the graph of a human life evolved, for I was undecided about all these things.

I made discreet inquiries concerning her at the desk, among friends, and even chance acquaintances with whom I had seen her talking, for her presence in the hotel was pervasive, and these facts emerged: Her name was Mrs. Edward Estlin, and she was the widow of a U. S. Steel executive. Estlin's work had kept them in Brazil for some years, and then they had left suddenly under the hushed rumor of scandal, something about a young Brazilian army officer and Mrs. Estlin. *"Une petite histoire d'amour,"* one of the Brazilian residents of the hotel told me with a twinkle in his eye. And just before the war, she had returned, "for good," so she said. "She's *muito rica*, terribly rich, you know," another Brazilian said, as though that meant wise and worthy as well.

I was not surprised to find the local appraisal full of deference and tolerance, for the Brazilian has more avuncular respect than the American. America is the land for the young if they know what they want, and I rather expected the boisterous Navy lieutenant to say: "Sure I know old lady Estlin. She's the one, you know, who shacked up with one of these niggers down here. With all her highfalutin' airs, just think of the old biddy doing that." And Carleton Andrews, a second-rate lecturer on America, sponsored by the Cultural Relations Office of the Embassy, told me shortly after a snub from Mrs. Estlin: "I'm leaving the Gloria. They ought to rake some of those old mummies out from behind the columns. Like that Estlin bitch. You know what she told me? Said I was doing more harm than good down here. She's a fine one to be going around putting on airs anyway. They say she liked some of these brown boys around town. Used to be a regular old whore, I hear." His story made me smile, for I could imagine her, angry, scornful, hard as an old powder horn, exploding in the face of the soft, silly Mr. Andrews who had perhaps neglected her in some way and incurred her displeasure.

But everything I heard was vague or vituperative. I looked her up in the hotel register and found that she had a New York address, noticing with a mixture of feelings that her apartment was directly beneath my room. Our acquaintance from day to day had grown by nods, bows, and smiles that never quite met, but I had come to want to really know her and even to like her, and I was glad when she made the first overture, stopping me as I passed her table: "Oh, this is Mr. Anthony Wilson, isn't it? Well, I'm Mrs. Estlin." She extended a hand in a quick, grasping, bird-like gesture. "I understand you're new here, and I want to get to know you. Do sit down and talk awhile." Evidently it was little girl's day somewhere in her moods, for she was dressed in a puffy, pale pink dress, and her face had been made up in a doll-like fashion.

"I'm very glad to know you, Mrs. Estlin. I've heard a lot about you," was about all I could get out before she began to play all the forces of her personality upon me at once. I was amazed to find that she talked about the present constantly with only here and there a name out of the past, like a jewel suddenly turned on her nervous fingers blinding me with its associations, so that the present seemed all the more in her command. She asked me a great many questions about myself and began subtly to give me compliments, but all the time I felt she was thinking about someone else, someone she thought should exist. "The Embassy needs young men of your sort, Mr. Wilson," she would say, and I found her manner as suave as an Ambassador's wife appraising the staff. "We have so many of the wrong kind of Americans coming down here.

No distinction whatever. Have you met that outrageous Mr. Andrews? Cultural Relations, indeed. He's the laughingstock of Rio." She looked cruel, feeling herself then, one could see, very much the white goddess of judgment so that all of the straining power of her wrinkles seemed to have gathered into the deep furrow between her eyebrows. But I felt that she was right. Surely she knew what Brazilians would feel, for wasn't she the oldest American in Rio, didn't she have the cumulative, backward look which was the only proper justification of authority? And I admired the conviction in her voice, the varying, mobile manifestations of herself, each assured, and her ability to imprint these impressions on me, but still I had not discovered the central source of her strength, the buoyant principle beneath all the years.

I tried to imagine what impression I had really made on her— this was very important to me. I knew I had a fine frame (over six feet tall, and strongly built—"a fine figure of a man," according to my grandmother, although it was strange how small I often felt), there was excellent bone structure in my face, and I had a good vital crop of dark-auburn hair and soft gray eyes. This I knew from the cage of mirrors in which I lived, but there was a discrepancy somewhere, for I could never synchronize my feelings with the convergence of reflections. Each view of my physical self, which I had thought about many times, suggested something different, and its inner echo was incongruent. Now, as always, I could see myself sitting with this old but oddly changing, withered and unwithering lady, and I was attentive, complaisant, and apparently charmed, but, as nearly always, there was a shadow in the picture, something in the reflection I did not understand, as though it might be the meaning of the little scene itself, as though there were someone unknown within me who was meant to comment upon that *tête à tête* and its hanging shadow, as upon thousands of others in the past, but had never learned to speak, so this picture, like all the rest, had no name.

The luncheon finished with pleasantries, and I could see that the young, auburn-haired man had afforded the white, columnar lady a *divertissement*. I had listened for the "wheres," the "whens," the "hows," and the "whys," throughout her conversation, as I would always do. But I still had only the slightest notion of who she was. If I found out, I told myself, it would help me in some way which was still vague to me and intellectually undetermined.

When I left her, I ceased to worry about her or myself—I had gone far enough for the time being. I felt content to be the auburn-haired young man who was making friends so rapidly, who lived in a pleasant world where nothing seemed to bar his entrance. There were these momentary congruencies when the man in the mirror was myself. I looked out of the great French doors which opened on to the broad, front terrace of the hotel. The whole girth of the building was sashed in with the blue of the sea as though its impulse were toward spilling itself in the fluent motion of the water. A wind was blowing, and everything felt drawn in its current toward the funnel of the mountains at the end of the bay, and beyond was the great whorl-mouth of the open ocean. The entire city seemed to pour toward that opening where the blue nirvana of the water was waiting for us all, and I felt fluid and gliding, and the burden of longing for some stasis within was for the time lost in the swoon of that strange beckoning.

III

After a few weeks, the Ambassador sent me to Manaus, a lost, torpid, town in the north of Brazil on the Amazon. I was going ostensibly to appraise the state of the Consulate there, determine the need for any further personnel, and make a report of its progress in general, but I had the feeling I was given the job because the Ambassador did not know what else to do with me at the moment. A wily, heartless old manipulator, he moved his officers into position like a chess player, and I disliked to be around him for he had the eye of a devil for what was not in a man. At any rate, I sensed that he thought I had not fitted in, or rather that he had failed with me as though an amorphous substance had eluded the mold of his hand, and that I was to be sent into the hinterlands to see Rio at a distance and know how much I should lose if I lost it permanently.

Manaus meant absolutely nothing to me until the fact that it didn't began actually to be unnerving. I went through my routine with the officials of the Consulate in a listless manner, hazily laying away certain facts to convey to the Ambassador. All was somnolence and torpor and the realization of how prone and limp man had become in such an environment. With nothing combatting the surrounding jungle, there was a prevailing atmosphere of the ancient mire of life in which it was necessary to delve one's sensations in the only discernible drive, the will to live, shared by the rest of the animal world.

I longed for Rio, which, once as lush and loose as a full-blown flower, seemed now hard and white as a jewel, a diamond-center of civilization which alone could have made that jungle meaningful. An experience, more painful to me perhaps than to another, was the feeling expressed in a line remembered from Shakespeare "that wisdom cries out in the streets, and no man regards it." Truth, Honor, Justice, Love—these were words I had thought I might find a better meaning for in a foreign country, finally giving up the Service, perhaps, settling wherever I possessed the security of that knowledge. "Chalice-terms," some professor back home had called them, but here in Manaus, more than in Rio, they were as dry as empty gourds.

My friends I missed most of all, though in missing them I suppose I missed myself. I spent much of my free time away from the Consulate trying to remember them in detail and how I had been with them. The fellows at the Embassy—what did we stand for together?—Perla Azevedo, my new girl, incomparable dancer and gay companion but haunting and elusive friend. Most often of all I thought of the White Queen, for, in the weeks before I left Rio, she had forged so many images of herself upon my consciousness. I hadn't seen her for any length of time on any given occasion—there was too much divergence in our ages for that—but, daily, in passing, I met her, and with the quick power of her personality she made herself memorable. I recalled her in countless ways: as the old white bird, the impish, albino monkey, sometimes silent, hard, and ungiving as a death's head, sometimes in the old costume of what was once a *femme fatale,* she was like a yellow rose pressed at its full-blown peak in a book too many years ago. Or, in the rich pleasure of her own personality, she was often like a fountain, pluming whitely, freely, and clearly, watering the ground around it, an unflagging, abundant source of life, confounding its detractors. Or, again, upon special occasion, in another reminiscent fashion, she wore a fillet around her white curls, and she could have been, in the glow of her own illusion, Juno, Minerva, or Venus.

I wanted to believe in the best of her story, to think that she embodied a sacred nobility, that she had sacrificed herself in some passionate and beautiful ordeal. It was Love, the highest and least known to me of all the worrisome words that I wished to attach to her. She had broken her life over an impossible affair, and had left in disgrace, returning to Rio as one always wishes to return to the place where one has truly lived. I preferred to believe that until such time as her secret would be mine. Whatever doubt and discord there was in my conception, her occasional arrogance, a sudden remark of chilling calculation, were glossed over and stored in the repository of nameless and unspoken suppositions which I had accumulated during the years. I knew that she had watched my appreciation grow and was pleased as a clever teacher might have been with an indulgent and willing pupil. Often, as we became less formal, she watched my eyes intently when I seemed to be dreaming in her presence, and I knew she was aware of their gray vacuity as though they might be filled with various sorts of soul. "Ah, Mr. Wilson," she would say. "You have the eyes of a dreamer. Be careful. Don't let yourself be the prey of the dreamless."

I finished my work in Manaus as rapidly as possible, the report comfortably couched in its Departmental clichés, and was on my way back. The coming reunion with my friends promised a true rehabilitation. I could see them coming to meet me, bringing back things I had lost. "Oh, Tony, you have been away so long," Perla would say, returning to me the motion and manners of our relationship until I was once again myself mixed with Perla. "Tell me all about it," she would continue, and I would have the thrilling sensation so rare for me that she also sought to recapture some part of herself. And the fellows at the Embassy would ask me about the trip jocosely, scornfully, or enviously, and perhaps they would reveal what there was that was new in me. But Mrs. Estlin would be the center of the return for, whereas Manaus was without age and without humanity, she was full of the years of man, and I looked forward to our reunion, for I felt that there was still so much to be learned from her.

The plane was late, and we got into Rio long after dark, but I could sense the city powerfully beneath me, the strings of light like little, pulsing, jewel-dynamos of its life, and all the tentacles of my sensation spread out to embrace it. Tomorrow there would be once again the old, recovered life with its new accretions yet to be claimed from the recognition of others. As I thought of the new blending of myself with the old associations, I felt an odd mixture of feelings welling up in me again: the longing to "stay" and the longing to "go." In the morning, there would be the view of the sea from the hotel and the winds and their nisus toward the channel of the mountains, the throat of the cornucopia which poured its faces and figures, like blossoms and fruits, into blue nothingness beyond. Yet something in me, a ghost of the real, would be standing on the terrace with waving hand, incurved, saying, "Wait, wait," even as now my hands grasped the arms of the seat in the silver plane that was falling like a bauble into the braided flow of pleasure and regret.

After a light snack in town, for I knew that the dining room at the Gloria would be closed, I went directly to the hotel and prepared for bed. As I lay down, I felt turbulent with memories of Manaus, what I had probably missed, remembering the irony of my disinterest while I was there. I was disturbed with the fact that at least parts of my experience seemed to have no value until they were past or until they had been recreated or given substance by the relating of them to others. What would happen as time passed if, habituated to recall as the necessary matrix of the emergence of that mythic being of strength, wisdom, and beauty which was always yet to be born in me, I could no longer draw assurance of its manifold nature, its inevitable coming, from those around me who had always been its heralds and perhaps the masks of its soul? Had I not always believed, like Joyce's Stephen Dedalus, that I desired "to press in my arms the loveliness which has not yet come into the world"? Or, was this only a way of telling myself the romance of things I would never do?

It was an unusually hot, still night, and I found I could not sleep. Since the forms of things were submerged in darkness, I decided, as I had often done before, to interest myself in the sounds of life with that sensuous avidity which had never forsaken me. On this particular night, my room seemed a very high perch, as though I were in a tree-house, and I could hear the night-birds close by, outside the window, and breathing up like a slow exhalation (since there was no wind) was the never-to-be-forgotten smell of the hill behind the hotel, its jungle-nature only half-concealed—it was the scent of root, lubricant dampness, and the voluptuous earth. A part of me sensed the pungent presence like the dark form of a lover, but something else cried out, "Is this, then, all?"

I was distracted from my causerie with the night by one of the sounds of life I had been wooing. I thought there was an animal in the woods nearby at first. It was a strange crooning, like a muttering of witchcraft from some dark cave. I lay quite still until I realized that it was the sound of a human voice and that it came from the room directly beneath mine.

When the tremor of surprise cleared from my mind, for I had never before heard a single sound emerging from below, until it had, indeed, become for me a "secret chamber," I heard a voice speaking in a mixture of English and Portuguese which seemed to increase its wantonness: "*Meu amor*, my love, my love. You're a beauty, *uma beleza*. Never forget that . . . never, never forget that. . . . Look how the young American beats his wings around you, *meu amor*, my beauty. Like Edward before he started to forget . . . Edward who would have forgotten, my beauty, until you taught him to remember with Armando. Ah, Armando who broke his heart for you, my beauty. Who cried and wished to kill himself because you did not love him. But he was like an empty gun in your hand, of no use any more, so what could you do, *meu amor*, my love? . . . But still they come, these Brazilians, dark, ugly, loathsome . . . but still they come. The flower still has its perfume. . . . The Americans neglect you, eh? . . . but, ah, there is Mr. Wilson . . . have you not captured his soul, my beauty? Is he not yours, my love?"

There was a sound of hands that were patting and pummeling flesh, and I could imagine her seated at her boudoir table in a cosmetic ritual, the ceremony of mummification long drawn out through all the years. The lamp would accentuate the whiteness with all corrosive rouge and paint removed, the cleansing tissue lying about like blood-smeared rags, and there she sat, unrelenting and supreme, the sovereign of her long and savage "struggle." Her room, I thought, if only she could see it, was hung with nothing but masks of victims, death's-heads of all the selves which she had killed.

Next morning I moved to another floor on the other side of the hotel with the idea of changing permanently to the Copacabana as soon as it was feasible. No one could deny that it was a more beautiful hotel or that it could offer me more in the long run. It was full of glitter and grace, a center of youth and endless activity and, perhaps, I would find an answer there for all my foolish indecisions. I remembered the elegant salons full of mirrors, and I could see myself there in the evening, dressed in my best for dancing, with Perla, white-gowned and shining in diamonds, the two of us together, walking quickly along as though life had no end of brilliance.

A Chariot of Fire

Oh, my dear, this is a holy trip, a pilgrimage. It'll be the one thing you'll most remember about Brazil." Trompowsky looked at the American girl with a misty, dreamy expression in his eyes. "I've made it many times, once every few years. Back to the source, I call it. A day in Ouro Preto and my heart beats red again." He laid a pale, slender hand across his chest.

The girl from Sedalia, Missouri, stirred a little in her seat and smiled to show a polite interest. Two hours ago she had told him that was where she was from, that her name was Ella MacDonald, and that she was an art student now living in Rio. Nothing more, but he was a man of a deep reservoir of conversation, thoroughly at ease in English, ready to release a waterflow of words across any aridity of silence that surrounded him. Now the story of his life was spread out around them in a great expanse, from the day of his decision to leave Russia and make a life for himself in Brazil, through his "storm and stress," to the venerable years of success and popularity. Ella floated in the warm bath of his personality, overcome as well by the torpor of her own timidity. But she was used to being the ballast of another's ego. Long ago her mother, in a fit of anger, had told her that she was heavy, lethargic. Maybe the old gentleman was like the others. Perhaps he was trying to buoy her up, awaken her to life through the sense of his own, "get a rise out of her," as they said back home.

He needn't have talked to her so long, she reflected. Such a monologue must have taxed his ingenuity and been exhausting even for one of his capacious self-interest. Perhaps he had taken pity on her, thinking her lonely—she nearly always managed to look that way. But that was better than aversion, which was the other side of her brief gamut of response from human beings. Yes, she told herself, he had understood everything when he took a look at her: the stringy yellow hair, the prominent spectacles like showcases of her harrowed introspection, the face bruised with an expression of self-hatred, the figure rather too angular for a woman, the plain, blowzy clothes like a final flaunting of the soul's despair. All of which had enabled him to enjoy his benignity from the moment when he sat down beside her this morning. He looked bland, replete, she thought, rather like a plump bluebird gone gray, a blue tam rakishly set upon his head in a remnant tuft of color and his eyes like blue blemishes on the residual pallor of his skin. *Plump and stuffed with worms*—the thought appealed to the macabre in her.

"Are we nearly there?" she asked, feeling taut, and yet very much alive beside his comfortable casualness.

"Yes, one more hump of the hills and we'll be at the train stop where we can take the car. But *paciência,* as our good Brazilians say, you're moving away from time not into it. It won't matter there." He waved a hand into the future. "Time's all bottled up back in Rio. Here we drink eternity."

"Can't they sometimes be the same?" she asked, once again hating him for his fluency. "Isn't the eternal merely the quality of passion we bring to time?" It was a peculiar spurt of eloquence for her, more like an eruption than a statement, and she felt like a "gaga" art student afterward.

"How well you speak!" he said, smiling mockingly. "Here I've been running on, and yet you have so much to say. Tell me about your life in Rio. Are you happy there, my dear? Tell me what you do with your spare time." He gave a little yellow grin, almost snickering, and she shuddered inwardly at the fulsome way he tended her.

"I paint. That's all. I just paint every day. I study at the Escola de Belas Artes. This is my holiday, the first in three years. I've come to see the Aleijadinho in Ouro Preto." She felt rock-like again and regretted more than ever her sudden jet of speech. Now she knew she would not go through her biography with him and give him another chance for pity. If he asked her about her life again, she would say, "It's been tough," looking at him arrogantly; and suddenly, instead of awkward and timid, he would think her rough, mannish, and would squirm a little inside, which would be all to the good.

"Oh," he said, having absorbed her interruption commodiously, "you must let me show you around Ouro Preto. What a treat to show it to an artist—you know so few of them come here from Rio."

"Maybe they're better off there. Maybe they've got sense enough to know that even if they came they'd stay at home."

"Not at all. Not at all." He looked at her a little archly, but even his pique, she decided, was pert rather than incisive. "They'd profit by taking a look at the past. They're mad all of them. Their work's a mish-mash. As for me, I come to Ouro Preto to talk with the past, to learn its great old secrets. Then I go home and paint my canvases—and look how the public buys them. They're thirsty for a drink of the past, the fine old wine instead of the absinthe of modernism which others give them. We're all infected, but a few of us have enough sense to take the cure. Ah, my dear, Ouro Preto is my sanatorium. Always I leave a part of my soul here for convalescence, and when the other sickens in Rio, I return and take my health again."

So this is a corpse I sit beside, by its own admission, a corpse, Ella thought with grisly humor, and the figure of the old man, loaded with his death, trundling back and forth between the present and the past as though his soul were working in two shifts, seemed ridiculous, comic, and—if she let herself go—pathetic. That she should have met him this morning just a few hours before the end of the journey gave her a feeling of having suffered a relapse, as though her thoughts had produced him in a kind of lost, back-ward-looking delusion, anticipating some exquisitely self-torturing contrast to be made with whatever lay ahead—whatever it was that kept pulling her toward it magnetically as though her body were made of a kindred but resistant substance. All night long when she sat up, alone, she had this feeling of vital attraction radiating through the heavy, lumbering train which sometimes seemed restrained and wound in the vine of the mountain or like a prong squeezing through a gap in the darkness. Then the caul of night burst into the peculiarly deflated mood of morning, and this spectral little creature had sat down beside her, proved him-self all too abundant and bodily, and left her at last glad of his presence as a foil of the unknown and angry that his volubility had robbed her of her "approach" to the old town. She felt dizzy now, as though from train sickness, and would have liked to touch him and even lean against him, but the very thought of his corpulence made her shiver for what was strong and firm—a stalwart, an-gular, bony man, for only that could have stopped the swaying in her mind.

Still they must ride to the hotel together, for taxis were scarce and expensive, but she resolved to shake him there. On the way, as Trompowsky sat smugly and silently beside her, once again she had a feeling of Rio, of having brought part of the city with her out of some perverse connivance of the soul, and the taxi, weighted in a mechanical somnolence, moved slowly, like a hearse through this quiet and sleeping town which might have been a tomb, a dream in glass, or a citadel without besiegement in a fantasy of the mind. But the conflict of its identity revolved in Ella's thoughts as though her own clear preconceived idea of it did a dervish, blending these facts of reality glimpsed from the car with Trompowsky's presence, the world from which she had traveled, into a vertigo whose peril as motion seemed equaled only by the threat of its peril as pause. At the center of the little whirlpool that was she, a voice, like a failing echo of her own, said: *This is not it, this is not as it should be, this is not as it was planned.* She pressed her foot hard upon the floorboard, clamping the body in its place, as though, despite the fall, the swoon, which might follow, that rotation must be stopped. The pretext of the lurching car allowed her to take Trompowsky's arm, and, though certain that it would be too unsubstantial to sustain her grasp, she clutched through the flabby flesh to the bone, and felt it hold.

"You'll find the hotel very comfortable, my dear," he said, as they rolled up to the entrance. "It was built by the Government five years ago. Good mattresses on the beds. A nice, clean place."

A minute ago he was spouting off about the past, she thought. *But when he goes to bed at night he wants to lie down in the twentieth century, sleep its sleep, and wake and look through the window—and voilà—the past, the beautiful past!*

The hotel jutted on the side of the hill, white and gleaming, faced with glass like a sterilizing box. She knew it would be brilliantly sunlit, warm, and a little steamy inside, languorous, but unassailably comfortable. It struck her as really more obsolete than anything in town, obtrusive among the unity of age, so that you wanted to reverse the perspective of the years and see it as a kind of cave-dwelling there on a ledge of rock.

"I didn't expect this," she said to Trompowsky.

"No one does," he answered with a silly little grin. "But it's here for use, my dear. There was so much complaint from tourists that the Ministry of Education had to do something about it. But you needn't let it interfere. When you go outside, the whole town's a cathedral.—Shall we meet for lunch? We might go to the Igreja de São Francisco afterwards. There's some of the best Aleijadinho there."

"Oh, thanks, thanks an awful lot." Caught so suddenly with his offer, she was more cordial than she meant to be. "I'm feeling a little shaken up after the trip. I think I'll have a sandwich in my room and rest awhile. I may look around town a little this afternoon, and save the sculptures for tomorrow."

"Just as you like." Trompowsky turned around and busied himself officiously at the desk. He did not bother to sign for them both, but handed her the pen and moved quickly down the corridor, rotund and buoyant, like a grayish balloon with a blue patch on its top.

When she had finished signing the register, the clerk looked at her card in the most professional manner and asked, "How long will we have the pleasure of your company, Miss MacDonald?" He spoke book-English, all the words correctly pronounced, but sounding like something memorized.

"Oh, several days, I suppose. It depends. You seem to have plenty of room." She spoke curtly, glancing around the empty lobby.

"Oh, yes, yes. It's merely for the Ministry's records. We hope you'll stay as long as possible. You are our guest, Miss MacDonald. We are honored."

"Oh," she said, and looked rather crossly at him, wondering why the Brazilian petty official always had to dress in black and display the manners of an undertaker. She was prepared not to like him, although she knew he was what Libby, her roommate back in Rio, would call a "cute boy." At the same time, she would have liked to say something to him, attracting him favorably, something that would make heat waver in his eyes and make him forget to call her "Miss." But he was like all the rest, sensing her hostility as an animal does, but all the worse for being so polite, so unctuously solicitous. She would have liked to slap him and stamp a look of anger in the smooth dough of his face. This streak of violence made her feel crude, ashamed of herself, and yet she longed for just that—to slug it out with someone and get an honest response, a slap in return, an oath, and afterward, perhaps, an impassioned truce, some basis for true friendship. But it hadn't worked with men or women, especially the young—she had known a few older men who were willing to exchange confidences, but they were too gentle and complacent, and she ended by despising them as impotent and weak. It was Whitman's *Camerado* she longed for, someone ardent in friendship. She had tried the direct approach, the blunt appeal for sincerity, even on Libby who had told her to go and "work out on a punching bag."

Her room was exactly what she expected: a square, sunlit cubicle of the twentieth century. After eating a crumpled sandwich from her bag, she threw herself across the low bed for a half hour's nap, partly to avoid Trompowsky, partly to make herself fresh for what she had traveled so far to see.

When she woke, it was dark, and there was a soft, misty rain falling. She could not imagine how she had slept so long, a deep, unfigured, dreamless sleep which was unusual for her. But the rest had not made her feel altogether free and unburdened—maybe her dreams were lying in wait for her—and she thought of the coming night with a little anticipatory thrill of terror. After eating the last sandwich in her bag and drinking part of a bottle of mineral water brought along for the train trip, she put on her trench coat and slipped quietly by the clerk at the desk, aware that he whisked his head around when she passed through the door as though a phantom had glided past.

The rain had stopped, but the whole town was enveloped in a womb of mist. It had been good to slip out of the hotel surreptitiously like a fading back into time. She walked down the moist cobblestones of the street carefully, admiring the old baroque buildings with their scrolls and contorted curves, their gilded woods and plasters, now partly rusted away. The richness and elaboration—the adorning hand was everywhere present—made her think with a shudder of her little modern cell in the hotel, constructed as though personal life, too, could be run like a machine. But now on all sides was the mark of humanity, nothing impersonal and merely functional. The mood of the town was very compact, she decided, one of age leaning upon age, and thereby ready to endure the pressures of time, knowing it held its story of youth and struggle intact behind a shield of persistence. *So this is the city of gold,* she whispered to herself, *Ouro Preto, Black Gold, the gold in the earth, the flesh of the slave. And the white hands twining, twining . . . the light and the dark braided together in an old chain of endeavor and suffering.*

Up the steep hill the figure of a man enveloped in a long black raincoat and wearing a broad black hat glided toward her with apparitional ease. Under the lamplight, his face was lean and sharp with an El Greco elongation in the bone structure.

"Boa noite, Senhora," he said as he went by, and Ella had the feeling that if she stopped him, his greeting would have been repeated in echoes of two hundred years ago. He was like a fume, a somber exhalation of the past. She thought suddenly of Aleijadinho, who was the real reason for her journey—the passer-by had aroused a specter of the crippled artist who undoubtedly had ascended this street on his way to work. The mist melted away around his memory, and she could see him on a day of clear poised weather, of balanced light and equilibrium in the world, helplessly borne by slaves, himself the son of a slave and a Portuguese master carpenter, the disfigurement of his face veiled and his body hidden in a flowing cape—the leper who had done his last work with chisel and mallet strapped to the stumps of his

fingers. His flesh had become the burden of chaos which the maker must bear, his illness and suffering were the smothering corset he wore, and all that the soul could do was the impossible, break out, break through, ascend: release the shining figure. Twist, turn the eyes of the lazar inward until they yielded the angel face. Twist, turn, until the stone revolved within itself and showed the countenance of the soul. The gyration of the true man outward, the torsion of the flesh until it freed the captive. No wonder the hand, tutored in ecstasy, could touch the stone with light until it mirrored the struggling and revolving vision turning to a calm. Ella thought grandly of how long that revolution in the soul must have taken, the artisan making himself artist, alone, without teachers, repeating in arduous conquest the whole history of man as maker, pent in the lonely hinterland of the world, caught in the prison of misshapen flesh. Somewhere in the Brazilian earth nearby the resinous torch of that body lay quenched, but tomorrow, and Ella glowed with the thought, she would see the captured and arrested light in the work of its hands.

When she returned to the hotel, Trompowsky was waiting in the lobby, his face startlingly pallid in contrast to the dark brilliance of her reverie.

"I've been missing you, my dear. Come and have a Guaraná or a coffee with me," he said.

"Thank you, no. I'm rather done in from my walk. I think I'd better go to bed early." She was determined not to be caught this time. It occurred to her that she might twit him about the Guaraná—a nasty mixture of ground seed, sugar, and a shot of rum if so desired—an old Indian drink supposed to stimulate virility.

"Come sit a bit," he insisted, grinning, wetting his pale lips with his tongue. "I want to talk to you about a proposition you should be interested in. I've been thinking you'd make a good secretary. You're intelligent, you're an artist, and you know Portuguese very well. The one I've got now is such a fool, mad about the young men. You should think it over. I'm very good to my girls."

He looked at her steadily, and—was it her imagination?—a leer flickered over his face, quickly undulant, covered by the returning wave of his paternal air.

"Oh, I don't think I would do," she said hastily. "I've had no experience. Besides, I'm down here on a scholarship. I couldn't walk out on that. There's my work, you know."

"Certainly, certainly, there would be plenty of time for that. I'll go over your drawings with you every day."

"But—" She looked at him, her face reddening, befuddled with anger.

"There's no hurry, there's no hurry," he said interrupting. "Think it over. We can talk about it tomorrow." He drained his glass and rose to leave. "You know, my dear, I could be like a parent to you."

Ella felt like crying when she reached her room. But once in bed, she flooded her mind with a pleasant fantasy of the past recalling her father, and soon she could hear the sound of his voice, gentle and manly. There in his old great chair he sat and she sat at his feet on a stool while he read from a worn Bible. His eyes were dark and penetrating, luminous with spiritual force, and they would have seemed terrible had they not been kind. But his body was slender and frail, burdened with its restless sensibility like a delicate candle with an enormous aura of flame. He was reading one of their favorite passages, the story of Elijah and then of Elisha and the Shunamite's son, letting his voice quiver with feeling: *And when Elisha was come into the house, behold, the child was dead, and laid upon his bed. He went in therefore, and shut the door upon them twain, and prayed unto the Lord. And he went up, and lay upon the child, and put his mouth upon his mouth, and his eyes upon his eyes, and his hands upon his hands: and he stretched himself upon the child; and the flesh of the child waxed warm. Then he returned and walked in the house to and fro; and went up, and stretched himself upon him: and the child sneezed seven times, and the child opened his eyes. And he called Gehazi, and said, Call this Shunamite. So he called her. And when she was come in unto him, he said, Take up thy son.* Ella felt this resuscitation tremble through her body, and she was terrified when her mother entered the room where she and her father sat together in perfect sympathy.

At first, her mother's mouth was long and hard like the barrel of a gun, and her first words would be a shower of bullets. Then her presence grew and spread, metallic and heavy, like an enormous candle-snuffer above the flame of her father's beautiful voice. Just as they were about to be enclosed in the descending mold of darkness, Ella screamed into wakefulness, and lay shivering in her bed. The solidity of her loneliness settled about her, and she thought of the old village outside that she loved but that held no friend for her except a dead man, and she thought of Trompowsky, somewhere nearby, the soft jelly of his body swathed in an elegant night suit, stretched out in complete compliance with the night, snoring flabbily, and she knew that if she should have to escape it would be toward him alone that she could run, and the world seemed ominous with his accidental power.

The morning was clear and flawless, and Ella woke "in focus," as she told herself, feeling the day to be a gift. Trompowsky would not be up till nine or ten, she was sure of that, so she dressed rapidly, rushed downstairs for a glass of orange juice, a cup of coffee, and toast, and walked out into the lucid globe of the sunlight. *I shall set a form upon this day,* she said to herself, recognizing how much this habit of communion was growing on her in such a silent world. *It has been given to me to remember. I shall carry it away like a bubble of clear gold. Twenty years from now, yes, twenty years from now, I shall be able to stand in its center and remember as though it were the depth of my own heart I stood in.* She thrilled to the extravagance of her emotion, but was glad that no one in the world could hear what she was feeling.

Across the hills the dual towers of the churches rose, white and trimmed in a rich brown stone the color of weathered gold blending with the plastered walls in a tarnished chryselephantine effect. There, in the pathway toward these towers, was a radius of her morning, Ella thought, and, everywhere she looked, another and another. She let the natural magnetism of the highest church lead her to it, beautiful and imposing in itself seen from a distance, but melting away, almost dissolving into nothing as she approached and looked at the delicate sculptured scrolls of soapstone ascending in a buoyant whirl of cherubs thrown like a radiant wreath across the doorway. Inside there was the baptismal font, once again with convoluted stone and spiraling cherubs seeming to draw the essence of matter upward with it, the wall of the church itself bodiless and unsubstantial. And so, from church to church, Ella saw them in themselves, dominant on the hills, and felt them fading away and falling back from the radiation of the sculptures, until the ground was set and the air hung with emblems of a vision, so compact in adoration that the very marrow of the buildings had been drawn into them. She could not remember another world so decked with garlands and trophies of its passion. It seemed to her that at the Igreja de São Francisco de Assis she found the pivot of it all. Directly above the door a huge circular medallion had been set, showing St. Francis, kneeling, looking upward to his Brother, the Sun, whose rays contained him in a lambent nest. She thought of the dark, crippled, leprous man there on the scaffold working at this kneeling figure of rapt love as though each stroke could transfer his soul into the enduring stone.

All day Ella felt herself moving in shafts of sunlight. The night before with its dreams of her father, the beautiful flowing of his voice through the Biblical story that had always been a kind of pact between them, had left her keyed up and almost hectically receptive. Trompowsky in his little tam shuttled back and forth across the stream of the day like a blue, recurrent mote, seen once against the hill and again looking down at her in the square just after she had left one of the churches. He waved gaily and beckoned to her, but she pointed in a misleading direction, and let the day glide beneath her once more. She did not return to the hotel until nearly sundown, throwing herself across her bed for a short nap, the impact of the day charged through every fibre of her being. Once again she slept flawlessly, dreamlessly, waking in a stupor of darkness and the incredible knowledge that it had begun to rain mistily again. She felt terribly disappointed, having planned to see some of the churches at night, particularly Saint Francis, wanting to see it drenched with moonlight. There was nothing to do, she reflected as she rang the *portaria,* but have a quick bite in her room and take a look around anyway.

When the sandwich and tea were finished, she hurried downstairs and through the lobby, but the clerk stopped her.

"Oh, Miss MacDonald, Mr. Trompowsky has been asking for you. He said to tell you he'd inquired." The clerk smiled—whether meaninglessly, or sententiously, she was not quite sure.

"Well, I'm sorry," she said, "but I've been terribly busy. Tell him I won't be able to see him this evening."

"Very well, Miss. He left this in your box."

"Thank you." She hurried on, looking at the little booklet, *A Guide To The Appreciation of Aleijadinho,* in Portuguese. The insolent old snob!

Once outside, Ella felt it could have been the night before. The same shrouding mist, the same silence, the figures in their raincapes passing at long intervals in a phantom chain. Her reverie as vague and clouded as the night, she did not know how long she had been walking when she saw, there at the far end of the lamplit arc, another black-swathed form come toward her, smaller than the rest, walking laboriously, seeming to hobble in the swirls of the voluminous cloak. She stopped, statically defined, while her heart dilated and was the only organ of her being. The figure came on toward her, dragging through the mist like a crippled ghost.

"Aha, Miss Ella. I've found you at last. You've been avoiding me." Under the rimmed hat Trompowsky's eyes were the blue-black of smooth sapphires. The light focused on his damp mouth which spilled out words like an old yellow spout.

"Oh, no, not at all. I had so much to see today. There simply wasn't time for anything else."

He came closer, and, as he leaned back in the light, she saw his whole face, so soft, so white, even the eyes drained pale, almost like a Halloween travesty of a ghost.

"I missed you," he said. "I kept sensing you everywhere—when I arrived, you'd just been there. It was like a chase. Quite the most exciting thing I've ever done here."

"Well, you've caught me at last. Here I am." She wanted to sound laconic, but knew, in desperation, that she probably sounded shy, confused.

"Yes, here we are. My dear, I don't know when I've been so struck with anyone. Such energy and such enthusiasm! So much you saw today! Really, it was quite a pursuit, I can tell you. And now I must hear all about it. Didn't I tell you it would be a holy trip? Didn't I say you would never get over it?"

On the way up the hill back to the hotel Trompowsky kept close, confidential, possessive, and she thought he would never stop telling her what she had seen, thought, and felt. He did not touch her, but she had the feeling that if he had, his hand would have struck her like a claw. The luminous box of the hotel seemed up an interminable hill of glass, and, though she wanted to push on alone, it was Trompowsky who had the spurs on his feet. When she sank immediately onto the sofa in the lobby, even he acknowledged her exhaustion and bid her goodnight.

The bed itself was like a box for Ella when she lay down, the final container within a container. She felt cold, heavy, spent, with little vibrations of heat flickering through her body in a mockery of life. If there had not been the fantasy world, like a fourth dimension of the mind, ample, unconfined, the empire of her safety, she did not know what she would have done. But there was her father speaking gently, soothingly, soothingly . . . then Elijah, the father, impassioned and powerful . . . Elisha, the son, asking that a double portion of the spirit descend upon him . . . Elisha walking across the room wearing a long cloak like a shield around his incandescence, a dust of stone flaking down from its folds. . . . He put his mouth upon her mouth, and his eyes upon her eyes, and his hands upon her hands, and she felt warmer than she had felt in all her life. When she reached up to him in embrace, the broad black hat fell backward in the light of adoration and Trompowsky's head slumped forward within the noose of her surrounding arms. Ella switched on the lights, reached for her glasses, and waited until dawn for the swaying of her body to be still.

No one saw her leave the next morning except the clerk who,

stiff, tall, dark, stood like an exclamation point at the silent frenzy of her departure. At her bidding the taxi drove fast though the red mountain road was still wet from the rain. The train stood on the tracks, black, ponderous, inexorably pointed toward Rio, and Ella knew it would contain her in a moment like a cylinder of her chosen fate, carrying her back to what old, what new, contention of desire. On the platform of the passenger car, she turned to see the taxi disappear at the rise of a hill, brilliantly streaked, splashed with color of flame, gone in a whirlwind of motion, and, as though a phantasmagoria of her journey were blent in that image, she whispered, "My father, my father, the chariot of Israel, and the horsemen thereof."

Boat with an Eye of Glass

As the years go by, there is a person, or there are persons, never more than a few, to whom we attach a special, endearing and enduring significance. There are certain things we have done which maintain an aura so that they stand out along the cloudy corridor of days in niches of radiant posture, a hall of heroes hidden in the mind, and each figure in that aureate concavity is a wonderful blending of ourselves with that which was, like a dual marble of the sympathy and substance of our past. It is thus that we gather perspective, acquiring treasures as we go along, keeping a light before the special acquisition by the devotion of our feeling for it in that time past. As the world around us tells us that we walk forward, there is an ever more alluring tendency to turn the head and, in an aggressive retrospect, recapture and relume the inspired moments of the progression saying, "That's how we were together, that was the place, those were the days."

I remember such a person, a time, and place in the Rio of 1923 when I was twenty-two.

But first let me yield the present to you, and leave myself all the freer to move around among things remembered. It is 1943, and I am on my way to Brazil again. If it had not been for the war, I probably would not have made the trip, but with the idea of Death as the great protagonist, gathering the world like supernumeraries into its magnetic scene, I felt the irresistible urge of the antagonist to recover an intensity of life I knew I had experienced in Rio. Moreover there was the memory of Raul, the prototype of friendship, the young Faustus of my more timid seeking, that beckoned to me as though a dark world must be balanced with the light if the poise of humanity were to be maintained.

I spent a good many sleepless nights over the decision, but I suppose unconsciously I had been longing to return for such a long time as not to have been able to allow myself another refusal. There were Doris and the children to consider—only one air priority was allowable—they would have to stay in New York, increasing my sense of guilt for what might have seemed a romantic "flying down to Rio" in a time of crisis, though Washington had connected my trip with the war effort. As an executive of Standard Oil, I was to put through a deal on oil rights which our office in Rio had been slowly attempting to accomplish against local opposition. However, it was not until Doris urged me to go that I convinced myself it was "important"—Doris, standing at the window looking far away, acknowledging this Southern longing in me as a floating vision that rose in a bubble of sea-colors and clashing palm fronds, something ineluctable and yet insubstantial between us, present and then gone, a release of images in search of a body, haunting and chimaerical.

Then when my doctor permitted me to go only on the condition that I combine business with a rest, I rather happily canceled my air passage in favor of the long sea voyage, once again freed by Doris to go alone, glad of being able to savor the slow ecstasy of approach, hoping to lose some of the armor and encumbrance of the years en route, as though the boat would leave New York ponderously and glide into the harbor of Rio as lithe as a wind-honed bird. The long contemplative hours on the ocean would be those of a devotee. It would be a novitiate, a cleansing time, as I prepared to reclaim the tropic of my youth.

For through the years that was what Rio had become to me—the visionary South of all my snow-bound Northern yearning, the fructive center of the earth's body, the pith of appetite, the climate of blessed mornings and benign evenings, the luxuriant frontier of Adventure that blooms at the edge of Order. The whole city had opened in my desire like an enormous loose flower, and there, like the heart of it all, was the island of Paquetá where Raul had taken me so often, which now in the depth of recall rose free of all the rest whenever I could summon this sunken realm of the South. For, in my waking hours, it was as submerged and buried that it appeared to me. It was not unlike a purer Pompeii of my youthful pleasure which some dark eruption in the soul threatened forever, changing in mid-air its flake of fire into reminiscent petals, muffling the island of bougainvilleas with the purple ash of memory.

Only in sleep was there motion and pliant life, seen in a glass-bottomed boat from above, the world of flowers bending and rippling in the current of dream like hands of enticement waving beneath transparence, the boat, white, functional, mechanical, a naked body of odious progression, struck with tremor, as though a mounting underswell were surging below that might lift the hard instrument of surface motion and break it across the purple pinnacle of flowers.

Though I speak of lurid dreams, I am not a man given to hallucinations. I think I know what is dream and what is reality—the magnetic counterpull of the one and the other has never sent me dizzy and reeling as it has with so many of my contemporaries. I have indulged in fantasy during the free times which I have allowed myself, but I have conquered the world around me as well—I am socially competent, I am culturally congruent. Doris, I believe, would tell you that, for she has helped me to weld the pattern. I got my start as an office boy with Standard Oil in Rio where, tired of college, I had gone to knock around and make a man of myself with youth's vague hunger for knowing and doing everything once. Through the years I prospered, and now have my name on a letterhead and all that goes with it.

Doris would tell you that I am "solid and substantial," for she has a proud faith in my supremacy and endurance and surely a need to believe in them. I would like to show her sometimes what I call my "island smile," the look of the free floater, but I wonder how it would go with the well-tailored suits which she considers so becoming to me, the well-tended manners, and my self-containment so carefully preened. I suppose with my height and dark hair, only slightly graying, my well-trimmed moustache, and compact look of health, I am what you would call somewhat "impressive," although in the morning when I shave, that face does not always seem to belong entirely to me. Though I have no delusions about my identity, strongly rooted as I think I am in the world of reality, there is a revolving expression in my eyes, bewildering me as those turning doors in hotels did when I was a child. I am not always sure what look I am going to show the others, although I am constantly, and I must say gladly, reminded that the wheel of introspection turns only for me. Doris never lets me think that she is aware, and I should be unhappy to think that she were, for I have stood her scrutiny for nearly fifteen years.

Though she has accepted this almost ghostly fume above our common life, this ectoplasm of unshared experience, it would not have been pleasant for her to see through my eyes, standing as I often do on a late winter afternoon in the library of our house in Beekman Place, melting the world of snow outside with the sunlight of another climate in my reverie, casting a tableau of purple and rose against the backdrop of white. But I often do just that, sensing her behind me as she enters the room, appraising my presence, taking the columnar view of me. Sometimes, as in the earlier days, I long to turn and run quickly toward her, and, in spite of the heavy pediment of our lives, stand close to her and let her see the hollowness behind the sheen, the tube without the core of valor, and share whatever doubt she hides behind her strength.

But I am wary of my knowledge of Doris. I am not sure whether she understands me, nor really whether I understand her in any growing, developing sense of personality. I have merely decided what she thinks of me and what I probably think of her. It would frighten me to test this postulate of Man and Wife by the standard of a resurgent and aggressive love which would, I am afraid, appear so primitive to her. For she does not seem to need me in this personal way any more. Whenever there is friction, she recites from her long dossier of respect for me, and I am left with nothing but an elegiac mood. As for my sons, Marshall, Jr., and Henry, I have learned not to be too possessive, and they, in turn, have accepted me merely as a necessary presence. Yet, sometimes when they stand before the fire with their mother, flanking the image of her golden good looks like little eidolons of protective concern, I seem to detect an accusation in their scrutiny as though their eyes had caught that turning flicker in my face.

But the drift of our lives moves with the utmost efficiency—our house is a machine for living. Doris has a schedule for everything, and I abide by the checklist, for I can find nothing vulnerable in her way of doing things. And so we stand evenly balanced in the scales, Doris with the strange and almost threatening power of her decorum, her strength of will, and I through a weight that is attributed to me as head of the family, though I wish that one of us would be weighed in the balance and found wanting, perhaps both of us in different ways, but I cannot shift one milligram of this equipoise of "gracious living."

So in a time of death, I am glad to be on my way, New York left behind, humped high with the rock of its buildings like the Stonehenge of a modern, manic race. As we go along in life, so much of the good, it seems to me, comes to us as recovery of what has been lost. When we are young, we have the sense of walking forward with confidence, and the backward look is unthinkable. So it was with Raul and me—we let out our minds like streamers at a masquerade, and if they fell in colorful chains around us, we broke through them with the exuberance of another faith. I remember how we thought that life could be summed up, understood, and contemplated in lucid adoration.

But in the darkening irony of maturity, so it seems, the Great Questions of our youth become vaster and the powers of heart and mind lose their projectility in a smaller, weakening, dwindling flare. So now I am taking "a walk," as they would say in New York—this voyage is like a leisurely stroll toward a world I believe has never changed. I am going back to meet Raul—this trip is a sort of homage to him. I think of him coming toward me with outstretched hand as though we were meeting on the docks before embarking for Paquetá. Though he died not long after I left Brazil and was, I am told, buried on the island, I discard that realization. I do not wish to believe in the mortality of his world.

It has been a pleasant voyage, a long sustained anticipation of a personal paradise. The boat moved slowly at first, hard and encasing, menacing as a destroyer ready to change its colors in mid-journey, then moving more quickly, sloughing its defensive shields, seeming less mechanical, gliding at last on the motion of jettisoned regrets. I love a harbor city better than all others. I like the way it drinks the waters of the world and how it gives itself as channel and passage, acknowledging the incoming and outgoing, using the imperceptible net of its soul to sieve the motions of men. When you are next there, in a town by the water, notice the exquisite sense of flow which plays over you like a crystalline current of time's dreaming, taking all but the best you have loved in its lustral wash, leaving a sense of your own essence until you know that this cleanliness and purity of line are what you have wanted all your life. As we pass through the gates of the mountains, I know again that Rio is my harbor city—not New York where I seemed far from the water, the harbor throat so gorged and throttled that though the great beaker was tilted, I waited and was thirsty.

But now all pent dreaming is set free. The color-vent of the mind from which the bubbles of fantasy float up is closed. There is no necessity for it. I do not need to look down at the deck of the ship and see if it is glass. I feel that I am below the world to which I had become accustomed, and am in that motion which I had found only in dream. I see Paquetá in the distance, and whatever vacuum remains is filled with my past which must be present again. I think of Raul, and I know that when I am in the city and then, most finally, on the island again, I will have the sense of a complete connection like a handclasp merging two continents of life. The last moments before we dock are spent thinking of him whom I must not lose for I have come too far in order to be sure that I remember. There is something agonizing in my feelings as though the mind were a fumbling sorcerer who could not quite bring off the transformation of recall, but I persist. I close my eyes and shut out everything but memory. I see Raul on the dock with his hand extended and his wonderful smile of comradeship.

It is Saturday, no work to be done, we are going to the island, and he stands there near the rail a little impatiently, not wanting to miss the boat. He is my friend, and I never think of how he looks when I am with him, but today I pause and take a mental picture, partly out of guilt at being late, wanting to register the gentle, though unsentimental, way he greets me, partly from a belief in "recording" which comes over me now and then. He is dressed in a navy blue, sleeveless sweater, white ducks, sneakers, and carries a package of lunch under his arm. His coloring is dark, but his eyes are a luminous gray, intensified by a tendency of pallor in the face. He looks frailer than I, and I remember with a twinge that he is an arrested tubercular. I can hardly believe it because of his vitality, and it is the one thing that makes him seem remote from me, as though he knew another dimension of experience which I have been denied.

On the ferry going over, Raul, whom I call "Ray" to bring him closer to my American comprehension, is everywhere, dragging me along, as always. He shows me every corner of the boat, speaks to all the people, with particular friendliness to the farmer folk who sit lumped together, ill at ease, their city purchases stacked around them. He tells me to speak to them and I do so in my pidgin Portuguese, glad to see their weathered faces crack into smiles.

I suppose this is why I like Ray—he reveals myself to me—he assures me that I can do, would like to do, so many things that I have denied myself. He makes me believe in my rapport with the world around me.

We are nearing Paquetá, "our island," to which we come as often as we can. We go everywhere in Rio together. We have girl friends in common, we go to parties together, but we like the island best. Ray, though, never thinks of it as "enough"—he loves the city passionately too. For him the effect of the island is lapidary, taking away the rough edges of daily living, but, finally, too detached, inward-looking, and self-centered.

We rent bicycles at the dock, and are off at a leisurely pace, riding through the little town which has yielded itself to flowers. The bougainvillea is everywhere, the main flower-tone of the island, purple and rose, leaving the subtler accents of color to the smaller flowers so that one remembers them throughout the day like piquant contrasts of a predominant mood.

"Let's stop here, Marsh," Ray says a dozen times. And he breaks off and hands me sprigs of a little, gaping, yellow flower with a big name, *bôca de leão,* lion's mouth, and in the condensation of imagined sound, there is a tiny roar across the morning. I who have known flowers only as familiar now find them intimate. From another bank he brings me a *brinco da princessa,* earring of the princess, a pendent red flower which seems to hang from the invisible form of a girl. He, the native, is helping me to see his country through the eyes of a stranger. As he keeps showing me the flowers, I do not feel foolish about it after a while, for they are as alive to him as people or animals.

We move on, talking to many people along the way, asking directions helplessly, and I notice how helplessness is so attractive to everyone. We talk with the peasant girls especially, and Ray knows how to treat them with a caressive courtesy. They laugh at his jokes and take no offense. We go for a swim, we climb the hills, we are a cartwheel of color and motion along the winding white sand roads. We pause on a bluff overlooking the water to talk and later to eat lunch. I reflect on our rapport, and I know that whether we admit it or not most of us like the idea of friendship between foreigners, as though sincerity among them were easier.

I look at Ray. He is tired; there is a shadow in his face. It makes me think of his illness which he never discusses but which broods about him in repose like a dark, attendant mother. I wonder if it is from her that he has learned such joy. I listen in the shadow-tarnished air for some message that he hears and I do not. He is pensive and quiet, then gleams across to me as though he had heard some news of Now which I do not know. He is the young prophet of Now; he has a way of judging that I do not know.

"Marsh," he says impulsively. "I've been thinking a lot about you today. You're the best friend I have, you know. You think me rather wonderful, I can tell that. I'm not, of course, but you see me that way. And that's what matters. I'm going to miss you terribly when you go, you old son of a gun. You will go, of course. And you should. You really belong back there." He pushed against the air as though opening a door. "You know, I think of even friendship as being provisional, although I don't like that word. It mustn't bind, it mustn't hold back. If we like our friends, we must know how to let them go. They are like clouds, I often think. We mustn't love them any less because the wind is in them and they move."

I do not agree with him though I let him think so. He has awakened me to Now, and I am caught in its shimmering net. I do not want it to change, to pass. I do not acknowledge his resolution of love and the flux of things. I resent this flowing away of the world, this Now that I have come to love so much. Though my mind is given to the concept that "the One remains," my heart denies it, clinging to "the Many that fade and pass." Even in the full joy of Now, I resist. I long to put ramparts against change around me while Ray stands in the rainbow stream of time like a filter of its beauty. Already he seems a phantom to me, and I think of his illness with terror, but I will not believe in his death which he accepts so calmly as though it has become a particularly radiant way of looking at life.

On the boat going home, I am full of controlled sadness and nostalgia, whereas Ray once again moves happily about among the others. I lean over the railing and watch the wake of the boat as it churns a huge foamy braid of dying color, and I think of it as holding in tow forever the purple island behind us, a rope which I have not been able to sever, though Ray shows me that it is possible, for he moves on, unmoored, neither imprisoned by things nor enslaving them. That's it—he takes the Now with him, while I leave it behind. Is it those alone who have something eternal to live for who know how to say farewell?

Today I am here. It is my first morning in Rio, not yet the island but the grand vestibule of embarkation, and I love it. I have come back from a long trip to a city full of greetings. There are so many here, like me, who belong to the time I love, who have perhaps saved it and stored it in the present-past forever. There's Helena Soares, Bibi Guedes, Henrique Paranagua, Carlos Bandeira, and many others. I think of their vital wreath of friendship which belongs to Ray and me.

But first I want to look around. I don't want to see anyone until I am entirely *in situ*. There's my work to do, of course, the contacts to be made, but I do these rapidly, efficiently, with blinders on, sealed in a tube of aggressive action. I do not let it set up conflicts; it is water rushing through concealed pipes in an abundant system of its own. It creates power for its own ends, it belongs to itself alone. There is no feeling in that part of me which it uses as a duct.

I am staying at the Gloria, and I like its dignified, traditional elegance which has been old-fashioned for a long time. It is an architectural time-pause which assures me that what I am looking for is here. During all my free hours I wander through the streets of the city with expectation, the old streets first, the Rua do Ouvidor, which is unchanged. I have the sense of looking for someone in the crowd and wonder if the next corner will bring us bumping against each other. But then, as I walk along, I have a slightly sickening sense of being utterly alone. I cannot seem to see in the way that I believe. Never before have I had such a feeling of insubstantiality. I lean against the side of a building to bruise memory into my being as the stuff of Now, for I feel the narrow abyss of the street that contains the stream of people in which I have drenched myself as a reviving baptism crumble and fade away, leaving me in a spatial desert which I must rebuild and repopulate with the eyes of change. It is as though I were a god on a plateau of nothingness and the great burden were mine. I must build a city, and I must sire a people.

Though I am not given to panic, and I know this is just a mood, I return in a state of exhaustion to the Gloria. I sit in a chair on the terrace looking toward Sugar Loaf, whose contours are like a shape of Forever, and across the blue water which changes only in terms of itself. The vista of the ocean makes me think of Doris, for only last anniversary I gave her an aquamarine which was like a congealed solution of its enchantment. At twilight, as her white hand moved in the dark, I used to watch it dartling the blue beacon of a world I could not forget. I wonder if she ever suspected that it was an amulet she wore for me.

I remember how much I have talked to her about Rio and that talking to her helped to insure me of its reality. We have spent so many evenings together on a couch looking at photographs, joint custodians of their vivid story. Perhaps the reliquary atmosphere began to bore her after a while. The night she got up in the middle of a film about Rio I was showing to some friends and slipped into her bedroom, where I found her weeping and complaining of a headache, convinced me that was so. I think she knew I never quite forgave her. Nevertheless, I half wish that she were here with me. Could she have helped, I ask myself, today on that plain when the sides of the world fell away?

The waiter brings me a Scotch and soda. I sip it slowly, feeling very much myself in the dreariest way possible without anyone around as the *bête noire* of it all. This entire voyage seems the most fantastic fiction of my life, a story that threatens to take the narrative thread in hand and loop it into some perversely knotted ending. This is the five o'clock slump, I tell myself. It will pass.

What I need is a trip to the island. Before I see any of the others, I determine to go. Yes, tomorrow.

I feel good this morning. It is an exquisitely clear day for crossing to Paquetá. On the boat going over, the old wing-feeling of moving toward pleasure is with me again. I conjure up the presence of two young men who are off on a lark, hungrily devouring every moment of time without a niggard trace in their affections. I am myself. I am Ray. I am clear as the morning in my feelings; they are a passageway again; the world flows through them, and look—I am holding nothing back! The strong pull of the island is in my blood. I am going back to Now, I am recovering what I should never have left behind. I am a man in search of the present. I believe it exists on the island.

Suddenly I am disturbed. Nearby there are two young soldiers, an American and a Brazilian, in their brown and green uniforms, talking and laughing. They are braided together in friendship that swings free in the motion of time. The young American has learned some Portuguese and the Brazilian a few sentences of English; they are talking about girls, games, and the war, in bright, dashing phrases. They are on a jaunt; they are making the best of time. The Brazilian is probably a member of the Expeditionary Force soon to be sent across; one of them, perhaps both, will die before it is all over. Their voices strike my reverie with the lash of a scourge and leave it in tatters. They have burst through its silken tympanum like wayward clowns who mock everything but the moment's moment. They live in a zenith-world of happiness which is ruthless without knowing that it is so.

The rising sound of their voices lifts a great wave of the war above me, a brilliant, curving thrust that would inundate and capsize the boat. But they are riding the crest, buoyant at the point they will remember all their lives. I think of the downsweep when they have rushed over the hump of excitement and happiness. I think of afterward, which is the greatest trap of all. I think of those, like these young men perhaps, who will win the short war and lose the long one. I see their wave of happiness above me; it has a classic gleaming light upon it; I listen, as in a tragedy, for the thump of its impact as it flattens on the leveling shore.

I look up and see the buffer-mouth of the pier looming toward me and brace myself for the collision I have longed for. The island is mine at last! I have forgotten the war for the moment as I let myself be spawned with the crowd into the island stillness. It is only when they have all vanished as through exits in a scene that I am forced to admit that I am here to play it all alone. The island awaits the great, good words of the protagonist, for such now have I become. It listens for the soliloquy which I alone can speak. There is an indescribable solemnity here, gravely beautiful, but without the sparkle I remember, like a jewel turning in the sun. I see that the island lies in a kind of eternal quiescence—everywhere there is a sense of waiting.

I know I must walk to the little cemetery where Ray is buried, and I do so slowly, with the curious sense of fictive movement. I believe that the radiance I lack is Ray's to give me again. If I can be sure that he is inviolable, that what he has become in diminuendo can return in the full diapason of memory, I will know that I am right, that where we were alive, we are alive.

It is a windless day, there is no motion anywhere but my own. The banks of bougainvillea, rose and purple, rise above me, encircle and enclose me, no longer seen from above, pliant and swaying, in the longing remoteness of a glass-bottomed boat. I am "down-under," I am within. I have come home to Now. The ceaseless prowling motion of the boat is over.

But, suddenly, there is a tremor of the wind, petals fall in a purple ash around me, and I look up as from a depth into the descending whirls, so thick that they would seem to bury me in their death of flowers. Here is the casting on of petals, I think, with an awakening sense of escape, and I look down at Ray's grave to yield him from it, but the earth is secure and sealed with the light of morning shining above it, and all that I think I see on the bright surface of the grass is the reflection of myself. I have come a long way to pay such homage. I feel like a man who has watched a tyrant laid to rest.

Now that I know, I can leave, for Ray has won again. He has expelled me forever from the island as he tried to do so long ago. He has brought me to that point where he lived his life with the sense of death around it. He has opened that final dimension of our friendship to me. He has taught me to hear the dark, attendant mother who speaks lest we starve in the midst of fullness, who tells us that to be able to live we must know how to die. I shall never forget the Now of all that lovely past for it has taught me at last to want to live again, and I know that that is what memory is for.

I think of Doris and her patience—now I see it—her unfaltering dedication to the world as it is. I think of New York, that massive pressure of man, built against the Unanswered and Unknown, straining mightily, sometimes obtusely, but convinced that in some mysterious way it lies at the edge of radiance. Perhaps it is not too late, perhaps there is still time, I tell myself, as though I have discovered the oldest and youngest strength of man, words to be spoken by the protagonist above the chorus that reminds: There was a boat with an eye of glass.

The Ugly Duckling

American diplomacy has its ugly ducklings, and, unlike those of the charming fairy tale, they are supposed to remain so and never become swans. They are the Foreign Service officers who are given the posts nobody else wants—the unhealthy, the unattractive, the unimportant places, always in the hinterlands, never in the capital unless it were some backward and unappealing city. The glamor post in South America during the Second World War was Rio, and it became the languorous pond where all the good little swans were kept unless they showed signs of becoming black, whereupon it was quickly discovered that they were ugly ducklings and were speedily demoted to an outpost. The Keeper of the Swans was, of course, the Ambassador, an expert ornithologist as far as Foreign Service birds were concerned. His career officers at least were all expected to be of proper plumage, handsome, opulent, ruthless, and to feed only from the hand of their Keeper, some kind of magical personage who had once been a swan himself.

Indeed life at the Embassy in Rio had many aspects of a fairy tale but with a sharp edge, as it turns out many fairy tales do. It was a construction of American power so decorative that, on all sides, it cut into the flesh of Brazil without the somewhat somnolent patient's being aware of the fact that an incision was being made. But like the original fairy tale, it would have lacked the contrast which is one of the real sources of identity if it had not had its ugly ducklings, its male Cinderellas who were supposed to sit forever among the ashes. These were the officers who, try as they might with every spiritually androgynous effort at their command, would never fit a foot into the glass slipper or if they managed to do so with great discomfort would only show their knobby bunions and repugnant corns through that lovely transparency.

They had known all along at the Department in Washington that Harrison Chandler Jones was born to be an ugly duckling, and they alerted the Keeper in Rio that he was being sent down for no other purpose, and it was up to His Excellency to set the fledgling down in the proper puddle or fabricate one if that were necessary.

The Ambassador, who had disposed of his sort many times before, knew just what to do with the new arrival. In a brief, dazzling audience that was so well managed that it even extended a totally illusory promise to poor Jones that he, too, might one day become a swan and fly back to Rio, the Ambassador gave him his first assignment. Vice Consul Jones was to open an office at Corumbá in the Mato Grosso which would serve as a "listening post" for the Embassy, and he would report regularly to the Ambassador on such matters as pro-Nazi sentiment, anti-Americanism of any kind, economic and political possibilities on the rim of power. The Ambassador did not expect Jones to discover any of these conspiracies or possibilities nor did he care, but he wanted him *there*. Diplomacy loves embellishments and evasions, and the term "listening post" was both a euphuism and a euphemism since in Corumbá there would be nothing but silence and lethargy while, on the other hand, Jones was not to be allowed to think that anything even remotely attached to the swannery in Rio could be futile or meaningless.

Harrison Chandler Jones, whose name like his life receded into the commonplace, had been born into an unimportant but ambitious Mid-Western family, and was schooled by his environment to swallow both the euphuism and the euphemism. He was one of the people who extravagantly admire those who may be morally and spiritually inferior to themselves, and to be in the Foreign Service at all was to be important, mysterious, an associate swan, at least in the eyes of the readers of the newspaper in his home town. Jones's mother, the romanticist who had given him the first two names as a cover-up for what she feared would be his basic destiny, was overjoyed when he passed his examinations with more than creditable colors and was sent down indiscriminately to Brazil to be assigned his duties at the discretion of the Ambassador.

At this point, I may as well bring myself into the picture as a swan, not of the very first degree but still the one who was to look after the ugly duckling. The Ambassador had appointed me as Jones's contact man for the Embassy, which meant simply that I was to keep him out of the Ambassador's hair after the audience that was to be repeated only on the rarest of occasions. By way of introduction, I will say that there were several reasons I was considered by my superiors as a bird of second degree. Though born an authentic swan, with Choate and Princeton in my background, after seven years, admittedly at excellent posts, I was somewhat less than chauvinistic about the Service. If only I could have just looked the part, as I most certainly did, and stopped there, nothing more would have been expected of me. I was still trim and resilient from athletics at Princeton, with dark hair, brown eyes, good features of the sort you might find looking out at you from the society sections of *Vogue*. My life had been cut out for me by my father and my mother, both excellent social tailors, and I had simply slipped into it as into a good suit and worn it for thirty years. Well and good, except that I have been accused of having a sense of humor, and the Ambassador undoubtedly suspects me of having a heart, an organ which he thinks should be left entirely in the possession of tradespeople and laborers.

A sense of humor I do have, but I do not think the status quo is in any danger from my heart. Or at least I did not think so until Jones walked into my lazy life as through a door that opened into a room which housed a deity. Crushes are supposed to live and die their essentially pathetic little lives at preparatory school during adolescence, but in some men and women this is the only form of human attachment that will ever really do. I suppose poor Harry did have just such a crush on me, and, unwittingly at first, I must have fed it and fed it until it took a direction neither of us had counted on. Much has been said about the hero-worshipper but perhaps not enough about the hero who lets it happen.

Be that as it may, the personality debauch we finally engaged in, and I can describe it in no other way since it was both addictive and, in the end, degrading, all came about because Harry wanted to be an authentic swan, and I was the only one of the birds of that feather who would let him come near. After taking one look at him, I should have said, "Look, Harry. Though you don't know it, the Ambassador is actually making fun of you. You'll never make it in the Foreign Service, not in the way you want. Why don't you go home to Ohio, become a grain feed salesman and enjoy beer and broads on Saturday?"

In those days in the career service you always began with looks and manners, and if the man had anything else, well, that might help keep the Republic going. Even for America, which is known the world over for its outlandish-looking types, Harry was something of a specimen. He was over six feet of extended bone structure which had earned him the nickname of "Length without Strength" in high school where he went out for basketball and made it a hilarious comedy of pratfalls and misplaced shots. He looked pressed out by a very bumpy roller, his long, narrow face a residue of substance forced to the top. But since I am partial to good complexion in both men and women, perhaps Harry's most unredeeming feature was his skin, which was so pock-marked that one imagined a long, sulphurous, and volcanic case of acne subsiding in craters. But I have acquired the habit, which I greatly rcommend as facilitating social intercourse with unattractive types, of concentrating exclusively on whatever good feature a person may have, and Harry did have good eyes. They were blue, sensitive, capable of a great range of emotional weather, and they made you think of that line of Browning's about "lyric Apollo." Except, otherwise, Apollo was just nowhere to be found. He had given his eyes and his body to two different people. Will you blame me if I tell you that I always talked to Harry's eyes while I had the distinct impression that he talked to my body. In a certain sense, this is the story of the difficulties of that sort of conversation.

I must admit that I did not do too much for the Vice Consul during his first few days in Rio while he was still Mr. Jones to me, and I was Paxton Davis, surrogate for the Ambassador, since there was his fervid misconception of the Embassy to sustain him and there was Rio which falls upon the new arrival like a hopeless disease from which he will not, and will not want to, recover. But if its beauty is, in the long run, cancerous, it is entirely painless at first. After a while, when you see that its physical fascination means to have mainly a moral effect, at least in the Anglo-Saxon, you begin to want anodynes, and the usual ones of sex and drink seem paltry indeed. You will discover then that it was an illness that did its work by arousing extravagant expectations and that you were not up to the demands. In a sentence, it suggests a grand passion and all you can come up with is a seamy little love affair. Americans are the world's greatest addicts of extravagant expectations, and I have never known one who did not at first treat Rio as a stage for personal realization. Well, Rio has only supernumeraries, casting itself as protagonist, and if you were wise, I suspect you would regard it as a peep show, not to be looked into too steadily, but I had not been able to sell myself on that sort of protective asceticism, and, at first, I didn't even try with Harrison Chandler Jones. Anyway, I half wanted the poor bastard to make me feel the town was for real.

I didn't even mind for a while his running on about how great "the Service" was, our staff, particularly the Ambassador. It was like having a child or a student around who thinks you're wonderful except that you want it to be someone else's child, and Harry was my child, my responsibility. Curiously enough though, I wanted him to like me. No dogs were allowed in the Embassy, but here was this lean, slightly mangy creature who wagged his tail all day long. After the rivalries and tensions of the Embassy, it was restful to be exposed to such canine devotion, for dogs are all such idealists.

One of the most pleasant things about idealists, at least in the early stages of their affliction, is that they are so complimentary. Though I had a pleasant apartment on the Copacabana, I had long since lost interest in it, knowing how unfavorably it compared with the more luxurious quarters of the Ambassador's favorites who always turned out to be the richest members of the staff. But when I invited Harry out for drinks every afternoon after work, he gave my place "the treatment."

There were things from my posts in France, England, and Iran, and he went around to each one as if it had a price tag on it.

"This is beautiful," he would say, and I looked smug.

"This Persian rug could be a wall hanging." Not if it could talk, I thought with a smile.

"Isn't she lovely? Don't you look at her every night before you go to bed?" he exclaimed before a watercolor of one of Marie Laurencin's *jeune filles*. Perhaps, my boy, but Brazilian girls are better.

When we paused in the study where I hung my family photos, father with his fishing gear, mother in riding habit, snapshots of myself on the hockey squad at Choate and the rowing team at Princeton, they had a going over too.

"You *have* had a fortunate life, haven't you?" he beamed, and I thought it was time to say, "Sit down, old man," for that was what he had made me feel like. In it all, too, there was a hint of expropriation. As long as a man can extravagantly embrace what you no longer admire, he makes an unconscious move toward making it his own.

By the time Jones left for Corumbá, we were "Pax" and "Harry" to each other, and our strange little saga was under way. I felt terribly letdown after his departure, and it occurred to me for the first time in my life how much those of us who have grown tired of ourselves depend for our construction on others. The best, as well as the worst, mirror in the world is another human being, and Harry had shown me what a swan I was. It was a shame in a way to let him leave so poorly briefed about the real situation in Rio, but what headway could I have made at that point against his dogged enthusiasm?

Depending on me to have his equipment and supplies flown into him from Rio, Harry established his consular office with great dispatch. I waited eagerly for his first report, half hoping he would react to the flies, the heat, the malaria, the bad food, the boredom, as I would have. Already I was beginning to see myself in Corumbá which was not at all what Harry would have liked. He wanted me *here* as much as the Ambassador wanted him *there*. His long reports were filled with specific details about the town, its possibilities and needs, and were written for experts, but, of course, none of us were. And I don't think Harry minded since he was too intent on constructing a Corumbá that would seem worthy of the interest of swans. He even filled us in on the workings of the water system, such as it was. I think he really thought we would come down in a flock one day, see him *in situ,* and congratulate him on the creation of a town which had never existed before. He asked me in his letters if the Ambassador read his reports with interest, and, of course, I said he did. As a matter of fact, they were circulated around the Embassy ostensibly to inform but really to amuse, and he became known as our Big Ear in Corumbá.

"How's the Big Ear doing?" became one of my greetings in the corridors of the Embassy. Some of the humorous aspects of the situation rubbed off on me, and I could sense that, in the eyes of fellow officers, there was a slight tinge of gray on my ruffled feathers. I grew defensive and had my little revenge by analyzing the reports with pertinent parts underlined in red as if for stupid children and recirculating them from the Ambassador's desk on down with recommendations for action.

No action was taken, of course, and Harry asked permission to come to Rio for consultation. When the Ambassador shunted him off to me, I put him up in my apartment and lived and breathed Corumbá for three days. He made me walk down every street of that miserable little town as if it were a potential Garden of Eden, brought into bloom by American dollars, and I was soon on a first name basis with all of its officials and town characters. There is unquestionably a kind of super-enthusiasm which can produce something which otherwise would not exist. Poets and artists are so endowed, and Harry had this feeling about Corumbá. It was obsessional and maybe even a little despotic so that I began to call him privately the Caliph of Corumbá. One had to think of Harry as many things, I discovered, to keep from thinking of him as he really was.

But even Harry finally became exhausted, as all compulsive

talkers do, and then I force fed him Rio. We took in all the cafés, nightspots, lay for hours on the beach where he stretched out like a hairy stringbean etiolated by the sun. I dipped him in the rich oils and dyes of the city's inexhaustible drums and vats. I gave him great handfuls of the glitter of the night streets. If Corumbá was going to do him in, as I suspected it might, I wanted to fatten him for the kill. Though he only reddened and peeled from the sun, got diarrhea from the food, I persuaded myself that he went back happier and better from everything I could give him, and I truly wanted to give him *something* in the early days of our encounter. If the goose, by some rare chance, did lay the golden egg in Corumbá, I would have provided some of the gold.

I still have loads of snapshots of Harry in Rio, but these days they remind me of pictures one might have found in Himmler's files after the war. He looks so thin, so corporeally not *there* except for his eyes, the life force from which everything else in him was strung. And how I could manipulate those eyes, so it seems now, simply by putting myself before him. Remember when you were a child breaking open a doll and finding weights on the back of the eyeballs that made them open and shut? Well, I was the weight in Harry's vision which made it open and shut. Or so the snapshots seemed to say.

In most of the pictures, Harry is looking into the camera, but he somehow gives the impression of having another pair of eyes on the side of his face looking at me. I am looking into the camera, too, no doubt about that, and I always manage to look so goddam superior and confident like an SS officer on leave who has taken along a man from Auschwitz for kicks. It gives you a creepy feeling that the lousy European war was going on everywhere.

But the funny thing is that in another way those pictures don't mean a thing. They are grotesques. They are gargoyles in the sun. And that's why I can't stand to look at them anymore. Except for Harry's eyes, they are so *still*. They give no quarter, no indication of anything that was attempted. The interaction got lost in the negatives. It looks ludicrously one-sided. There is only one victim. It leaves no room for interchangeability, that source of so much of the real drama of life. Harry looks like the last beggar while I have all the money in my pockets.

But that was not the way it was, at least not at the beginning. When Harry went back, I felt I had come into something; he had left more than he had taken. At idle moments in the office, I found myself wandering the streets of Corumbá. I began to improve upon it in ways Harry would never have imagined. His

practicalities of sanitation and engineering were not enough.
Niemeyer would have to be imported to erect some of the stunning modern architecture he had built in Rio. An idealist's town
would need an idealist's setting. I saw myself *there* instead of
Harry, in my crisp white suit dedicating a new building or opening
a new school. As Paxton-*cum*-Harry I would need a mistress, one
of those slightly dusky Brazilians, luscious as a milk chocolate
filled with fruit and cordial in a box of hard centers. I even gave
her the name of Amalita which sounded properly amorous.

But a strange thing happened. I discovered that I was sometimes jealous of Harry and that my jealousy took the form of
erasing him. He was just not in Corumbá anymore or if he were,
he walked inside of me. No one had the right to be like Harry and
not look like me. *Clear the hell out of there, Harry. You are not wanted.*
You are a dead duck, Harry. Amalita loves me not you, Harry. Beat it,
chum.

Such mental shenanigans, fostered by indolence of which there
was a great deal in an Embassy whose processes were overelabo-
rated in relation to their substance, did no more harm at first than
a bad movie. But then as if I were trying to read two sides of a
page at once, my ambivalence began to clash in the center. What I
would not tolerate in Harry there, I would indulge here. I defended him on every occasion from my fellow officers. I would
not let them enjoy their scapegoat. I brought him up at every staff
meeting and espoused his every cause. I ruffled the feathers of
every swan in sight by praising the ugly duckling. The Keeper was
not amused.

So it didn't work, not in one way or another. I am convinced
that there are an infinite number of possibilities and would-be
combinations in life that do not. I think we live in a great unseen
sea of *disjecta membra,* a floating world of things that never came
off, love affairs and friendships that did not endure, partial meanings and half-truths that never melded. I think all of history is
heavily drenched with disconnected passions and ideas that might
have been better than those that do unite. I think that life, in this
sense, is both abysmally cluttered and dreadfully loose.

In the year that followed, Harry came to Rio as often as the
Embassy would permit. But as time went on and the Ambassador's
indifference deepened into hostility, Harry and I more patently
shifted roles. It was I who talked about Corumbá and he who
came as a scavenger to Rio. You see it was I who wanted him *there*
so that I could be there, whereas he seemed to have lapsed into a
melancholy homing instinct for Rio. He seemed to listen less and

watch me more. I had the feeling that he annotated and reannotated every gesture I made, every smile I gave him. When I lighted a cigarette with my Dunhill, I was for a moment a well-kept hand and an expensive lighter suspended like a spirit-part before him. I was a Sulka tie, a custom-made shirt or shoe, a suit from the best tailor in Rio. His vision, I felt, swam with these things, but he could not quite discover the secret of their combination. How on earth did you put together a swan? He asked me prices and places, and he took it all in, but I never saw that it changed him at all. If anything, he looked shabbier and more emaciated as time went on, a crooked-faced Pinocchio put to the rack and stretched out further than his material substance would allow.

"Harry," I said one afternoon over liberal Scotches, "I think I am going to get us some money for a Cultural Institute in Corumbá. The English are considering it, so the Ambassador will probably follow suit."

"Really," he said, looking at the star sapphire on my finger. "Shall I draw up a plan?"

"Yes, please do. And ask for more than we need like a good little consul, and perhaps we'll get what we want." I didn't mean to sound proprietary, but that perhaps was the effect.

"Oh, I'm an old hand at asking," he said, and that was that. He had had enough swan-talk for one afternoon. So I took him out girl-hunting. I would find us an Amalita. I would know what to say to her for him. I would take her back to Corumbá. *Beat it, Harry. Go home, Harry. No ducklings allowed.*

That night, a lovely cool one in the rapidly diminishing Brazilian winter, we took two of the girls to the Urca for a final fling. In a burst of generosity or inner confusion, whichever it was, I paired off with the less attractive of the two. Goddamit, I suddenly wanted Harry to strut his stuff. You see, I was still capable of this sort of reversal. The trouble was, the next moment, if things didn't go right, I could have made a lampshade of his skin. When you come to the conclusion that the original may be false, you are likely to have a turbulent relation with any would-be reproduction. But Harry's date had no such misgivings. She spent the entire evening flirting with me, and I could have strangled the little bitch. When we danced, she clung to me in her red dress like a long flowing bloodstain while Harry sat there and watched, getting quietly drunk. I could have kicked him too. I could have tossed him on the dunghill of history right then and there. My date, of course, refused to cooperate, flagellating him with the fact that she also preferred me. No one cursed or slapped anyone else or said anything obscene, but the whole evening was like something out of de Sade. I went home exhausted and in a foul temper, and when I tried to undress Harry and get him into bed, he just lay there moaning and mumbling. "Don't do it. Don't touch me, don't touch me, don't touch me." That's friendship, I thought, when all the man's got in the whole goddam country is me. I threw my jacket over him and went to bed.

It was the last time I saw Harry for quite a while. There were no reports and no requests for consultation in Rio. His letters which would at least have fed my personal situation ceased. Rio, which gives few clues to the fact that there is anything in Brazil besides itself, was once more circular in its beauty. The Embassy was a stagnant pond lurid with a huddle of swans. It strained, it entangled, it finally snapped my fantasy. I was pure swan again. I was Paxton Davis-*sans*-Whatever-His-Name-Was. I felt light and floating and disjoined in my own world. I hated Harry Jones for all that I was worth. I called home Amalita forever. I razed the Niemeyer buildings. I took away the glass bell and let the jungle in.

When you go back to being a swan full-time, you are likely to discover that you are all feathers and no flesh. Whatever a taxidermist puts inside his specimens, I must have had in me. Rio was still Rio, the sensualist's paradise, and there were still Ledas everywhere, and I slept with my usual succession, but it was all shadowaction. Jove's bird does not lend his myth; he yields to those who can forcefully take his place. My assignment in Rio became a life in costume, but Harry's touch had been insidious. I could feel the melanosis of the black swan setting in.

I did not have to wait long, however. The war in Europe was drawing to a close, and the Ambassador, who, it was rumored, was to be a representative of the Liberation, began to put his house in order. An excessively tidy man, he did not intend to leave any loose strings from which his successor might make a noose. He had fattened the staff of his empire beyond all necessity except that of vanity, and he began to expedite the trimming. He called me in one morning and told me as the one person who had the slightest interest that he was closing the office in Corumbá and had already telegraphed Jones to that effect. I was as stunned as the prostitute must have been when Van Gogh sent her his ear. Jones was to be given a month or so to conclude his affairs and would be sent back to the Department for reassignment.

During the next several weeks one could hear nothing around

one but the nervous flutter of wings since it had become known that the Magical Personage would be picking and choosing from among us those he would call to Europe in whatever post he was assigned to reopen. Jealousy was so rampant that the Embassy writhed with an atmosphere of white snakes coiling around the feet of the Ambassador. It was rank and murderous, and I had to get away from it for a while. But still no word from Harry.

I was due for a short leave, so I decided to simply fly in on him unannounced. It was the wrong thing to do, of course. It was like dropping in on someone too early the morning after. But I sold myself a bill of goods about going by beginning to fantasize again. Harry must be in trouble. I would organize a rescue party of one. The concept of Brazil thrives voraciously on the notion of rescue parties. Those you don't hear from in some time could be, and often are, in the hands of many sorts of enemies, natural and human. As an extension of my own hostility, I preferred to think, however, that something shady was going on in Corumbá. Old Harry might very well be planning to abscond with Embassy funds in the company of Amalita or a reasonable facsimile thereof. I even checked with the Embassy bursar and discovered that in the last few months Harry's financial accounts had indeed not been adequately reported. This was good news. I remembered that the headmaster of the American School in Rio had recently brought off this sort of ducking out with school funds plus mistress, and was presumably living it up in some part of the country people like our Ambassador did not acknowledge. Bully for the headmaster! He had taken things in his own hands. He had made a little loop in history that wasn't supposed to be there. He had made an unconventional combination.

I was positively ebullient as I made my travel plans. If you knew Harry, as I know Harry, oh, oh, oh, what a guy!—that was my mood. It was Harry-*cum*-Paxton again. The formaldehyde was flushed from my veins by the time I got on the plane. I needed to go to Corumbá. It was like a rehabilitated addict's going after a fix again.

But the trip sobered me up. It was an old plane, it bumped roughly when it hit an air pocket, and I was thoroughly sick. When we arrived, my white suit was spotted and rumpled, and I felt as if I looked like Harry. *Beat it, Harry. Clear out, chum. No swan songs allowed.*

Nevertheless, it was time to open the ripe fruit of my imagination. This is the thing that every sentimentalist who ever lived would almost rather die than do. But, we open everything in time, the bodies of women and then their spirits, friendships that reach an impasse, the stalemates of our beliefs—Or we have them opened for us. The modern world that has devoted so much of its energy to opulent surfaces is irresistibly drawn toward the disclosure of centers, and, in general, plans in advance not to like or admire what it finds there. Open and destroy. I am a child of my time with this difference. I cannot be reconciled to what I am likely to find at the center of my experience even if I have put it there myself. If you find a mist in a box, close it up and it may harden into a jewel. But I am hasty, I am somewhat heartless, I, too, undo the box as often as I shut it. I do not give it time to jell in my imagination. I do not persistently imagine it there whether it is or not. I cannot make history with the strange, bewildering parts that are given me.

Corumbá was a miracle of repulsion to a person like myself. How on earth could poor, dear Harry have put it into a box for even a moment? I don't mean to suggest that at one time a considerable human effort had not been made. There were homes, service buildings of different kinds, churches, but they all looked as if they had suffered from a long wasting illness. Perhaps the war had had a peculiarly deflating effect, for in spite of people and animals passing by, occasional vehicles stirring up the dust, there seemed to be an abysmal silence. It was as if a whole town had the muffled tone of a sickroom, and yet sullen too, as some people become when illness defeats their every move toward health. One could not get over the feeling that this town was not meant to be.

I found Harry's office without any difficulty since it was the only place that showed any signs of recent painting. It was ten o'clock in the sort of tropic morning that makes any white man feel made of rancid wax. With a gin and tonic at his side, Harry sat at the desk I had sent him. He was sitting profile so he did not see me for a while, and I had time to take in the scene. It showed signs of having been, as near as he could make it, a replica of my office in Rio. And then I noticed how he was dressed. The shirt which was open at the collar and not very clean nevertheless reminded me of my shirtmaker. The rumpled white trousers did not belong to any of the suits he had worn in Rio. Finally I saw on a rack in the corner a coat which could not have come from any tailor but mine. Glancing at him, I noticed beside a pack of cigarettes on the desk a Dunhill lighter standing upright like a silver monument. I felt totally trapped.

"I've been waiting. I've been expecting you," he said, and indeed it looked as though he had been there for a very long time. I let him have a final look at a swan and then I closed the box. I went back to Rio by the next plane. I did everything I could for him by remote control. I sent out a clerk to help him pack and to sober him up. I did not any longer want Harry *there.* I wrote a special report on him for the Department praising his work. I lied to the Ambassador about what I had found, and, of course, he was very happy to have me do so.

For the Keeper of the Swans is a maker of certain history. He discards the parts that most likely will never combine. He is unaware of the rich saturation of death around him. It will never matter in the least to him that Harry-*cum*-Paxton never emerged.

Well, that's that. Some of us are stuck with the incongruities of the imagination. I like to call us the "mythological people." We lurk at the fringes of experience, wanting to be let out. We support each other in our roles as if providing for escape. We are the ones who conceive griffins, centaurs, and mermen. Or we yearn for a swan with the heart of a duckling. We open and close the box.

The Edge of the Fountain

On the terrace of the Bolero, Dr. Edwin Woodley sat looking out over the Copacabana beach, sipping a *cafézinho*. He did this often now after his afternoon class at the University of Brazil since it gave him back that largesse of soul which he had preserved as carefully as he could through forty-five years.

One could tell at a glance that he was a person of culture and intelligence. His baldness merely served to increase an imposing intellectuality as though incessant thought had cleared away the tangle and growth of hair in order that the bone structure might shine through more powerfully, and his skin, though of a pink and pleasing good health, showed no trace of jowls. It was a countenance reminiscent in overall impression, though the detail was different, of the shorn power, the denuded grace, the handsome, glowing mentality which appear in some of the photographs of Henry James, on whom, so it happened, Dr. Woodley was an authority.

This was the fourth week of eight which he was spending in Rio on leave from his professorship at Northwestern to teach a seminar group and deliver some public lectures on Hawthorne, Melville, Poe, Whitman, Dickinson, James, and the other "greats" of American literature. He was there on invitation from the Brazilian Government, the sort of "guest" which our State Department underwrites, allowing the entertaining country to save face by paying a token part of the expense involved.

As it happened, however, Dr. Woodley had been having an extremely difficult time extracting even this small gesture of the University's faith in him. Consequently he had been forced to go from one to the other to see about the matter, each man seeming to be an office without an occupation, until it had all come to be a little sinister, like an anecdote from a Kafka story, as though there were a monstrous tyrant behind all the rooms of officialdom to which he must pay some particularly degrading tribute before he could receive his due.

Matters were not helped at all by the fact that the Director of the Faculty of Philosophy, his immediate sponsor, was visible but non-accessible. He was a fat white worm of a man with sorrowful black eyes, but apparently someone to be reckoned with, a clever master of political maneuver who never got up until twelve o'clock in order to catch the world at the height of things. It was he who started the process of passing Dr. Woodley from hand to hand as though the incorruptible American might be worn down into some amenable shape of moral fatigue and capitulation.

Moreover, neither the University nor the Embassy, which took a dim view of professors and aesthetes scurrying around in time of war, had provided any publicity for the public lectures, and, though these were brilliant, quite the best that any American had brought there, Dr. Woodley found himself faced by a rapidly dwindling audience dropping like beads from a broken string until there was the mortifying experience of catching oneself "counting the house" as though in some evil sort of way the number of heads present was to signify the right of survival, the whole business becoming finally a kind of spiritual Inquisition.

These strata of the "situation" in Rio streaked Dr. Woodley's mood as he looked out over the water, letting the gulls draw the delicate strands of his loneliness to some indeterminate point. He was neither Embassy, nor Colony, nor the professional man with a demonstrable and practical defense of his presence, the engineer, the sanitation man, the "expert" of one kind or another. Nor, of course, could he align himself with the most powerful group of all, the businessmen who had swarmed into Rio on the waves of the war, making deals on the one hand, preaching democracy on the other, each one like a taut rope of the American way, stretching the material of the Idea to include everyone like a sort of mythic parachute that would save the world. Such an intellectual coverall Dr. Woodley detested, and he had refused to dangle in the big balloon of misrepresentation and nonsense with all the rest.

It was curious in a way that he should be in Rio at all—he admitted that to himself freely—recognizing the mixture of motives not altogether fitting into a single pattern. The decision to come to Brazil was one of his freer, more impulsive, basic moves—perhaps an unconscious answer to the chaos of the war, impelled by the notion that order and the sense of beauty as well should be tested in such a time. Perhaps, also unconsciously, he had a "southern exposure" in his soul, brought up, as he had been, in the cold country of Minnesota, and there was an unrecognized longing to warm himself in a more ardent and beguiling climate. Possibly the lure of Rio, a word blended of dazzling beaches, dark folk, the moistures and fecundities of desire, had stirred in him the slumbering wish to wear the many-colored robe of abandon.

His reflections as he finished his *cafézinho* and called for another had become more agreeable. Yes, thank God, he told himself, life and discipline had done that much for him. He knew how to dismiss the unpleasant as well as to force himself to return to it. And, in spite of the Ministry's anonymous bewilderments, the Embassy's indifference, he was determined to find the Brazilian experience rewarding—he would enjoy himself and get his work done. He would "possess" Rio, its startling crudities and unexpected beauties, mainly, as he had observed, transplantings from Europe, the old garden of the imagination to which he had been for so many summers a "passionate pilgrim." And he would observe the people, get to know them whenever possible, learn some snatches of their language, and become an *aficionado* of the best that was in them. All that mattered, as Ezra Pound had said, was "the quality of the affection."

As this caressive mood spread gently around him, he turned, looked out beyond the crowd again, over the crushed white of the surf, to the far emptiness of the ocean's sweep, assuaging himself with its containment. But, abruptly, he was brought back for there had been a thump nearby like the sound of a heavy fruit falling on stone.

A woman had sat down clumsily in the chair on the other side of the wicker table. She was not one of those Dr. Woodley had been resting his eyes on, the lovely Carioca girls who were like sticks of perfume on a simmering fire of pleasure, but looked indeed as though she had been cast down in anger, a lump of humanity, seeming all the more fleshly solid from having struck the sides of the world too often before arriving at what was apparently the bottom but which might yet give way into lower stories of disaster.

"Monsieur," she said, shifting heavily from her crumpled position, her whole body bulging from the chair like a final belching sigh. "I want to talk to you." She leaned forward in a conspiratorial hunch. "You will give me a few moments of your time, no?" It was curious that she combined French address and English discourse, the latter spoken with the intonation and accent of some *école* of long ago, giving Dr. Woodley the impression that she had mistaken his identity.

"Pardon me, *Madame*," he said, rising hastily, aware that his neatness, his modest blue suit, presented an unusual contrast to her dishabille, creating the tension of two worlds in the little café. "I'm sorry. Perhaps I have taken your table."

"No, no, no, *Monsieur*," she said with unexpected violence. "Sit down, please. I want to talk with you. You are an American, no? Then you can help me." The inert mask strained for a smile as though the lips were loaded with stone.

"What is it that I can do for you, *Madame?*" he asked as he sat down slowly. "I'm afraid I don't understand." But the signal of "handout" flashed ahead and he began to feel wary, fumbling at the same time toward his pocket.

Another careful look at the woman convinced him of his first impression. She was unmistakably European, naturally a refugee, one of the lonely and forlorn horde which he had seen in the streets. Over her wisps of sandy gray hair, she wore an old blue sun-scorched tam which gave her an even more squashed and dumpy look at the same time that it seemed to have shorn her of the halo of civilization which beautifully coifed hair gives to women. It was the head-covering, even the helmet, of necessity, the downward fall. Her woolen trench coat bore no relation to the weather, for the afternoon was warm. Apparently it was worn constantly, even slept in like the pelt of an animal—a rumpled, dismal affair of dingy tan, smudged with tawny beach sand of some abandoned siesta or evening sleep of a demoralized sense of locality. There was a brooch of red and white crystal at the neck-line, rather chic in its time perhaps, but a horrendous gewgaw now, a gaudy pustule of life's deceit. There were also visible between the lapels of the coat and below its border the remnant of a silk dress like a tattered flag of her *ancien régime*. Beneath, the bony poles of bare legs, burnt black as mummy flesh by the sun, pushed down into the filthy swaddling of a pair of old sneakers.

Out of this packed imagery of degeneration, the face loomed somewhat, but not greatly, startling in its sense of life not all yet hammered back into the animal pulp. This was most frightening of all to Dr. Woodley, the flicker, the spasm of humanity, which was worse than death, like the twitch of an insect jolting the mind into a last minute appraisal and regret for that snapping at one point in its network of the basic thread which unites all living things.

"You must help me, *Monsieur*," she said. "I have been wronged, horribly mistreated. They have beat me, they have put me in jail. They are pigs, these *brasileiros*, filthy pigs! Look at me, *Monsieur*. I am a woman of class, I am a graduate of the Sorbonne. But look at me. See what they have done!" The face puckered up in a grimace of tears which would not flow, but the effect, summoning more strength of passion than could be spared, had the force of a phantom-geyser. "But you, *Monsieur*. You have a good face. You will help me, yes?"

"But—but, *Madame*. I do not know you," Dr. Woodley said with reluctance, feeling curiously ashamed a moment after. "I'm afraid I don't know what your trouble is."

"But you will help. You can help me. You are an American!" The last word she flung at him like a dash of some final stimulant as she watched the closing expression of doubt, mistrust, and bewilderment. And then the walls of communication, throttled so long, rose in a shrill babel of French, English, German, Portuguese, as though the fusion of all language, rising and gorging the disused tube of the throat, were necessary to lift the mighty wail of her heart.

The rushing spout of words attracted a white-coated waiter who, evidently familiar with the woman, started to usher her out. She cringed at the sight of him, refocused her face and gave him a withering look that died of its own extravagance. Dr. Woodley waved the man away vigorously, maintaining his grip on an impulse which might have taken just such an opening of escape as had been offered it.

"Go ahead, *Madame*. I'm listening. I assure you no one will disturb us," he said, but the very connivance which he thereby cast around the unknown, this at least provisional acceptance without possessing the facts, was disturbing, for it put him in league with the chimaeras of destiny.

"Oh, *Monsieur*, thank you, thank you. You are not like the others. I have found a true American at last," she sighed, and laid on the table a greasy handbag, stuffed out of all proportion like a peasant's sack, a swollen tumor of her wanderings.

Then the story came out in ejaculations, rivulets, sudden passionate torrents of accusation and limp stretches of self-pity—disconnected, rambling, splenetic, febrile. It aroused a strangely glimmering feeling of the havoc from which all ideas must once have raised themselves. The words rose free, rational, and shining, cleansed of the entangling muck for a moment, and then sank back to the diffusion and defeat of their struggle.

But, in spite of the thrashings of her distress, the fragments of a past emerged. It appeared that she was not French but Yugoslavian, having come to Paris with her daughter after the death of her husband many years before. With income from work she obtained there, they had lived happily, using their free time to take courses at the Sorbonne, discovering all sorts of hidden affinities with the French, content to be expatriates forever. But the war had thrown them into a panic, and they had escaped to Lisbon just before the fall of Paris. There they had waited on the ominous threshhold, pondering the possibilities endlessly, finally deciding on separate explorations into the immediate future, a division calculated to avoid a single catastrophic defeat. The daughter, a successful photographer in Paris, was to go to New York, being perhaps more able to buck the bewildering enormity of the city, whereas she was to seek the more genial climate of the south, and the one who fared better would send for the other in a final healing of sundered forces.

As it turned out, there had been nothing in Rio for her. The city appalled her as blatantly primitive or superficially civilized, a jungle travesty of Europe. Unlike many of the refugees who had scurried under the cynical protection of *gran finos,* she could not pay lip service and had gone down, down, making, as it were, an excavation into ultimate possibilities of misery until her life had become a temporary footing in darkness down which the aimless hand was lured to throw a stone.

Her daughter had done better, though her position too was extremely precarious, and it was a question, not yet resolved, as to whether she should let go of the slender rope from which she dangled, go to Brazil and get her mother, only perhaps to flounder with her in a final embrace of defeat, or stay in New York and hold on with all her might until some feasible way of reunion could be worked out.

"All that I want, *Monsieur,* is just a visa," she said finally, and the last word fell from her mouth like a jewel hoarded there. "I have talked and talked with your Consul. And now they will not let me see him. I have not enough money, he says. I tell him that I have a lovely, kind daughter who will take care of me. But, no, no, he says. There would not be enough. She cannot guarantee my support, and I would only make her starve. I weep and cry, and he tells me the truth. There's a matter of your record with the police, *Madame,* he says. They have told him I am crazy. Twice I have been in jail already because I do not like the government here, because I want to go to America. And they beat me and tell me I am crazy."

"Well, *Madame,* I am very sorry to hear this. If you think I can help, I'll see the Consul tomorrow," Dr. Woodley said, for he could not deny this woman. Everything he believed in told him he should not. "Perhaps he'll listen to me. Perhaps—"

"Oh, thank you, thank you, *Monsieur,*" she broke in. "You will do it for me. You will get me the visa!"

And then her speech went to pieces altogether, mingling past, present, premonitions of the future, dashed against each other in negating phrases. Dr. Woodley did not know what to think. He wanted to feel for her, to take her side. But perhaps she was mad after all. It was getting late, and he excused himself, leaving her babbling and burbling like an old cauldron of despair and vengeance.

Standing in the bus line tumid with the crowds of a war society, he was astonished to see that the "woman" had added herself, a grimy, dessicated segment, to the fat caterpillar of people strung out along the walk. Well, she, too, must be going somewhere, but the whole thing had begun to give him a sticky, crawling feeling, and he longed for his bath and dinner. As though waiting for a receptive mood, the voice of one of the "authorities" with which his mind was stored, Santayana, the old philosopher among the Blue Nuns of Rome, quite unexpectedly drifted into recall: "It is possible to love human beings only in solitude." But he rejected it promptly, as he had always done, contesting the Olympian aloofness of such detachment.

Once ensconced in a seat buttressed by a rather gross Brazilian, he glanced behind him occasionally and saw her, still muttering away, waving, smiling, then looking at him blankly, while the gray bus lurched along frantically. As he got out at the hotel with relief, he remembered that she had forgotten the most important thing of all. She had never given him her name! All that run-on talk and not the final words that say "I am."

When he had bathed, and dined in a lovely *salon* of the Gloria, now a place of enchantment, a turret of pleasure on an angry hill, he felt much better, letting the plumes of his feelings shake out their radiance again with that focus on the agreeable and beautiful, as long as circumstances permitted, which more than once had "saved" his life. Remembering that he was going to hear Jennie Tourel in a concert of French songs at the Teatro Municipal, he descended to the *portaria* briskly. But as he hailed a taxi, the woman emerged from the shadows beyond the columns like a taunting denial of his well-being. This was ridiculous, absurd! He was not to be haunted. But he held on to himself, remembered his wish to be kind, and spoke pleasantly. Driving away, he looked back furtively as though wings of pursuit might unfold from within her, but she had leaned on the bulging belly of the lower wall, a wizened child against a heavy mother.

But it was not until he returned from the theatre and found her still leaning against the mottled yellow façade, her tan-brown dinginess like a protective coloring, that he got some inkling of what he was in for. This was too much! He had hoped to slip in unnoticed, but stirring from her stupor as though a secret mechanism had awakened her, she came weaving through the shadows, losing him just as he gained the revolving doors. The little thrill of escape took him back to his childhood. It was like Halloween. He was being chased by a witch!

But as he got into bed, he remembered her with overwhelming pity. He should not have run from her, he would do what he could for her tomorrow. He wanted and needed to sleep after an exhausting day in the maze of the University, but his famous power of concentration had finally deserted him. The voice of Tourel was still ringing softly in his ears, richly evocative of the old days, Paris of the "then," Paris of inviolable beauty, and he could have let himself float down to sleep in the flow of these memories, but they were constantly crossed and deflected by the muddy current of the woman's life, and it seemed that a thrombus moved in the stream of all things beautiful.

The next morning he went in early to see the Consul, a tall, big-boned man with an air of casual strength, who listened to him professionally, yawned a little as from a story heard too often, saying finally, "Yes, Professor Woodley, you needn't worry about not knowing the name. I know who she is. It's an old case. Been running on for several years. Dona Carlota, the kids in the street call her, though that's not her right name. They've even made up a samba about her, I understand. Quite a character around town. It's been one long headache to me. The old lady simply won't listen to reason, won't get it through her head that we can't grant her a visa under present circumstances."

The Consul raised his hand slightly, requesting the indulgence of silence as Dr. Woodley tried to interrupt him.

"You see, Professor," he went on, "there's simply no legal way of doing it. She has no money here or in the United States. I understand she lives on a pittance sent down by her daughter. Then there's the problem of her mental condition. The Brazilian authorities have declared her unbalanced, and this disqualifies any prospective entrant to the United States. It's a pity, of course, but, Professor, if you want my opinion, I think the police are right. The old lady is bats, simply bats. It was good of you to come in, but, if I were you, I'm afraid I'd just forget about it." He turned away from his visitor and glanced through the windows across the bay, lazily dropping the subject into the vat of blue, dissolvent color.

Dr. Woodley was stunned and angry when the Consul stood without shaking hands, surgically detached like a man in charge of a corrupt program of euthanasia. But there were classes to be met; one's emotions must be buckled in. The day beckoned to him out of its cloudless beauty, and he must trust it again, he told himself, as he walked toward the University under an avenue of palms whose swirling fronds had nothing but ease and forget-fulness in their rustling luxuriance. And yet he knew very well what probably lay ahead. One of the professors would stop him in the hall and tell him the story of an intrigue or persecution among the faculty, perhaps compare his salary with the prevailing stan-dard as a suggestion of encroachment. To his colleagues he had become a sort of magic lantern into which they could insert "slides" of the intramural struggle against the Ministry of Educa-tion. Often he was prepared to commit himself, when the contra-dictory view was convincingly inserted into the other side of his thinking by another colleague.

Late that afternoon, as he left the Faculty of Philosophy, having been spared the conspiratorial *tête à tête* for once, he was con-fronted by Dona Carlota who waited on the walk. She gave him a carved little grimace of recognition and imminent reproach as though she knew some bitter joke about everyone and everything. How had she known he would emerge at just that hour, how had she tracked him down before he had had time to compose an acceptable reason for his failure? He must meet the situation anyway, he must be kind, but this would have to be a conclusive scene. He must tell her he could do nothing for her, he would have to lop her off and drop her away from him into some vat of his own, the festering cloaca of life's irreconcilables, and he shud-dered inwardly with echoes of the morning.

"*Madame*," he said, fumbling for words. "I saw the Consul this morning. He told me to tell you—" But he didn't need to finish for, with a look of arrogant fury, she wrested the story from him like a stolen belonging.

"You lie, *Monsieur*. You did not try. You believed him, not me. You are worse than he is, because he does not pretend. He is cruel, but you only pretend to be kind." But suddenly the structure of her anger collapsed. "Forgive me, *Monsieur*, I was angry, I was disappointed. You will help me still, no?" You will speak to the Consul again. You will not let him believe the lies."

But Dr. Woodley had backed away. He could do no more at the

moment. It was six o'clock, the lowest hour of the evening. Above him the palms still swayed, revolving heads of clashing green knives that cut the sunset sky to bits and let in the dark. He walked to the bus stop, quickening his pace without seeming to run, while the frenzied old woman, now blurred in the twilight like an enormous brown hand waving at him, called out. "You are an American, *Monsieur*. You can do it if you will!" And she seemed indeed beyond her reason as she shouted the shibboleth of his nationality like the name of a god or devil in the contracting twilight.

Whatever finality, freedom, and sense of extrication Dr. Woodley carried to bed with him seemed not so certain in the queasy moments before breakfast, and when he emerged into the yellow morning light, there was Dona Carlota pacing back and forth before the columns, almost satisfying some perverse appetite of anticipation and prediction.

The "chase" was on. There was no doubt of it now. In the days that followed, Dr. Woodley was to wonder at his prowess in evasion, like a dexterity recovered from youthful games of "Cops and Robbers," as he dodged in and out of doorways, down out-of-the-way streets, taking cover in little frequented *botequims*, giving his pursuer the slip in a hundred artful ways. But he had not counted upon the resources nor the endurance of Dona Carlota. She was his shadow, his alter ego, the phantom of his other self. The possibility of deluding her became an absorbing consideration of each day, usually ending with their strange juxtaposition in some unpredictable place, a *cul-de-sac* of laughter or exasperation, according to the pressures of the moment.

If he met her going the other way, she wheeled around immediately as if drawn by a magnet inside his heart. Her schedule of wandering could be adapted to his precise sense of time and direction at a moment's notice, reminding him half humorously of the old semtimental song of Rudy Vallee, "My Time Is Your Time." Her "stickability" was maddening, and, in his bitterer moments, he could have shaken her off like a leech that sought some special syrup of his blood. In another mood, she appalled him as a kind of inescapable human evidence from which he had no right to flee "down the nights and down the days, down the arches of the years, down the labyrinthine ways."

He might be walking in the Praça Paris on an amber afternoon when the landscape was held in a pause of gold, and there was

Dona Carlota streaking every clarity of air through which she moved as though she expelled a potent, murky brown incense, a trailing banner of the world's derangement. On Saturday, if he went to the Copacabana for a swim, he was aroused from a sunbath by a rumbling blend of vituperation and supplication and saw her stretch out beside him, very much at home among the rocks and shells, almost whimsically aware that she had caught him naked in the white and winter refinement of his flesh.

Instead of riding on the bus, he took to catching a *bonde,* a wild, open-air jungle cousin of the American streetcar, always so loaded that the men hung along the sides like tatters of flesh lacerated from its body, while their wives packed themselves inside. Though he pushed deep into the womb of sullen women, Dona Carlota managed a place not far from him, a squat figure of opaque topaz among the soft neighboring flesh, and the *bonde* rolled maniacally along while she "smoked him out," exposing him to the concentric concentration of feminine displeasure. When he stepped from the infernal machine, he felt himself hounded out of the human situation by shrill womanly laughter and the sly smiles of the men.

Sometimes, though rarely, he would see her across the plaza, lost in herself, having cut the umbilical attachment even to him. She sat on a bench simmering obtusely in the heat, looser now, her clothing spattered with blood as from stoning and all awry, looking very much like a female Lear of the tropics as she clutched at her wisps of hair and buttoned and unbuttoned her coat. She had become indeed "the thing itself."

All the while another turn of the screw was being given by the invisible hands that controlled the University. The lectures were going even more badly and a distressing knowledge of failure plagued him and thwarted his excursions among accustomed pleasures. One afternoon toward the end of his two months' assignment after a particularly humiliating experience of delivering a hard-worked lecture on James to a token audience and an exasperating bout with Dona Carlota which, after long pursuit, had ended in a trap of a favorite bookstore, he took refuge in his room at the Gloria, dropping a load of newly bound books on the bed without his usual care. His nook, at last, he said to himself, not far from a private indulgence in tears.

The room was delightful—there was some comfort in that. It was at the back of the hotel looking toward an impinging mountain, chosen for its closed, intimate, garden effect. His things were around him—even here he had made some progress as a connoisseur. There in the bookcases were his handsome, hand-bound volumes of French and Portuguese to which he had added today. On the wall, in the best light, hung a small Portinari, bought after much deliberation and financial misgiving, showing a flamboyant cock in the foreground and two brown-skinned natives touched by the shadow of red light, exquisite as surface decoration and yet having poignancy and depth in its folk yearning, the lyrical contrast between ruddy, natural exuberance and muted human suffering. Upon a shelf there was a glowingly carved saint from the old religious city of Bahia. In a drawer in his desk, heating it like a secret love, was a box containing a lovely aquamarine, which he was taking as a gift to the "beloved friend" whom circumstances had never quite permitted him to marry.

These few emblems and trophies of his faith made him long for his bachelor apartment in Evanston, which was lined with books and decked with the treasures of his many tours. He would be home soon, thank God. The Brazilian venture had failed miserably. But why, why? He had come with the best of intentions and had tried to be finically conscientious in the discharge of his duties. But first there had been the trouble at the University and then this fanatical woman who would not let go. She had swollen in his consciousness out of all proportion from an annoying mote to a tumid bladder of disordered passions. When she came from Lisbon, she had left that tiny door of Europe open, trailing behind her the distempers of the time. Would it be the fate of the New World to wear such a macabre and strangling garland around its throat at war's end? Could it give everything that would be asked of it?

He thought of Virginia Woolf, another of his "authorities," who had recently committed suicide, prophesying, "All lovely things will be destroyed." He remembered Spengler's dire foreshadowings, his prediction of the return to "the brute blood of the world." He thought of the "monuments of unaging intellect," which in the mounting wash of horrors were tiny obelisks of marble, as pathetic as the white, upward-straining fingers of a drowning man.

It was the enormous sense of the breakdown of form in life which lay so heavily upon him, and somehow the whole, wild, dark emanation seemed to funnel through the unyielding tenacity of Dona Carlota. She was the frightening *avant garde* of the fauna of universal proliferation, the "lost link" between worlds, the slouching, slovenly, bruised, and pitiful embodiment of some terrible evasion. He felt for her and longed to feel more, wondering if somewhere along the line there had been a failure of sympathy. He had been willing to help her; he had tried. But had he tried enough? Had he given in too easily to the belief that she was beyond the pale? Yet, he asked himself, how can the heart be given everywhere? For through his blood he could hear the slow seepage of the century which left one singularly drained and incapable of response, ending perhaps in a heart-castration, an impotence turned away from the baffling complexity of human life to the safety of insentience. And, at the pith of the noxious reverie, stood Dona Carlota like the incarnation of all his questionings, a residual, unaccommodated object, a leftover tossed down by God just when love reached an abstract and absolute purity.

A week later the door of the big Pan American plane closed on Dr. Woodley, and he was thankfully leaving Brazil forever though a mist of tears in his eyes made him marvel at how suffering endears. The downward suction of the take-off brought a faint nausea of regret, breaking off finally the entwining cords, leaving so many ruptured ends streaming in the wind. The last days had been most affecting. Some reservoir of pent feeling had been tapped, and there had been a round of good-bye parties and testimonial lunches and dinners, and the soft, encircling arm of Brazil had clutched him in a sudden *abraço* he would remember all his life. The University officials had appeared out of nowhere to thank him for a job well done, claiming him as a friend of international education, *bem querido,* and the students gave him a touching gift, timidly and unobtrusively, with the hesitancy of a little hand in a large one. The air which had seethed with devils shimmered with the wing-beat of another sort. The warmness of his nature responded fully, and he could have even wished for more time to stand under the burst of glory.

On the eve of departure, he had seen Dona Carlota seated at the edge of a fountain in the Praça like a cracked, earthen vessel, still talking aloud as though not to forget language. She saluted him with her indomitable spirit which amounted almost to gleefulness, striated by expressions of scorn and redoubtable anger, as she parroted her eternal performance: "*Ah, Monsieur,* the American! You are going to help me, no?" He had looked at her with a foolish feeling of affection like an old acquaintance, perhaps the oldest that he had. Now memory held her face longest while the plane relinquished the dim outline of the great mountains as though she stood at the edge of the continent, permitting no farewell.

The Girl from Ipanema

The disadvantages of reaching fifty are obvious, but perhaps not enough of us consider the rewards, not the least of which, I would suggest, may be a certain paradoxical optimism. A reasonable survivor is the possessor of a unique experience which not all of the generations of man can produce again. He has brought a human story this far forward. Streamers of many lengths float back from him, and he is susceptible to the most varied and subtle pulls of time as if a puppet took living mastery and drew the manipulative world after him.

But since we cannot, and should not, remember everything, a man in his fifties is likely to begin to sort out his memories and say: yes, there, and there, and there, I was more truly alive—and all of this as a way of hanging exempla on the bare walls of the future. Perhaps one of the reasons so many people come unstuck in middle age is that the modern viewpoint does not encourage us to value our past. A man is supposed to walk shedding images, an attractive and vigorous figure for youth, but a mature man at last wants the adhesive touch. He wants to be able to walk back into memory and find that the beautiful and meaningful things have been permanently transferred. We are on all sides advised to wonder at the present and the future, and no one wants to discourage this quality even when it may be applied as blatantly as a one-way searchlight, but is it not a special prerogative of men of fifty to think there may be as much to be said for a light that reexamines as one that explores?

I like to think so, particularly as I am about to tell you, like a seasoned soldier, what I consider a war story, not only because it took place during the 1940s and I was, in fact, in the American army. I call it a war story because I find, at fifty, that all of my most vivid memories have been related to campaigns of one sort or another, and if I should ever write my autobiography, which, in any formal sense, I shall never do, I would think of it as the memoirs of a soldier. It is all the wars of life that I feel patriotic about, and I wonder if a palliative for the malaise which seems to deepen as history progresses is not to remember that the peace we say we love so much is, in fact, as H. G. Wells pointed out, "war smouldering."

Now in 1968, we are once more actually at war, and since I will not have an active part in this one, in that sense, too, I cannot give to the future the claim to more vitality, more light, if you will, than it deserves in my own case. So I have been more than usually preoccupied during recent months with old encounters. Perhaps, also, my reminiscent mood is partly due to the fact that Vietnam seems to me to be a "dark" war, more confusing and more confused than most. It is the first time that the scenes of combat have actually been brought into the living room so quickly after the fact that it can be called without too much exaggeration our first Instant War. But specific detail, no matter how concurrently transmitted, does not necessarily provide meaning, and I believe that Vietnam up to this point remains to most of the American people shadowy and remote. I am reminded of the remark made by that shaggy old combatant, Ernest Hemingway, for whom the other struggles I have mentioned finally proved too much. When he said about Korea, "This is not my war," I wonder if he did not also speak for many of us today.

Nevertheless, somewhere, perhaps out of reach of the television camera, there is the war struggling to define itself, and one day the soldiers, in particular, and ourselves as well, will be stuck with remembering it. And some of us will want to justify our ways of counterbalancing it as though each of us had his own private *résistance*. It is with this in mind that I would hope that the story I am about to tell would one day be meaningful to an officer stationed in Saigon or a foot soldier on the Mekong Delta as well as those who turn off their television sets and watch the shadowy figures go dim on the screen as if it were a not-so-crystal globe that absolutely refused to tell the future.

Since, in this case, I want you to remember vicariously, I am fortunate to have a substitute for Proust's *madeleine,* and I can send you back to where I was in 1943 by one of the loveliest songs to have come our way in years. Let me say right here that I became a devotee of *bossa nova* the first time I heard "The Girl From Ipanema." A haunting, seductive, musical hybrid, it is like a love affair between America and Brazil. If you enjoy popular music at all, you probably know it and like it, but what you do not know is that I lived it. Play it for me some time with Antonio Carlos Jobim and his wife Astrud singing it alternately in Portuguese and English and Stan Getz on the saxophone driving home the American message:

Soft and tender, young and lovely,
The girl from Ipanema goes walking
And when she passes, each one she passes, goes, "Ai."
But when she walks it's like a samba
That swings so cool and sways so gently
That when she passes, the one she passes, goes, "Ai."

Oh, but he watches so sadly.
How can he tell her he loves her?
Yes, he would give his heart gladly.
But each day when she walks in the sea,
She looks straight ahead not at he.

There is something poignant about forcing the grammar to make the rhyme between *sea* and *he*. It is making the language give in where it should, and keeps the story down to a level of common humanity. By the time the lyric reaches the reprise, I am back in Rio on the beach at Ipanema, and I am remembering who I was:

Soft and tender, young and lovely,
The girl from Ipanema goes walking
And when she passes, she smiles, but she doesn't see.
She just doesn't see,
No, she doesn't see.
But she doesn't see.

The beach at Ipanema was, and I trust still is, the loveliest in Rio. Farther out than the more popular Copacabana with its rows of apartment buildings, it was a residential beach, conforming, without perhaps being aware of the principle, to Frank Lloyd Wright's notion that houses should be horizontal in feeling and cling to the landscape. There were no casinos or places of amusement, just nice homes mainly, and the Ipanema Country Club, which was not café society at all but represented the best and most stable traditions of Brazilian life. In short, it was a family beach, neither a bikini nor a hamburger heaven. The strand itself seemed to have been passed through a special grinder for texture and through a filter for whiteness. The mountains in the background repeated the famous motif of the Sugar Loaf in the harbor, and were named "Os Dois Irmãos"—The Two Brothers—concording with the familial atmosphere like a thought of an anthropomorphic people who would like to imagine that something was left on guard over the beautiful girls on the beach while the men were at work. The sea was the bluest I remember ever having seen. It looked as if it had run out of a colossal ink bottle, overturned, you could suppose, by a lover's hand. It was in league with the sensuous opulence of the country, abetting the notion that Brazil was one of the few places on earth where the word *fulsome* could conceivably be thought of as a term of praise. Looking at that color, one could believe that it was here that Venus walked in from the sea.

But, best of all, it was a place for girl-watching. If you are interested in "hot stuff," nubile flesh roasting in the sun, the Copacabana would suit your tastes, but if you were looking for the girl of your dreams, Ipanema was the place. In my quiet way over the years, I had become the sort of expert that would make most bird-watchers lay down their binoculars in envy. I could go to a beach and in a matter of minutes survey and assess the situation accurately and settle down to the most unobtrusive but intense concentration. I am by nature a pronounced visual type, so much so that if I were dying, I would hope that the last thing consciousness would cling to would be the image of a beautiful woman. I will not go into the intricacies of my technique except to say that it involved the use of the eyes as if they could see around corners, through obstacles, abstracting the close-up from the distant view, all the while putting full faith in subtlety. In short, if a man could not see as much with the sidelong glance as though that were all the vision he had, he might as well turn in his eyes. If, as I think, every young man's life, no matter how frustrated it may be, is a basic search for Venus, girl-watching is a very serious business. It intends to sort out the possibilities of love, it means to establish one woman as a standard. It is ritual, evangelical, and more often than not, tragic in some of its implications. It is both the happiest and saddest thing a man can do.

So don't say at the end of this story I didn't warn you about girl-watching at the same time that I invited you to join in my obsession. By the time I reached Rio I was, to steal a phrase from ballet, a girl-watcher *noble* and I had twirled, boosted, and done *pas de deux* with an enormous *corps* of girls, but I was still looking for the *première danseuse*. Obsessions, it seems, reach their greatest intensity when much militates against them, and, of course, the war was supposed to be everything in 1943, especially for a lieutenant in the Office of the Military Attaché in Rio. I had tried to get into active combat, but it was no go, for someone had to do our job. But my Commanding Officer never let us junior officers forget that our patriotic coloring might at any moment turn into a yellow streak. Perhaps his own secret guilt hung in him like a swelling bag of venom, for he pressed at us constantly to think of nothing but war, war, war. I honestly think he would have had me court-martialed if he had known that, while I intended to do my job, I refused to give everything to the one war. I intended, if nothing else, to come marching home, a girl-watcher in good standing, intact, confirmed.

So every day at noon, when it was possible, I caught a quick ride to the beach with a fellow officer who was married and lived in Ipanema and who had a car. He was a good Joe and never once squealed on me to "Captain Hook," as we called the C. O., and I lost no time changing at his house and trotting out to the beach with my box lunch which I prepared each morning just before breakfast. He even let me keep my umbrella, portable radio, and other gear in his garage, for I wasn't going to look like a beach bum, not on Ipanema where the best girls came.

You had better know too what else I brought on to that beach besides my paraphernalia if you are going to understand this story. Perhaps by now you have settled down to the comfortable notion that I have been shooting you a line about this girl-watching business and that I am just a crew-cut womanizer with a talent for rationalization. Well, you're wrong—I'm not a short- nor a longhair. At the barber shop, I call for a medium trim, and the barber knows I mean it. I have brown hair, gray eyes, am of medium height, and, though I have done my share of weight lifting, I would look a little understated on Muscle Beach. My name, Gordon Sands, suits me, Gordon, mind you, not Gordo, and yet, saying all this, I have a feeling that you still would not pick me out in a crowd. It might help, though, if I told you that one of the other officers, the sort who went to the Copacabana, once said that I had "one of the world's tidiest minds," but I had the feeling he meant one of the dullest as far as he was concerned. It's true though—I am a man who has always tried to keep his comb and his conscience clean. I am more than usually susceptible to the notion that when the physical goes rancid it seems to leave a spreading oil stain on the spirit. I keep a neat room and a meticulous desk. I change my shirt and my underwear every day. I am not a compulsive hand-washer, but I suppose a psychiatrist would say I have a love-hate relationship with the physical. I am the sort who would feel he needed an entire change of body if he caught a venereal disease. Nothing in this attitude, however, ever seems routine or methodical to me. I like the challenge and the struggle of being fastidious. The daily bath, the careful grooming, are the rites of one who will not accept the fact that the physical expects us to engage in a losing battle with it, which is not to say that constant attention to morale can always carry the day. All disciplines renege from time to time, and sometimes I found myself feeling a little too dry-cleaned, particularly for Brazil, and wondered if I could do with a trip to the dyer instead. The comforting thing about living in Rio was that you knew the vat was always full and the mottled hand and arm that plunge you in were tireless.

Since, apart from traveling time, I had only a half hour at my disposal, it took even an expert like me several days to get to the heart of the matter of girl-watching on the beach at Ipanema. I have learned that people, particularly women, have a special place they like to return to on their favorite beach. One wonders if this is a foible or if it has something to do with a basic territorial instinct. I have seen girls return to the same spot day after day with unerring accuracy as if their shadow had left a secret imprint on the sand or their particular perfume had hung in the air overnight. In any case, without this sense of place, the difficulties of girl-watching would be increased enormously. Once interested in a girl, you would have to start all over every day, and the reduction of possibilities might never be accomplished. But, if you want to get mystical about it, it is as if most girls are determined to be "found," and they mean to simplify your work for you. I am a great believer in instinct, and I believe that it is still as forcefully at work in girl-watching as it was when we lived in trees and were "swingers" in the most literal sense. I like to think that the actions to which we have given the most modern terms have the pressure of history behind them. So it made me feel less like a pauper of destiny to imagine that I was backed up by a monumental experience in my effort to find the girl from Ipanema. I was not only dragging forward the form of life like a burden from an ancient quarry. It gently pushed and guided me like a girl with lovely hands.

At any rate, thank God, life is recurrent and formalistic in ways we do not have to impose ourselves. The crowd fanned out from the Ipanema Country Club in an irregular circle, and I inspected and filed away parts of it geometrically. A Cubist picture of my mental state at this point would show squares and angles containing beautiful girls which I had clipped from the whole. Another part of my particular mystique is that I have usually found the loveliest girls just a little off-center, out of the path of the swimmers rushing down for a first dip, but still focally situated, and this time was no exception. Since it was Saturday and I had the afternoon off, I penetrated the larger than usual crowd like a fruit that had a husk. Not more than twenty feet from where I pitched my little laboratory, there she was. I did not have to hold up my emotions in tubes to the light to know that they had changed color.

Do you like beautiful women, reader, do you really? Does it change your chemistry, does it make "all systems go?" Or did you decide that this is where a good part of the world's troubles lies and throw away the headdress of your heart, content to be what I call "a bald eagle?" Unless you are one of those who still wear plumage, or remember that you did, which is another way of being cock of the walk, you won't understand my story at all.

I shall always remember that first image of her under a pink umbrella like a pin-up against the blue sky, totally, and I wondered instantly, if forever, unaware of me. I struck a medallion right then and there, I commemorated her on sight, then let her live. She sat on a beach-rest looking out to sea, a little radio at her side playing the inevitable samba. She looked made up of the natural colors of Brazil in her blue two-piece bathing suit and her general impression of light and shadow. Her eyes were like blue looking through blue; her skin was lightly tanned but you knew it would be milky white across her breasts, and her hair was like a compression of the glossy shadows with which the mountains imprint our impressions of Rio. I had found my "romantic" beauty.

Was it Henry James who said somewhere that the art of portraying passion in fiction was knowing what to suggest by the pressure of a hand. Pressures have indeed gotten out of hand since his day, but I should like to go him one better and suggest that we may not even have to handle the merchandise. The imagination is often lonely and perhaps, basically, always alone, and it has eyes and hands that do not depend on contact sports to alert their prowess. One of its finest feats is the drama it can extract from pictures at an exhibition.

So I surrounded this girl with a *mise en scène* which would be suitable for the sort of story I wanted her to tell. She was a family girl, an upper-class Brazilian of the sort that can still be thought of in that country as being taught singing, dancing, and manners. She gave off a sense of inclosure as if she did indeed exist in a painting. There was an air of delicate brushwork about her in every respect. Even her make-up looked as if it had been transferred when she pushed her face in a flower—it was that lightly done.

I watched unobtrusively for a long time, but no amount of mental telepathy was going to get through to her, and yet I felt that she was thoroughly aware of everything that was going on. Finally she got up, slipped off her sandals, and went down for a dip. But as the song says, "When she walked in the sea, she looked straight ahead not at he." She swam on her side for a while, turned over easily on her back as if for a siesta, pulling up the blue and white-fringed coverlet of the water. It took most of my professional restraint not to rush right down and lounge in that big blue bed beside her.

Since all living creatures concede in one way or another, I wanted to suppose that when she got out and stood for a moment near the umbrella to dry herself, she was giving in to me a little. With drops of the sea clinging to her skin, she looked like a fountain-figure when the water has just been turned off, and I had a moment of pure possession. So when she gathered up her things, it hit me with the shock of a robbery in a museum, and I felt like a detective who could do nothing at all. I had projected a car and a chauffeur for her, but, oddly enough, she got on a bus which carried her out of my vision like a van which contained the loot of longing.

Nevertheless, every day she was in the same place when I arrived, and I had the impression she had been there a good part of the morning, but just as regularly she left before I did, even on Saturdays. She never ate lunch on the beach or brought a thermos of anything to drink, and, as far as I could see, never spoke to anyone. My daily exposure to her lasted all of fifteen minutes. I think I read somewhere in college that Marcus Aurelius said that you should live each day as if it were your last. At the rate I was going, it would have taken practically a lifetime to spend that day with the girl from Ipanema, but I lived those minutes so that they lasted me until the next time I saw her. The thing in life, as I see it, is to find something that sustains you. What Emerson called "the hypocritic days" do most of us in, there's no doubt about it, and there must be something that restores. The Long War is purely and simply this struggle to keep faith in the stuff of life itself. As I have tried to suggest, I am not belligerent in the ancient combative sense, but I do want to hang on, and it was in this very urgent way that the girl from Ipanema made Captain Hook bearable and provided the war in Europe with a small shining figure which nevertheless balanced it on a lever.

Maybe it was two weeks, maybe three—I wasn't keeping score since statistics have a way of adding up to despair—but one day she acknowledged me. Patience, as it does with birds, had paid off. Before she went down to swim, she turned briefly my way and smiled. I suppose I should have been insulted that it didn't happen sooner, but I wasn't; it made the whole thing into an old-style Latin romance implying the authority of the duenna, rather than a pick-up. I didn't, thank God, charge her right then and there as some of you fellows who think you are such studs might have done. I let that smile sink in, returned it, and that was all.

But the next day was Saturday, and I meant to make it the day I released us from the song. Should I tell you now, gentle reader, and I hope you deserve the epithet, or let you find out later as writers of popular fiction advise, that the complication of the plot began at that time? Let's compromise. If I admit that the trouble began when I took her out of the song and made her "see," I am only giving you another point of departure and leading you in another direction. You see, this is really two stories tied together, and it was my fate to try to make them one.

That Saturday, and I shall never forget as long as I live how much the simple fact that she smiled made me feel like a conquering hero, I went over to her umbrella, opened the doors of her life, and walked in. I had won the war of silence, and I intended to win the harder one. It did not surprise me that she spoke English, for I knew that nearly all Brazilian girls of her class did. But there were surprises. There was not any blemish on her that I could see, in contradiction to Edgar Allan Poe's notion that there should be at least one on any beautiful woman. But intimacy did breed something new, something I had to get used to. A woman twenty feet away is one thing, and within touching distance, another. One can immediately sense the subtle, physical glue of life at work, and there is a haunting undertone of concern which refuses at first to define itself. I was working in close now, and I felt like a diamond-cutter—one false move, and everything might be shattered.

My Brazilian Beatrice turned out to be named Lucia. She lived, she said, with her grandmother and a younger brother in Ipanema but farther back toward the mountains, which seemed symbolically appropriate to me for she had a good woodsy smell about her. I knew it was a perfume, perhaps one with a famous name, but I would have been willing to bet that it had been altered somewhat in contact with her skin. I enjoy my nose as much as any dog, and I could have closed my eyes and believed that we were in the Brazilian forest together. You see, all I needed was the slightest physical prompting, and Green Mansions here I come.

But something else was different about her and I realized that it was the first time I had seen her adorned by anything. I saw swinging from a slender chain around her neck a *figa* made of ivory, a little forearm and clenched hand with the tip of the thumb showing through, set in gold at its amputated end. It plunged down toward her breasts, suggestive of a whole mental life I did not share. I knew that it was a folk charm, supposed to bring good luck, and, in a fresh release of egoism, I wondered if she had worn it for me. The girl from Ipanema was still, somewhere, made up of dreams.

Modern stories are all supposed to be stacked with descending ladders of conversation which take us down into the depths of the narrative and make it more "real," but I have found this to be just another limited convention that sometimes works and sometimes doesn't, so I shall not delude the reader into thinking that Lucia and I talked about anything more than little things or made very much conversation at first. Not that I wasn't working toward that—*au fond* I am as much a ladder-man as anyone—but she didn't "give" in that way. She seemed perfectly content with a static relationship, seeing me briefly each day, though I must admit that I cheated on Captain Hook's war when I could. Then on Saturday I persuaded her to share my box lunch and a longer part of my afternoon.

Of course I pressed for a chance to see her in the evening, but her grandmother was always ailing or her brother, to whom she was apparently a part-time mother, needed her in some way. So I let her put me off for a while, not knowing at the time what a smart thing I was doing. We existed like pure beings with no other purpose than that of pleasure, we had no prior or future associations, we functioned as I have said, almost without semantic burden. All that we had was that circle of protective shadow beneath the umbrella to make One World and the walk down to the sea for adventure. Reader, have you ever divested yourself of ambition and possessiveness, time and language, and given yourself up like a stripped warrior to love? Have you ever won the war and made the peace all on your own in this way? Have you ever said to your belligerent soul, "Step outside with me," and then showed it the reduced arena of one ineluctable desire?

I did for a long, long moment with Lucia. But the truth is that for many of us nothing is ever enough. James Thurber had a point when apropos of "The world is so full of a number of things, I'm sure we should all be as happy as kings," he observed, "And we all know how happy kings are." So I had Lucia, but I did not have her quite enough. I began to try to dislodge the hands of the clock, stuck together like two little swords at high noon, and probe the circumstances around us.

I may be slower than some of my countrymen, but, once I get started, I have the temperament of a wedge. Little by little, I pried out of Lucia every little bit of information I could, and I shudder now at that excavation. If Schliemann had hoped to discover Troy for no other reason than that Helen was supposed to have lived there, he would not have brought up with any more fanaticism each stone of information I delved out of Lucia. If I had only been interested in archaeology, that might have been that, for she complied reluctantly, sticking to her original story which I thought I already knew from looking at her—she was a nice girl with a traditional education and background who lived with her grandmother and brother in Ipanema. She embellished the later version slightly as she retold it under pressure, but it was still circular—it still came back to a plot of sand, a view of the sea, and two people who now seemed to me unbearably Platonic. I was more of a contemporary than I thought. I wanted to see the shadows in the cave. How was I to satisfy myself that this was the real Lucia unless I could see all the copies that flickered in a nether world?

I am afraid that from girl-watcher I would have gladly turned *voyeur* if there had been any conceivable way in which I could have looked into her private life. I simply could not stand the tensions of hermetic love, though, theoretically, that is exactly what I had longed for. I needed a "culture" in which my emotions could breed and live.

In order to connect her with something more when I got nowhere with repeated suggestions that I be introduced to her family, I offered to meet her any time at any place just to see her in another environment. I even invited her to bring her brother to the beach one Saturday, thinking he would deepen the perspective. But no go. If I had awakened Sleeping Beauty, she was determined not to set one foot out of the charmed circle. At the risk of mixing my fairy tales, I might say that I had begun to feel a little like the Beast. Didn't I, after all, appeal to her except as someone to pass the time with on the beach? Or was she a snob and did not think me good enough to meet her *gran fino* family? I knew that the Good Neighbor Policy had been generously lubricated with dollars and that some Brazilians, resenting the notion of boughten friendship, did not like Americans. Was I, then, playing a little scene from a Brazilian parody of *Romeo and Juliet* without knowing that this was so? The whole thing had become too mythical and literary for me.

So one day I betrayed her. I waited until she got on the bus, and then I took the next one that passed, and followed her. But Brazilian bus drivers are among the greatest individualists on earth. They earn so little that they find freedom in their own way, driving murderously fast or rattling along like a cart according to a personal mood and rhythm. My driver at that particular moment favored carts, so we lost the bus in front. I could have choked that villainous-looking man who was the first character in the drama I was devoting to the "real." All I accomplished that day were difficulties in the subplot when Captain Hook dressed me down for being late, and I had to lie my way out of it.

Dumas once said that all you need to make a drama is three walls and a passion. Well, next day, I decided I could do without the walls. I was going to have it out with Lucia, but when I got to the beach, she was nowhere in sight, and I knew what had happened. I didn't even allow myself the suspense of thinking she might be late for once. My sense of withdrawal was immediate and terrible. It was as if the earth had worn thin in that place where we had always met and the sand was only an artificial cover over a pit into which she had fallen. I had my cave, all right. I needn't have hunted for it. It was always there beside us.

The entire beach now seemed a place of alienation. I stood over our circle as sure of its location as if it had been staked out with pins on a strategic map. It seemed absurd that the sand had not kept the outline of her body and the air did not contain her scent. But the process of obliteration was already under way: This place had not any right to be. What had seemed a focus on health and wholesomeness turned out to be an embossed scab which had now been torn away. People on the beach were humps and lumps which once inhabited the peripheral cutout of a beautiful vision. I was left with the stuff of life like a demented baker with his dough who cannot form anything because he has lost his favorite mold.

Remembering my last connection with Lucia, I got on a bus and rode aimlessly through Rio for hours like a worm which hoped by segmenting itself endlessly to leave a trail of the mind's desperate calligraphy. Once, thinking I saw her as we swung back through Ipanema, I got off the bus, grabbed her by the arm, and turned around a startled girl who did not know she was a copy. After that, I went back to our place every day until one day I saw children playing there and they had humped up a mound of sand like a grave. When I shouted at them and saw the surprised, then angry, look of the mother, I knew I had better quit.

The war I had been privately waging was irrevocably lost. If only I had been able to extract one fact that linked her in any traceable way to something beyond my imagination and her quiet acquiescence in what it had constructed around her, I would not have been struck so baldly with the fact that Rio, as far as she was concerned, was a city without meaning. The Brazilian earth, for me, was branded forever with that circle where we had existed together—otherwise, it was an enigma of sea, sky, mountains, and human flesh to whom that secret monogram of love meant nothing. I would like to have taken the brilliant parts of that city and thrown them down repeatedly in kaleidoscope until they yielded the figure of Lucia. For the first time in my life I hated the imagination, what it had done, and all that it left undone.

But if Rio was something I might have dreamed, Captain Hook's world stayed firm as basalt. My fellow officers were all amateur psychiatrists, as who hasn't been in recent years, and they decided there was just one thing wrong with me. I was totally back in a man's world now, and it was "real" indeed. When they suggested going out on the town, I knew what they meant the way every man always knows every dreary and so-called basic "fact" about life, our contemporary informants in the absurd and the extreme notwithstanding. I sometimes wonder if diffidence in sexual matters did not arise partly from a desire not to make it boring. Does the sexual athlete, fully exposed, turn out, even to himself, to be Cliché Man who would make a Neanderthal seem a creature of varied interests?

But I went along with the boys. Why not? Cliché Man was the only friend I had. But when we got to the red-light district, I let the other fellows go into their favorite place and waited outside. I didn't feel smug, I didn't feel clean, I just felt powerless. If I had come to an impasse on the beach at Ipanema, I had come to the end of something here too. Or so I thought.

But not quite. Basic actions take such a pathetically short time. They are as concentrated in their way as a lyric poem with a death-wish loaded in it. I knew I would not have to wait long. I spent the interval noticing for the first time how revoltingly ugly Rio could be. It had been a city of startling contrasts to me, a place of mystery but not of estrangement. It could, I had decided, take more ugliness and squalor than most cities, tucking it like dirty underwear under a beautiful dress. I was not, like so many tourists, one of those who go home and talk about the *favelas* first.

But that night I became a tourist. In this poorly lighted district Rio seemed darker than any city I could remember. The rickety buildings looked like tatters hung on poles, the fag end of the

Brazilian dream. It was as dank as a ravine through which all of your bad thoughts had passed. One had the sense of being down-under and yet in a pervasive place as if it were a bog upon which the glittering and artificial city I had loved floated like an illusion. A red light seen here and there would have served if I had needed, at this point, an *ignis fatuus* to tell me how I had been misled.

Farther down the street, I noticed a young boy motioning to me, and I automatically responded for no other reason than that I wanted to move in that darkness, like an enfeebled swimmer, to see if it would support me. He was a handsome but frail-looking young Brazilian, and his face was white as a blister on the dark skin of the night. But when he motioned me to go inside, I reacted blindly and raised my fist to slug him.

"Don't hit him. He's my brother." I turned around at that voice and saw Lucia standing in the door. She had on a cheap and sleazy kimono, and her face was so heavily made up that it looked as if it had been pushed into the flowers of evil. She had an artificial rose in her hair and smelled of an aggressive perfume. It was as though the venereal armpit of life had been raised as I turned round.

The brother began to cry, and he spilled out "the story." Iron-ically, he began just as Lucia had done. There was indeed an ailing grandmother, but they did not live in Ipanema, and from that point the story unraveled like a worn and dirty piece of twine. Since the death of their parents, they had lived, it seems, at the very edge of poverty, and Lucia was their sole means of support. I could not have asked for any "truer" ending to the story except that Lucia gave me one.

She quieted her brother and then turned to me and said, "Oh, Gordon, what have I done to you?"

There was nothing more. She went into that house with her brother, and I was a tourist who had wandered into the wrong part of town. The next day and thereafter, she resisted all of my attempts to see her or communicate with her, and I was left forever with two stories. In an irony, almost too modern to bear, the story of Pygmalion reversed itself. The living girl had turned into a statue. Or, looking back more ruefully now, one could say the story returned to the song as if it had not been sure of itself in any other place.

Nevertheless, every story needs a conclusion. One might even say that it inherently longs for and is indeed a little sick without one if we accept the fact that it is only a conclusion along the way.

Clarification with its commentary, no matter how temporary, is the only cure we have. We do not look at the world only to absorb its immediacy. We spend our lives writing captions, and, whether we like it or not, we are incurably didactic regardless of how implicitly we phrase our language and our lives. Lucia left me with only a picture, but you can be sure she wrote something under it. I walked in that song, too, you see, and perhaps, without knowing it, "looked straight ahead not at she."

What do you suppose, gentle reader, and I hold you dear by now, Lucia made *me* see? Doubly confined as she was, she stretched my conception of morality and life; she made me see that because a person is one thing, it may not mean that he may not have to be another. Above all, she made me understand that it is a sign of great moral victory to keep believing in an ideal while doing without it. Nowadays I cannot look without tenderness at any woman who has made any effort toward beauty. She partakes of those ritual trips Lucia made to the beach with as much resolution as any general on earth has conducted a campaign. She is a part of that sustained effort toward health and order which insists that a half may indeed be a whole. In the house of ill fame which the mind and imagination can so easily become, she gives us a hint of another fable. And, for a moment, when I look at her, I can see the girl from Ipanema.

Whatever happened to *him*, the man on the beach, you may perhaps ask, gentle reader (now finally evoked), wanting more of a conclusion than life usually allows at a single sitting. That is another story, and perhaps several stories, tied one to another. Suffice it to say that he is still in the world, and he is still remembering. The war goes on.

II. The Carrollton Stories (1989)

The Hidalgo

"The hidalgo"—Brice Evans might very well have taken it the wrong way if he had ever known that this was my private name for him. His sense of his own image was so precarious that he was known to search the most obvious compliment for traces of criticism.

Tipped just the right way, however, with the proper tone of voice, it might have pleased him enormously, given him, in fact, a lift from the depression to which he was often so subject.

"*Hidalgo . . . hijo de algo . . .* son of something"—from his six-foot height he would have mused over the Spanish derivation. "Not bad, David, not bad at all. Better than being a son of a bitch, wouldn't you say?"

But it was too risky, and I never gave him more than the implication of the thing. Brice was so stigmatically scarred one wondered that his friends could find a fresh spot in which to wound him, but he could always unroll new geographies of sensitivity. The Nazis made lampshades of human skin; Brice could have lent his to the world.

If a tender ego is wrapped around the globe, all of its inhabitants are savages. I suppose I was Brice's best friend because I seemed less than others to approach him with spear in hand. We had joined the faculty at the university in Carrolton, North Carolina, the same year, in the same department, Romance Languages. Sharing an apartment with him for a while, I learned what jokes could be jokes and how one could improvise in the middle of a remark that was going downhill, ruffling it the right way. As one of my colleagues said—if only I could have been married to Brice, he would have had a happy life.

But that fell to the lot of Alberta Grimes. Berta worked at the university library where she was significantly know as "Grimy." How did it happen? I don't think anyone knew. They simply did what Henry James, stuttering toward his implacable certainties, would have called "the almost, the utterly, inconceivable thing," and one of the wits in the department said of the union: "Roman-

129

ticism and Realism, seeking revenge, saw no answer but marriage."

This, of course, was not altogether fair to Berta, consigned to the role of realism in a dowdy dress, for there was no doubt that she "looked up" to Brice at first, but was not entirely aware of what she saw. Conversely, Brice unquestionably "looked down" and was sure of what he thought he saw—a devoted and unquestioning admirer. The angle of vision goes a long way toward making a marriage work if you can sustain it.

Poor Berta—it may be as simple as that—her geometry failed her. If she began with a theorem of relations, why couldn't she stick it out? Why do some women do themselves in, increasing the impetus the moment they get married?

Green-eyed Berta with black hair as heavy and thick as grape clusters—instead of keeping it musty, tied in a knot, she might have combed it out like something from the Song of Solomon. Instead of wearing glasses needed only for reading, why not let those catlike eyes look up with a mysterious touch of old Egypt? Was Cleopatra so beautiful that she did not need to throttle the clandestine heart of every blandishment for its secrets? Egypt, ah Egypt—surely Brice, looking down from his romantic mists, would have been glad to hallucinate some flexuous shimmer along the Nile.

But Berta, who had not been a math teacher for nothing in her earlier days, made the fatal adjustment of the angle of her head, took a straight look at Brice, and determined upon what she would have called "an honest relationship."

I was privileged to see the effects of this positive philosophy one afternoon not long after they settled into a basically simple but charming house on the edge of town. Brice, all for atmosphere and attitude, had brought along his bachelor trove of *objets* and artifacts from Spain, but Berta meant to be an intellectual companion with a vengeance—books everywhere indeed, but no soft lights or soft sofas that hinted of the bower, and her idea of a boudoir was *two* beds, a table, and a hard chair. As for the bathroom—that sybaris of the overprivileged, if the pun may be permitted, was simply the place where you moved your bowels.

But it was not the lair but the language, as Brice might have put it in his alliterative soul, that provided the ultimate impasse. Thickly moustached, saturated in his dark, hawklike good looks, standing in the middle of the room in his lordly way, looking down at Berta who sat crouched heavily in her chair but crouched to spring, he would advance what would be taken as a major premise, something so simple as whether the cats, Cervantes and Calderón, should sleep in or out.

"I want the kitties to come in, Berta. You know that I like sleep-in animals."

"And who's going to clean the litterbox? You saw what a mess it was when they did sleep in the bathroom."

"Poor dears. They eat, and they emit, just as you and I, dear Berta, whether we like it or not. Who was it said about the functions?—*Hélas, nous ne sommes pas comme les anges.*"

"You needn't translate. I understand French, and David teaches it."

"All right, *querida.* It comes down to this. I like a bit of ermine in the house. A little luxury. Something I can stroke."

"That's just the point. The house is too hot. Dr. Gregory says the only reason they have such beautiful coats is that they live outdoors."

"Il faut souffrir pour être beau?" I said, tipping my smile from one to the other—but I wondered, was Brice thinking what a night on the porch might do for his wife?

"Forced into beauty? That's a savage notion." He glanced at me with gratitude as if I were a student who had given him a chance to pontificate.

One could see from the look on Berta's face, now that he had latched onto something he thought was philosophical, there would be no beating him. Once he had a footing, Brice had a way of building elaborate bridges of language out into the unknown. In these early days, Berta did not try to stop him, from either a certain baffled wonderment or wariness. She crouched but she did not finally spring, Besides, where was the catwalk for her tentative accompaniment? Assuming that he could build out beyond her, when it fell short of destination, and it always did, she was inevitably, unaccountably, there to catch the debris.

Just another faculty wife not up to the eminence of her husband? Not on your life! Give a woman like Berta ten years—she will take twenty, and will have given a good account of herself in that sabotage which makes so many marriages finally a matter of static engineering, at best, or all bridges exploded before an undetermined but advancing army.

Meanwhile I had married Adeline Cartwright, a music teacher in the public schools, and by hook or crook Brice and I obtained Bynum Professorships. Carrying considerable prestige as well as an extra stipend of $1,500, a large sum in the 1930s, they put us both in the upper echelons of the establishment, and Adeline, dispensing an implication, said that we could "rest on that." But in the Evans household, it precipitated a violent quarrel. Brice wanted to replace the pine mantle with marble and put a tiled fountain in the garden. Berta, though she could not appreciate the sensuous possibilities of either, insisted on another bedroom and bath for herself. Of their joint occupancy of the latter, Brice had quipped, "More than five minutes and Berta thinks I'm philandering."

Berta—who else?—carried the day, and Adeline and I were invited for Thanksgiving dinner not so much to thank the Lord as to see the terms of surrender.

Nevertheless, as we walked over from our house a few blocks away, Adeline and I let ourselves expand a little into the newly acquired feeling of being among the Bynum elite. Why not? Certainly a part of the wisdom of life consists in stasis—the not being done, but having done, the pause in a moment of pleasure to regard an achievement, no matter how modest, as if nothing could touch it. *J'y suis. J'y reste.*

Moreover, November in Carrollton has always been one of my favorite months. I like to think of the lucid weather, not too cool, not too warm, as post-Montezuman. The empire of burnished leaves is gone from the sky, but its spiritualized memory lingers on. The ghost of Tenochtitlán wanders a little in the heart, and one has a fluid sense of lucidities clandestinely stored.

The equilibrium of release—would it have touched our two tense friends? Berta, red-faced and rebellious as if she were still being cooked in the crucible, an idol of uneasy autumn, met us at the door with a kitchen mitt on one hand. Brice, who loved improvements and expansions even if they were not to his order— would he be allowed his gesture of Cortez who got away with the loot? I noticed again how "Spanish" he had remained but now more El Greco than Velasquez. The large circles around his dark eyes seemed to be extravisual—it took two sets to keep looking for the world of the hidalgo.

The flowers Adeline brought were dumped rather unceremoniously into a vase, and we went on the "tour."

"Berta's been reading Virginia Woolf. She thought she should have a room of her own," Brice said, preening a little in his brown cashmere jacket, fondling the gold silk tie like a seasonal comment.

"I didn't need her advice. Brice has to have a literary reason for everything." Berta, a season ahead in a blood-red dress, spoke without any of its sentiment.

"Wrong wolf," Brice hummed as he stuffed his pipe. "Berta's doing a monograph on the great Thomas."

"You mean *trying* to," she said as she pushed open the door of a very monastic little bedroom. "I like an uncluttered room. Brice has the rest of the house up to its eyeballs. I wish just once he would try dusting."

The bathroom, too, was purely functional though sporting a bidet which, in a touch of black humor, Brice had secretly ordered the contractor to install.

"This, too, will do very well for me," she said, "except for that ridiculous-looking thing in the corner. Everyone thinks it's a foot bath."

We really should have had that Thanksgiving turkey with its tail feathers intact, spread like the bonnet of an Indian, for Berta was on the war path. We "viewed the bird" under Brice's eloquent surveyal, but that was the last vision of mellow thankfulness two pilgrims from down the road were allowed.

He had had yet another drink to steel himself for the ordeal of carving, and when he could not find the second joint, Berta jumped up, sloshing her own glass on the table.

"I do like a man who can carve a bird properly," she said in the generalized manner she often employed with him.

"Or be the bird perhaps you mean, my dear," he shot back. "I shall not offer myself for dismemberment."

She tried to shove him aside, but this time he shoved back, almost grazing her hand with the knife.

Pretending that he had made contact, red-faced, rubbing the back of her hand, Berta sat in her chair and would hardly touch a morsel. But what appeared to be an explosion imploded itself— Brice ate his turkey ravenously and silently. Always alert to the vagaries of his defiant moods, Berta saw that he had shot his load, and took over.

To be treated to an exhibition of Berta's mature technique was to realize that a woman can harbor resentment until it creates a new person. Day by day, year by year, as one builds a colossus, Berta had become a figure of immense negative force.

She started off on a long rambling monologue on her study of Thomas Wolfe, rather like a parody of Brice's "bridges," but with the difference that no wind in the world could have shaken it.

Brice got a little air into him at last and tried to awaken his wife to the fact that others were present. Her response to the feeble intrusions he attempted were monolithic:

"What's the use? You never let me finish a sentence."

"I'm speaking, Brice."

"Will you please have the courtesy to let me go on?"

Most lethal was her "pardon me," spoken with ironical contempt even when Brice seemed to be handing her a modest piece of steel for her construction. Moreover, she demanded undivided visual attention as well. Brice must *see* her build a firmer, finer bridge than he ever could. If his eyes wandered toward the bottles on the sideboard, she said, "I'll wait, Brice."

Eye riveted to eye, one must acknowledge the verbal welding until the most passive listener longed for the suicidal leap. Poor Brice—one never struck in Berta's union, nor did one improvise the slightest bit for the boss. A suggested alteration in the project, and Berta would say, "I don't want to go into that."

Through it all, the impression lingered that Berta did not really care about Thomas Wolfe, that she may in fact have selected him because Brice did not particularly like his work. All that she wanted was a point of departure. By now, however, Brice was laid out like the departed one, eyes open only because no hand had bothered to close them. More than debilitated, I noted as we were devising our means of escape, he was utterly demoralized. He had come down in class. The hidalgo looked like a Dago, or a Diego, as he might have etymologically informed me, if, reading my thoughts, he had had the strength for a derivation.

But, withal, we didn't dislike Berta. We had the feeling that at the beginning she really had tried for an honest relationship, seen it, perhaps, as her duty to balance Brice's more grandiloquent nature. Romanticism would not pay the rent, and it was a known fact that Berta's politicking behind the scenes was partially responsible for the Bynum. But since we had to choose—they both put it to us in these terms—we chose Brice.

Nevertheless, I regret the dichotomies we are constantly making between a pair of personalities, and am aware that Brice is only half of the story. There is always another figure standing pleadingly on the banks as the narrative river rushes past: Save me! Save me! But what is one to do—push the protagonist off the narrow raft? Any story is only a writer's partial view of things. Someone else must come along to collect the unevacuated.

Still, all of us have those we choose to "bring along" in the course of things. They have incurred our favor, inspired us to believe in them, because they mirror perhaps some ideal movement in our own souls or simply because they are good company on the raft. Brice, standing in the middle of his living room, in the days when Berta would let him stand, hemming and hawing as he calibrated his sentences across some Golden Gate, was an endearing figure. Berta, crouched in her chair, an impervious, inert mass of words unless she was allowed to be kinetic entirely on her own terms, gave us no access.

However, the question about Brice periodically arose: Except in his worst moments, we could savor him, but could we, in fact, "save" him? There were times during World War II when we thought we could not. He was not of the age or condition to serve, and grew increasingly morose that the younger and more fit could escape. I knew my limits and did not fret, but then I had no unredeemed desire to be a cavalier. It would have helped, as I often thought, if Brice could simply have worn a dashing uniform around town, except there would have been no fictive maiden on the streetcorner to cheer him on. After several drying-out periods in a sanitarium for alcoholics in Southern Pines, Brice tried to slit his wrists in Alberta's infamous bathroom, and we all had to admit that he had become a full-fledged manic-depressive. Did he choose her bathroom as the only place where she was likely to come and find him before it was too late? He was sitting naked, propped up in the tub, one hand hanging over the rim, the other diffusing a fan of blood. Did he want to leave in her prosaic imagination a picture as violently impressive as David's *Marat*? The unkind—but were they also the intuitive—said that he wanted her to see him without his clothes on once more before he died.

Apparently Berta got the message she did not want to receive, and herself took more heavily to drink, but quietly, so that at first no one knew the extent. Some enormous impaction of spirit, without easement, demanded an anodyne. Since she had become socially difficult and no one would hear her out, when important visitors at the end of their lectures in Memorial Hall agreed to questions, she took to standing up and haranguing them, endlessly unfolding a construction of non sequiturs as if she were filled with garbled Erector sets. She had grown heavier, and, in her psychological *extremis,* loomed larger, a great hulk of a woman with the delusion that attracting attention is the same as securing a bridgehead. The audience craned their necks at the loose suspension. My most lasting image of her is flushed and furious as she extended herself at last toward the hapless surrogate for Brice.

Carrollton is one of the worldliest places in the world, and endearingly so, I think. There is a certain avuncular charm with which it endures saints and harbors sinners. It takes care of its own, marking time when careers idle, standing back discreetly from the fire when they blaze too brightly. It has been known to tuck away the mental case, the adulterer, the large or minimal ego, the *flâneur,* the deviate, even an occasional addict, if they are not too publicly displayed or onerously imposed. Lie with whomever you please, but do not leave the correspondence or the condom on the doorstep. It is laissez-faire indeed as long as you have the wit to keep your affairs somewhat to yourself.

For this reason alone the Evanses became a worrisome case not only to me but to the town. How often at the end of an evening can you pour your best friend *and* his wife into the car without a hopelessly diluted sense of proprieties? Berta, the canniest drinker I have ever known, never seemed bibulous, but she must have arrived loaded, retired to the powder room periodically, and touched herself up all evening. "Of Time and the River"—some do not mean to be left standing on the shore. She had caught up with Brice with a vengeance.

Must one brutally say there was no other solution than the final one? Should we admit that a snake lies at the source of words, and if one cannot make it rise from the basket to dance on its tail while the other admires the accomplishment, waiting his turn at the flute, half in love with the swoon of the obbligato, the role of the fakir seems stultifying and the spectacle hazardous? Common domestic knowledge concedes that the longer anyone tends a serpent alone, the greater the risk of sting.

Berta, hermetically distended, took the tip of the odious thing in her great crammed mouth, and gave Carrollton the closed circle, the concluded circuit. No symbol of the eternal life of communication could have been more enigmatic and more dubious. After her death, Brice went into the forbidden sanctuary of her bedroom, opened a large closet, and out poured an avalanche of empty brandy bottles. I think he cried more over that than anything else. There was something about the hideous sound of glittering glass crashing down, spreading out like a spewed snake, that gave him, in sudden impasto, the thick, unsprung sorrow of Berta's life.

In any case, for most of us, it darkens toward evening, and the river races with shadows. What, then, could that inconceivably be ahead where the water rolls unpredictably in a saraband of light? The figure of a woman standing not much farther down along the bank?

I will never again discount the fecundity of the future that could produce Irene Crawford at just the right moment. Irene belonged to another of the university pairs to whom Adeline and I could give only unequal devotion. Her husband, Beaufort Crawford, a university dean, was a handsome, able man whom Irene had met when he was in Harvard graduate school and she a Boston debutante. The label of the marriage cited the most successful ingredients: good family, good looks, *some* money on both sides. But on one side it lacked good humor, that fixative which finally keeps even the most sumptuous domestic picture glossy and enduring. "Beau" Crawford's temper was legendary, and he had merely to scowl at Irene, or a friend for that matter, and one knew the wrong thing had been done.

Even so, Irene registered at cocktail parties as a rare and winning sort, in those brief encounters dropping handkerchiefs along the way so as not to be totally lost to others as her husband penetrated the dark woods. Daniel Boone's sister could not have been more cautious or canny, and we knew where to find her when Beau went off the trail with a Wave he met in Washington where he served in the Navy during the war.

White handkerchiefs notwithstanding however, Irene went through some very rough times. While Beau was in the service, she worked in a defense plant in Baltimore, ironically to be near him; and when he left her, she was not sure—for who can ever be?—that she had designated the trail all that accurately. She tried an affair in Washington but it did not work, for Irene was not a promiscuous sort. As she later told me, there were only two options: Should she jump off the Washington Monument or go back to Carrollton and marry Brice Evans?

After the divorce, Brice had called her when he was in Washington at an MLA meeting, drunk as a lord, which always made him, in the right company, just that much more lordly; and when she had dinner with him, she decided that he was unmistakably a man who had a handkerchief in his hand.

It looked like the perfect solution for both, but would it really work? The worldlings of Carrollton gave it only half a chance, for they knew, or thought they knew, Brice too well. Relieved of competitive Berta would he find a released and uninhibited Irene a bit too glamorous and sink once more into drink and doldrums? Or might some of the bloom have rubbed off Irene herself? The young man in Washington—did his hands still smell of the luminescent firefly, caught and bruised? Such are the accidents and the odors of the garden of love.

Nevertheless, in due course, the ironical, the witty, and the wishful thinkers like Adeline and myself picked up the markers and went to the house on the edge of town to see for ourselves.

Carrollton may be worldly, but not altogether world-weary, and I do not know of any place where a lively interest in people flourishes more abundantly. You don't gossip until you go. Two slabs of hearsay won't make a sandwich; one must have meat. Or, as Kant more drily put it: "Concepts without percepts are empty."

And who could be a more perceptible creature than Irene? She moved into the house with much more delicate filling than the stuff for carnivores—trunks of lovely clothes she had mainly made herself, barrels of fine china, chests of old silver and family linens. But Irene could not, and cannot, be explained in terms of possessions. Able, at last, to pulse and emanate, she released an aura of the sophisticated North, the nightclub, post-Fitzgerald memories of a world where flappers jumped into fountains fully clothed and young men drank champagne from a silver slipper.

They had married in December, luckily for Brice who yearly went down into the sloughs of Christmas syndrome perhaps for no better reason than that Alberta always dressed up as Santa Claus for her Brownie troop, and by springtime they were ready to give a housewarming for all those who had saved a crumpled bit of cloth, and even some who had seen it as an obvious plant.

Spring in North Carolina makes mummers of us all. We want to act out our dreams, to revive "the dead"—all of those personae which the Other (an imperious wife, an importunate child, an overweening colleague) has put down. We like to pretend that we are reading for a new role, if not happy then passionate. The whole town of Carrollton becomes a greenroom.

The Evans house sat in a grove of Judas, that most enigmatic of trees, and in Alberta's time they seemed to enclose it in a gloomily impassioned atmosphere as if Judas, fellow victim of Berta's indecisions and impactions, had taken refuge there instead of hanging himself on the namesake tree. By contrast, Irene, with the Eastern glow of an odalisque, met us at the door in a long gown of purplish pink chiffon one could have supposed was steeped in its blossoms.

Coleman Jones, Chairman of the Department of Romance Languages, took me to one side and said, "Looks as if Brice is in luck. Last time it was a thorn. This time it's a rose."

If Coleman, dry and androgynous, could resort to floral metaphor, Carrollton, which loves flowers almost at the religious level it devotes to trees, would never think of her in any other way.

Brice was swashbuckling over his prize, his sensual, sexual nature marauding into the clear. I had always felt there was more than a touch of the buccaneer in his temperament, and all that he needed at this point was a gold ring in his ear to have arrived down the years from the Spanish Main.

Irene saw that everyone had a drink and someone to talk to, then sought me out on the sofa to say that Brice was dedicating his new book to me.

When I protested that the honor should be hers, she insisted, "You're the one who has stood by him all these years. Besides—perhaps you've forgotten—it was at your house we first met."

"So it was." I pretended to remember while in my worldly way I began to search her motive.

"In any case it would be silly to dedicate it to me. You understand his work far better than I. I'm not an intellectual."

"You're something much better. You're an instinct." Was this her oblique way of saying it wouldn't have been right either to dedicate the book to Berta who had held back its completion for so many years?

"You mean my stockings are pink rather than blue?"

"Yes, indeed, they are, Irene, ravishingly pink," I said, and we laughed intimately together as if, other things being equal, we might have been lovers.

So there you have the essence of Irene. In a single conversation she had accomplished three things—bound Brice's best friend to him more warmly than ever, effected the transition from one wife to another without indelicacy toward Berta, and obtained my blessing on the role she meant to play. I stopped searching for motive, for I wanted it as translucent and transparent in the uninvidious sense as it could be. Almost any woman would have smoked the glass with some little show of malicious triumph, some unfortunate references to past or future. But Irene, intuitively, with the lightest of materials knew how to build those bridges Berta's ponderous engineering never could accomplish. I had the feeling, rare with anyone, of talking with a woman *à coeur ouvert*.

We compare notes in Carrollton—oh, how we compare notes!—and I found that Irene had gone from guest to guest in an aura of the true self offered. A new variety had at long last been allowed to bloom in Carrollton—"Coleman's Rose" smelled sweet in every nostril.

But the most incredible thing was how she stayed in contact with Brice whose dips in moods could have parted the web so disastrously. It was touch a friend and then back to him. After the party, I did not need to make room for her on the raft: without crowding she extended it on her own and sat there incongruously congruent as a shining figurehead.

Still the art of continuity must learn to drop more than a few stitches and go on. There was still a snake stuffed and stymied in Brice's craw, and the staccato rhythm of sudden ejaculation had to be expected. A year after their marriage, in one decline and fall he hit the bottle again as if he meant to shake in Irene's face the rattle of that creature which poured from Berta's closet. Too much charm, some secret demand on his ego he could not meet, had the lady killed him with kindness? Poor Irene—the rose must come to terms. Like Berta, would she become a thorn after all?

But Irene carefully retraced her steps, and as far as it was visible to anyone deployed their lives as confidently as ever. She made a new dress, cooked *paella* and *arroz con pollo* for dinner parties where Brice sang, played his guitar, and conversation seldom palled. Painting the bathroom, the kitchen, one room after another, she went through the house until without making an offense of it there was not a smudge of Grimy Grimes left anywhere. At the Mardi Gras ball, mounted by the department, her dress and mantilla were stunning, and there was Brice in a brocaded suit, every inch a nobleman.

It did not, however, last all that long—ten years or so—but in retrospect, it looks like an era. I think most of the men in Carrollton were a little bit in love with Irene, and the wives didn't seem to mind. She could brush any pair of friends with a nuance of *ménage à trois,* and it was no more than a sophisticated charade, a reassuring scent of Cupid's presence in the academic air. Irene caused no serious estrangements, broke up no homes. No one went off by himself to sing *chagrin d'amour.*

The narrative river flows on forever, but each of us has his cove. Brice got lung cancer, and it was once more back from Velásquez to El Greco. Irene kept him ambulant almost to the end, but his lean hand seemed to reach ever more yearningly across a span he had never quite crossed. I stop right here. Never try to describe in too much detail the demise of friends. Memories, as much as they can, should return to the whole cloth, not give us a tangled remnant.

Irene herself had said everything she had to say about Brice as if every day with him were an open and declarative sentence. The rose petals she scattered over him did not need to be gathered up in a hermetic potpourri. It had been a life of open gestures, and there was peace in the sympathetic nervous system.

Irene still lives in Carrollton, rather monumentally beautiful in her totally unmonumental way. We still compare notes—will she or won't she? But I am among those who say she will not. It is a fairly balanced experience of mankind to have lived with one man who had, essentially, the soul of a peon and to have made another into a hidalgo.

Nevertheless, there may be some man, even a husband, with a white handkerchief tucked away somewhere, but I have an idea Irene would accept it, fold it neatly, and put it in his pocket with just the right amount of triangle symbolically peeping out. For Irene is still so infinitely Irene. She will never turn away a man without just a touch of *ménage*.

There will always be, though rarely, an Alberta, or Berta's brother, to see her differently. Meanwhile, the rest of us keep "bringing her along." The Groves of Academe are not noted for ladies of instinct. But when the time of the congested snake is upon us, we are aware of a relaxing presence in the community, taming us out of tension, making us say things we would and could not say, drawing out the slithering implication until it looks like a harmless and malleable silver band. A little *haute couture,* a little *haute cuisine*—Irene, we say, can do anything, but what we really mean is that we do not need to make room for her. Give her a broken man and she will build him a bridge. Offer her a raft and she will make a barge. Ah, Egypt—does the river, as it passes through Carrollton, look somewhat like the Nile?

Saint Cecilia's Son

Everyone agreed that Craig Matthews was "Mr. Music" himself. It was not only that he was head of the department at Carrollton University in North Carolina. Craig was a confirmed case with a father who was a violinist, a mother who toured with the San Carlo Opera, and an uncle who had known Ravel. Moreover, no one but Craig would have attracted a ravishing beauty who played the piano, also happened to be named Celeste, and managed to produce an only child he could name Cecilia after the patron saint of music.

A touch more, and it might have been too much, but Mr. Music knew just exactly where to draw the line. Moreover, in the five years that he had been at the university, he had revitalized the department without firing anybody or making any drastic changes. The committee which selected him, impressed with his credentials, nevertheless envisioned a diplomat, and were attracted to his having acted so successfully in just such a capacity at a small midwestern college where the musical faculty had also been hopelessly divided.

The sciences and the medical school, as at so many universities, were on the ascendancy at Carrollton, grabbing the lion's share of state money and federal grants, and some of the discontent in the music department, itself low on the totem pole in the humanities, could be traced to reduced morale. Like any good plenipotentiary to small powers, Craig negotiated among the staff an entente dedicated to a peace as pleasant and uncomplicated as music played in the campus campanile on golden afternoons.

But if faculty meetings were exceedingly bland, the Matthewses did what they could to make their parties brilliant. Celeste, alone, everyone agreed, was worth the price of admission, namely an allegiance to Craig. She was among the prettiest women in town, the implications of her name blooming even in her seraphic mass of honey-colored hair though, in antithesis to the serene golden cloud above her head, her blue eyes darted nervously back and forth whenever she was around her husband, like a bird eyeing a feeder to see if it were really filled with food, too near a source of danger, or perhaps just surrounded by too many for its resources.

It was this sense that somehow the bluebird of happiness might end up in a cage that saved her from a too mild and ordinary charm. Her husband was everything to her, but St. Francis of Assisi he was not quite.

Nevertheless, Craig was the *pièce de résistance;* even his enemies conceded that he glowed and glowed, and never gave out. But much more than a static effulgence, he was a whirlwind without an eye, always solidly in motion in any given room, in the town, indeed out into the state. No activity was too minor for him to become involved, and he did not confine himself to music, ready to talk on almost any subject if he were given a few days notice. With his smiling, arm-waving hyperbolic manner, he seemed to inflate the most flaccid occasion with helium. What did it matter if he brushed the subject lightly if one could carry home this image of a large, forceful man with thick, wavy dark hair, brown eyes with a glint of amber in them, a generous mouth, so savored that it almost, but not quite, threatened to drip its suggestion of a bit too much sensuality on the observer.

But what gave him an interest and attraction beyond conventional radiance was something no one could quite put his finger on, a pull into something other than his own circle of light—a depth, a darkness beyond the surrounding nimbus. One could not define it, but there was a suggestion of the errant in his ardor. He seemed to be casting sequins on a carpet which his admirers were supposed to pick up as they followed him in search of some harder, gemlike flame. Did it even have a touch of fatality in it, one wondered, this desquamation among the lacklustered? Was it just this nuance of the Pied Piper that really gave him his power to dominate—the thrill that all this academic boredom might end somewhere in a mire of radium? No one could quite say. But there seemed to be something—a Fata Morgana in the Groves of Academe. He was not just a grown-up boy twirling sparklers at Christmas.

As Saxon James, professor of piano, asked at one of their parties, "What fuels the man?" Heavy-set, pontifical Saxon was also known as "Jimmy" for the reason that it did not suit him at all.

"Good spirits," Rollo Lyons, director of the choir, quipped as he helped himself to another drink.

"I know he likes to drink, as who doesn't? But I've never seen him come into the office with a hangover."

Telepathically advised, Craig came over, casual, lucent, a wandering wick casting light equally on the two adversaries he had persuaded to kiss and make up.

"Jimmy, my boy! How's the Horowitz of Hines Hall? Rollo, you old yodeler! How are the choir boys *and,* I might ask, the girls these days?" He thumped the back of the plump, blond, little man, and squeezed his arm suggestively.

And then it was time to touch up Sandra Murphy who taught composition uncomposedly, having always thought she was meant for greater things.

"Sandra, darling! You look stunning tonight. I wanted to tell you I ran into one of your students, and he thinks you're great. Nadia Boulanger isn't even in the running."

Sandra, also tall, dark, but alas the triumvirate, responded at eye level. Should Craig turn out to be Janus, the two-faced god, how nice to have one her size. "Oh, Ricky Jones? I gave him an A on a little piece for the piano, and he thinks he's Chopin."

"And you're his George Sand?"

"Well, hardly."

"Don't be too sure. Don't be too sure," Craig said, and drifted off into another corner of the room.

Ah, the luminescence! The carpet and furniture seemed smeared with his trail. Soft and insinuating—no asbestos needed. A moment with Craig, and Sadie Jefferson, known to the students as "the Sadist," dripped with phosphor. Just the waves of his voice made her feel like a mermaid in the moonlight streaming little stars from her breasts.

Even Saxon, whose private name for him was "Tinkerbell," had to admit the man had panache. Without having published a book or written a single composition, Craig was the department's "celebrity."

Moreover, since things always worked out the way he wanted them to, before the end of the party someone would ask him about "the picture."

Emily Adams, who had heard him hold forth before, wanted out of sheer love of the man to give him his fix for the evening. Short, plump, dressed as usual in muted tones, she might look like the end product of thirty years of teaching in a girls school in Massachusetts, but had brought down to retirement in Carrollton more than a left-over life to kill. Her little body contained a vigorous intention to find in the southern community someone special she could admire and care for, and Craig, who had not yet fully acknowledged her despite the fact that she had been to his house once before and met him on numerous occasions since she attended everything, looked like the most promising candidate.

"I've always admired this magnificent painting," she said, smiling all the way back to the gums. "Could you tell me something about it?"

"Saint Cecilia, you know," he said, looking down at her.

"Yes, of course," she continued. Didn't he remember she had told him she studied at the Juilliard and would know who Cecilia was? "Was it a family treasure?"

Yes, indeed, it had belonged to his mother who willed it to him, and he made it sound as if she had much to bequeath. Hung in the living room just as it now did in his house, it dominated childhood dreams even more than his parents, and was the source of his interest in music.

Always a good listener, Emily did not interrupt him, and the painting seemed to substantiate the reverent manner in which he spoke about it. Nimbused Cecilia in her long blue gown played the piano and looked up to heaven where a choir of angels and cherubs poured down a shower of roses. She had a beautiful soft face that everyone in the world likes to think of as belonging to an ideal mother, and Emily could bet that if the saint ever stopped playing, Craig, big as he was, would like to climb up in her lap like the *pietà*.

Looking into the picture, he did not bother to turn her way often enough, and some words were lost, but he need not even have spoken intelligibly, for Emily, who had heard it all and heard it from others—how many times before?—was not listening. Anyway, it was as good as an assignation in the Louvre until Craig went to get them another drink.

But the moment he left, the light over the picture looked more subdued, even sallow. Of course, it wasn't that good, but what a liar one had to be to keep dear Craig going. Still, it was imposing in a way, six feet by seven, possibly the largest painting in Carrollton, including the university museum, and one had to admit it was appealing, but rather in the manner of Eastman Johnson in one of his more saccharine moods. The Saint looked much too suavely sanctified ever to have been martyred, her aura as meretricious as Woolworth's. The face reminded one of Celeste—or was it, in fact, Craig's mother who looked out in such sweet sorrow from the photograph on the mantel. There was absolutely no historical pertinence or propriety. Cecilia was every inch a late-nineteenth-century conventional beauty, perhaps permissible only as an antidote *en passant* to what passed for art these days.

But when Craig returned, the picture glowed with warmth again. Who could argue the fact that a living painting did something for a house? And this, after all, was no rank amateur. So large, so much there, it simply knocked down the wall and opened into mythology. Once you got inside a picture like that you simply did not ever have to stop. It embraced, folded in behind you, burrowed onward. The world it presented might be suspect, but so was the "Tunnel of Love."

Anyway, reservations didn't matter. Craig's enthusiasm, once you got him going, was so infectious. Evasive as to provenance—no, he did not know who had painted it; it had simply come down in the family—he surrounded the picture with all the glory of Saint Cecilia's legend. Was Emily familiar with the two odes Dryden had written on the subject? But, of course, and he seemed now to remember that she had been a music teacher, she would know about them, for Handel had set one of them to music. Did she, however, know the Raphael at Bologna, the Reubens in Berlin, the Domenichino in Paris? He would go anywhere in the world to see a good Saint Cecilia.

He reeled off the paintings, none of which Emily had seen, and the names alone, buttressed by the specific places, made him sound like a connoisseur.

She was dazzled at how he had embroidered the familiar story for her, and would not have been surprised if he had recited one of the odes all the way through. She went home three drinks later thinking what a wonderful man Craig was, what a marvelous family he must have come from. The picture, as she thought it over, was much better than she had allowed. Wouldn't it be exciting if Craig discovered it had been painted by Somebody after all? That man deserved to own a masterpiece. After supper, when she had settled luxuriously into bed, she could feel that this evening had done it. Now that she had taken on Craig's saint without any apparent reservations, she would not have to flap around him quite so exhaustingly to attract his attention.

When the guests had all gone, Cecilia, cherubic in her white nightgown, came in from the wings, or, as Emily, dreaming, might have etherialized, on wings, to model for her father's thoughts.

The party had been an enormous success. Celeste looked celestial, and Cecilia, Ceciline. What more could Craig ask?

But he always did, a little. The music had stopped, the picture was static. There could have been a billboard at the end of the room, and he wouldn't have cared. He was tired, bone-tired, from selling the Saint.

To Cecilia, all arms and lips, he said fretfully, "Cissy, hadn't you better go to bed?" And though he hugged her, the contact had no more reality than he might have extended to a Christmas angel stuffed with cotton.

"Daddy's exhausted, honey," Celeste said. Though it was always like this, she would never get over the fact that the most confident man in Carrollton, after the ball was over, simply folded up and plummeted. She turned to see him, brooding in a late-Luciferian glow, looking at the picture, so closed to him now, and she had the feeling he would like to walk into it and disappear forever.

But the next morning, in the house, at the office, singed, but only singed, with ambiguity, Craig was an imposing man again except to those who were innately disposed to reservation. Though he went to some of the levees at the Matthews house, Billy Hanes, music critic for the local paper, had refused from the start to be impressed. Craig was just too perfect. He was like a bright medal hung in the soft Carolina sunshine. It was easy for him to make his effect with the impressionable. One longed to nudge the metal and make it turn. Heads we say—did it have a tail?

Small, ferret-eyed, where Craig was richly chromatic, Billy was determined to know the score. "The picture" was one thing, possibly not the main thing—what was the man really like who palmed it off on the public? Nor did he listen to the submissive sounds of what he called "Craig's harem." Billy was the sort who would like to have said to Celeste, "Gee, you have beautiful blue eyes, but have you ever noticed how bloodshot they are?"

Consequently, he began to keep a little black book on the "Archangel." Was Craig a womanizer? No, apparently not really. Was he a closet homosexual? Billy could hear the chorus of Nos from the distaff side. Did he drink too much? Yes, but who didn't, and with him it never interfered with his profession. But just how much of a scholar was Craig? Who was he anyway? Did anyone really know? Where did he really come from back beyond the midwestern college?

Billy seemed to remember certain gaffes, certain gaps. Once at a party, for example, didn't he pronounce the name of Purcell with the accent on the second syllable rather than the first, and hadn't he been vague on the subject of the music itself? But then there was leeway. He had been drinking. Still, Billy, structured as only local critics longing for the bigtime can be structured, was skeptical.

But nothing came of it. Craig shone, and Billy got a kick in the shins when he questioned the halo. Nevertheless, men like him seem to have a certain amount of luck. They just happen to be around when the light flickers.

During the intermission of a symphony concert, Billy, who liked to get the feel of an audience, struck up an acquaintance with a Dwayne Maddox, professor of music at a small college in Virginia, who was visiting his son. As they were talking, Craig and Celeste brushed past, and it looked to Billy as if he ducked his head.

"Do you know him?" the professor asked.

"Sure. Craig Matthews. Big man on the campus. Head of the music department."

"Then I must be mistaken. I thought he was somebody else."

"Yeah. Who?" Billy perked up.

"Oh, someone I knew in college." The professor, flipping through his memories, seemed to have come to the place where the pages stuck.

"That's interesting. I didn't think there could ever be a look-alike of Craig's. He would not be flattered."

"No, I don't think he would."

"Oh?"

"It's perfectly ridiculous. It couldn't be. I thought for a moment he looked like a classmate of mine named Jack Caldwell. It's a complicated story. You wouldn't be interested."

"*Au contraire.* Go on. You interest me exceedingly."

"Well, if you must know. He was not much of a person. I didn't know him too well—but we were both music majors. He dropped out his junior year. I seem to remember something about cheating on an exam."

"You mean he never did graduate?" Billy asked as if graduation were next to godliness.

"Not that I know of. Of course, he could have gone somewhere else."

Yes, as who couldn't. He could have gone somewhere else. That was the problem. Was this gangling, asthenic, nearsighted academic with his essentially languid curiosity to be taken at all seriously? What else did he know?

Still, Billy could not be precipitous—he had been keeping his little black book too long and too carefully for that. But a week later when he ran into Craig at Sadie Jefferson's cocktail party, he asked him casually if he had ever known a Dwayne Maddox.

"Dwayne Maddox?" Craig did not blanch, but he did not flare up either in his usual way at the sound of a human voice.

"Yeah, Dwayne Maddox. I met a guy in Hines Hall who said he knew you." Billy longed for more height to tower over that face like a candle snuffer.

"Where? When? Did he say? I can't seem to recall him. Is he in music? So many people come to my office wanting jobs."

Big deal—was he going to get that I'm-too-busy-to-remember

brush-off? "I don't think it was there. Said it was a long time ago. Said to give you his regards."

Did Craig instinctively realize he was being toyed with? He hesitated, then smiled with that indulgence which always enraged Billy and made him feel he was being treated like a moth which in the natural course of things had been drawn to the flame.

"Let me think," he said. "No, I don't recall any Dwayne Maddox. Not a usual name is it?"

"No, not like Jack—or John. One doesn't come across many Dwaynes. That's why I felt sure you would remember."

"Sorry," he said without hesitation, and the storm globe came down around the light. Pure, unwavering Craig looked at Billy a moment. "You know how it is. I'll probably wake up in the middle of the night . . ."

"Sure, I know how it is. If you do just happen to remember, give me a call. I've got his address. I think he'd like to hear from you."

Billy, who was not really very fond of music, though he did not know it, thought he heard Saint Cecilia playing that night— something called "Craig's Swan Song." The music was there, no doubt about it, the motif kept reverberating, but what were the words?

He wrote to the little midwestern college. No—Jack Caldwell had not graduated. But the registrar would not say why. Who cared after all these years. Billy looked up Craig's degrees in the university catalogue: A. B., University of Illinois; M. A. and Ph. D., University of Rochester. Billy wrote to both of them. No record of Jack Caldwell or Craig Matthews ever having been there.

He went to the dean first, and the dean listened and did not believe a word—Billy was known around town to have a tongue like an adder. Besides, Matthews had come to the university with the highest credentials, recommended not only by his former employers but any number of musicologists, and he ticked them off while Billy waited with the tension of a parking meter ready to flash a violation.

Billy had never written so many letters in his life, already sure that none of the musicologists would have heard of the man. His face as rigid as a little red metal flag, he went to the president with this concrete evidence in hand. The president said, as presidents often do, "There must be some mistake. Talk to Professor Matthews. I am sure he can explain everything."

Billy got the same brush-off wherever he went with his story. One has to go rather deeper into things than most busy academicians care to when confronted with the fact that what has been accepted as authentic may possibly be false. What we want from our stars, and, *au fond,* Carrollton shared with the general public a love of theatrical glamour, is that they never fade nor fall from the sky. It calls in question the inviolability of one's glittering firmament to be faced with a clinker in the hand.

But Billy was willing to risk it, not at the office when Mr. Music would have every reason in the world to make short shrift of their interview. It had to be in the evening when Craig was slightly turned down, relaxed, softly radiant in the enclosure of the family.

Billy found them grouped together in the living room, after he telephoned, and he had to admit Sargent would have done them proud. At the end of the room the picture which he had always thought so dominant seemed absurdly superfluous. Celeste, Cecilia, pulsing in their chairs or intermittently moving around the room in spiral attendance—they, not he, were the moths "devoted to something afar." It was too bad so much gauze and gossamer had to be destroyed. It was even a *little* too bad, if one paused a moment longer and let the tableau tempt unwonted feelings, that a "masterpiece" like Craig had to go.

"I think you know what I have come about," he said after Craig had offered him a drink.

"Yes, I think I do." Craig's face changed to a study in tarnished planes, or so his visitor liked to suppose.

"Do you want Celeste and Cecilia to hear?" Billy relented, and would always tell people he did, as if the saint in the picture smiled at him for the act.

"Why not? Better here than elsewhere," Craig said.

Billy handed him the letters.

"Yes," he said and passed them to Celeste. "I'm Jack Caldwell. That's the heart of the matter. That's all there is."

The bellows did not, or did not care to, work anymore, and the room sank psychologically like a brazier going down. At one point, Celeste, whose history began at the midwestern college when the light was turned up high, looked at her husband as if an eclipse were passing over him, and Celeste began to cry, unused to this sudden twilight that seemed to have fallen around her father.

The president, the dean, and, unhappily, Carrollton turned off the current altogether. What else could they do? And who had time, or wanted, to remember that Craig had been the best chairman the department had ever had? Who would wish to search an enigma that the unreal, in certain circumstances, might be better than the real? If they remembered what they should remember, how could they so conclusively think what they now must think? It was indeed an obscure matter.

But Emily, in whom so many conflicting emotions were aroused, had to have a strong drink to get up enough nerve to go by and see Craig before he left for God knows where. Why did the only man in town she had truly admired have to be exposed as an impostor when all the little phonies would go undetected? But, most of all, how was she going to get along without him? Where, in fact, would she ever again find *her* "saint?"

On the way over, it did not help either that the April afternoon was heavy with the perfume of wistaria, ambiguously hung with the color of mourning. Emily remembered that Craig said wistaria was his favorite flower because the last dress he remembered his mother wearing was of its color, and around his property he had the largest concentration of vines and bushes in town.

Great purple sails hung from the trees, and Emily thought how much they spoke to her of voyage and journey, release and regeneration. A huge, staggering, lavender fleet, becalmed in the woods, thrilled with stymied hopes, stagnated ambitions, and every frustrated person in Carrollton was part of the indentured crew. It was strange that a deep, almost rank scent like this suggested the human hegira. Not "all the perfumes of Arabia"—this musk would go with us everywhere.

When she rang the bell, Craig came to the door in shirtsleeves, a hammer in hand. Nearly everything was gone from the house except a few packing cases and the picture which would have to be professionally crated. Celeste and Cecilia sat on one of the boxes having a cup of tea, stiff as dolls, dazed and red-eyed, sisters of Undine to whom Craig had given souls rather too late to matter.

Almost tearfully glad to see her, he impulsively closed her in his arms, big, suffocating, but now surreal, like a child enwombing the parent. He went out to get her a drink and sweeten his own, and when he returned, Celeste and Cecilia made their excuses, thank God, fading into the vacuum of the empty house as if their part, after all, had been mainly spectral. She and Craig sat down facing each other on two crates near Saint Cecilia, and, as she would say to herself later, she "got it out of him" at last as they looked into the painting as if it were a phantasmal window.

It all began—oh God, didn't the odious phrase summon up every wrecked life in the world?—in a small town in West Virginia where Craig's father was a plumber. His mother had come from somewhat more, though the "genteel" had grown shabbier and shabbier down the years, and she had married beneath her. The only thing of worth she brought with her was the painting, done by a great-aunt from the right side of the family who had studied in Europe. If one has dreams, one must focus on something, and it became the catalyst for mother and son.

A piano was somehow managed; she played a little, and they sang together. The smile of the saint in the picture encouraged them to think they did it rather well, and an impoverished old maid was engaged to visit the house and give Craig lessons.

This phase of the story could have broken Emily's heart for she knew too much about dreams that were stretched too far and wide. Why couldn't we have some built-in sense of what we could really do with the materials at hand? Mothers all over the world who believed in the democracy of genius were trying to extract more from their children than was there, and yet if "your reach did not exceed your grasp—" It was just too brutal to think about. Modern life that so callously promised everything to everybody, suggesting that one must be "successful" and "good" at one and the same time, left boys like Craig without recourse. The wick was meant to burn in everybody's window apparently without oil. One was expected to go on striking matches endlessly even if it produced no flame.

All that Craig had at the time in the way of fuel were the ardors and blandishments of his mother and Miss Agnes centered on himself. How could any child, and they put it to him none too obliquely, backed by two such propulsive dreamers, fail? Craig could not, just could not, offer them a dark and vacant window.

Moreover, the painting attracted the child like a lifesize illustration of his own myth, a book of a single illuminated page with the mother-figure represented as saint and savior. Other adolescents had their pin-ups, but he had his Saint Cecilia. Jesus, what a mixture of sex and survival: talk about "a stairway to the sea where down the blind are driven"—had Craig ever acknowledged that Cecilia was also *their* saint?

"I always felt I belonged to her," he said. "I always hoped she would lean down and kiss me."

Emily needed another drink after that, and, when he went to get it, was horrified to find herself saying, "That goddamned saint!" No, that wasn't what she meant. It couldn't be. Why, without her, Craig might have been nothing. Nothing at all.

When he returned, he put them both through three years of

college. At first, things had gone rather well. Something in his genes had signaled to the frail, skinny boy at the piano that he was not going to make it on sentiment alone. He went out for soccer in the fall and track in the spring, and his body responded with an overplus of rich masculinity. Hair, skin, muscle, bones took up the struggle as if the soma, in an effort of compensation, knew that it must draw on all its reserves to produce a beautiful young man. If he could have left it at that, his professors, who did not handle star material even on a physical level very often, would have passed him on through the ranks with a gentleman's C. But his mother expected him to be more than an average student, perhaps even Phi Beta Kappa, not counting on the fact that poor preparation would finally take its toll. By his junior year, he felt he was never going to graduate with honors, particularly since he had to moonlight in a variety of jobs. He realized that he had been trying too hard, that he need look no further than his own handsome presence for the keys to the kingdom. He began to "flirt" with his classmates and professors, kiss ass, copy passages for themes from books, glance at another's paper—apparently one had to do a lot of little things when the saint wasn't looking!

Emily felt exhausted at this point as if she had been laboriously climbing a dark stair toward a light only to find some steps missing. She could not control a sense of tremor, a refusal of further suspension in her ganglia; the purpose of ascent collapsed, and the whole spine of the thing seemed spurious. It was almost atavistic, this identification, the empathy she had experienced with Craig's attempt to make it on his own. One had to go down into the pit of aboriginal memory to feel that ascending staircase in the backbone.

Was this what the failure of the so-called moral life meant? You went as far as you could legitimately, and then instead of setting about the depressing work of slowly building the missing supports, you let those glorious, those goddamned dreams take over, eliding the gap fictitiously, pretending it was not there at all. Then one had a "rush"—there was nothing more thrilling than putting one's foot on the first, high, hallucinatory step—but it was an addiction. A kind of ambivalent glamour, the thrill of not getting caught, of carrying it off just one more time, one more day, blushed through the system with a sense of heightened existence.

But, of course, someone like Billy Hanes could fold up the stretched steps like an accordion, and the sound, the music that came from the compression, was very like the stuff you heard in every concert hall these days, residual scrapings and scratchings, reductive, aleatory. So you wanted to be a hero, sonny boy. Clean out your ears. This is the music of time.

Rattling the ice in her glass, Emily could have been sick on the floor but not until he got her another drink (Just a half, Craig, darling). The horrible thing was that he could have made it on his own. The steps were there, steps made of stone, right before his feet. Why was he so afraid? Lord love a duck! How these mothers built you up and at the same time destroyed any sense of identity you might have had on your own. Still, it just didn't compute. He *was* Saint Cecilia's son. Why did he have to act like such a bastard?

Craig learned his lesson from the cheating episode. He didn't try anymore to deal with—what was the word—reality? The faked credentials, the forged letters were done in the same soft climate in which he worshipped Saint Cecilia. They were simply union cards which had to be procured at any cost, to enter into the atmosphere of the picture. And it had all been so easy. He had not even, at first, felt particularly dishonest about it. It was just something that had to be done. And the son of the saint could do it better than anyone else. Then Celeste and Cecilia had taken over where his mother and Miss Agnes had left off. These women in his life might look rather flimsy, but they had a picture in them, by God, and he pulled it out of them by main force. The rest was cinematically easy; all that he had to do was supply the anecdotal figures with unflagging animation.

Within that continuum Jack set about making Craig better than, so he thought, Jack could ever have conceivably been. The irony was almost too much to bear. What kind of world did we live in in which the imitation could function better than the genuine? Craig on the basis of a lie had "spoken with the tongues of angels." How many more Craigs who might have been Jack were there in Carrollton? He was simply the unlucky bloke who got his tongue jerked out. Did one have to let it go at that? Too much might-have-been and one would get locked up in the kind of representation even Goya couldn't have handled. Time to go.

"That damned picture!" he said as she got up to leave. "That damned picture!"

"No, don't say that," she almost shouted. "It's the most beautiful thing you own."

That was all she could say to him, but she was glad she could say that. It was too late for him to turn against the painting. He must hang it somewhere, and, then, somewhere else. Would he understand? Would he see it now? Not at the top but at the bottom of the stairs, but still a step—the compressed significance more than able to bear his weight.

But having emphasized and underlined his obligation, could she ever quite grasp the astonishing power of his pathological courage? To keep going at all, he must finally have lived in a world almost without moral reference, collapsing everything into his need to succeed. Out there, alone, all those years, poor Craig with his incredible power of genesis! When he was finally exposed, it must have been like a concussion from an alien planet with its devastating scene of a man falling through space clasping a burning picture.

Outside, Emily paused in the wistaria-drenched darkness. All over town the great purple snakes coiled in the trees, writhing with the richest ecstasy of spring, the powerful, pungent scent connected with something final, something fatal. Laocoön could not have been more violently embraced. Could she endure for even a moment longer these waves, these fumes, this fetor of slithering purple?

As she walked home through the campus, the stone stairs of Hines Hall loomed iconically, but stasis, at this juncture, was not all that she wanted. Sound, released, ranging, continuous—that was it. One needed the aural support, the implied thrust, the imminent passage, if one were going to push one's way through the seductive stupefying perfume.

God, the world was swarming with child prodigies, little angels—poor sods who thought there was a saint for everyone on earth. Still some of them must hear *something*. Was it music from an accordion that Billy Hanes could never crush between his hands?

A Prince in His Time

The "Prince"—perhaps the name the college boys gave to Holt Hamilton III will partly explain why I could never judge him.

We were in the same class at Carrollton University, belonged to the same fraternity, but anyone, including myself, would have said that in those days it was only an accident which permitted Keith Rogers from a middle-class family in Charlotte to associate in fictive equality with native royalty. It was not only that Holt was the son of a textile magnate from Winston-Salem who had given vast sums to the university. He was a princeling on those levels which undergraduates most admire. A star on the football team and a stud with the girls, Holt performed against the mysterious backdrop of money which sets up theater at any place at any time.

Even so, since there were one or two others in the fraternity who also moved in front of a velvet cyclorama, Holt might not have been able to put himself beyond criticism if he had not also been the best-looking man in our class. Blond—but many are blond. Six feet two—but what is height alone? Blue eyes—millions suggest the original seawater in our soma. But Holt held them together in some absolute physical confidence. I could never get over how big he looked when he walked into a room. Perhaps the best way to express it is to say that he put you at ease with your dreams. He was the objective correlative of undergraduate glamour. I could never look at him without remembering what his grandfather had said when asked if money brought happiness: "No, I wouldn't go so far as to say that, but it certainly does help to quiet the nerves."

The fact that our fraternity, which was not high in scholarship except for a stray aspirant to Phi Beta Kappa like me, had such an assured, one might almost say composed, place on the campus was largely due to the good luck of having Holt Hamilton as a member. Holt, who did not need to be snobbish, made us feel good about everything. When, as the saying went in the fraternity, we went over "to get our balls off" at a brothel in a nearby town, we felt seamy and sordid unless Holt went along. *Noblesse oblige*—we came home more gilded in our manhood.

I hazard the guess that at the university in the twenties we inhabited the right place at the right time as not many generations have been able to do since. Traditional Carrollton, a place of veneration and venery on its mound as thick with trees as a hunting preserve, was a mold for the liquid of young men's desires. There is something about a combination of old buildings and young bodies which seems to reach back and forward in time. The ivy-covered Greek Revival classrooms and dormitories with their architectural emphasis on the horizontal suggest a striving for perfection in this world not the next, and Carrollton, not uniquely, alas, had been dubbed the Athens of the South. But undergraduates adore such clichés, managing somehow to invest them with new meaning, and most of them tried to work out some approximation of *mens sana in corpore sano*. In this tradition, Holt did not entirely neglect his studies, and even a "brain" like myself worked out at the gym.

The fact that Holt, so classic in body, did not seem gelded in brain may also explain why I could never judge him. Though I observed him minutely, I could never tell how intelligent he was. As a physical manifestation, he stood obvious and final, but his mind was a mystery. He could make the most obvious quip, and it came out sounding like Congreve. Something happened when he spoke, a mysterious power coated his words, and they moved through the mind of the hearer invulnerably. Was it money or male virtue that provided the lubrication so that one listened and was enlightened—or lulled? I could never decide.

While we were at college I never saw Holt really out of character but once, and that was in our senior year when he came into our room to ask me to help out with his father and mother who were coming down prior to the day when the university would present Holt Senior with a Distinguished Alumnus Award. Most of us dreaded parental intrusion into the hunting preserve—what do you do with a father and mother so long banished from the court of dreams?—so Holt's troubled mood seemed normal to me.

Having pointed out the difficulties of protocol, he said one thing I would always remember.

"You'll like Dad, Keith. He's more like you."

"Bullshit," I said. "What have I got in common with *the* Holt Hamilton?"

The tall figure of gold seemed to melt a little inwardly, and I could see he was offended. "I'm Holt Hamilton, too, remember?"

"You sure are, old buddy," I said quickly, using his term for me to put him at his ease. "So how can you lose?"

Nevertheless, at first, when I met his father, my self-esteem took a real beating. Admittedly, I was short, dark, and wore glasses, but was it to the likes of this little balding man with the pince-nez that Holt had unfeelingly and, I thought, unperceptively consigned my destiny? Had the descending line of power and promise, saving up spore, skipped a generation to produce Holt? But the eyes behind the pince-nez bored in, and I found I had a hard, compact commodity on my hands. I traded with him, and he "bought" me. Son and mother kept their distance, and I could not get over the feeling that the old man's condescension was in some way paying me off for looking after the student prince during his golden days.

After that, the year in the university town was what it had always been—genial, gestative, southern but not too southern, touched by the North but not too severely. Young men can stretch themselves full-length in Carrollton, and seniors, brimming with four years of accumulated dreams, pull the elastic until it pops.

Holt knocked up a local waitress, an abortion was quietly accomplished, and nobody cared. In the winter quarter, the accusation of cheating on an exam stigmatically threatened, but since I sat behind him, I came to his rescue with the Student Government. What if I did see that big head move from the sphinxlike attitude we were supposed to maintain? Hadn't I coached him for hours on the subject? Coincidence was the prerogative of the sons of kings—to ask riddles, not to answer them, their inherent right.

That spring in Carrollton—and where can one match its concomitant flowering of camellias and azaleas?—a symbiotic opulence seemed to breathe through the pores of seniors who were both enterprising and amative. "We learned and we were laid," as I wryly said to myself. The town had a kind of heraldic beauty wherever you looked whether your color was pink, purple, or white. If democratic competitiveness palled, Holt and I could repair to the stone castle in the deep woods owned by a secret organization to which we belonged, and drink from a private grail. Flowering Judas wept tears of blood, dogwood extended the white cross of ambivalent purity. If parting were such sweet sorrow, it was tempered by the crusade ahead.

Penultimate April brought ultimate May—the various vivid campus with its prospect of weekends at the beach, the blue shock treatment for minds to whom so many enchanting ultimatums were offered. Hot, ecstatic days! We came back to Carrollton weighted with lapus lazuli, Blue Knights ready for our final tournament on the wooded hill.

After graduation, when we were packing up to go home, working in our B.V.D.s in ninety degree heat, Holt, so heavy with collegiate honors that he still seemed suited in mail, moved with a curious, immersed, absent-minded lassitude.

"Well, old buddy," he said as he slammed down the lid of his trunk still redolent of masculine accouterments and last year's mothballs. "What do you say we come back to graduate school. I've gotten kind of sweet on the old place."

Then he spoke like a young man in his underwear. "Of course, I don't know what Dad will say. You know how he is—all of this Holt-Hamilton-the-Third business. He never will get over the fact that I look like my grandfather. Could you write him a letter, old buddy? Tell him I've got the stuff for graduate work and so on. Maybe law school. That ought to go over better. Shoot him the real bullshit."

If it had been anyone else but Holt, I would not have been so noncommittal, but I simply could not buy his future as a dubious security. Neither mundane nor metaphysical anxiety befits a prince, and I did not want him to descend to the level where I so often lived. If the sweat on his body were to remain golden, it could not be mixed with tears.

Nevertheless, I did write that letter, but it was no go. Holt returned to Winston-Salem to work in his father's business, and I went back to Carrollton alone to study for my Ph.D. in English. The sons of rich men not only can "go home again," but generally do. You could say Holt had too much to return to while I had too little.

As I grubbed away at my doctorate, married another struggling graduate student, and even after I was lucky enough to land a position at Carrollton, I regretted the loss of my "confidence man." Of course, we saw each other on football weekends when Holt rolled into town, each year in a new Cadillac, and he looked and acted the same. He was soon vice-president of the company, and, in line with family tradition, gave a new wing to the fraternity. I had heard there was to be an "arranged" marriage into a tobacco family, and I began to suspect that Holt did not feel the family mold too much of an Iron Maiden.

Then he did a surprising thing, the only one I can remember during those years, and it made him look larger or smaller according to the way one considers the matrix of men. The tobacco heiress was ditched at the last moment, and Holt eloped with Valerie Tatum, daughter of a history professor at the University of Kentucky. Val was bookish, a good student—it was almost as if he had married my sister. True, she was indulged in a horse, but only because Dr. Tatum harked back to a heritage of Kentucky gentlemen; otherwise, like me, she got her notions of the high life out of fiction. So once again, when I might have judged the Prince, he had done the unexpected.

I remembered Valerie, from occasional double dates in Carrollton, as rather lanky, unprepossessing, and was not prepared for the tall, handsome woman with long auburn hair parted in the middle who treated Holt and his family as if they might be rather her inferiors.

In those days, gossip, as it still does to some extent, thrived in the South as a genuine form of human interest, and though I did not see much of the Hamiltons, I heard about them constantly. Val made a hit with Holt's father after all, and he loosened the purse strings. They had a large place of their own. Valerie founded a hunt, deployed a string of racehorses, and gathered a notable collection of nineteenth-century English paintings. Having been cut down in size by the elopement, Holt took enormous pride in how Valerie extended his life. The two men provided, and she proposed. Where in North Carolina could one find a more splendid syllogism: major premise, minor premise, and conclusion?

Like the golden ball the ancients said hung down from heaven, a kind of static wonderment surrounded the intense activity of the triumvirate—Mind, Money, Mind, the malicious syllogized, but no one really knew what oiled the combine or how it spread itself among them. I still bet on Holt, the lubricator; I still saw him as mediator. I had not written my thesis on the Romantic Movement in our literature to disavow the possibility of an American hero.

As my own life prospered somewhat more and I became a full professor, I even began to enjoy the respite, to see the advantages of contemplating Holt from afar. Academic life, when it works, narcotizes us somewhat to the ambitions of extramural experience, and yet it was great fun to hear the stories about the Hamiltons that drifted back to the campus and only every now and then be faced with the evidence of a life larger than life.

Holt Senior, the old triumvir, lived on and on, philanthropic, predatory to the end, and the state shook with a kind of Roman fall when he finally died. Deflective and disarming, the figure turned in the mold again, this time more violently, *volte-face*, as if the head meant to grow new features. Holt retired, gave "Winhaven," named after his dead mother, Winifred, to his oldest son, and came back to college at last.

"Holtwood" was built on a slope outside of Carrollton to the specifications of Valerie who had chosen the name to suggest, I suspected, that the caesura in the clause of power had moved into the position of Caesar.

Would the Prince, however, be able to seduce a faculty not noted for their love of the rich as he had enchanted undergraduates, or would Valerie to the prejudiced seem little more than a handsome Horse with Carrollton as her paddock?

To introduce them to our friends as casually as possible, my wife Sally and I gave a series of small cocktail parties. *Soror et frater*— Holt soon had them aligned in his favor as he did the college boys in voting time. It was true that Valerie sat on the sofa a good deal, suggesting a court mentality, but Holt brushed the subject of an old hip injury, and that was that.

"Old buddy," he said to me, and I could have sworn the golden mist was floating back around us. "I'm home again."

"Holt, you old scoundrel." I clapped him on the back just for the joy of feeling how solid he still was. "You always get your way. What did you say to Maggie Perkins? She hasn't smiled in ten years."

"Keep a few rose petals up your sleeve, old buddy. It's not what you say to women. It's the way you handle them."

Maggie, on her third drink, sidled up again, and Holt, who could extend a moment as well as any man I have ever known, sent her away as a confirmed constituent.

Not one false step had been taken, not one motion lacked its smooth synovial fluid. The fabric of the town had been tested and found to have a soft hole in its center where an ambiguous but alluring figure could lift the entire swathe like the pole of a shimmering tent. At the next party, Holt, who knew every move in manners which could properly be made, limbered up so attractively that you could have said our man of metal, spuriously attributed, was really made of local pine. Carrollton, with all its trees, is essentially a town of dryads, and its people like those who can bend in the wind.

Sally and I simply set out drinks, saving the bartender's fees for our retirement. We needn't have worried. Holt watched every woman's glass like the declining mercury of party spirit, but he never let anyone drink too much either, keeping the temperature at a pleasant 70 degrees. That is, except Val—I noticed that she managed to be rather too sedulous in her cups, and short and complaining when he forgot her on his rounds.

"Miz Val," he drawled and invalided her down a bit, "don't you think we had better hang up the dipper and go home?"

Gracious, gregarious Carrollton could not do enough for the Hamiltons. Hadn't Holt, after all, chosen to build his mansion among professors rather than the Dukes of industry? Didn't Valerie read the best books and invite all the artists in town to her house? Could the undergraduate dream that so many of them had shared come true in a man who wore a crown and at the same time respected curriculum?

No party was complete without them. If Valerie had a "cold" and Holt came alone, people somehow loved him better by himself. He seemed all the more free to go up to everyone and leave his imprimatur, but lightly given. Some few who simply could not stand the incomparable blend began to call him "The Butler," but Maggie Perkins, in whom Holt had released some hidden spring of generosity, declared, "There are butlers and butlers, my dear, but who can object to one who works for nothing? I couldn't give a party without him."

How many men can live as long as I and have a boyhood admiration publicly confirmed? I was delighted to see that Holt, who had never hawked his wares even in college, now hushed them up completely. The boy who moved before velvet had learned to wrap his smallest gesture in it. Instead of standing in solitary splendor on a burnished plaque, like one of the trophies in his gameroom, he seemed merely to have encircled our town with an almost imperceptible chain, the finest of gold wires. He could pull ever so slightly and the shape of events fell to his touch.

Since things had worked out as I had hoped, it was a comfort to have him come in reasonably close once more. Politics in the department, of which I was now chairman, were at their most divisive, but there was the rewarding and resplendent figure of my friend who belonged to my world and yet was not embroiled in it. We love those who are always *in medias res*, immersed in the thick, moving stuff, but who can remove themselves at will, luring rather than lured by life, remote and magical as a figure just beyond the reach of the waves and yet somehow in command of that great diapason of color. When the seizure of experience rolls back for most of us, draining the caves of the heart, we can mitigate the sense of subsidence by merely the thought of one whom the sea loves and still leaves alone.

When I was tired, I thought of Holt's rising influence, and it calmed me like a full tide in the morning. Moreover, it was a very pliable prince indeed who could sit in council with the president, be the favorite speaker of the undergraduate organizations, and shuttle back and forth to Winston-Salem, for he still kept his hand in, without invidious connections being suggested.

Touch and go—and so it went for several deliquescent years. Very few knew Holt well if they thought about it, but who needs to localize a pleasant scent which permeates a room? All any of us had to do was rub the bottle, and the genie would appear at our side.

Not that there were not some apostates whose unadmitted quarrel with him was perhaps summed up by Sally when she said one evening after a party that he was "untouchable." Or, as she corrected herself, was it that he seemed to be pinch-hitting? For whom? Himself?

But not long after, as if he received her telepathic message, Sally felt his pressure, and so did I, but still committed to the demulcent view, I refused to admit that it lingered long enough to leave a small blister.

We had been out to the country for a cocktail party, and Valerie, on the spur of the moment, invited us to Holtwood for supper. I thought Holt hesitated, assessing Val's temperature as somewhere between late, late happy and early hostile, but he acquiesced graciously, suggesting that I drive Val while he took Sally in his car.

Was it the warm spring night, the wicked drinks, or the wayward woman? In any case, my old buddy and I, it seemed, might get down to our underwear for the first time since graduation.

One could say, in proper sequence, that I had my tie loosened by Val on the way over in the car. Holt refused her one for the road, and she had climbed that final degree to hostile-belligerent.

"I'll have one when I get home anyway," she said. "You know why he doesn't want me to drink?"

"Holt's a prudent man."

"You're goddam right he is. Prudent and worried. He's afraid I'll talk."

"Don't we all?"

"I mean say something he won't like. Spill the beans."

"Oh?" I echoed lamely, for I could not associate Holt with that homely vegetable.

"And I don't mean Boston baked. You should try some of the southern variety—yellowed-eyed with salt pork."

"I don't quite see Holt serving them at his table."

"Well, look under the table, honey. He's got a pot between his feet."

Blessedly, it was a short ride, for Valerie suddenly grew plaintive about how bad she felt most of the time these days and insisted that Holt never helped her at all. "Oh, he acts like my specialist in public, but when we get home I can cry my eyes out—no doctor in the house."

Alcohol and the aging woman!—I flinched for my fastidious friend.

But Holtwood itself seemed a little decadent that evening, touched with the atmosphere of those hunting lodges where European crown princes divested themselves into basic neurosis. Was there just a trace of Mayerling, enhanced by the accidental fact that this was the night off for all the help except the butler, and we four seemed almost furtively gathered? The pink and lilac tulip trees looming through the dining room window in the dusk put me in the mood of something foreign and fatal. Both Holt and Valerie were expendable after all. It was as simple as that. For the first time they did not carry the weight of empire so forcefully as one had always believed was their common style. Rather amazed at the disparagement of my thoughts, I could ask myself if life at Holtwood were perhaps too marginal, too crepuscular. There was a muted lavender glow in the room just when a searching bright light of deeper understanding was needed. Was I, was I indeed, beginning to judge the Prince?

Of course, he did his best to carry the evening off, but I suppose he always needed an assemblage for his most finished performance. Val, dispensing male hostility indiscriminately, played strip poker with him all during dinner—here a jacket, there a shoe.

She had hardly gotten in the door when she demanded, using the nickname she knew he loathed, "Why don't you get us a real drink, Hoe?"

But when he touched us up lightly, she snorted, "That's nothing but holy water. Can't you do better than that?" and colored her own heavily with bourbon that streamed through the liquid like brown blood. Ah, what a communicant our Val had become!

In my let-down mood, when he went out for some more ice though the bucket was still half full, I let my disaffection debouch. Why couldn't the man keep still for more than two minutes? Must he always even in his own home act like "The Butler?" Men in their underwear are not gracious companions for well-dressed women attended by a butler in fact.

The old colored man who had served Holt since he was a boy labored not too efficiently or rapidly among the dishes the cook had prepared.

Holt tried to keep it light when he sang out, "Nobody's in the kitchen with Dinah" as Valerie held out her glass for a refill. "Val, why don't you go out and give William a hand?"

Sally got to her feet. "Val, not Sal," he said like a rhyming schoolboy, laying a hand on her wrist, but for an instant he looked rather thickly at his wife across the table.

"Beans. That's what you're going to get tonight, Hoe." Valerie winked at me. "Just plain old North Carolina beans."

Holt looked quickly at me, and I knew that he had decided it was time to pick up his pants, a shoe, the works. Without meaning to, Val had given him an entrance, a proper cue, and, a master of tone, once he had modulated his persona, he would out-southern his wife the rest of the evening. It was easy in fact, one of his seasoned performances. I had often seen him in a group, the putative clods concealing the nuggets beneath the dust, proclaiming, "I'm just a North Carolina country boy." Lil Abner was having no part of Svengali—not now or ever. Was it his fault that Daisy Mae had gotten into the blackberry wine?

Word began to get around, everyone accepted the betrayal and made the transition for the Prince. Poor Holt—stuck with a neurotic wife, not to mention the touched-up hair which now looked dipped in elderberry juice or the poor teeth suggesting snuff stain. Daisy Mae should have known that the wine was laced with wormwood. Why didn't Holt get a divorce?

Why indeed? Was it that royalty never admits a mistake? I seldom saw Holt waver in his composure toward her after that nearly divestive dinner at his house. And it must be admitted that her attitude toward him was inconsistent and ambivalent. No one was allowed to say a word against him except herself, and if you were so unguarded as to agree with any of her scurrilous remarks, you found that Echoes were not welcome in that house. You would not be among those asked to his sixtieth birthday party when Val invited the governor and arranged for the University String Quartet to play after dinner. Also, when she was not drinking, I noticed she fed him just the right lines. Struck with a practiced hand, when he might have sounded glib his mind could appear to muffle those around him with the resonance of a gong.

Only once more, at the end of a party at our house, did Holt suggest the nude beneath his clothes. Distracted by departing guests, he forgot to give Valerie his arm, and she slipped and fell, letting out some vituperation of truly naval magnificence.

"Nobody to help me," she sobbed in diminuendo. "Nobody, nobody."

Holt lifted her into the car and came back to talk with me in front of the house for a moment.

"Don't be too hard on Valerie. She's never gotten over the death of my father." His forehead was beaded with perspiration from the effort of hauling her to the car, and I thought how incredibly he could still produce the look of vulnerable innocence. He had left with me the perfect exit line, enigmatic and enlisting. The sweating boy standing over his trunk could not have done better.

Val did not live much longer after that, though her condition was kept as secret as the health of a dictator. The sofa was not a subterfuge. She really had never fully recovered from a hip injury inflicted when her horse fell and rolled on her. Over the years her sedentary life had aggravated a circulatory problem, and she would not follow her doctor's advice.

I went over to see her not long before she died, and wondered why I had not made even more of a friend of a woman whose bedroom was so buttressed with books. She wasn't up to much—just some surface chat—and to keep things moving I asked her if Holt had liked my book on Wallace Stevens. No. He had not had the time to read it yet, but she would keep after him until he did. And then she said something which had a curious echo in a house that did not like them.

"Don't blame Holt too much . . . I think I've done enough for us all."

I will not let thee go until thou bless him—I felt rather stunted in my imagination as I left. Why hadn't I thought about them, both of them, more than I did? Why hadn't I lifted the roof of the Georgian mansion and looked into the doll's house? Had I, as much as Holt, stayed chained to Carrollton as if it were Heidelberg? To dream and to know—one of the most poignant regrets life has in store for us is that we can seldom do them together.

Holt waited a proper year, and when Sally and I were in Europe, we heard rather raucously from Maggie Perkins that he had married exactly the wrong woman. Nothing more than generalized aspersion, no details since Maggie did not want to diminish the shock of our first encounter. Nevertheless, she wrote, though she did not mean to go along, Carrollton was *trying* to effect another transition for the Prince.

"Nevertheless," however, had apparently subsumed "never," for it was at Maggie's house that we met the new Mrs. Holt Hamilton III after all. Meanwhile I had had time in Europe to think about the Prince, and reflection, once begun, never stops.

Though he knew we were in town, he did not ask us over for a "preview," and since we had not been invited to the wedding, performed by a justice of the peace, but had been sent an announcement which trailed us all over France, we did not call him. I decided that the Prince wanted it that way—a dispersive encounter at another large cocktail party—and, perspectively, I looked back to recall that this was the milieu in which I had mainly seen my best friend since our college days. Did he think the whole thing could be lost in the shuffle, and after a few parties no one would care? Would it work? Wait, as Maggie said—and I answered my own question—until you see the wife.

Inside and out, Maggie's place in the beautiful October weather looked handsomely equipped for a succession, radiant but touched with nostalgia, as changeovers, seasonal or societal, frequently are. In a town where they would rather put a curve in the road than cut down an oak tree, autumn is both temporary accretion and potential calamity. As long as the leaves stay golden, a dryad has an equity overhead, though a threat of impoverishment hovers in the air.

But while it lasts the equipoise is infinitely appealing. Maggie had her dining-room table heaped with autumn camellias, Daikagura and Debutante, as if to say that the sun in Carrollton never closes its greenhouse until Christmas. The Prince was undoubtedly to be honored—Maggie was not generally so lavish. But this time he did not come up with our prepoured drinks in his hand. Did it mean an uncharacteristic call to obeisance? I saw him, always the tallest, standing in a corner among a levee of those who never intended to have anything to do with him again. Our eyes met, and I suppose I obeyed rather in a trance some call to comity he had given me more than forty years ago. I went over with Sally for the presentation.

He looked startlingly well. If a man must turn gray, consult Holt Hamilton who knew how to go all the way and make it the natural color of a full head of hair. No slump, no shrinkage, though I thought his suit a little more boldly and atypically patterned than usual—he was still the fully distended male, well balanced on his hips as athletes are, a synergy of masculine resources. You could cut off any part of him as a perfect specimen—head, an arm, a strongly articulated hand where the fine hair still glinted in the candlelight. I suppose I shall never again know a man with such incredible physical *suffisance*.

But no more seductions? Having been unmistakably summoned, I was surprised that he hardly broke ranks, barely widened the circle to admit me. Though I suppose he did not like my not having written, I thought he spoke rather abruptly when he said without the usual amenities, "I want you to meet the *new* Val."

Take it or leave it, old buddy, this is it—was there really a shade of truculence in his voice or just my own embarrassment ventriloquizing?

I could swear he made only a comprehensive motion toward a group of women surrounding him and did not really indicate her, as if to say that it did not matter, that we were to accept her as a generalized notion no matter what she looked like, what she was. The wife of Holt Hamilton need be nothing else but that.

But I had no trouble identifying her among one or two strangers in the group. Incredibly particularized in spite of fiat, she was the only woman in the room who did not look like Carrollton.

She did not look like Winston-Salem either, the tobacco heiress *rediviva*, that would have gone over perfectly well—a gulp at too much money, but then a swallow. No. It was a milltown down the road. Not quite though. A competency of some concentrated sort came at you like a filing case—she had been his secretary for a year and then his mistress for three or four.

If only she had been beautiful! Sex that all can enjoy on the surface suggests at least one certitude. But the short, somewhat weathered-looking blonde in the loud flowered dress was no Circe.

If only she could have been bright! Shrewd she would turn out to be, of course, but Wallace Stevens might have been a man who ran a department store as far as she was concerned.

If only she could have been kind! How do I love thee? Shall I count the ways? What had happened to Holt's spiritual arithmetic? Was he counting backward? How could the Prince do this to us?

Still too set on automatic not to pass a tray of canapés before he left, he also managed alone with me one of those moments which had formerly seemed so fabulously extended.

"We must get together soon, old buddy," he said. Is the tone of a man like Holt always tentative and subject to reassessment? I must have been more baffled by Valerie *Segunda* than I realized, for he sounded like one of "the boys in the backroom."

"Tell them I'm having the same." Had our Val's difficulties stemmed from the fact that she could never have answered in the words of the song?

Nouvelle Val—*nouveau* Val, as one of the French professors dubbed her—found that the backroom opened into the front room if you just pushed hard enough. But who could blame a lady for wanting to let in a little fresh air? For starters, the Landseers and Leightons could come off the walls of the living room in the guise of a gift to the university. New scenes, new fabrics—the Georgian mansion began to look a little more like a place where a man in his underwear could relax with a girl friend.

Saddest of all to me, the old-timers in the stable were put down, and Val could look around her and say: This is good.

If the possessive pronoun had a new mistress at Holtwood— "My Cadillac, my house, my gardener"—the master did not seem to mind. No one had heard primary Val mention any of these. She had a history that antedated them all. Nor had she let Holt sit easily on a pedestal.

Not blackmail, not premature senility, as some foolishly suggested, searching for reasons, made sense. Was it only that Holt found someone who could let herself be possessed purely and simply on the level of possessions? Sons of the sons of Midas tend to lose their sense of tactile glamour, and Valerie *Primera* and Holt Senior looked upon the stuff as something to be molded. They were goldsmiths, the in-between of mind and money. Had Holt longed all his life for the original lust of his grandfather as though that alone might enliven a weaker sense of form? *Nouveau* Val was indeed well-named: All things new. I winced at the thought, but would Holt at last be allowed to relax and enjoy the crassness of wealth? Who, who indeed, would not bend his knee when he acknowledged that the Prince had found the partisan he preferred?

That, of course, is a continued story, and at this point I relinquish my focus. Perhaps I had moved it a step too far from the running sea. Anything we attempt to secure in a higher place, a figure, even a "fact" for that matter, will lure the almost amorously combative invasion of the violent blue water. The action finally requires that everything should be drawn down, back, into. The statue, no matter how handsome or remote, cannot resist the indigo grasp. Anyone who sees those loose blue fingers fringed with white, almost lazily, but powerfully, deployed up along the shore, groping the earth, instinctively runs away, but they will reach higher. There is not an Achilles among us who has not felt, or will not feel, that indelible blue stain upon his heel.

Nevertheless, I do not begrudge myself my youthful admiration. It is not beside but beyond the point that second lives, fenestrated by the sea, may seem to sluice some irrecoverable weight of gold or that second wives may not turn out to be remontant roses. The remarkable thing was that a high, youthful place lasted so long. But then Holt Senior, Valerie, myself, and, I believe, Carrollton, tending the retaining walls, wanted it to last. None of us, for the world, would have missed knowing a prince in his time.

The Rival

Until Eudora McVay came to town, Myra Moorhead regarded Carrollton as an extension of her ego. Some thought it was because she was an artist that people let her get away with so much; others said it was because she was an Irish artist.

An ambiguous sexual metaphor might have stated the case more fairly. If Myra had her way with Carrollton, she let the town have its way with her as long as it came across with the right tributary caress. Dining at Gertrude Hinshaw's house, she recuperated the following morning from the heavy drink and rich food with Old Red who came by with a bottle of scuppernong tucked under his arm to clean the pine needles out of her gutters.

Myra's men friends were "old," "big," "little"—father figures of all sizes and shapes. Steve Wilson referred to this nomenclature which seldom had any relevance to her corresponding age and physique as "Myra's Mother Goose." Never mind. She had never cared too much for Wilson who came as near as anyone in town to being a rival. Old Red, while she granted him the privilege of drinking his wine, agreed that Steve had never amounted to much as a novelist even if he did teach creative writing at the university.

Hardly anyone seemed to think it at all odd that the end product of so much male contact was a relentless series of Cassatt-like paintings of women and lovely young girls. An easy transference of fantasy, they sold well, and few bothered to ask if she really liked doing them anymore. Even Steve admitted that no one could put the bloom on a female bottom like Myra. If for a change she did a landscape of cotton fields or the dunes at Nag's Head, her connoisseurs let them go by, and waited until she was back to normal again.

As well as anyone, Steve knew that how Myra looked and how she *could* look was also how she could be. There was the Myra who wore Yugoslavian blouses, bright skirts, and Duncan sandals, the self-stylist who wore her still beautiful, burnished brown hair in braids tied with bright pieces of wool so that a precocious child had asked her in the post office if she were a woman or an enlarged girl. Most impressively, there was the Myra who looked like the figurehead of a ship pushing through the storm. When presented with this image, Steve, ironic even about her grandest moments, said, "Yes. That's Myra. Breasting the waves and waving her breasts."

One could choose, but was there really as much to choose from as there seemed to be? After the laughs were over, Steve, at least, had double, even triple, thoughts about Myra. Had she gone so far with her image that it had taken on a life of its own like a sorcerer's apprentice? Perhaps, sooner or later, there had to be a Eudora McVay, but he was willing to admit that she was more than Myra should have had to bargain for when he saw them together at Aviva Russell's large, white-columned house in the country, a gathering place for an assortment of the cognoscenti, mainly minor examples of the breed, sparked by one or two like Myra who would accept no other cachet than major.

Though they would never have admitted it even to each other, for they were dogmatic liberals, the Russells considered themselves the Medici of Carrollton, dispensing a magnificence, which they did not realize was thoroughly arriviste, made up of curios from all their travels, exotic food, and the accumulation of anything they thought you possibly might not have. Moreover, Aviva, whose husband was in the medical school and could well afford his columns, his tennis court, and his congeries, was able to count on Myra's acceptance of all this by making it clear that any party at their house at which she was present was built around her. But, this time, that architectural plan needed a trip to the drafting board after Eudora arrived.

Myra's first reaction was physical, her face wrinkling back like the shuddering map of an invaded country when Eudora presented the tight, plump bloom of a more youthful simulacrum and said in a Southern drawl, "Why Myra Moorhead! I've known you for years."

"Oh, have I met you somewhere?" Myra wondered how successfully her question managed to create distance. She looked out over the fields at an old tobacco barn the Russells had moved from a neighboring farm. All the "effects," and now this motion picture character.

"No, honey, I mean your work. Those beautiful girls. I'm just crazy about them." She waved her hand, buoyant in spite of the burden of a large, square-cut aquamarine which plunged depressingly into Myra's mood down among all the other unattainables in Davy Jones's locker.

How long was it going to take Sonny, the Russell's so-called butler, to bring another tray of drinks out onto the terrace? Meanwhile, she must try to give herself to the October afternoon which had been worked by a smith whose range included the modest and the grandiloquent piece, a bush of vermeil, a breathtaking tree of gold. It was a perfect setting for anyone who loved maturations and conclusions, but she could feel the gilt flaking from the frame she had meant to put around the occasion. Something about the honey-chile drawl did not ring true. Was this absurd person making fun of her?

There was no doubt that she had been hearing, "I'm Eudora McVay, honey, the sculptor. I don't have to tell *you*, thank the lord, not to say sculptress. And I won't have to tell you not to call me Dora. When anyone does, I tell them I'm not *that* dumb. Get it?" She laughed and rolled her large blue eyes like billiard balls she meant to sink into the pockets of Myra's wandering attention.

"Yes, indeed," said Myra and gave herself time to take the measure of this woman who had hair nearly the color of hers, and was also dressed in a peasant blouse and skirt, courtesy of some department store which went in for ersatz foreign attire. "Eudora McVay," she mused with just the right touch of *froideur*. "I don't believe I know your things." Would the subtle depreciation of *things* be lost on her, she wondered?

"You should, honey. And you will if I have anything to say about it. I do women too. We're sisters under the skin." Eudora laughed and winked at Dr. Russell, a compact little man who had been on safari in Africa but was still most proud of having captured tall, long-necked Aviva, a wicked, blue-eyed giraffe, standing high in the middle of things, ready to pick leaves from the tree that appeared most succulent.

"Really? You must come by some time and let me show you the murals I'm doing for one of the new buildings in Raleigh." She drew herself up, realizing when anyone became too American with her how Irish she still was.

"You don't have to tell me, darling. I know you're big around here." Did she emphasize the adjective as she looked down at Myra's breasts, caught like two large pulsating doves under the net of her blouse?

If it were meant as double-entendre, Myra chose not to accept it as such. The illusion of a life-sized ventriloquist's replica brutally thrust in her face had been dispelled. This woman really did admire her, she was not to be worried about. In the afternoon light which settled like amber around the wasp of her hostility, they spent a mellow cocktail hour talking about Myra, and Aviva congratulated herself on having succeeded once more in her specialty of bringing impossible people together. She had made the pear and the peach into a viable still life.

For some months they were inseparable. As long as it was clearly recognized that Myra was the real thing and Eudora the parody, no harm could come of it. Myra, liking beginnings next to conclusions, helped Eudora get settled in her studio, a converted barn on a hill not far from her old, run-down farmhouse on the outskirts of Carrollton, told her where to buy whiskey, groceries, books, get her car serviced, and then introduced her in rapid succession to all of her unimportant friends. Eudora, in turn, coming on like a young ox, planted her garden that first spring, laid a flagstone terrace, ran errands, drove her to New York on business, and even found time to do a study of Myra in creamy, golden stone, a bit campily conceived perhaps but handsome as a Demeter if you were in a benign mood.

But just as people began accepting them as a pair, the trouble started over men. Steve Wilson was not prepared, however, to find himself in the causal role since he had never thought his long, lean body topped with a thick thatch of blond hair would put him high on Myra's list of erotic objects. But, in an expansive mood that did not often come over her, she decided that the three of them should get together and share some blue fish Old Red had brought back from the coast. She regretted her generosity all week, however, since Steve was so unpredictable and Eudora had begun to "drain" her with her demands. The day turned out hot and humid, full of what Myra called imminence, and when they arrived together in Steve's battered car, she was already having one of her sinking spells. That was the trouble with the South—it exaggerated, and it made one exaggerate everything. Just the day before, when the weather was better, she had written lyrically to friends in the North about her "plantation" in Carrollton, and now the whole place looked like Tobacco Road.

"Isn't this an awful day?" she asked. "Could you work?"

Steve was noncommital, but Eudora said with a smile, "Why, honey, I worked like a horse. I'm a Georgia peach, remember? A day like this just oils my motor."

Had the heat gotten her, or did she actually see Eudora bumping and grinding her hips? Ignoring it, performance, mirage, whatever, she persisted, turning to Steve anxiously. "How about you, Steve? Did you get much done?"

"Oh, I don't know, Myra. I never *finish* a piece. I just work at it."

How, he wondered, did her friends ever admit they accomplished anything?

Myra looked tentatively satisfied, but Eudora laughed maliciously. "Why he's only kidding, Myra. He told me in the car he finished the best chapter he's written all year." She stood there, positively shimmering for his attention like Danae in her shower of gold. "Now you stop worrying about yourself, darling. Just sit down in the shade, and Steve and I'll fix you something long and strong and cool."

What they would do in the house was anybody's guess. As she sat under a large magnolia tree, hung with blossoms whose sensuality seemed to have prostituted itself more heavily than usual this year, the laughter and hooting that drifted out convinced her that the whole thing had been a mistake. The fact that Steve was also a Southerner only made things worse. They shared all kinds of innuendoes and private jokes which they could scatter on her like itching powder the moment her back was turned. Why had she tried to do something nice for them? They just tried to take advantage of her.

But Steve, as he was the first to admit, did not really count. It had always been understood that he would never have more than a walk-on part in any story that concerned her. She put it androgynously to Eudora. "He's always been a gentleman with me, and I've been a gentleman with him." Actually, she frequently felt like scratching his eyes out when he gave her a cool, penetrating look which moved up and down her like a fluoroscope.

Once when she had spread out on the floor a large drawing of one of her most voluptuous nudes, he had walked over it absent-mindedly as he left, and she told Aviva it felt as if his large boots had squashed right down into her living flesh. The fact that he had never fallen for her was publicly explained when she observed, wiggling her behind, "Steve's all brains. No end rhythms." Nevertheless, secretly she had put him aside for the rainy day when she was hard up and just might make a concentrated effort to liberate that black magic which thin, scrawny men with prominent Adam's apples were supposed to contain. "Just watch the apple, Myra," her mother back in Ireland had always said, "and you'll know what you're in for."

June continued hot, humid, fungoid. With all the moisture in the air that hung over the town in a dense cap, Carrollton could have been a captured environment like a station in space. One had this strange feeling that one couldn't go anywhere or do anything without the reluctant permission of the sun. You sank into stereotype, immobilized in the ambitions of the last, clear, cool day. Some liked it—it was like a moratorium in the endless search for meaning and mastery. Myra didn't.

When all the signs were right and no one was acting up, she was a dynamo of productivity. But let the weather go against her or one of her allergies return, and she became a languid hammock stretched between the world as Will and Idea. While he trimmed the grass, Big Joe contentedly watched her in yellow toreador pants, swelling out like a pumpkin from all the therapeutic drinks she was having.

The summer would have lacked all romantic tone and the Southern Belle might really have driven Myra out of her mind if Anna Wainwright had not stepped into the gap and invited her to a party where she met Colonel Baxter. Of course, Anna had to invite Eudora too for no other reason than the fact that she had made some tiny little curtains for the windows of her doll houses.

Only recently arrived, the Colonel had come to Carrollton ostensibly to write, telling various stories about himself. He had been in the Air Force during the war, a test pilot afterward, and then ferried planes to South America until he took a job as a white hunter in Africa. He was a tall, brown, adventurous-looking man with a bushy moustache which he called his "lady's hair brush."

Myra, torn between possessiveness and the desire not to have to do anything for anyone, let Eudora get the jump on her and line him up for dinner at her house. Though she did not exactly designate the Colonel for herself, she pointedly invited Steve in Myra's presence and asked him to give her a lift.

When Steve picked her up, she was wearing a pink and purple chiffon that might have served Mata Hari in her prime but made Myra look a little bruised and Grand Guignol. She was in an irritable mood, and complained all the way over about how clutching Eudora had become. "When I get up in the morning, she's there with the milk bottles. And, of course, she's trying to take over every friend I have."

They arrived to find the first signs of an extension Eudora was adding to her studio. When she insisted that they examine the plans, which was even worse than looking at someone's slides of a foreign trip one will never make, Myra realized that a barn with these superior ambitions would make her place seem rustic indeed by comparison. The Colonel, however, had brought along his basset puppy, and this promised to get things off on a level Myra thought she could handle. But Carrie went straight to Eudora, smothered her with kisses, and would not go anywhere near Myra no matter how she cooed and mugged.

"Does she do this to everyone?" Eudora asked, simpering at Baxter who did not wish to play favorites just yet.

"Let go of her collar, Eudora. You're strangling the poor little thing," Myra said peevishly. Moreover, the cross-hatching of glances between Eudora and the Colonel had not been lost on her, and Carrie, having continued to refuse her advances, squatted and peed copiously in front of her. She let Eudora run for a rag, and was thoroughly annoyed when Baxter spread out some news-papers like Sir Walter Raleigh throwing down his cape for Queen Elizabeth.

When the situation persisted through several drinks and a sumptuous dinner, which Baxter fell upon like one of the African lions he claimed to have shot, it looked as though both the dog and the man would go to Eudora. Unnerved by Eudora's offer to take care of Carrie while the Colonel was away for the weekend, she boozily brought the subject around to her love of animals.

"I've never known an animal who did not love me," she said, eyeing Carrie like the canine dropout of the year. "Carrie's just a little shy with me because she's in Eudora's house. Why don't you let me keep her, George. Eudora's been here such a short time. I'm so much better equipped."

Baxter finessed uncomfortably, ogling both of them oafishly. Myra might have more class and put him in touch with the right people, but, oh, that good booze and the trencherman's meals Eudora would provide!

"You know, I have this mystical thing. Even the field mice love me," Myra went on implacably and Steve splashed his brandy on the rug. "One night last winter, a little male mouse—at least I think it was—crawled into my bed, and I let him warm himself between my breasts. He just lay there as if he were in heaven." Myra looked at Eudora as if to say: Top that one if you can.

The next morning Steve foggily remembered that Eudora had put on some samba records and they had all danced, bumping around like huddled boats in a storm, and that at one point, he, Baxter, and Myra had made a threesome. He seemed also to recall that Eudora broke free from another weird combine and did a solo, cupping her breasts, no doubt in response to Myra's mamm-ary challenge, and crying out, "I'm so primitive! I'm so primitive!"

On the way home, Myra looked subdued, ten years older, and there was a moment as she said goodnight when Steve had a poignant sense of a private world debouching. She had begun to have such a nice thing going when Eudora appeared like a figure out of Pop Art, pasted in outrageous collage over the image of herself she had achieved in Carrollton. Standing at the door with the light turned on, she looked at Steve diffidently as if he had already begun to see her differently. Could he be counted on? Could anyone anymore? Waiting for him as he went back to his car, she hesitated as if she might call him back for a nightcap and one of those long, in-depth sessions of reaffirmation without which she did not seem to be able to hold Myra Moorhead together for any length of time. Steve almost returned without invitation, but he was tired, had a splitting headache, and something advised him he had done this once too often and Myra must sometimes bite the bullet like everyone else.

But she was not prepared for a blow that came from another direction. Eudora, never subject to power failures, had worked steadily all year and turned out several new pieces which, taken with the work she had brought to Carrollton, were enough to persuade the owners of a local gallery to give her a show. They were large, crudely done sculptures for the most part, but directly appealing, and the show sold out. In the local and state papers there were articles and interviews in which Eudora let it be known that she was "an internationally famous artist." Myra was apoplectic but went to the opening anyway just for the pleasure of the asides she would make, only to find that Eudora had placed her statue obtrusively in the center of the gallery where it looked less Demeter and more Madam to all the youthful nudes.

Myra left for her vacation on Cape Cod a week earlier, making up sufficiently with Eudora to leave her in charge of the vegetable garden. But Eudora turned the place over to Big Joe and followed within a matter of days, taking a cottage in Wellfleet for the month of August. Nothing could have gone over more poorly with Myra. The Cape, particularly Truro, was her refuge. The days were devoted to lustral rites and renewals with long walks in the dunes, nude swims on secluded beaches, and she would not have this intolerable woman clinging to her like a wet bathing suit.

One of the joys of the outer Cape was associating with her peers, a choice collection of writers, painters, architects, and a few European refugees like the Count and Countess Zamoyski. She passed the word around that Eudora was bad news, and, knowing Myra, they agreed to hold the fort while thinking privately how amusing it would be to see the competition.

Eudora fell in love with the Cape and proceeded to give it the octopus treatment of embrace and exploration. When she ran into

Myra on the streets of Wellfleet, she expressed no animosity for the cold shoulder treatment, but gave her a rundown on all the places she had been going, the people she had met, including the "darling Zamoyskis," and acted as if Myra were the new arrival and might be in need of an entree and a cicerone. She raved about the dunes, the Highland Light—"so powerful, so phallic"—and Myra wondered if this creature were going to make a travesty of everything most sacred in her life.

While they were talking, Old Charlie, the town drunk, came up, unshaven, hectic, glittering-eyed as the Ancient Mariner, put his arms around her, planted a mackerel-smelling kiss, and called her "My baby." Reaching into dirty dungarees for his wallet, he showed Eudora a photograph taken twenty years ago Myra had sent him one depressing day last winter when she felt nobody loved her. Eudora, who looked more like the photograph than she did, took that moment to announce that Colonel Baxter would be coming to Wellfleet for a week.

Myra spent a distraught afternoon trying to figure out who in Truro had done her in, finally deciding it was the Russells whom no one for the world could have persuaded to do anything so ordinary as vacation in North Carolina. Ensconced in their house near the bay, they proceeded with the mixture as before, except now with a New England cast—Indian pudding instead of the curries of India—and held open house almost every afternoon. How else could Eudora so quickly have met the Zamoyskis, even Avery Richards, her special friend, the Pulitzer Prize playwright who lovingly called her "Little One." She saw the Russells as seldom as possible on the Cape since they were not important, and the days were few and golden, but she rang up Aviva anyway who at least invited her for drinks the following afternoon but made her stomach feel like a cold pudding with her account of all of Eudora's successes.

The next day was clear, beautiful, unlike her addled and beclouded feelings, and she took an early morning walk just to clarify her attitude. The bay was full of sails, white tents of a mystical encampment. From the dunes, people on the beach looked like well-crafted figurines—all gold and bright enameling. Paintings could be excised from the landscape everywhere: here, an intimate Boudin, there a clear, astringent, enigmatic Edward Hopper. But when she went back to the cottage, the rest of the morning promised to belong to Francis Bacon whose work she had always loathed, and she might as well kill time by making the rounds to see how much damage Eudora had done. She stopped

by for Bloody Marys and breakfast with the Zamoyskis, ran down
to Corn Hill for a drink with Simon Johns, the noted art critic, and
managed to invite herself to stay on for lunch. In the afternoon
she dropped in to see her architect friends, "the Bauhaus Boys,"
and had tea with Maggie Cabot, the doyenne of Truro society. It
was a full, exhausting day, but worth it, for, though everyone had
bitten into the Georgia peach deliciously, their teeth had grazed
the hard core of her vulgarity, and the damage to her own position had been slight so far.

Still, she must work fast, faster than Eudora, and do what she
could for herself. At the Russells where everyone would be
gathered, she must put her best foot forward and quickly follow it
with the other. Putting down Eudora would be like strangling her
own problem child, and no doubt in Carrollton she would regret
the attentions, but it had to be done. She would wear her yellow
and orange Pakistani dress, long amber beads, do her hair up on
her head in a braided crown, and, for a change, give herself in
pure drops rather than oceanic waves. In view of the competition,
the tidal approach would not do anymore.

Nevertheless, at the last moment, feeling desperate at the prospect of seeing so many people who had now met Eudora, she rang
up several of her "young men" whom she knew had been invited
and offered to give them a ride. Moorhead might lack a coach and
four, but there would be someone to drive, a footman at his side,
and an aide-de-camp in the back seat of the Volkswagen which,
cramped though it was, would serve her as well as Cinderella's
metamorphic pumpkin.

The Russell's terrace looked out on the Pamet River of which
Myra had done a painting which now hung in the Museum of
Fine Arts in Boston. The scene gave a strong support to her
emotions. She was, in a sense, standing in the midst of herself—
and since it had been reproduced several times, it would be vivid
in the minds of those she really cared about. She would not have
to say: There I am.

Moreover, everyone came up in the friendliest fashion—she did
not need to rush breathlessly around. The Russells set a handsome table, had provided her favorite Scotch, the house was full
of flowers, and Myra could suppose she was the honored guest.
Why not? Who else?

An Episcopal Bishop by the name of Patman Moore, a large,
imposing man in his early forties, who deepened the bright effect
of the party in his clerical clothes, took a special shine to her, and
she told him at length about some murals she would be doing for

a church in Charlotte, enlarging on her life in Carrollton, "the old plantation" where she lived, "the darkies," until it sounded a bit like a page from *Gone With the Wind.* And why not? There was small chance he would ever get to North Carolina, and if he did, because of his feeling for her, she could make him see things the way she wanted him to. Apparently a Moorhead fan for years, with the least little bit of judicious prodding, he raised the possibility of her doing some work for his church, treating her with a deference she had not been getting enough of lately. But, most of all, he was such a dear, a big teddy bear of a man, and he soon began to call her "My child," and his voice was like a lullaby. She responded frequently with "Bless you," and would have loved to have knelt down and kissed his ring.

But her eye caught Eudora's florid figure operating at the edge of the terrace. Charlie Grimes, who had been her chauffeur, was sucking up like Baxter's puppy, showing his rotten teeth and looking more defective than usual. Poor man, he was suspected of being "one of the boys." Let Eudora have him. He could be spared.

She went back to the Bishop, but the cathedral hush had been shaken. A few minutes later she saw that Eudora had moved on to Pierre DuFour, her footman for the occasion, and was giving him remorseless attention. Pierre, who lived on a pond and posed as a sort of French Thoreau, was something else again, and action was called for.

"Eudora, I see you're meeting everybody," she said, pulling at her beads like a rope that could not budge the heavy bell of her large head.

"*Now,* I am," Eudora gushed. "Why didn't you tell me about Pierre, honey. He's a doll."

"Oh?" Myra glanced away toward the back of the garden where the sunflowers, à la Emil Nolde, looked sulphurous and demonic.

"Yes, indeedy. He's just one of the most interesting men I've met anywhere."

Dark Pierre, who could not blush, bowed, and Myra began to wonder what she had ever seen in this man who lay mooning about all day and invited his friends to dinner prepared with the pond water he bathed in.

"He wants me to see his paintings." Eudora managed to make it sound as if he had asked her to pose in the nude.

"You'll find them very interesting. You admire Douanier Rousseau, don't you, Pierre?" Myra asked, hoping that would suggest to him the rank imitator he was.

Simon Johns rescued her, bumping stomachs as they embraced, but suddenly looked fat, foolish, the seventh rate critic he really was, and Myra felt the oceanic swell gathering. She simply sat down in a chair and began to talk in all directions at once. People were startled, but knew that it was about that time for Myra, and paused to listen. All except Eudora who now had in tow Frank O'Flaherty, a talented but unsuccessful novelist and the choicest of the three young men. The Bishop, completely enthralled, went over, did everything but raise an ecclesiastical hand for silence, and got them to join the group. The Zamoyskis commandeered the most comfortable chairs since they knew what was coming. Simon poured himself another stiff drink, and the Russells had a squashed look as if to say: There goes the party. They were still smarting from Myra's remark as she passed the hors d'oeuvres table on her way to separate Eudora and Pierre: "What a strong cheese! Just like smelly feet."

But, once she had gotten her captive audience, Myra faltered. What was she going to say? Why had she made such an effort with this perfectly idiotic group of people who were now tugging at her emotionally as if she were a sow.

The Bishop, however, prompted her about the murals, and she plunged in and did a job on them. By the time she was through, she had made that church in Charlotte sound like the Sistine Chapel. In the heat and glow of it all, she saw Eudora wink at Frank, Simon developed hiccups which sounded like a backed-up drain, but no one dared interrupt. Carried away, she went on to describe her relations with the Rector.

"Such a dear man. He thinks I'm very special."

"And you are, my child. You are," the Bishop said.

Myra gave him a quick, grateful, but nonetheless deadening, smile and hurried on. "He's a sweet, wizened, dried-up, little man. But so emotional. He insists that I feed him, that I'm good for his sermons. He says I am the Earth, that I have stars in my hair."

The Bishop looked ready to pronounce the benediction when Eudora started clapping. It was worse than the "Surprise Symphony." Everyone looked up, startled, and then, incredibly, joined in. It was just the touch that made the whole thing look corny, and Myra wanted to lie down and cry with one of Fuseli's nightmares crouched on her bare breasts.

No one wanted to be the first to be caught running out on her, so it was up to Eudora to clear the house. Having already issued invitations for dinner, she corralled Charlie, Pierre, and Frank, and hauled them off to Wellfleet in her station wagon. The Russells did not ask Myra to stay, which she was counting on, and she went down to the waterfront for a lonely bowl of chowder. The waitress gave her a seat by the window, but, in the dusk, the bay was a melancholy color that looked poured out of Picasso's Blue Period, and, huddled alone at the little table, like an absinthe drinker with her bottle of wine, she let her thoughts match that palette.

There was no relief in sight until two days later when Aviva rang her up to say that Colonel Baxter would not be coming to the Cape after all. It seemed he had been charged with cashing bad checks and had to strike out for more salubrious climes. Georgy Girl would be taking her lumps like everyone else. But Eudora recovered by arranging a show for herself at The White Sail Gallery in Wellfleet, publicized with blatant articles in the *Cape Codder* and *Provincetown Advocate,* and had the nerve to ask Simon Johns to give a little talk about the sculptures. When she heard this, Myra felt as though Edvard Munch's "Scream" were rising in her throat.

She bowed out by taking off for the Gaspé Peninsula with Maggie Cabot. When she returned, August was almost over, and there was an end-of-the-season sadness in the air. She went around half-heartedly mending her bridges, and then decided to give the whole thing up and go home early.

The Russells, who noted every change in her fever chart, were quick to recognize when they returned to Carrollton after Labor Day that they had not come back to the same old Myra, and, as a result, had returned to a somewhat different place. Carrollton, coming up out of its summer sleep, a little sheepish at having sacrificed so much to somnolence or having secretly savored it, seemed to want something more than an influx of students and returned travelers to give it a rejuvenating stigma. Some of the former might have stars in their eyes and the latter have stickers on their luggage, as Aviva alliteratively phrased it to herself, but it was not the same as being "stuck" by Myra in one of her moods of acute perception. No one saw much of her for a while, and, though her shock treatments of hostile electricity were not regretted, the members of her inner circle did not relish the vital slump.

The rival continued to flourish but not through any acquiescence or opposition on Myra's part. Eudora still turned up at all the parties, but she was now just another specimen, ranker than most, in the social garden which if it cannot experiment with new hybrids loses its sense of purpose. You had Eudora, but you did not have Myra, and what kind of show could the season promise if you did not have them together to enhance, heighten, and humiliate each other? Had Myra arrived at some quiet, resigned knowledge that "the violent bear it away?" No one knew. Someone was simply not pulling on the other end of the rope.

Finally she emerged, a month, two, three months later, no one was quite sure, since it was never clear where or when she had surfaced. Was it when she stopped by Aviva Russell's with a jar of her exquisitely clear beach plum jelly like a big, cylindrically carved ruby in her hand? Or was it when she cleared out her plunder room and assembled various minuscule artifacts Anna could use in her doll houses? Or had she simply made it authoritative and official when she spoke to the Association of University Women, looking like a Saxon princess in her lamé dress and amber beads, and gave an illustrated lecture about her Charlotte murals, the best speech anyone remembered having heard?

Myra had always said that her brains were physical, and perhaps her morality was too. She had lost at least fifteen pounds, which seemed more, for she had apparently tightened herself up with exercises. Even in her informal moods, and they returned, slowly, youthfully, she was in her own bright meadow, her hair done up in a tail like a high-spirited pony.

Though it had its share of metaphysicians, Carrollton was not going to suppose that Myra had gone through some sort of thesis, antithesis, and synthesis. Aviva discussed it with Steve who could explain if anyone could. But Steve did not know quite what he should say to her. He knew how acquisitve she was of anyone's thoughts if they could be grasped on her own terms, gewgaws and debased objects from the country of the mind, and he did not want her running off with them like bargains picked up at a bazaar.

No one could be more radiant than Myra as long as she could keep herself in the proper frame of reference. Her problem quite simply was one of proliferation. But what would Aviva make of it if he said she was like a shining fruit that had been put in too many lights, subjected too often to the heat of too many inferior circumstances.

When he sensed that she might suspect that he was woolgathering and press him for an answer, he said laconically, "Myra's picked herself up."

It was useless to predict at that point, though he was sure of it, that the rival would not be easily vanquished. People tire, and it was perhaps no more than that, of the best moralities of others.

Unaffected by his lucubrations and finical distinctions, Eudora would let the connoisseurs have their hard-won model while she proceeded with a vigorous dispersal of the popular version.

So it had to be admitted, and Aviva should surely know by now, that "their Myra" might not last. One tired, one buckled, the true self offered found brown eyes looking out from some unstanchable darkness within.

Steve, for one, did not want to teach Myra anything. If she wished to live her life in multiples, that was her own affair. Moreover, there was something, if sometimes in his opinion only something, to be said for Myra *in toto* for no other reason than that she was bold enough to illustrate how far one could go and perhaps come back. The only question was, and it was a curious one since she was an artist, would she, had she, in fact, remained plastic enough? Was her freedom as wide and deep as it looked?

He kept drumming into himself that the trick was always never to close on too little too soon. In the archaeology of images, the hope lay in the fact that the best, not the oldest, or the latest, might rise. It was enough to know, and surely, he thought, Myra would agree with him now, that somewhere, somehow, like a catalyst of freedom, the rival emerged.

Daughter of a Poet

A publisher has a complex relationship with his writers which, on its subservient side, is somewhat like that of a valet to his master. They are seldom heroes to him, and among the chief tests of his character is the struggle to like them enough to stay in business without a sense of revulsion. On the other hand, he must be a figure of authority, and one reads with nostalgia of the relationships that existed between Frank Doubleday, for example, and some of his writers. But by the time I came along, publishing was big business, and this was a thing of the past. Most of the writers I have known, taking for granted their right to be curried and cherished, sign on like a crew of pirates whose only interest in their captain is money which can be translated into power and glory, and voyages together come abruptly to an end if Blackbeard falters for a moment in his pursuit of booty.

Consequently, a retired publisher like myself, a veteran of many mutinous voyages indeed, tends to ask himself where are the "seas of God" toward which he hoped to steer his ship when, fresh out of college, he started as a reader for a publishing house. Alas, while I was still active, I came to the conclusion that as long as money and publicity were such important factors, no very satisfactory human relationship could exist between writer and publisher, and I began to look for purists in this respect only to discover that none came my way except poets and scholars. So, discounting the cynical consideration that their purity might be based on nothing more than lack of bargaining power, I did what I could for them. When I became a senior editor, in opposition to my more hardened colleagues, I insisted that we publish two or three volumes of poetry a year and one or two first-rate scholarly studies. We never hooked a Robert Frost or a John Livingston Lowes, and for this reason I have always regretted the colossal blunder I made in refusing to publish Fairfield Raymond when he sent me the manuscript of his first volume.

Fairfield Raymond, as everyone knows, is one of the masters of modern poetry, and I can now see that my rejection of his work was due not so much to a lack of literary acumen, as to extraeditorial considerations. I did not *want* to like his poetry because I had certain reservations about him as a man. At the time I could not see why he had sent such a boldly experimental work to me in the first place since I thought of myself as somewhat of a middle-of-the-road man, but now I suspect his motive in approaching me was the reverse of mine in rejecting him. Apparently I was someone he admired from a distance because he had heard I was partial to poets. Raymond was then forty-five, and his choice of a potential publisher must have been very deliberate indeed. He offered me the only opportunity I was to have of exploring a publishing relationship with a writer who was going to be one of the great figures of our time, but, in complete contradiction to my usual stand, I persuaded my colleagues to reject the book because "it would not sell over 300 copies." I was right, of course, as far as sales were concerned, for the first edition sold somewhat less, but published by another prestige house under the title of *Scintilla*, it went on to prove how well-named it was by providing the spark for the "New Generation" movement which has dominated poetry ever since.

So I missed my chance to watch how a great man worked without imminent hope of power and glory, for *Scintilla* did not do its work overnight, lying instead like a spark among damp leaves until forces in the air of the times brought their strong winds of change to bear upon it. After that, no one came along to interrupt my career devoted mainly to piracy, and the young, ardent readers of my later years with the company knew me chiefly, I suppose, as the man who rejected Fairfield Raymond.

You are likely to wonder what were the extraeditorial considerations that induced me to commit such a gaffe. I now know that it can be entirely explained in terms of my idealistic aberration. I simply did not like what I knew about the man. Raymond was already an underground figure in modern poetry well known to the cognoscenti, and I had met him socially once or twice, read his poems in magazines and admired some of them for their sensuous opulence and sophistication conveyed through a strikingly original technique. I persuaded myself, however, that they were morally vapid, the work of a talented dilettante, because I did not want to believe that a man who was president of a bank in Newark, New Jersey, could write genuine poetry. He had already conquered the establishment of which I was part, and could not, in my sense, be a purist. I also knew that he was married to a noted beauty and socialite with whom he did not get along too well and that he had a daughter who was something of a problem. This much had leaked out from the monumental reticence with which he surrounded himself, and I decided he must be a marauder and operator in terms with which I was so familiar. How could a man make all that money and still be a poet with whom I might establish a congenial relationship?

So when I left Jackson and Low, all that I had left of my subsidiary little dream was a handful of letters from Fairfield Raymond written on bank stationery in the dignified, urbane manner which was the hallmark of his epistolary style. Even his letter following my rejection contained no recriminations, and I would never know whether he would have been a hero to his valet. The matter rested there until his death, at which time he had become the acknowledged "Emperor of Modern American Poetry," having held together until the very end the divisions of his life with unwavering, imperial hand. Not even Robert Frost, who often boasted about the "poet as an Executive," had been able to carry off what Raymond had done, establishing himself with equal vigor, and on his own terms, in two totally divergent fields of endeavor.

But curiously the door into his life did open to me posthumously after all, slowly as befitting an entrance into an emperor's tomb. By this time, however, I had retired with my wife Natalie to a charming old fieldstone house near the university town of Carrollton, North Carolina, and was perhaps in a more fittingly reliquary mood toward opportunities missed than I was during Raymond's lifetime. I had heard vaguely that his daughter had pulled herself together after his death and was working on his papers. Then one Sunday I saw in the Book Review Section of the *Times* a brief letter signed by Lesley Raymond requesting that anyone who had any letters from her father get in touch with her in Newark. But I did nothing about it. My own papers were in a deplorable condition, and I suppose it was a combination of laziness and guilt that prevented me all that winter and spring from going through my files.

Still, when I looked through the mail one afternoon in May, I was surprised to find a letter from Lesley Raymond, very formal, very dignified, saying that she had been going through her father's papers, which apparently had been kept as scrupulously as affairs of state, and found my letters to him, carefully dated as to when they had been answered. Not long before his death, for some strange reason of his own, he had destroyed a very businesslike file of carbons of his outgoing mail. Might she see any letters I had kept so that the correspondence between us could be reconstructed? Since she would be combing the South for letters, and would be in Raleigh for several days, she would be glad to drive over any morning or afternoon at my convenience.

I consulted with Natalie, and we decided to respond graciously with an invitation to come around four o'clock in the afternoon so that there would be time for a look at the letters, perhaps a refreshing swim in our pool, and then dinner. It was Natalie's idea to suggest the swim, giving us something to do if the going got rough. The letter to the *Times* and her original letter to me had been signed Lesley Raymond, but the one accepting our invitation was signed Mrs. Lesley Raymond Larrabee, and we were not at all sure whether Mr. Larrabee might also materialize. Natalie was titillated but not upset by the uncertainty, since she was an old hand at stretching a dinner for an extra, unexpected guest some writer brought along.

So Lesley Raymond arrived at our place on one of those exquisite days in early June which always remind me that Henry James said that "summer afternoon" were the most beautiful words in the English language. She was driving a rather ramshackle compact, surprising to us since we had heard so much about Raymond's wealth, and was attended only by an elegant Saluki named Omar. We thought for a moment with some misgivings that she had come prepared to stay overnight, but discovered she was merely carrying a portable typewriter in one hand and a briefcase in the other. Natalie and I are great window-watchers, and we thought her rather oddly dressed in sandals, a flamboyant pink dress and stole, and several brightly colored bracelets and rings. At a distance, walking up our gravel drive from her car, she might have been one of those itinerant vendors of cheap cosmetics or a representative from a religious sect who would give us a tired little sermon through a firmly closed screen door.

But the close-up startled us with an emaciated parody in a long blond wig of photographs of her father in his younger days. I had the feeling that Fairfield Raymond had come back to haunt me as a transvestite. The big frame, the handsome prominent nose, the full, sensuous lips, the vital blue eyes, ready, it seemed, to roll in the fine frenzy of the poet, were all there, and the voice which said, "Mr. and Mrs. David Low?" had some of the sonorous tones we remembered from the recordings.

Suddenly we knew she was not common at all, just rather desperately put together. Some of the jewelry was fairly good, the dress was not cheap, though it might have had a more recent cleaning, and the stole was there to hide the rather bony shoulders. Fairfield Raymond, famous for his representation of unconventional women, had provided the couturier, but Lesley had simply not been able to carry it off. Nevertheless, I remembered rumors of what a hellion and tomboy she had been and marveled at the transformation.

Natalie and I prepared ourselves to accept her as a damaged sheep who had returned to the fold. Chipped polish on fingernails and toenails strengthened this impression, but a deeper, more poignant note was struck when she drew back her lips in a nervous smile and we saw the worst set of nicotine-stained teeth we had ever encountered and noticed her fingers looked stained in a tanner's vat. The hand and the teeth a mountain woman who dipped snuff might have owned produced a curious montage effect of a woman within a woman. One moment the face was really quite handsome, and the next, it had a touch of Goya in it.

I wondered, of course, what were her first impressions of us. Would my white hair and beard, large and rather sorrowful brown eyes, which someone once said reminded him of an Old Testament prophet, though a kindly one, I hoped, make her think me stuffy or passé, or merely remind her that this was the "prophet" who had turned down her father's manuscript? Would Natalie, lively and handsome as she was, with green eyes and hair still auburn, withstand the look of the gimlet which came into Lesley's face when she was offered the gracious, well-manicured hand that also might have handled the enfabled pages?

Since it was too early for cocktails, Natalie offered her tea, and we sat down on our porch overlooking the pool, I with my ironical reflection that this was the part of Fairfield Raymond which had been apportioned to me. Lesley lit a cigarette, blowing out the smoke through that mouth which looked as if it should have been guarded by a tiny Cerberus. Though our place was certainly the sort of setting her father would have enjoyed, she looked around the garden and the pool but said nothing, not even the usual complimentary remarks Natalie received on her roses and flower beds, and one sensed that she was an old hand at miserly response.

Nevertheless, I expressed our pleasure in meeting her and suggested that I hoped it had not been too much of a chore to drive over and see the letters.

"Not at all," she said. "Wherever possible, I am visiting all of the people with whom Father corresponded."

"That must take you a good many places," I said.

"Yes," she agreed. "Though not as many as you might think. Father was pretty much of an Easterner. I haven't had to cross the Mississippi yet."

"Perhaps Europe, then?" I hoped my tone conveyed a hint of the absurd.

"No," she said. "You know Father never went to Europe. He merely transported what he wanted of it to Newark."

"Then you must be having an interesting life," Natalie broke in. "I wonder that you have the time."

"It's all I do," she said, and waited to see what effect that would have.

"I see your point," I said, though I didn't really. "It must be fascinating to meet all the people your father had any contact with. A fine tribute to him, I should think. I know he would be pleased."

"I'm not so sure he would." She looked at me with a glint of malice in her eyes.

"But it must be fun meeting so many people," Natalie came forward with her usual determination to put a positive value on any endeavor. "And how quickly the days must pass."

"It helps. I'm off to Tennessee next week. All those New Generation critics, you know." She smiled as if that were a box of candy yet to be opened.

Natalie, I could see, had, at least in part, hit upon the simple but fantastic explanation. It was sheer loneliness. Obviously the poor girl had never known any of her father's friends or acquaintances. In a long drawn-out way she was now crashing a party she had not been permitted to attend. It was pathetic but smacked too much of psychotherapy achieved at the expense of others.

"A very original approach," I said. "Collections of letters can be quite dull. Perhaps you are going to give the reader some idea of their human setting."

"Perhaps," she said, and blew out a cloud of smoke. "I haven't gotten that far yet. I'm not a scholar. At the moment I'm just making the rounds. I've got at least two years to go. Maybe longer. Sometimes I go back more than once."

This thought was so unsettling that I said more abruptly than I should have, "Perhaps you would like to see the letters now."

"Oh, yes, indeed." She laughed and gave me a penetrating look. "You're special. When you didn't answer my letter in the *Times*, I thought I would save you for a while."

If she had said *savor*, I would not have been surprised. I felt as squeamish as if I were in the presence of a cannibal who had been dining on vegetables and had at last discovered meat.

An irresolute "Oh?" was all I could come up with.

"Yes," she went on. "I wanted to meet the man who refused my father."

For the first time in my life, I wished I looked more menacing than I do. I had some foolish impulse of wanting to satisfy her in that way.

"I suspect you have confused the man with the book. It was purely an editorial decision, a rather poor one, I'm afraid." I could tell from her face she knew I was lying. She was absolutely certain that I did not like her father.

"I want to see what he said when you didn't accept *Scintilla*."

"There are more than one. Six or seven letters, I think."

"Yes, I know. That will be all the more interesting," she said.

Suddenly the notion occurred to me that Raymond may have wanted his daughter to make this absurd far-flung tour. He was the sort who would have known any child of his deeply enough to suppose that she might dream up just such a bizarre journey if he gave her any reason at all for doing so. But why did he do it? What was there in the relationship which would make this most reticent and distant of men suggest if only obliquely, like an unwritten part of his will, that she undertake this pilgrimage to places and people, most of whom he had been in contact with only through letters?

"You may not like what you read," I said, getting up to go to my study.

"May I be the judge of that?" she asked, a trifle too peremptorily, I thought, and I was glad to leave the little scene in the hands of Natalie until I heard with horror her telling Lesley that it had all been a terrible misunderstanding in the office and that I really admired her father a great deal.

The letters were read in silence, and, sitting in the peacock chair I had given Natalie as a birthday present, Lesley finally made me nervous with her total concentration. It was as though I had presented a petition to a surrogate for the Emperor, and was waiting for some sign of condescension. I was relieved when she finally took off the lid of her light-weight portable, sat forward in her chair, balanced the container on her knees handily, as if from long practice, and copied the letters.

"They're disappointing," she said when she had finished.

"Oh, I'm sorry, dear," Natalie gushed. "And to have gone to all this trouble."

"Not at all." She turned to my wife as if she would like to put a stopper on that solicitous little fountain. "I suspected as much. I just wanted to be sure."

"But they have the Raymond touch," I protested. "They're just like his poetry."

"Yes, I know," she said. "That's just what I mean."

I began to think how brilliant, after all, Natalie had been in planting in her letter the notion of a swim. I was not prepared, however, for Lesley's reappearance in a bathing suit printed with hibiscus on a white background. I thought of Raymond's Cuban poems, and wondered if she must always go around with such obvious references to his work which somehow seemed to cheapen it. Her body was too white for all that striking color, and she seemed suited in transfers which might wash off.

Grateful for our well-tended garden which not even the whore of Babylon could make tawdry, I imagined, however, that Lesley would find it too beautiful, or, perversely, not beautiful enough, and I noticed her picking a stray weed out of an urn of geraniums on her way down to the pool.

Omar, however, as if he had been reading his mistress's true thoughts, suddenly went on a rampage, running back and forth, nipping off the heads of flowers, and digging up the ground. Lesley, already in the pool, did nothing to stop him, and merely laughed when he dropped some of the mangled flowers in the water. It was just like her, I thought, to have a beautiful dog who was a reincarnation of the impossible child her father had not been able to control. The irritated imagination began to wonder how many rugs he had peed on, how many dirty paws he had laid on impeccable dresses, how many calling cards he had left on lawns or in spotless rooms when they stayed overnight.

Natalie has almost a mystic touch with dogs, and went down to see what she could do. But Lesley, who was floating on her back in a "tomb" of sapphire with a beatific smile on her face as if she were a princess receiving a votive offering of eternal flowers, stood right up, put out her hand for him to lick, and would not let Natalie touch him. He crouched down like a stone figure on guard.

When she got out of the pool, I went down to fish out the flowers, daring Omar to make one move, but some secret communication seemed to have reminded him after all that he was a representative of Fairfield Raymond, and he did not budge.

Lesley took her time coming down for drinks, and one wondered if she were not an old hand at intermezzos so that her hosts could regain their composure. She took in the bottles and cocktail things with approval, and sat down as if to say the charade was over and the real reason for her visit ready to begin.

The first drink can often release in a person what is most charming and most endearing just below the surface of repression. The second, third, or fourth, however, may go deeper than anyone cares to follow, and so it was with Lesley. One drink of my good Haig and Haig, and she blossomed, and it was easy to see what a radiant, charming woman she might have been, not just pretty and appealing, but one of Henry James's "great girls." There was no further mention of the letters, she made several graceful observations about our place, and complimented Natalie on the hors d'oeuvres. One forgave her that intermittent brown touch of horror in her face, one began, as a matter of fact, to forgive her everything, the intrusion into our life, the gauche remarks, the fact that she was not Fairfield Raymond himself. The interjection of the parent in the child, so halting or spastic before, spread fully and benignly through her gestures, the rich voice, the way of focusing attention upon herself as on an interesting picture which deserved it.

But by the fourth drink, her nature had begun to coarsen as much as her pores. She took out her compact and redid her face, but too thickly and brazenly. She dropped an oily canapé on her dress, and the stain spread, dark as a plum over the pink. Her ashtray looked like a little bombed-out city where her fingers, tall as vandal giants, toyed with residual fires. As images of disarray multiplied, I began to wonder if we were going to get all the way down to that hellion I had heard exploded a firecracker in her father's bed the night before he was to receive the Pulitzer Prize, so that, due to severe burns, he was unable to attend the ceremony.

When we sat down to Natalie's excellent lobster mousse, with a bottle of Pouilly-Fuissé, Lesley drained her glass in one draught and said, "You didn't approve of Fairfield Raymond, did you, Mr. Low?" as though now we were conspirators and could speak of him with complete impersonality.

"I wouldn't go so far as to say that, Mrs. Larabee," I answered, and I suppose my own impersonal tone finally released the *enfant terrible*.

"Well, he didn't approve of you either," she said as bluntly, I thought, as he must have sometimes foreclosed a mortgage.

"But, Mrs. Larrabee, surely you know we didn't really know each other, and I'm afraid I'm not a public figure so there was not much hearsay for him to go on."

"Oh, I didn't mean you specifically, though when you rejected *Scintilla*, he must have hated your guts specifically enough. I mean, just your type."

"Every man in his Humor," I said.

"Oh, don't look so shocked," she said after Natalie refilled her glass, since I was too distracted to do so. "He didn't approve of me either. Nor his brother, nor his sister, nor his aunts. Fairfield Raymond didn't approve, period."

She paused but only for a moment to say to Natalie almost as if she were a servant, "Another glass, please," and then continued, "And you know he was right, so goddamned right about you, me, everything. The funny thing is I never heard him say a really mean thing about anyone in his life. He was a *doer*—that's where the bank president came in handy. He let me get drunk and smash my car just once, and then he saw to it that I didn't have enough money to do myself any harm, at least while I was around him. When I married Larrabee, he sent us to a branch of the bank in another town. Nice little things like that. He caught Mother flirting with another man just once, and back to the nunnery for her."

In spite of her vehemence, I got the impression that she did not entirely believe her own exaggerations. The remark about her father's marital life was indirectly qualified later when she said that her mother was "vain, frivolous, just the sort of mannequin Fairfield Raymond would have set up to act out his dreams." A remark about his cruelty to her was balanced by a reference to his difficulties as a writer and the observation that "of course" he had to have "a little stinker like me."

We were also subjected in ruthless detail to an account of Raymond's personal financial indulgence in his later years—his collecting of paintings, the expensive jaunts to Cuba, solo as far as his family was concerned, his insistence on maintaining a large house and several servants when he could no longer afford them. So far, the connections had been made from sentence to sentence, thought to thought, but then came the last rational sequence of the evening like a crack of light over a total darkness she was about to penetrate.

"Why couldn't he have been just a president of a bank? I could have understood him. I could have adored him then. We could have come to grips. Why did he have to try to make a goddamned silk purse out of every sow's ear, including me?"

Several after-dinner brandies, which she demanded, finished her off for the evening. Physically she was still very much on stage, striding around the room with her glass like a female impersonator who had a terrible grudge against Fairfield Raymond, but her mind babbled desperately in the engulfing darkness. We hauled up dangling bits and pieces from her chaotic condition like endless stretches of a climber's rope, never retrieving the climber.

One got the impression of a man walking like a god in the eyes of a child who had done everything to prove to herself that he was a devil, only to discover that this horrified her more than if he were a god. Worst of all, one had the feeling that she had spent all of her life moving in circles around her father, close up, intimate, stuffy, at first, and then widening into larger and vaguer ripples around an impenetrable idol. If it had been as simple as that, she might have gone the way of many children into total indifference toward a closed, unsympathetic figure. What she finally found so unsettling was the experience of endlessly circling round a Janus-like personality looking out on the world in two such different ways. The moment she approached him as a poet, she had already moved into the gaze of the banker. Life was a matter of living in a revolving myth where the duplex figure of veneration stayed stationary, and one would have had to have the wraparound eyes of a Picasso face to focus all of the sensations of the man into a stable viewpoint. Up from the alcoholic depths came the disconnections and disruptions of that experience. By making rational connections between vituperation and self-condemnation we put together a picture of Lesley's simplistic, but by no means languid, attack on the problem. First she had tried to be a secretary in the bank, but every day was overshadowed by the thought of that *éminence grise* in the great office upstairs who kept in his desk copies of untyped poems he had somehow thought out the night before. Miss James, his secretary, typed them out during the course of the morning as neatly as his memoranda to junior officers. Lesley never remembered actually *seeing* him write a poem. There was no pathetic figure she might have sympathized with, stumbling in on him at night, disheveled, with a glass of whisky in hand, staring at a smudgy page. The poems simply appeared at regular intervals as methodically as a bank report.

Then Lesley had tried to be a painter, only to find she had no talent. She had even tried to be a poet, and the most slanderous fury of the evening, tossed up like pieces of a submarine which had exploded from its own inner pressures, were reserved for those encounters with her father. No objections had been raised, every form of patience and courtesy had been extended, and a very superior form of kindness when it became apparent to both of them that the undertaking was hopeless. After that began what Lesley, spewing out the name, called her "Ten-Year War with Fairfield Raymond." It was her way of introducing her final, disconnected ravings—smashed car, smashed marriage—a burning satellite which could not release itself from orbit and, even now, still smouldered in circles around a dead star.

It was unthinkable that she should drive back to the motel in Raleigh in this state, so Natalie and I put her to bed in our guest room, fed Omar, and let him sleep in the kitchen. Stretched out in a pair of my pajamas, since Natalie's nightgowns were too small, Lesley gave me the feeling that we were looking at Fairfield Raymond in an exhumed state.

We went to bed ourselves with misgivings, wondering if such a compulsive smoker might not set fire to the house. I, of course, did not sleep a wink. I kept thinking of the obsessive rounds Lesley was making, and would make, to all of the people with whom her father, in his remote fashion, had been in contact. It was clear, on the one hand, that she wanted to "get the goods" on him in the way a disaffected angel in the company of Lucifer wanted to discredit God, and, on the other, she wanted to fight her way back to that close, intimate circle where a figure with *one* lucid, discernible side—a man who worked in a bank, a man who wrote poems with his back to the Great World—dandled his daughter on his knees. My interest in Fairfield Raymond, which was as remote as anything about him, had come home to me in this lacerated, engorged, tumescently suffering manner, and now seemed retributory. How did he do it? How did he remain until the very end so implacably divided and yet never once show any signs of disintegration? I shuddered to think how the great connoisseur would answer me while his daughter lay upstairs in a stupor which was the after-effect of a sustained encounter with genius.

Lesley herself awoke with the sun, and I could hear her coughing, moving uncertainly around, a disabled, minor planet which had fouled perhaps beyond all future use one of the circuits which were still open to it. I got up myself immediately and, while dressing, had very rueful reflections indeed about the varying fates which befall us ordinary mortals—fates contingent on nothing more than where we are set down to add our little personal note to the elaborately harmonious, discordant music of the spheres. I thought of the children of Winston Churchill and how Robert Frost's son had killed himself, and I thought of what the world would have been like without either of these men.

Natalie and I made discreet domestic noises, but Lesley did not appear. Finally, Natalie, who in her uncluttered kindness and bravery could have faced Rimbaud after one of his more debilitating evenings, knocked at her door and left a pot of strong coffee on a table outside.

Several cups of coffee and many cigarettes later, Lesley came down the stairs, portable in one hand, briefcase in the other, no doubt glad of the balance. It was affecting to watch her descending, for we knew the poor girl would have to say something, and we wondered what it would be. She actually looked quite well, as people sometimes do after a powerful purgation of the emotions, and I have no doubt she had made a special effort as a cosmetician. We did not quite know how we should treat the gaudy, disaffected angel slowly descending, almost as if she were on an escalator. What could this *deus ex machina* possibly offer to a drama so entangled and unresolved?

Not even Omar, still beautiful but rather spectral now, rose to the occasion, standing quiet and close to his mistress as if overnight he had received a visitation and reprimand from her father.

"Thank you for a very interesting visit," she said. "By the way, may I use the letters in my edition? They were quite good after all."

Nothing more but spoken like the daughter of Fairfield Raymond. Still, when she had left, curving down our drive like an astronaut uncertain as to whether orbit can be achieved, my final thoughts were of him. Something in us all does not want to see the hindparts of divinity, even at one remove. We do not really want to be the one to tell the emperor he has no clothes. Perhaps it fell to Lesley's lot to tell him more than once.

My word of the night before came back to me. What an implacable man! To meet the Great World so successfully on its own terms while at the same time constructing an alternative culture of such beauty and intricate moral depths was no small task. Fairfield Raymond could be permitted some regrets that once he had brought that second kingdom into being, there was no one around to fully understand and accept it. The beautiful sorceress he had married had turned out to be Circe, and the child who had started out as a princess became an ash-stained Cinderella without any possibilities of reversing the fairy tale into its normal progression toward grace and radiance. And, of course, in order to exist at all, a world which would feature enchantresses and princesses must accept the necessity of incursions into the domain of bankers and publishers.

Too late for anything more than moral enlightenment, Fairfield Raymond had made me understand somewhat better the rowdy crew with which I sailed uneasily for so long a time and their confused and far less successful efforts to cope with the situation. It was Raymond's clearest insight that one side of the world will always be, to some extent, the adversary of the other and that an artist, in clear recognition of the facts, must set up his parallel lines and mark out his rival city. But it must also have been his deepest tragedy to realize how little can be expected, at least in one's own lifetime, in the way of crossover and exchange, particularly nowadays when so many factions and ersatz cities of art invite participation. But time draws all lines toward it where they blend. Meanwhile, the artist builds his city only to discover there are few, if any, inhabitants. It is he who must make the crossover, it is he who must sustain the daily rebuffs and indignities at the checkpoint. The greatest moral triumph would be in handling the necessities of division without bitterness, corruption, or damage to others, and yet with the plaintive knowledge that some of this must inevitably creep in.

There must have been many times when Fairfield Raymond wanted to let go of one end or the other. My greatest respect for him derives from the fact that he did not do so and did not let us know, any more than he could help, how much it cost him. In his large way, he was a purist not a pirate after all.

The Caryatid

Albert Henry Howell did not appear to be a mystery to his colleagues at the university, nor to his wife, Cora. Handsome, affable, learned—these were visible and ascertainable assets which had moved the administration to make him a Distinguished Professor. That he was also tall, pink-skinned, vigorous, impeccably staunch in appearance, had made Cora cling so that he would look down on her benignly, and then lean on him to see if she could bring him down. As the years went by, her belief in him had become a devalued currency, and she was, so she thought, glad to suppose that she had had her part in turning his hair and bristling bronze-gold moustache to silver.

When Albert married her in an excess of passion and protectiveness, almost defensively she had responded like a caryatid, finding her role in an antinomy of what she basically longed for. Short, dumpy, her long, copious blonde hair coiled in a capital, she looked pushed down by her supportive role in the world—synonymous, in the early days, with Albert, and only Albert, though she had not meant it to be so. He was to have been richly columnar, made of such Ozymandian stuff, since Cora's archaeologically attuned imagination could wander equally between Egypt and Greece, as would never fall. But in the end, Albert had not "cooperated," to use her word, and she had for a while retired to the Porch of the Maidens, stunted by the implacable burden, to stare in the direction of the place he should have superbly sustained but where the "lone and level sands stretched far away."

Cora's fantasies conjoined with the fact that Albert was a professor of Ancient History, had gone on some digs in his graduate days, and had been asked to lecture in Archaeology as well. Moreover, she had read widely in these subjects in the hope of similarly fulfilling the role of Toynbee's wife as amanuensis and research assistant, while Albert, dominant through it all, would make the transition from college professor to philosopher-prince of the television screen. Too much Challenge and too little Response? Cora would never have transposed these categories to suggest that anything she had done, or did not do, could have kept Albert only Albert or prevented him from becoming her *éminence grise*.

But university communities are strewn with the archaeological ruins of high ambition. Other men have failed to become a Toynbee, win the Pulitzer Prize or the National Book Award, and had wives like Cora. Albert had dozens of friends who had not been offered even the honorable but minor recognition which had come to him. Good, gray, dependable men in serviceable dark suits, quietly preserved in the vinegar of discontent, or saturated in alcohol, they became vague, inoffensive, bottled-up creatures standing like totems in the opaque corners of cocktail parties. So what possessed Albert Howell to become a night prowler? For one thing, had they known it was he, some of the seasoned might have said it was because he did not drink.

In the early years of his marriage, he had drunk a great deal indeed. But one night when he had polished off more than a fifth, he roughed up Cora a bit—a slap, a push, but from big, gentle Albert, they seemed like blows of King Kong, and Cora, who got the first inkling that the psychological wind blowing through their lives was too strong for the column, ran from the house to spend the night with a neighbor she thought she could trust.

Abject Albert came to get her the next morning, and she agreed to return on one condition—that he never drink again.

"I won't have it, Albert," she said when they got back and settled down in the kitchen where she poured herself a precisely measured bourbon. Cora drank every day, but she was as careful as Mithridates in her portions.

"You mean not even a beer?" he asked and tried to loom over her some shadow of his fallen strength.

"You could never stop at that. And then look what happens," she said, rubbing her cheek suggestively.

"What was it that I did that was so bad?" Too plaintive for a man who still glowed like an ingot, he could sense that he was nothing but paper, gold paper perhaps, but no more to this determined little woman than a cutout she could paste in the window of her contempt.

"What did I do?" he pleaded again. "I don't even know why I got drunk."

And then he remembered. Little Cora, charming little Cora, whom he loved so much and of whom he would have liked to make a diminutive pet, a snuggler, a real heart-warmer, had shown her claws again. After dinner and a few drinks, he had felt amorous, wanted to come in close, but Cora said she was too tired.

Looking back, he could remember that even during their courtship, she had not been demonstrative.

No sex, no alcohol—Cora moved on in other ways, laundering him of all of his old cronies who liked to meet after classes at Jack's Bar on Main Street for a few beers and some dirty stories.

"I won't have it, Albert," she said one evening when he came home with the rich, warm smell of Michelob on his breath, ready to nudge, pat, pinch her, and make a rollicking little scene from Breughel in her aseptic kitchen. "It's not dignified for a teacher to go in a place like that."

"Everybody goes there, honey," he protested. "It's a tradition in Carrollton."

"Yes, everybody who is not going to be anybody. If the Dean knows you go there, do you think you will ever become Distinguished Professor? Why it's nothing but a porn shop. I see the students in there giggling and laughing over those awful magazines."

"They're just dreaming, Cora. All they've got to look at when they get back to the dorm is an ugly roommate."

"There are some lovely girls on campus."

"Yes, most of them are virgins like you," he teased.

"Oh, why don't you grow up, Albert? I don't understand how you can go to class and teach on one level, and then go down to Jack's and make a fool of yourself."

No sex, no alcohol, no children—the years went by, and Albert began to feel as passé as his own field, to which fewer and fewer students were attracted. He was superannuated even among his colleagues, for Cora did not like this professor or that for very definite reasons of her own, and the younger men he could tell clearly did not think that he was "with it." A new hybrid, strangely old-fashioned and yet modern in appearance, they had begun to have longer and longer hair, grow beards, wear jackets with shirts open at the neck, sandals even to classes, and "let it all hang out" in the company of their students. Seeming to crowd him into an even more marginal place, the enrollment of the university grew to nearly 20,000; buildings sprang up everywhere, great pseudo-Egyptian blocks that closed in the lovely views or glowed at night with weird and greenish lights like an outpost in space.

There was never a year when the bulldozer and the crane were not at work. Great gashes in the red soil made parts of the campus look like a huge operating room, and there was no possibility of sewing up the patient without loading his interior full of instrumental steel. So bleed him copiously, let him rise from his bed, the many-storied monster with the heart of Mars, overpowering in his ambitions to supplant the colonial style. It looked everywhere like an architectural war to the death. Albert, who, like Hawthorne, regretted the lack of ivy on the buildings in America, restricted his walks to the inner bastion of the old campus, but it gave him more of a "Williamsburg" feeling than he would have liked, ringed round, reductive, and threatened. Why couldn't the old and the new join hands more gently?

Cora, however, winnowed out her version of the contemporary—she was not going to be left behind with a dawdling classicist. She might return each night to the Erechtheum where her soul could brood over the unfair and unacknowledged weight that women were forced to bear, but in the day, she went out to see if a little dynamo like herself could not turn a wheel or two in the modern machine. When she had run through her interest in numerous civic and charitable organizations, and even after she was elected to the Board of Education, Carrollton, adjusting with good grace to the age of tokenism, a black here, a Jew there, accepted her at least for the time being as a pictograph of the new woman.

On high platform shoes that somehow gave her an even more squashed appearance, she walked very straight and unbending as if she were indeed balancing a flat stone on her head, wore long gold necklaces intermingled with beads which sometimes swung like the loose chains of her freedom. At cocktail parties she closeted herself with a single person to talk about some problem in the town, some said so as not to have to acknowledge Albert any more than necessary, but to others it seemed a way in which her fiercely generalizing nature could reduce the world to a single issue.

Some of the time Albert let her go alone, and she would come back charged with what he called "the juice of another" which meant that she had obtained total agreement, the lifeblood of a fellow doctrinaire. She could even become somewhat affable to him on these occasions since her success confirmed that he didn't matter. But one evening she returned and found he had gotten into the cooking sherry, and wanted again to be "sentimental." Moreover, his cat Nefertiti, tawny, slinky, so much a princess that Cora hated her, had been allowed to roam the house, and had left slashes in the rug. Cora hit her with a rolled-up newspaper, refused to cook any supper for Albert, and would not speak to him for two days.

Curiously, Albert did not entirely object to these quarrels.

There was a rowdy vitality to them, and, at least, after the silent treatment, they had to come in closer to each other if only to spit and claw. The next week, when he was sure she was going to be out late, he opened a pint of whisky he had stashed away, let Neffy into the den, and sat down to dream a little. If only she could understand that the world, to him, was so far away that alcohol could bring it up close, at first like a telescope which brought in the distance, and then a magnifying glass which allowed him to examine it genially and lovingly.

He was set for an evening of revery when Cora came home early—the board meeting had bogged down in an impasse—and found him with a silly smile on his face, fruitily off somewhere in a dream miles away from her, she supposed, though he had not felt so "immanent" all week. She flew into a rage, poured the rest of the bottle down the drain, and chased Neffy onto the porch.

"Every time I turn my back, you get drunk," she said with her conveniently anhistorical cast of mind which made anything displeasing to her a continuum of the past, present, and future.

Slumped in his chair, Albert looked up at his little Cora, looming psychologically as large as the Colossus of Rhodes. Loose, unbuttoned, how could he counter with any show of strength?

"I'm not drunk, Cora," he protested. "You know I haven't been drunk in fifteen years."

"I don't know what you call yourself now. I wish your students could see you. They'd do a piece on you as the lush professor in the next *Lampoon*." Cora's white hand rested among her gold chains like a *figa*.

"They might welcome it. I think I'm just a stuffed shirt to them." He buttoned the top of his trousers, and buckled his belt again as if gathering the folds of his body together.

"What about all those times at Jack's Bar?"

"All those times, Cora? You put a stop to that years ago." He wanted to rouse himself, wander into the kitchen to finish off with a ginger ale, but he was indeed architecturally inferior to Cora who stood with her legs apart to support the additional weight of her exasperation.

"And just as well I did. Do you think you would ever, repeat ever, have been a Distinguished Professor if I had not?"

"No, Cora. But am I so distinguished after all?"

She let that one simmer since it struck too close to the heart of her disappointments, and went brooding off into the house only to return in a more towering rage. Nefertiti, during Albert's "dream-off," had slipped into the living room and left another aristocratic mark of her displeasure on the sofa's silk cushions. Let in once again, she sat smugly on his lap like the Egyptian cat-goddess Bastet astride the plump belly of a Buddha. Only someone with the wit which Cora lacked could have appreciated the scene, acculturative across time and space, two gods for the price of one.

"I won't have it, I won't have it," she screamed. "It's either me or that goddamned cat."

Spitting at Cora, Nefertiti escaped under the chair, and Albert was forced to relinquish the shimmering glass which he pressed to the world as lovingly as a cheek. Just as he was "in close" at last, Cora had to gush up from the rock of ancient history, and he wondered how he had trodden so long and heavily on her feelings that she could produce this black geyser from the fossilized remains of dead emotions.

She soared on and on, and he could not put a cap on her. He retreated, they met in the kitchen, she struck him across the mouth, and, lifting a geyser from some released, black reservoir of his own, he hit her with a TV dinner he had left out to defrost. Marble upon the head all these years was one thing, meat, mashed potatoes, and gravy, another. The guck and liquid flowed down from Cora's hair like a disintegrating structure of what she had been supporting. Now all that she had on her face and dress, like an excretion, was the intended nourishment of a man she had clarified as Albert the Simple. As she stood there staring at him, he wanted to hand her a stone.

But the caryatid would not forgive him, nor speak to him for over a week, having declared when none of their friends would take Neffy that she would not break silence until he had gotten rid of her. Finally Albert, at a prehistorical distance from everything, put his little princess in a gunny sack on Saturday morning, drove out to the lake, and dropped her in. The world, the warm, loving world stood back so far from him now that when he looked memorially at his slides of Egypt, the cat-goddesses brought tears to his eyes. Nefertiti, drifting in her topaz death-slump, would hang for a while, a bagged remonstrance, and Albert dreamed one night that Cora was suspended in her place.

Not long after, he was up in the attic looking for some old papers which he had stored there, wondering what he was going to do with his life with no Nefertiti and no possibility of a replacement. How was he going to bring anything in close again, how could he, in fact, in any way caress anything at all? Something was wrong with him—he could not seem to succeed in any kind of intimate contact. The social mechanism of looking and grasping, of being seen and taken, simply did not work for him.

He loved women and would have liked to amuse himself with them harmlessly and variously as a man goes hunting for wild-flowers, delighted to find a new specimen. But again it did not work. If you failed with one woman, did you fail with them all? Could they smell some deep lack of masculine sexual perfume whose essence alerted them to the conqueror? Did they sense that he had a kind of hidden autistic nature which prevented his mind and body from working together congruously, that he was a man of rapturous moments who never learned to become a raptor?

Still not having located the papers he was looking for, he opened an old box marked Notes and found instead a large, broadbrimmed hat, a black sateen mask, and an old opera cape, remains of a costume worn to a Halloween party long ago. It startled him like an unexpected proposal from fate. He felt much as he did as an adolescent when he read about sex in forbidden books. He longed to put on hat, mask, the long, loose, securely attached condom of the cape and have secret relations with the world. It had a curious, relieved, released sensation about it as if part of him had been living in that box all these years.

"Do anything with a desire but repress it"—authorities as divergent as Oscar Wilde and William Blake advised him, and the following evening, he left the house after dinner, and Cora accepted the familiar excuse that he was going to the office since she planned to be out anyway. The night was cool, he could wear his old London Fog, and he carried in his attaché case the rest of the paraphernalia except the cape, which was too unusual and identifiable. He did, in fact, go to his office, put on the light, nearly always the only one in a conjugal and convivial department which had few evening stars in its intellectual constellation, and went back to his car to dress up.

Walking to one of the residential areas in the woods near the campus seemed one of the most natural things he had done in his life, combining the feeling of an exhibitionist who has finally given in to his inclination with the knowledge that everyone was, in fact, protected from his "exposure." He wandered and circled around among the houses, so cozily lit, the inhabitants happily ensconced for the evening, until he found one into which he could look without detection.

A young man in shirtsleeves and slippers, smoking a pipe, was sitting with his beautiful blonde wife, listening to Ravel's *Daphnis et Chloé*. Two lustrous children, a boy and a girl, played in the room, and an incorrigibly affectionate Samoyed went around insisting on its tribute, a pat, a hug, a tumble on the floor—an immediate identification, a sanction for Albert, glossing over any suggestion of prurience in what he was doing as if any clandestine focus were a plea for some original purity of the world.

After a while, he felt permeated by the scene. Similarly, as a child he had pushed his face into lilacs and been taken into their embrace, a complete encounter in the way Georgia O'Keefe enlarged her flowers until they engulfed you. He felt powerfully charged, full of "transfer." Press him against a surface, and he would leave a replica of some vivid, moist detail of his glowing submission. He could hardly pull himself away.

Cora had the lights on all over the house, but she was not keeping the home fires burning nor did she intend to give or receive a pat on the head. Her meeting had not gone well, and where was Albert to take the blame. She looked at him suspiciously, he thought, but then she always looked at him suspiciously.

"You don't mean to tell me you've been working on that paper all this time," she said, pulling off her long, heavy earrings, her little head seeming to drop to one side with the shifting weight.

"Oh, it was such a nice night. I took a stroll around the campus." Still enraptured, Albert held on to his good humor.

"Why didn't you walk over in the first place and save the gas?" Cora was Carrollton's most ardent conservationist.

He didn't answer, but kissed her dutifully, and they went to bed without a quarrel. But as he turned over on his side, the room into which he had been looking flashed into his mind again. What were those Neanderthals doing underneath the scene—the lowering man, the squat woman dropping earrings into a scooped-out stone, the hirsute children, and the mangy dog with teeth bared? Could one never hold on to any pictorial position that suggested an ideal? Was the mind itself a transitory place, entertaining eons of human history within an hour?

"Don't snore," Cora said, needing one last negative, and Albert felt as if the room were filled with vapor from a bog.

Still, with his mood basically refreshed, the next morning little Cora was like "Mary in the morning." He liked her bustle and hustle, her no-nonsense approach to the day. Though she pushed him around in the kitchen more than he would have liked, perhaps he deserved to be pushed into life again. If it could have been push and pull, a slap and then a tickle, drops of that vapor might have settled on her little ears like diamonds. He had always felt uneasy about keeping anything from her, and now he had something to feel really guilty about. Except he didn't. Not enough never to do it again.

The picture of the young man and his family sustained him for almost a week. It calmed his nerves, sweetened his mood, gave him a mental surface to rub amorously. He was able to lobotomize an unpleasant situation by inserting it like a slide which cut across his mind with an alternate view. Sitting in his office, he could imagine himself to be the handsome young man, having rummaged around in his desk and found a pipe which belonged to the era when Cora allowed him to smoke. With the stem clenched between his teeth, he could tousle the heads of the children, nuzzle the white dog, think of the night with that lovely young woman in his arms. It seemed to bring a kind of perfume up out of the earth, indeed out of his own person, an elevated ambiance of some delicate feeling as if his cortex exuded a corona.

But Cora kept at him, and he found the tensions mounting. It reminded him of his lusty young fraternity brothers who used to say that they could go for a week and no longer. Evolution, as Cora nattered on, went further downhill. There was something almost saurian about their enlarged and futile hostilities which rose against the sky in terrible silhouette. If he had been trying to create his own personal Noosphere, which Tielhard de Chardin had spoken of so eloquently, it had evaporated into basic brutality.

That night he went to the office again with the picture now so grossly distorted that he must lance it with another. Why was what he was doing considered so abnormal? Why couldn't he just go out and look? The little black strip he put across his eyes was like a band of mourning he wore in honor of some kind of visual death.

He went this time to a new part of town, carved out of the pine woods, where hideous modern apartments predominated as if applied to the lesion in dermatological overkill—another of many unfortunate grafts the body of Carrollton could not reject. Suddenly he saw a young instructor in the History Department coming toward him from the parking area of the complex, and he had to duck behind some bushes. Deciding to cruise the dormitories, he gazed fleetingly at several coeds in mini-nightgowns and watched the housemother of a sorority putting curlers in her hair. The former were too self-absorbed, the latter reminded him of an older version of his wife, and he saw in the distance a cop making his rounds.

By ten o'clock, he was about ready to go home, aware of the seconds pulsing on Cora's little arm, but instead decided to take another turn around town. At the back of an apartment house abutting on the woods, he saw an unshuttered window casting an obelisk of light out into the night.

It was like an archaeological surprise. A young woman standing only in her panties was looking at herself in a mirror. He felt as if he were plundering the tomb where a princess practiced the art of dying before she lay down forever. She was smoking a cigarette and studying her breasts as if to see how much gold would be needed to leave their impression to the world.

In the enclosure of the window, itself enclosed in darkness, she did indeed look "Egyptian," and with the high light around her shoulders, slender, almost boyish, she reminded Albert of Tutankhamen in his golden funerary mask. There was something sad, world-knowing, world-weary in her face. "I have seen yesterday—I know tomorrow"—King Tut had said it for her long ago.

Albert wished that his hands were cups of gold that could give the "princess" the breast piece she desired. Was she hidden away in the recesses of America as he was? There was not even a photograph on her bed table to suggest someone who would lie down with her in the "ever-during night." She reminded him of Nefertiti with her blonde hair and suntanned skin, his own Lady of the Lake risen out of topaz sleep, a reincarnation, a tenth life granted to his lovely little companion.

When the woman pulled down the shades, Albert went home wondering how much further he could go. Were such extreme fantasies the mental fumes of a psychic desperado? Did he simply want to go raging out of his mind, or was he a new breed of dreamer, ready for lift-off, a "saint" of some kind of ultimate, exhaled longing. He would like to think so. The troposphere, the stratosphere—where did the veils of his strange and inordinate emotions belong? Would they simply wrap him some day in a cocoon of solipsistic feelings coded with a fatal message for all bright creatures which wanted to emerge?

Meanwhile, the "tomb of the princess," as he came to think of it, seemed cut and lodged in stone. He did not go back again on purpose, for he felt that he himself had the weight of a statue as he moved or sat at his desk, huge as a Pharaoh looking over the Nile, guarding that vision. Did all desire want just this kind of ponderous sanction? Perhaps the tragedy of every personal history was that it could memorialize so little. He had pleaded and pleaded with Cora that time was going by and that they were giving each other nothing worthwhile to remember. He could not recall a single entirely happy day with her. Just one would have stuck in his memory like the lotus seed that could bloom again in a thousand years.

During these weeks, sensing that some large figure of her

original longing, but now inaccessible to her, had hardened inside the man of paper, Cora battered him unmercifully, and her erosive temperament swept over him like the winds of the desert.

"You've been acting very strangely, Albert," she said to him abruptly one morning.

"What do you mean, Cora, honey?"

"I don't know." She observed him feature by feature. "We're not connecting somehow."

"Have we ever?"

"Oh, don't go into that. That's not what I mean." Just unwound from sleep, without her make-up and heavy, hortatory jewelry, Cora, remarkably, still posed a considerable weight on the kitchen floor.

"What then?" he asked laconically.

"You go around slap-happy as if I didn't exist."

"Oh?"

"Yes. I could swear you are up to something, Albert. What is it?"

"Cora, you know I am never up to anything. That's one of my troubles."

"Don't be stupid."

"No, it's true. I am one of the have-nots. I belong to the only really underdeveloped country—the land of the lonely." Even as he spoke it he felt the disparity between this old, vacant, stretched-out view of himself and the new and secret one, visually impacted, glowing with catacombs.

"I could crown you, Albert. I could crown you," she said as she went into her bedroom and slammed the door. "I'll find out though. Sooner or later. You can be sure of that." Then a seal of silence—Albert did not try to follow her into the mephitic air of that immurement.

What did Cora already know? Had she gone to his office one night and found that he was not there? Had someone recognized him and told her that he was out pranking on the wrong night of the year?

Nevertheless, that evening, he had an irresistible desire to take another look at the princess in her tomb. When he got to the apartment, however, the room was dark, and the shadowy side of the building, whose inhabitants were either out or had gone to bed, seemed impenetrable as a pyramid. Had he stayed in the office too long, brooding over his compulsion? He felt immensely let down as if grave robbers had been there before him and plundered the sacred room. He thought he saw the shades move a little but did not wait to see since the moonlight made him more visible than usual.

As he walked back home and onto his own lawn, feeling unbearably keyed up, strangely naked without his hat and mask, he still needed a fix, and went around and looked through the window of the den where Cora sat under a lamp, cubistically planted, startlingly recessed, like the woman in the apartment. Dear, little Cora, relaxed and with a dreamlike expression on her face, was listening to Debussy's *L'isle joyeuse.* Stretched out on the chaise, her shoes kicked off, a drink and some snacks on one side and the little heap of jewelry and trinkets she had removed on the other, among these furbishments she might have been propped up in a funeral boat. Though she looked happy, floating toward her joyous island, as he never saw her when she was with him, he felt unutterably sad.

But when he entered the house, stepping in midstream from the barge of her revery to turn off the stereo, she rained down abuse on him for being so late, and the next morning her unusually surly manner was like an aphrodisiac to his habit. He was determined to go once more to the tomb of Nefertiti, for he had given the woman at the window that name.

The room was full of light this time—was it even more so than before? The same appealing figure naked to the waist, the same fondling of her breasts with one hand while she smoked with the other. But did it somehow look more posed and therefore less intimate? Did it speak of another presence now and, as a result, quiver with illicit suggestion—intimations of the bloodshot eye looking into the cell of a brothel? Had Cora's displeasure been able almost mystically to poison this for him as she did so much else, or had his own increasing sense of guilt lifted up out of the tomb a basically modern pornographic scene?

The woman kept stroking her breasts, walking back and forth in the room, disappearing for a while, returning, pausing at the window with what looked like an inviting smile. Had she seen him, Albert wondered with dismay, was she, in fact, soliciting? As he glanced at his watch and realized that he had been standing there for more than half an hour, he heard a sound up on the street and saw a police car pull up, flashing its weird, revolving light, a huge voyeur's eye plucked from its socket riding on the roof.

"Quickly, Albert, give me the mask." Her handbag open like a large mouth, Cora stepped out from the shadows and pulled him behind a tree. As always, she wore no hat, and even in the dark, the mass of her hair was impressive.

"Cora?" Albert hesitated. He could not really accept the fact that it was she though she had never looked more substantial. It was as though the night sky had weakened, and a small statue, delusive in its sense of power, had walked out of the deep woods to support it.

"Hurry! Hurry! And let me do the talking." She slipped the mask into her bag, brushed a bramble off his coat, and turned on the flashlight in her other hand in the direction of the officer rushing into the woods.

"Why Dr. Howell! And Mrs. Howell. What on earth are you doing down here?" The man in uniform bore down on them like a huge, dark blue bear, crashing through the trees with all the portentiousness of Carrollton—*Dura lex sed lex*—and his voice managed to be an unsettling mixture of deference and dubiety.

It was Jeff Wallace whom they had known since he was a child and lived on their street.

"You scared us to death, Jeff. What in heaven's name is the matter?" Cora, standing under his bulk, offered her golden head as if it were a hive stuffed with honey.

"Some woman in the apartment building called the office. Said there was a Peeping Tom outside. Claimed he had been by more than once. I told her to keep him interested until I could get here. That must be her up in the window. Have you seen anybody suspicious anywhere around?" He played his own flashlight through the trees where the beam danced and flitted, ghostly as an eye in search of its body. Albert shuddered. Except for Cora, it might have been stuck on his face like the projected eye of the Cyclops.

"Why, no, Jeff, we haven't. But then we haven't been here long." She looked, however, as though she had been there forever, the foundation figure of some new arch.

"Oh?" Jeff paused, and Cora stared at him as if she was turning his mind by main force. One more huge concentration, and she would have him faced the right way, a large gynandrous brother with her manner of looking at things grafted on to his masculine nature.

"That's right. We'd been to the movies, and took a little drive it was such a nice night. Dr. Howell wanted to get out for a breath of air. We parked the car around the corner, and were walking along when an owl flew into the woods. You know what nuts we are about birds," she said, perhaps hoping he would remember how he had helped her tend her feeders when he was a boy. "I got the flashlight and we decided to come down and have a look-see. The woman must have thought we were a prowler. We saw her up there in the window without any clothes on. I don't think she would like to know what we thought of her."

Let others lift *all* the Pharaohs to higher levels up from the river. *She* had moved this heavy Blue Man and set him down safely before the Temple of Belief.

"Oh, is that it? I'm sorry to have bothered you folks. We get a lot of crazy calls like this. But we have to investigate. You never know these days when one of them is for real." Now that he had been securely placed, Jeff spoke as if he had been ventriloquized by the little oracle who stood at his feet.

But remote control was dealt a severe blow when the woman pushed up the window and shouted, "That's the man. That's the Peeping Tom." Would this, Albert wondered, bring down the temple.

He need not have worried. Once the magnificent dummy had learned to talk, he assumed the authority of his articulator. "Oh, calm down, lady. You've been imagining things. This is Dr. Howell and his wife from the university. They're just out for a walk."

"I don't mean her. I mean him—the one with the mask on."

"Nobody's got on any mask, lady," Jeff growled sarcastically. "You've been seeing things. If you don't calm down and stop insulting the Doctor, I may have to run you in for causing a disturbance. Maybe for indecent exposure."

The women let out a stream of obscenities, slammed down the window, and turned off the light.

Albert nearly fainted. Did Jeff, after all, suspect anything? In spite of his good will, would he drop a hint here and there until the rumor spread? Would he, without meaning to, relegate him to the same category as the professor arrested for having heroin in his house, the coach picked up for soliciting young boys? Had they, too, seen that surreal, disembodied eye flashing in the street, as it turned, gathering beyond the third, some fourth dimension of visual degradation? Had the man prosecuted for forging a prescription for amphetamines seen it, in its diminuendo, glinting in the glasses of the pharmacist who had fingered him?

Albert would never forget it. Carrollton, dear Carrollton, to whom even two dimensions of this sort of thing were more than enough, what would it say, what would it do, if it knew that the eye had almost tracked him down to stigmatize him with its winking jewel?

And, most of all, what about Cora? What about Cora indeed?

She got into the car, took the wheel, and drove home without a word. Was she waiting for the privacy of the house to release her pent-up anger and demolish him? Wound and wound in her silence, as they moved through the silent streets, Albert felt like a mummy she was preparing for some ultimate tomb of her own. Her powerful control and reserve made her glow like a priestess who would come up the stairs and close the doors upon her victim. He would quite simply be left in the soundless depths forever.

But when she got him safely into the house and had taken off her coat, she stood there without a trace of rancor.

"Why didn't you tell me, Albert? Why didn't you tell me?" she asked.

Albert felt he had never heard a more cabalistic question, huge with irony since he had told her so much and apparently so little. It reverberated back and forth between them, both weighted and winged, but finally unanswerable.

The caryatid would perhaps explain one day how she had come to step down from the Porch of the Maidens where she had lingered so long, so stolidly, and wandered into the woods looking for him. Having, at last, dismissed the archaeological past, she had not hesitated. Perhaps she had sensed that a figure within her reach was as mystifying as any she had known and that her legendary force had found a worthy object. Albert could allow her any number of motives.

She was like two people in one to him now in a unified consciousness without chasms, without catacombs, and he found with growing surprise that he could, after all, hold them together. She would always be the little woman who was Mary in the morning and the one who had turned Jeff into a Blue God. The big coil of hair which sat on her head could in its vengeance, like the headdress of the Medusa, still threaten to release its golden boas, but, in a fantasy of another sort, it was the pad on which the fall of a suicide could be broken.

Though he could think and dream this now—what else was he good for but sending nuncios to Eros?—none of it came from him. It belonged to Cora. Something had finally warned her that the heavy structure on her head was largely chimaerical. Perhaps seeing him there in the dark, abject and suppliant, taught her the true weight of the world: no mass like the far-flung implications of another's lonely dreams, nothing more satisfying than being the pedestal upon which the life of someone one loves can rest.

III. From *The Case of the Missing Photographs* (1978)

The Case of the Missing Photographs

The experience of feeling like a punching bag is endemic to cocktail parties. People pass by, take a well-aimed jab just to show who the competition is, and leave you swinging wildly back and forth only too aware of what hit you but unable to do anything very decisive about it. Marjorie and I often come away with a sense of having been knocked about by champions or left to hang unnoticed in a corner of the social gymnasium.

Thus it can hardly be described as anything less than a "beautiful event" when someone turns the metaphor, surrounding us like a pleasant summer breeze where we are suspended, available and unthreatening, like those Chinese chimes that used to hang on old-fashioned porches. The pendent pieces of glass painted with flowers or little figures reminiscent of ideograms were at once transparent and appealingly exotic. There is nothing more congenial than equating one's feelings with such an image which can be approached, and is receptive, from all angles, responding with light-hearted music.

The day we were going to the Cowdens I was determined to maintain just such an affirmative mood. Lying in my bath, pleasantly relaxed, I initiated my usual ritual with Marjorie. Going over the list of our friends, several of whom I thought would be there, I planted in her mind the notion that we might meet someone new. We did not know the Cowdens all that well, and they must have a portfolio of at least ten or twelve people who were good prospects. Marjorie is patient with me in my bath, as though she understands what it is to be a supine male in his late thirties, subject to her intrusions from the dressing room where she carefully selects and applies just the right armor a Connecticut woman should wear in a given situation. I think, too, she rather enjoys the ritual of preparation, as if it might, indeed, exert some kind of mystical control over coming events, and, as I towel off, she looks at me as if *there* were a man who should be able to ring anybody's bells. Thank God, Marjorie and I are on very musical terms with each other, and I have no qualms about being "viewed in the nude" by a woman who long ago surrounded me like a summer breeze.

When we arrived at the Cowdens, Marjorie looked and smelled as fresh as one of the peonies which bloomed along the walk, and I might say that we could have been taken for a pair of champions if you only glanced at us. The party was in the garden, the light a filtered radiance of the sort one feels has been earned by the purification of the long winter, and the voices rose like a confessional of bees. But underneath the canopy of sound, more melodious than it would ever have been indoors, the reality of the situation set in. To whom were we going to talk—Mrs. Arlington Smith who had the longest nose and the oldest house in Meadowmount, the Laynes whose minimal art matched their personalities, the Daleys who pushed the collecting of old maps, the Irvings who seemed to breathe a cloud of geographical halitosis as they expatiated on their travels? Instead we soon found ourselves talking to each other. Marjorie began to look like a damp peony dipped in some social fountain of dismay, and I rocked back and forth on my feet, reflecting that an impasse of this sort can do sad and irreparable damage to a lovely Connecticut afternoon.

Janice and Nat Cowden looked utterly punch-drunk from their efforts to bring people together, but Janice finally got wind of the fact that all was not well in our corner of the garden, and snatched a couple from under the long nose of Mrs. Arlington Smith, applying them as a tourniquet to our ebbing spirits.

It was a brilliant decision to match us with Claire and David Steadman, for we prospered the moment we accepted the transfusion of their company. I am a literary critic, writing fairly successfully for the quality journals, and Claire, it turned out, had read one of my books, which in itself is always a summer breeze. David, an Englishman, applied just the right touch of gallantry to the damp peony which gladly entrusted itself to his subtle, grooming hand. While I was allowing myself to be praised, standing in a scented wind that dried up all my nervous perspiration, I discovered that I found the praiser physically attractive as well, not so much as Marjorie, but then a man's imagination must have its harem of second bests. Claire was tall and slender, but one could have wished for a bit less plain and a bit more promontory. She had gray-green eyes and hair of a rusted strawberry color tending in the direction of gold. Though her two front teeth were slightly pushed together in the point of a V as if her face had at one time meant to be broader, freer, then had contracted and crowded the oral cavity, it was not unattractive, suggesting the quality of a child who has yet to have her teeth straightened.

When we switched partners, David let me do most of the talking, perhaps in gracious acknowledgment of how attentively I had listened to his wife. But no one seemed stanched or repressed. We were brimming cups as our mutual interests bubbled up and over—books, music, painting, theater, swimming, walking in the woods. David, who brimmed the least, nevertheless nodded frequently, looked wise, and, though he was not tall, his fresh English complexion, regular features, and imperturbable manners created a solid impression that provided weighty periods for his wife's ecstatic sentences. All of us went home happily assuaged as though four people had been making love in public. The garden had rung with our laughter, and Janice Cowden, tired as a sheared sheep, beamed gratefully at us when we left.

Claire was the first to call and invite us to dinner the following weekend. They entertained, she explained, only on Saturday, since David, an English master at Choton, was always busy with extracurricular activities during the week. Her directions were precise, and we found their house without difficulty, a charming old saltbox, huddled in a larkspurish and snapdragon sort of garden. There were two other couples, a young poet and his wife from Choton, and a doctor whose wife Claire had known in art school. Claire introduced us with just the right amount of pride in her voice as Evan and Marjorie Harrington, and managed to give us the impression that the party had been built around us.

As it grew cooler, we went inside for dinner, finding the tasteful interior one would expect from Claire, country-house Connecticut without any corny, pseudo-colonial effects, though we were surprised to find that they occupied only the first floor. Claire alluded to the fact when there was a loud scuffling above by saying that "our mice have big feet," but I noticed that her wit had an element of strain in it.

This was the first indication that she was not as much at ease in her own environment as she might have been. She served a delicious but complicated curry which was later to have such disastrous effect on our digestions that we were ready to answer Ruskin's famous question, "What do you have to say to India?", entirely in the negative.

It was pleasantly obvious, however, that Claire felt particularly drawn to me since she arranged for us to sit together both during and after dinner, and I had the foolish, though not ungratifying, feeling that she looked to me for some almost extrasensory communication not afforded by the others. Though everyone else called me Ev, she always addressed me as Evan, but the formal approach did not always harmonize with her ardent, almost hectic desire to get her thoughts across. Consequently, she tended to enter a serious conversation without preliminaries, rather as one might split a melon.

Noticing that I was glancing through a book on modern painting, she came over, put down her coffee, and observed, "I think Vlaminck was right when he said Picasso was the perverter of modern art, don't you?"

"Well, perhaps," I hedged. "If you mean he was obsessively devoted to change."

"*Après* Picasso, *le déluge*," she persisted. "Nothing but a runaway river of change. Nothing but fads and fashions. Abstract Expressionism, Pop Art, Op Art, Minimal Art. The works." She picked up another book which had a painting of a large, unsavory hot dog and bun on the cover and handed it to me.

"What about the Blue and Rose periods?" I asked lamely, returning the book to the coffee table. "Paintings like *Femmes au Bar* and *Les Saltimbanques*?"

"They were done by another man. Vlaminck wasn't talking about them."

And that was that. No compromises. No concessions. Only the high, thin laughter that floated around us when I looked too troubled. I sensed that in some way I was not satisfying her, but, for the life of me, I could not discover what was lacking. When she turned to talk to her other guests there was an aura of psychological excitation about her which made me feel vaguely guilty as if I caused her to react in a manner that was not altogether good for her.

But the evening, nevertheless, was a "beautiful event" as far as we were concerned, and we let only a respectable three weeks pass so as not to seem pushing before we returned their invitation. Marjorie keeps a sharp lookout for what she calls "the drama of the garden," and tries not to invite anyone over between the acts. For the Steadmans, the jeweled scepters of the phlox were in bloom and, in another part of the garden, the mounds of pink and red rambler roses seemed to cover the barrows of ancient kings. Our house is also old, but we have made less effort than the Steadmans to remain true to the period, mixing old and new, preferring to let it live its life in the present century as well. Hoping to make them feel at home, we invited their poet friend and his wife from Choton, inarticulate as we found them to be, and Maisie Freemantle, an English artist in her sixties, who looked rather like a cocker spaniel fed all year on plum pudding.

We did not give them the tour of house and garden we sometimes inflict on champions for want of a better way of getting the occasion off the ground, but Claire visited each flower bed like a butterfly until Maisie, entirely unaware of the floppy canine image she aroused, stood in her way before a final one as if to say you have seen all the flowers in the world except the rarest: "Smell me. Admire me. You don't know what you've been missing." But Claire soon sought me out, turning Maisie over to David, and, taciturn though he was, I saw him occasionally open and shut his mouth like a pair of shears as if even he were tempted to cut the stem of her garrulity.

Again I noticed this ectoplasm of nervous irritability which surrounded Claire whenever she came to grips with me. I pass for good-looking and have some reputation in the literary world, but I have never thought of myself as either a lady-killer or a Saint-Beuve. But was I, without meaning to be, some kind of eidolon to Claire? Was it that I had the qualities she associated only with artists and yet had a comfortable and agreeable background, a combination that might annoy a strict moralist such as I deemed her to be?

Several times while we were having cocktails, when I flirted a little or took her less than seriously, she made me feel I sat too casually on the rock of my insouciance, a happy, sunny, but wayward toad who overlooked the lily pond where the mysterious, disklike leaves of her thought let down roots into the opaque water. No one wants to be thought of as an ornamental toad, no matter how gleaming and glistening with life, and I suppose I went out of my way to illustrate that frogs were the equal of lily pads. But none of this helped. I began to sense that the first, fine, careless rapture was over and that she wanted to take me down a peg or two.

During dinner this became awkwardly evident when, unable to keep the conversation light after compliments on Marjorie's excellent food went around the group, Claire introduced the notion of genius and asked whether an artist ever really *knew* when he was one. Various theories were proposed more or less idly by the rest of us who were at the moment more devoted to the first half of that maxim "Dine with the rich, and talk with the wise," when Claire turned abruptly to me and asked, "Evan, do you think you are a genius?"

With my mouth full of deviled crab, I laughed and said, "Of course, can't you see what a big head I've got. Geniuses always have big heads. Look at Churchill, Paderevski."

"Maybe some of it was hair in Paderevski's case," Claire went on with dogged seriousness.

Maisie, uneasy that this curious conversation might redound to my advantage after all, swallowed an enormous mouthful of food in one gulp.

"Talk about big heads. Have you ever seen one larger than mine?" she asked, and put her hands to her cowl of brown hair as if it were a great rock of genius.

Ignoring her, Claire stumbled on, addressing me as though no one else were there. "So you *really* do think so?"

"Think what?" I said, slightly annoyed by now.

"That you are a genius."

The poet dropped his fork, and Marjorie broke in with her warmest smile, "Ev has no doubt whatsoever about his abilities, but he doesn't overrate them either. I find it restful. So few people have the courage to be realistic about themselves. Have some more aspic, Claire, dear?"

"Thank you, Marjorie, my love," I said with a wink. "All that's necessary to have a happy life is to delude one other person. Whom have you deluded, Claire?" I continued, turning to her without a trace of apparent rancor, congratulating myself on how beautifully Marjorie and I worked together.

"Me, of course," David answered as he watched a deep blush spread over Claire's face like a contagion from her hair. "I agree with Marjorie though. I respect self-confidence. Do you remember E. M. Forster saying somewhere that he admired most the people who acted as if they were immortal and society eternal?"

Good old silent, watchful Dave, I thought. He had saved the day, diffusing the tension into something literary and general. He was my man from that moment on.

"You're so right, Mr. Steadman," said Maisie among whose many roles was the ultimate one of peacemaker. "We can all be geniuses in that way, can't we?"

Suddenly, as if someone had just slain the dragon, we found ourselves admiring Marjorie's Bavarian cream molded into a white castlelike tower, and Maisie was able to go home thinking that she had made the party.

But, in spite of Claire's penchant for recognition scenes which dress the drabbest ego in the motley of bruised self-esteem, we saw a lot of the Steadmans and were determined to like them. I became more adept in sidestepping the conflict between Claire and myself, whatever it was, and, if the going got rough, Marjorie would advance like Salome and distract us with the beautiful veils of her wit and grace, and David was our philosopher.

Nevertheless, when Christmas came along with its round of parties, the Harringtons and the Steadmans were exposed to each other in circumstances that could not always be so delicately maneuvered. Maisie Freemantle went into her yearly deep mourning at the approach of the birth of Our Savior as if no man, mortal or immortal, should be given that much attention, and Marjorie and I joked about the "Christmas syndrome" when we noticed Claire growing paler and more staccato as the social pace quickened.

Someone had told us that she had a very beautiful sister who was the family favorite. Another suggested that she had brooded over the fact that she could not have children. In a psychologically oriented world, these little facts about each other seep out and seem to explain our actions as well perhaps, and as superficially, as the ancient humors did. We began to feel a little sorry for Claire, and, if she were not going to provide a summer breeze for us, our kindness and understanding might help to keep some of the winter chill from her heart.

This attitude still prevailed when we saw her on Christmas Eve at the Weavers, a charming couple who always try to give their parties an original twist. That evening it was to be the passing of a Christmas Box from which each couple would take a slip of folded paper, and whoever had the winning number would win a series of photographs of one person in the family. The prize had been donated by Jacques Rimbaud, a rather unsavory character and sometime photographer whose wife Maureen (née Rafferty) ostensibly ran an art gallery but actually specialized in acting out episodes from Krafft-Ebing.

I who never win anything drew the winning number, and I suppose there were others who thought "Them that has, gets," but everyone was perfectly agreeable about it. Only Claire spoke out in a loud voice, "Well, I hope you are going to let Marjorie have *her* picture taken."

Perhaps it was the word *let* that did it, but I had a nice Christmasy desire to slap her.

This time Marjorie was considerably quicker than I. "Claire, dear," she said, "you make it sound as if Ev keeps me in a dark room."

"Darkroom," one of the more potted guests snickered. "Isn't that where all the developments take place?"

Claire let the rest of the group move back to the punch bowl, and said again, "You *are* going to let her have her picture taken, aren't you?"

I could not think of any answer that did not have a four-letter word in it. But Marjorie once more came forward. "I think it's a family affair, don't you, Claire, dear? But since you insist, I think you ought to know I have already decided it is Evan's turn. He has a new book coming out in the spring."

Claire blushed like the little girl who peed in class, her eyes misted over, and I could have sworn she did not herself entirely know why she had persisted. I got a little drunk that night because I, too, did not know why I aroused such infantile animosity in someone I basically admired. It was as though somewhere in the darkness of the soul Claire and I were children together, and I had been given something for Christmas which she wanted and of which I was unaware. No doubt for some people Christmas, in this sense, is the only day of the year.

After the holidays, there was no direct confrontation between Claire and myself, partly because the ties that bind were no longer so blessed, and we had begun gently to loosen them. Even so, whenever we did run into the Steadmans, Claire made some reference to "those photographs." If Marjorie had swerved one inch from her persistent marital decorum, I think Claire would have been all over her with protectiveness and solicitude. One sensed that her desire to ferret out some difficulty between us was overwhelming and that it had taken this bizarre outlet.

Meanwhile, posed as we were off and on before the camera of her obsession, we did nothing at all about the photographs themselves, admitting that we had developed a slight complex. We felt as though some bad luck would be hidden in a photograph which had become such a strange idol to someone we had so much wanted to like. It seemed to shuttle us foolishly back and forth between appearance and reality that we could be judged by the mere taking of a picture. If either of us decided to have the photograph taken, we would be yielding to Claire, who would read something into an act which was totally superficial in its implications for us.

Another disturbing aspect of the whole thing was that if this sort of febrile mythmaking could go on in the mind of a friend, what caricatures of ourselves must exist in the thoughts of casual acquaintances. It suggested to us in our less sanguine moods that people simply projected others as they went along, posing them as subjects of a private pathology. Claire wanted a mug shot of me, and was determined to have it at the cost of a more pleasant "reality" I had been trying to present to her.

Nevertheless, at the end of February, when we received an invitation to an exhibition of Claire's paintings in the tiny gallery of the local bookstore, we accepted. It was one of those bleak winter days when the radiant Connecticut I so much love shows the sorrows of her soul, and the vivid colors of the paintings with their welcome warmth seemed like so many heaters of various sizes embedded in the walls. But the little room itself turned out to be crowded and stuffy, the paintings, at second glance, were considerably less than first-rate, and one had the uneasy feeling that that was where the work would always remain. Mostly of beautiful young women, conceived, one felt, in too precious an idealism, they revealed a certain interesting documentation of longing. I could not help thinking of Claire's sister.

Maisie Freemantle, dressed in a purple dress which made her bosom look stuffed with a bushel of mashed plums, was the first one to vocalize her feelings.

Pushing heavily against me, plums and all, she whispered loudly, "Aren't they awful? Hasn't she got a nerve giving herself an exhibition?"

The poet from Choton, thin and pale as a paper straw, was poking himself nearsightedly into a strawberry-colored painting as though stirring a soda. Suddenly I was touched with the pathos of it all. This was Claire's collection of friends, about each of whom no doubt she suppurated some "photograph," better or worse than the subject warranted. They were the real exhibit in all their weird vitality and variety, most of them totally unwilling to be developed in the darkroom of her temperament.

Astringent, fastidious Claire was beaded with sweat, her high laughter puffing out of her like steam, and she looked martyred with bewilderment. Not a single painting was sold, and the nonexistent profits were consumed at the large punch bowl. I knew I had to make a special effort and that, in this case, it would not be the "truth that set us free."

As we were leaving, I kissed her, tasting the cosmetic flavor of her damp cheek, and said, "Claire, what a handsome showing of pictures. We do want to come and see then again. Congratulations!"

She looked at me as though she thought I were lying, and closed abruptly that hiatus of cordiality and good manners, sincere in its insincerity, in which we reveal and discover those representations which mediate between the world as it is and we would like it to be.

"What about those photographs? Have you had them taken yet?" she asked, her face whitening. I was too confused by the harsh geography of the closing gap to do anything but smile, bow, and back away with my receding half of a friendship.

So the photographs that meant so much to Claire never got taken. I half-heartedly tried to persuade Marjorie to call Jacques Rimbaud and make an appointment with him to come over, but she said again she loathed the man and that he would merely use the sitting as an excuse to visually undress her. He did not pursue the matter either, and I had every reason to believe that the fact that I worked at home would have inconvenienced his philandering instincts. We agreed, however, that we would not let Claire know one way or the other. We felt we owed ourselves at least the vengeance of keeping the photographs forever in the files of missing persons.

Why didn't it end there? Why do human beings keep toying with each other past the point of reason and civilized endurance? Loneliness provides part of the answer, but I think one must look elsewhere into some basic lust for human encounter, some fascination with what's difficult in the face of the absurdities of human coexistence. Claire could not let go of us, and we would not let go of her as long as the unknown still had any potent charge left in it.

Maisie Freemantle's birthday came up in April, "the cruellest month." Maisie claimed to have known T. S. Eliot, and one of the local wags said that he had no doubt penned that line after encountering her on her birthday. Next to Christmas, it was the hardest day of the year for her to get through, and Claire decided to cheer her up with a "surprise" dinner party of some of her closer friends. We accepted but, the situation being what it was, Marjorie warned me to watch the drinks and steer clear of "the darkroom," the expression we had come to use about anything relating to my difficulties with Claire. I agreed and tried to put on the suit of *bienaise* I had first worn to the Steadmans', now stiffened, it seemed to me, beyond all style or comfort.

Maisie was to arrive late, but we found already assembled the Weavers, the poet from Choton, to whom Maisie had taken quite a shine since he said almost nothing and all of it complimentary of her, his wife, and the usual odd couple who would presumably provide the spice for the occasion.

By that evening, however, Maisie had worked herself into one of her moods, claiming that a storm which had passed through the evening before had upset her "vibrations." Maisie's perceptions extended to the ends of the earth, and a volcanic eruption in Japan produced a tremor in her. Consequently, she was not amused by the surprise party, for she had hoped to come over to the Steadmans', drown the knowledge of the passing years in alcohol, and "cozy off," as she would say of an evening which presented an unbroken aspect of adulation and acquiescence.

Downing a drink, she said to me, "Why didn't she say this was going to be a party for me? I would have worn something else. I don't like surprises. I think they are aggressive. They mean to throw you off balance. How did she know it was my birthday anyway?"

I couldn't resist saying, "Why, Maisie, she probably looked you up in *Who's Who.*"

She blanched as if I had produced a birth certificate and promptly called for another drink. I mentioned to Marjorie that Maisie was seriously in need of some expert "cherishing," and managed to escape and spend a silent, restful cocktail hour with the poet from Choton.

It turned out that I needed it. Claire had gone all-out for the occasion, and was an incandescent bundle of nerves, particularly after she sensed Maisie's ingratitude. The dinner was delicious but promised for me a long and fiery trip down the alimentary canal. It was topped off by one of Claire's spectaculars, which consisted of little clay flowerpots filled with chocolate ice cream like earth into which at the last minute she inserted an iris from the florist. It represented such a striving for effect I felt like eating the iris as I am told Einstein did in the case of an orchid a fancy hostess had put on his service plate. Maisie, overcome in spite of herself, wiped hers clean and stuck it in between her bosoms where it seemed to take root in the richest of soils.

After dinner I sat on the love seat with a generous glass of brandy as compensation for the fact I had had only two drinks, hoping that the poet's wife would settle down with me for some discreet politicking in behalf of her husband's career. But Claire, the grand effort of the dinner over, beat her to the draw. I stiffened perceptibly, and we sat there looking out into the room like two people in a daguerreotype, capable of only the most mechanical small talk.

But it was destined momentarily to be a modern color photograph after all, for Claire soon began touching up our study in black and white with little caustic personal remarks. I instructed my diencephalon to hold its fire, but I am afraid it listened to the brandy instead, and the moment perhaps both of us needed arrived like a late, paltry, but nevertheless irresistible impulse from a Greek drama.

"Oh, Evan," Claire said, her face as feverish as Phaedra's. "You never did tell me whether Marjorie had those photographs taken."

"No, I never did," I said impassively, but my brain stem, having folded the gracious umbrella of its cortex, throbbed with mayhem.

"But you did let her have them taken, didn't you?" she continued, giving me her self-righteous Pallas Athena look which I so much loathed.

"God damn it, Claire," I said with a relief that had a curiously vital sensation in it. "Why don't you mind your own business? You've been hounding me about those photographs for months. What's your angle?" I had at long last torn up the likeness of myself I had tried to maintain and given her the pieces.

Claire promptly burst into tears and left the room as if I had assaulted her. Barbaric little flakes of a relationship I had apparently exploded seemed to float down around me like fallout.

Too late now to do any good, the poet's wife came over to me, and I think I may have been fairly rude to her as well. David, who never rushed, did so this time to see to Claire, and Maisie gargled some foolish remark to the effect that Claire too must still be feeling the proximity of that awful storm, so hard on "us sensitives."

I knew I should have held on, but I simply couldn't. I wanted to pour corrosive developing fluid all over Claire as well as myself—See, this is what you are, Claire. This is what I am. Two can play at this game of photographs.

A rueful David reappeared after a while, looking like "a verray, parfit gentil knyght" who nevertheless had a serious woman-problem on his hands. Maisie, warm-hearted at her best, rose to the occasion, said all the appropriate things as she gathered up her birthday loot, let me nuzzle her iris in its very special place, and managed to make David think the party had been a success.

But that evening closed the darkroom forever, or so it seemed. Our friendship with the Steadmans had lasted less than a year, and, since it had every possible affinity to insure its viability, the loss was all the more regretted. The incident was gossiped about in Meadowmount for a while, and then nobody cared. In August we heard that David had given up his job at Choton and that they were living in New York where Claire could pursue her art studies. Later we were told they had gone to live in England, then Europe, and finally we lost track of them altogether.

Perhaps three or four years later, on a beautiful day in July,

Marjorie and I went to a large cocktail party at Grandview, a club thickly sewn with the seed of champions. We were in a lucid, confident mood, and our skill at giving as well as taking the briskly delivered social punch was better than usual. But since I can never be a wholehearted competitor, I withdrew after a while to smoke a cigarette and enjoy a moment of psychic distance so necessary to anyone who feels that most of his life is spent shadowboxing with elusive ideas and images. Marjorie, beautiful as a marigold in yellow silk, relaxed and released from having delivered her share of uppercuts, was dutifully embrocating Maisie, who looked bruised and loose all over, a punching bag gone to seed. As I was on the point of joining them to add my adhesive touch, I felt a gentle tap on my shoulder, turned and saw Claire Steadman, not looking a day older in a lovely green dress, but somehow more muted and insubstantial, like an image that had blown in from outer space.

One hoped to see David moving slowly through the crowd but sensed with desolating certainty that he was now inoperative in Claire's life. Perhaps it was this intuition that contributed to her insubstantiality—the look of a woman without a man, as if she mattered less to others because she mattered less to herself. It was horrifying, as I was later to think, that dear, kindhearted David had been the most expendable of any of us, so soon to have become a hardened, crusted memory, like a suit of armor from which the meat of a man had been extracted.

Though Claire kissed me lightly on the cheek, and I responded with an earthier vigor, something was missing. I realized that it was the cloud of intense nervous excitement that had always surrounded us. There was nothing obsessive in the air, but there was nothing else milling around either—no suffocating martyrdoms, no tortured mythologies. She told us she was now living in Philadelphia and working at the Museum, coming back to Meadowmount for occasional weekends.

I kept waiting for the question, which now seemed age-old, "Evan, what about those photographs?", but it never came. In the slow, suffering chemistry of her emotions, Claire had finally "developed" me. It was probably not the image I wanted to give her and certainly not the one she offered me, but it was a photograph we could both accept. Marjorie and Maisie came up to be kissed and to receive Claire's final version of their likenesses, and we talked together like perfectly normal human beings for half an hour.

None of us gave in to our latent feelings that it was "too late" in the cohesive sense of nows and tomorrows bound together. What might have been in its full, generous entirety would remain forever in the files of missing persons. But it was still time in that Claire had come back if only for a moment to meet us in that hiatus of representations where we suspend the opposing cliffs of personalities like the terrible, frozen music of avalanches which might crush beyond all recognition those fragile surrogates with which we mainly communicate with each other.

When Marjorie and I left Grandview without a noticeable bruise upon us, still looking like champions, Claire was already oddly mystical, even recessive, but it was, no doubt, all for the best that we had not stood too long under opposite eaves, neighborly though they appeared on the surface. The unknown constantly recharges itself, incubating its challenges and rebuffs, and Claire and I, perhaps, were not meant to endure together its struggles and depredations more than once. In retrospect, the mood for everybody concerned had been sensible and civilized: "Let's leave it at that." But when we remember, as we frequently do, how Claire "came back," a visitant to an enigma, Marjorie and I feel our hearts, like the futurists they insist on being, respond to their old fond dream of summer breezes and Chinese chimes.

The Faun

Lura Lewis ran the drugstore in Meadowmount, but would have been right at home in the Mermaid Tavern. Lura loved life, people, Connecticut, but most of all she loved her drugstore, which was a microcosm that encompassed the other three.

It was a matter of pride that everyone who was anyone traded with her—the first selectman, the Congregational minister, the officers of the brass companies in Shaftsbury, Bill Byron, noted novelist, and Maisie Freemantle, painter, and all-around town genius. Nights when she couldn't sleep Lura ticked off their names on her fingers like a plurality of little gods in a godless universe, and it gave her almost as much pleasure as the money clinking in her cash register.

No remote control for Lura. Any morning you could find her presiding at the counter, sharing a cup of coffee with Bill Byron who had hit a writer's block or Maisie stalled on her latest painting. Her particular pets were the artists since she had had a fling at writing while working her way through college, and now could specialize in empathy. She collected Maisie's work, had a stack of Byron's latest book right by the cash register, and the lesser fry could always pay the monthly bill with an etching, a sketch or, better still, the promise to spend some time with her son Ronnie. Lura knew the ailments, real and chimaerical, of all her sensitive plants, and, if Ben Grafton, the poet, came in for a prescription for one of his allergies, she took him back into the drug department for a session about Ronnie and overlooked the fact that Ben hadn't paid his bill last month. Maisie, who was one of the healthiest people in the world but could smell pollen on the air even in winter or a Freemantle-directed germ in the cough of anyone nearby, gladly gave her mother-of-the-world advice in exchange for a succession and variety of pills. Confident that she could get by with it, Lura finally labeled one large bottle "For Small Unimportant Viruses" and sent Ronnie over with the placebo for an afternoon of communing with the afflicted-great.

Lura, the redhead's redhead, with her hair the color of a coxcomb and metallic blue eyes, life-loving and life-giving, ready to be the Rosamundi to all of her "family," as she spoke of her customers, thornless as she could keep herself and still move around in the world and make money, had one thorn in her flesh which sometimes seemed like the spine of her entire life. Ronnie. If she could have attracted all the mothers and fathers in the world to help her bring him to manhood, she would have done so. It was Ben, adoring in her the *élan vital* he lacked, who concocted the rose of the world image, and she thought it was great, simply great. Like the mother in the Robinson poem Ben so much admired, she meant to shower down on Ronnie "a crimson fall of roses thrown on marble stairs." Great poetry, simply great, and Ben had her crying in her beer when he read it in that high-toned voice of his, but what were you going to do when you stripped yourself down to the buff giving off petals and there you stood, Mother Rose, ready for the next thorn from Ronnie to whom she was as devoid of pain as a pin cushion.

Now, it seemed, she was saying for the thousandth time over her morning hemlock which everybody else thought was the best coffee in town, "What am I going to do, Bill?"

Byron, tall, dark, Southern gothic, hung up on his latest nonfiction novel, *Life in a V. D. Ward,* repressed a desire to vomit in his cup which Lura liberally laced with bourbon, sensing he had been on one of his colossal three-day drunks. Exuding the mood of Poe's Raven, he nevertheless managed to gulp down two words instead of one, "Generation Gap."

"What do you mean gap?" Lura asked querulously. "I've kept that boy as close to me as my corset."

"Yeah, I know," Byron said, remembering his own mother who had kept him as far away as the moon with what would have been the same result if he had not had a little talent into which to pour the witch's brew which still sloshed around in his mind. "But he thinks he can see through you, corset and all."

"What's he looking at? A blank wall?"

"The future, he thinks. Of course, it might be a blank wall at that. Maybe he knows, and that's what bugs him." Byron rubbed his face where the stubble reminded him of what a dirty old man he must look like this morning.

"What's so wrong with looking at me? At everything I've done for him? At Meadowmount?"

"Honey, I really love you. You really think Meadowmount is where it's at, don't you? Every lovin' letter in red, white, and blue. How about a little more tonic, sweetheart? The day's beginning to look like the color of bile to me."

Lura was pouring a generous jigger into a second cup of coffee when Ronald came into the store.

"Mother's little comfort station," he said with a smile, kissing her flatly as if she were a drawing on the wall. "Good morning, Mr. Byron."

"Mornin', son. You've got a real mother there. Don't make any mistake about that. One in a hundred."

"Yes, I know. And I'm the son of all the other ninety-nine."

"Don't get smart with Mr. Byron." Lura turned toward Ronnie, her upswept hair shimmering like an overheated burner. "He's not feeling too well this morning."

"So I noticed. I like coffee too. Just like Jackie Gleason."

"You're telling me," Lura interrupted, warding off the wise-crack with which Byron would most likely defuse the situation. "Well, let me tell you, young man. You're not going to get so much as a sniff of dandelion wine around here."

"Mother, mother, mother," Ronald said like an incantation. "You promised."

Byron, sensing that this small clenched fist of anger was likely to mushroom into an emotional cloud of nuclear intensity, quietly swallowed the rest of his coffee and slipped out, leaving "his pal" Lura with the best-looking son in Meadowmount on her hands and a desire which came over her several times a day to brain him with "the jawbone of an ass." There was nothing like the Bible for expressions that sounded high and mighty and yet came from the guts. Even rage at Ronnie had to have something special, something out of the ordinary, about it.

Every time she looked at him, angry or glad, he dazzled her. He was just so good-looking with what Maisie called his elegant *tournure,* and she called a damn good build, though she secretly preferred Maisie's term. Byron said he had the charm of an ephebus, and Ben Grafton was reminded of the athlete in Housman's poem. Naturally someone came up with the old one about a "Greek god," and Lura accepted every epithet, plain or fancy, as his due. Maisie who dearly loved an Edwardian simile said that the color of his eyes was "essence of periwinkle." The wonderful, fresh skin, the fine white teeth, the long slender hands—just sitting in her drugstore talking to her customers, Lura could gather together enough extravagant images for a "Song of Songs" about Ronnie.

But her own private term for him was "the Faun." He had been such a lovable child, such a nuzzler, such a dreamer. Perhaps it had something to do with her love of Debussy, whose *L'Après-midi d'un faune* could send her off into a world of voluptuous loveliness, the world of youth where everything bloomed in a kind of Fauve luxuriance. She knew there were some in town who thought her a little on the crass side, those who had never had to go it alone the way she had, and they would never know that her best times were at the end of the day when she could pour herself a drink, put on some Debussy records, and think about Ronnie. And it worked every time—the sunlit, sensuous meadow which was kind of an idealized version of Meadowmount on a clear summer day, and the figure of Ronnie ready to do a Nijinsky leap into the spotlight of fame and fortune. What the hell if there was a commercial side to her dreams? Who was it anyway who said that it was all right to have castles in the air, but you'd better start putting foundations under them? Well, the only foundations she had ever known anything about were money and possessions. Ronnie was going to make it big, and, with her help, he was somehow going to do it without losing his place in that sunny meadow.

If anyone had said to Lura that the facts told another story, she would have said it was how you *felt* about the facts that counted. That's how you made them come round. And nothing was able to shatter the process of metamorphosis until the death of her husband Hart whom she loved dearly. He had been a kind of manqué faun, too good to run a drugstore, not quite enough of an artist to be one. With his bad heart, early in their married life he had returned to the wings to watch the other dancers leap, ready to catch them if they fell, never losing sight of the fact that the stage which simulated a glistening meadow was splintered and treacherous with loose boards. It was he who had started the coffeehouse atmosphere of the drugstore. It was he who had attracted Maisie, Byron, and Ben Grafton. She had simply carried on after his death, subtly changing things, making the atmosphere less rarified, adding her own special blend of ribaldry, resourcefulness, and respect for the arts, which was unlike anything else Meadowmount had to offer. Lura thought nothing of interrupting Ben Grafton when he was reading aloud Wallace Stevens's "Sunday Morning" to ask Ronnie if he had had a good bowel movement.

Ben might blanch a little, but this was the kind of vigor you had to pump into the situation to keep the whole damn thing going, and everybody seemed to thrive on it. Maisie sort of felt she was spiritually back in England at the local pub when she went down to Lura's and discussed her hysterectomy along with *She Stooped To Folly,* which the Nite Lite Players were doing at the Town Hall.

Nursed through a thousand hangovers, Byron, secretly saving a Nabokovian fantasy of Lura for his old age, called the drugstore "Amity House." Ben Grafton tripped over her name one day and called her "Flora," the best Freudian slip he had ever made, and from that time on she was just that to him, the Tintoretto masterpiece, the eternal earth-mother figure tumbling in leaves and flowers. Everyone got what he wanted from her except Ronnie.

No one in town could figure it out—Lura gave that boy everything. And it was enough until the trouble, the big trouble, started at Hotchkiss when Ronnie was caught smoking grass in his room. The affair was hushed up, he wasn't expelled, but those who traded at the other drugstore said she shouldn't have sent him to such an expensive school in the first place.

That was the first indication to Lura that somewhere lurking in the faun was the shadowy figure of the satyr. Before he graduated, there was another incident with a girl in Lakeville, and her family raised a stink. That Lura could understand. That was normal. The boy was simply growing up. Ronnie came home, nuzzled her, kidded her along, and secretly she was glad it was nothing more complex—her son, the lover boy!

But that summer Mrs. Arlington Smith, who lived in a gabled house across the green and looked like Hawthorne's Hepzibah, started a rumor that Ronnie was seeing a lot of Archie Scott, a wealthy older man who had once danced in the ballet. Lura was furious, and loosening her carefully apotheosized image of her son, sent Mrs. Smith backing nervously out of the drugstore with the suggestion that Ronnie had also been accused of getting several girls from Lakeville in a family way. Nevertheless, she insulted Mr. Scott the next time he came in the drugstore wearing a purple shirt—No goats in her meadow, thank you!

"You know what that old Smith bitch said," she complained to Maisie. "Intimated Ronnie was a homo."

Maisie, who could dream for everyone, said, "She's just jealous that she's too old for him to give her a tumble. I saw her talking to him like an old soubrette several weeks ago, and he treated her as if she were his grandmother. I suppose you know her husband caught her sleeping with the milkman some years ago."

But if Ronnie's preparatory years, as symbolical to Lura as their name, had been sown with wild oats, the years at the University of Connecticut, which were to have been the floral ones, proliferated beyond expectation. His grades were poor, he was caught cheating on an exam, there was another marijuana incident, and he was finally suspended for a year.

After he returned to Meadowmount and loafed around for a few days, Lura had Ben Grafton in for a session at the counter.

"What's happening to the kids these days?" she generalized. "No respect for anybody. Nothing's enough or everything's too much."

"You know what I think, Flora. I think Ronnie's testing you. He wants to see if you're just a big noise or if you've got limits."

"Hell, Ben. I believe in every old-fashioned value in the book. He knows that."

"Maybe you're a little abstract on one hand and a little too concrete on the other." Ben glanced at himself in the mirror over the counter. Who was that dark-haired, seedy, middle-aged character who looked like a handyman? The town poet?

"What in hell does that mean?"

"He knows you slip Bill Byron all the drinks he wants. He knows you sell raincoats under the counter to the local Don Juans. Things like that."

"You mean I'm a hypocrite?"

"He might see it that way."

Lura gave a lifting, releasing motion to her breasts as if her girdle were hurting down below. "For Christ's sake, if that's what it is, these kids are getting so moral they are downright immoral. We've all gotta live, and Ronnie knows I never gave anyone anything that would hurt him. I treat everybody the same."

"Then why have you made such a special case of him?"

"Because he *is* special. He's got to be better than good. Boys like Ronnie are the flower of our youth."

"Lilies that fester smell worse than weeds." Ben stretched out his long, bony legs like a man who would much prefer sitting in a boat headed for Camelot.

When Lura glared at him, he whitened like the endangered lily, and he found that he was *persona non grata* at the drugstore for several weeks after that. Lura went around for days thinking that Ben should talk with his grubby little poems about nymphets and his life that stagnated like a pond choked with reeds. Why didn't he break off some of those reeds, kick up his heels, and let go. Meadowmount could do with a touch of Pan!

But things were moving so fast that by the time Ronnie got back to the university the administration was more adjusted to his sort of young man. Smoking pot seemed a mild enough offense, almost a prank, for some of the kids were shooting wilder stuff now. Authority was something you saw in an old statue in front of the library; the Age of Negotiation had come to American education. Lura would have been pained to think so, but the campus sheltered more than one handsome, blue-eyed son whose favorite slogan was: "We want the world, and we want it now." Ronnie was more tentative than most, and he had charm which his professors were willing to settle for these weary days. They graduated him with a C average, and passed him back into the system which his generation so much wished to control.

But the problem for Ronnie, under the watchful eye of Lura, was what was he going to do about his small cut of the world. He loafed for a while with the vacuous feeling of the young that time will stand still if they do, positing against this desuetude an intermittent, militant outburst of energy which went mainly into arguments with his mother's customers. Someone gave him some love beads, but he felt foolish as a cow waiting to be belled with them hanging around his neck, and long, greasy hair was not his thing, not when he had been used to a bath every day of his life. Of course, the drugstore was even worse; it was the scene of the great American put-on. Or at least that was the way Bill Byron explained it to Lura.

"What are you going to do, honey, if you're not a hippie and you're not a square? Just hang loose in the middle?" Byron had been trying to work both sides of the street himself for such a long time that he projected this dilemma indiscriminately.

Since he was no help at this point, Lura sent Ronnie round to see Maisie who sat so securely on her generous ego that she could give a vacillator a sense of where the omphalos was if anybody could. But Maisie, having lost a commission to do a portrait the day before, felt the stone beneath her washing away in the Heraclitean flux, and was in no mood to be "drained" by anyone so dispersed as Ronnie. He upset and irritated her with his hectic sensitivity and tacit appeal for help. One should not have that much sensibility without an equal amount of sense, she told herself, and spent most of his visit wondering when the loose but powerful cyclical motion of her own nature would bring back that great rock of stability which was floating like a thing of papier mâché in the stream of resentment and disappointment. Besides she had no faith at all that Ronnie could ever be an artist on the strength of nothing more than an art course he took at the university, though he made his pitch to her like the purest of aesthetes—all for art or the world well lost. And, of course, the ferment *was* there—one could sense the seething color and frenetic energy of his temperament, quivering, shimmering like specks in a pointillist painting, but they formed no pattern. As far as people like Ronnie were concerned, the Seurats of the world were dead. His mind was full of floating sparks and, without the furnace, which was the form of art, to contain them, they were simply aimless and dangerous. They were the real modern anti-afflatus, ready to light anywhere and ignite God knows what.

But when she felt better the next day, half off and half on the marvelous stone, Maisie tempered her account of the interview to Lura.

Barging into the drugstore, heavy as the dark side of the moon in the eyes of Lura, who had had to deal with Ronnie when he came back from her house in an unusually distracted, dismantled form, Maisie said, "I think I put Ronnie on the right road, Lura. He's a lovely, sensitive boy. But he needs to know it's not going to be easy. *Ars longa, vita brevis.* It's work, work, work. God if that boy knew that every painting I've ever finished had been a blood sacrifice. There's a piece of me in everything I've done." She concluded with a vigorous gesture, unaware that the spectator might wonder that there was so much of her left.

Lura gave her a cup of Bill Byron's "coffee," got her some iron pills without comment, and let the center of the earth roll back to the Volkswagen, mystically strong, as hermetically sealed as ever.

A few days later, Ronnie returned to his old notion that he wanted to be a poet, and Lura sent him off to see Ben Grafton since she *knew* the answer had to be somewhere in Meadowmount. Ben liked Ronnie, even understood him, perhaps, better than anyone in town. He knew what it was like to be off in the middle somewhere—poets were always there no matter what the state of the world was—and he knew that you had to stretch yourself like God Almighty to stay in touch with the extremes and yet remain oneself—that was where Coleridge's reconciliation of opposites came in. That was part of it. But he also knew "what Maisie knew"—that not many people could do it. Robert Frost's son had killed himself trying. It not only took a lot of living, but a lot of controlled living to write one quatrain someone might want to read a hundred years from now. Could Ronnie stretch himself without breaking, that was the question, or would he, as that cynical son of a bitch Byron was always so fond of saying, "just hang loose in the middle"? Ben wouldn't bet that he would or wouldn't. Ben liked failed poets almost as much as those that succeeded, sometimes better.

Maisie, of course, rang him up to warn him that Ronnie would be coming by, giving him a preview of what to expect. But apparently something had gone wrong at Maisie's and Ben was totally unprepared for Ronnie's approach. Expecting the same aesthetic pitch, he felt instead he was listening to Lura when Ronnie, standing all the time, walking briskly back and forth like a commuter ready to catch a New York train, talked to him about the dollars and cents of poetry. How much did *The Saturday Review* pay? Did they pay by the line or by the word? How, specifically, *how*, did you get into *The Atlantic* or *Harper's*? Did pull help? Would Ben mind writing a letter of introduction to the *Yale Review*? Could Ben go over his poems and tell him which ones would sell? How long had it taken Ben to break in? Did he make a good living at it now?

On a scarred veteran these questions fell like pins hurled by a child, and Ben wondered where, oh where, were Ronnie's bow of burning gold, his arrows of desire. But to let him down easy, he gave him the practical advice he wanted, interspersed with wry comments which Ronnie took in the opposite manner from which they were intended.

When he saw Lura the next day, Ben realized that Ronnie had been on one of his confident "highs," perhaps in reaction to Maisie, and had gone home and sold his mother a bill of goods. Lura looked elated, Flora ready to take first prize for her special blossom, and she even offered Ben a cup of "coffee" rather than the usual tea and lemon when his bill was two months in arrears.

"Ronnie thinks I'm the Vanderbilt of poetry," he said, holding up his sleeve which had worn through at the elbow.

"Oh, God. Not *that*." Lura looked as if somebody had hit her in the stomach.

"'Fraid so. Already planning to get his poems mimeographed to send around all over creation. Wants letters of recommendation. Prices and prospects. Got me to give him my Annual Report on Poetry. I think you've got a businessman on your hands instead of a poet."

"Jesus, Ben. That's not what he told me. I thought you were giving him the real stuff. I mean real *poetry* poetry." Lura pouted so that the lipstick bow which overlapped her lips did a little snake dance. "He would ask *you* for that sort of stuff. Why didn't he hustle Maisie instead? That way she might have thought he was serious. He's just like the wrong-way lover. He never knows what he should do to whom."

Something, however, of Maisie and Ben melded in the uncertain alembic of Ronnie's mind, for he told his mother that he wanted to go to Columbia that fall for graduate study "in the craft of poetry" and "to look over the market in New York at the same time." Lura thought it was great—Ben, Maisie, and Bill gave their blessing—and she set him up in a cute little apartment. He wanted "to be his own man" and, since he was nearly twenty-two, what mother could begrudge him that? When he came home glowing on weekends with Rona, plump, earthy, vigorous, a compact edition of Maisie, everyone at the drugstore marveled that New York could produce such a wholesome peasant girl, and Lura did everything but hand her a veil and scatter her with orange blossoms.

The euphoria did not last long. Ronnie began to look hollow-cheeked and pale, Rona more jaded, and Lura beat it out of him that they had gone on speed together. They were also shacking up in Ronnie's apartment and had rung up a big liquor bill in the neighborhood at Lura's expense. The story of the would-be poet had turned out to be one of wine, women, and very little song. Not a poem written in months. He wasn't even going to classes anymore. Lura went down to New York in an enormous rage, expelled "that Circe in a peasant blouse," as she now called Rona, and cleaned out the clutter of the apartment, the empty bottles, the soup cans and uneaten hamburgers which looked like models of a Pop artist. Packing Ronnie and his fumigated possessions in the station wagon, she drove him home with the letdown feeling of, having shorn him of this, grimy as it was, what did she have but a basket case on her hands?

But one thing Ronnie could still do was *move,* and with or without Lura's permission—nobody knew—he soon took off for California. Archie Scott had now settled out there and was the head of some Zen Buddhist cult which had attracted attention back East, and he had even written a book that had given him the status of a guru among the young. Ronnie began to write poetry again, mystical stuff which Ben privately thought was the hash in the hashish mentality of our time, but Lura relented and gave him a small allowance. Stacks of Archie's book were placed beside her cash register in place of Byron's best seller, which had shot its load, and finally there was a little volume of Ronnie's poems which she had paid the Exposition Press to publish.

One had to adjust to the young, she decided, or, as they were fond of saying on college campuses, establish a meaningful dialogue. Ronnie had to be allowed to live his life in the twentieth century. She didn't talk so much about him to Maisie, Ben, and Bill anymore. They meant well, but perhaps were old hat. She began to read Archie's book and the other far-out stuff Ronnie sent her regularly, and, strangely, they seemed to go well with the drink in the afternoon, the Debussy records, the dream of the faun. One had to admit that perhaps these kids knew something after all. Maybe there *was* a whole new world opening around us which squares like her knew nothing of.

Some of the flower children who had begun to permeate Meadowmount were permitted to hang out at the drugstore. Lura laid in a store of posters, beads, and psychedelic trinkets—just a little window dressing for the new clientele—nothing that would offend, nothing Mrs. Arlington Smith could complain to the first selectman about. In order for things to remain the same, she told herself, they have to change. Meadowmount with a little coloring of the East.

But Lura's posture of den mother to a new breed did not last long. One night Archie Scott telephoned from San Francisco to say that Ronnie had gone on LSD and had had a bad trip. He was in a hospital. What did she want done with him? Archie's words were serious, contrite, but anything he said managed to sound affected, and Lura remembered later that she had poured a stream of obscenities into the phone, but that Archie had refused to answer in kind. Realizing that this creep was all she had to rely on, she got hold of herself and gave him instructions to put Ronnie on a plane as soon as he could travel. Until Ronnie's departure, Archie called her every day, and Lura got the impression she was talking to someone who was really fond of her son. How had a misfit like Archie been able to reach him when her mother's love, powerful as a laser beam, had only been reflected into her face to blind her with frustration? What did it all mean, this gathering together of the unwashed and the emotionally crippled like a cult of shamans or primitive Christians looking for a Second Coming?

Ronnie lingered in the California hospital three weeks before he returned to Meadowmount, acting very much like a case of shell shock when Lura met him at the airport, and she immediately made the decision to send him to the Institute for Better Living in Hartford for a month. He drooped a little less and they sent him home, but he was like a man with total burns—he did not want to touch the world or be touched by it. From the emotional swaddling with which he seemed to be bound up, only his blue eyes looked out bright but vacantly like jewels in a mummy's head.

Slowly he was able to do odd jobs around the drugstore, and one afternoon Ben Grafton saw him listlessly painting the front of the building, staring at the boards as if they were a white minimal canvas of his reduced responses. He talked a little, smiled as always, giving off that combination of sweetness and helplessness which reminded one of Dostoyevsky's Idiot, and Ben felt that his familiar figure registered on Ronnie's acid-singed brain as nothing more than a shadow-replica. Ben would have given his right arm if he could have even brought back the brash hustler of poetry which Ronnie had presented as a possible persona to a man he liked who admired his mother.

But a girl who was a reporter for the *Shaftsbury Republican* and had a difficult family life of her own began to take an interest. Ronnie had youth on his side, and though the unwinding was slow, bandage by bandage, toward the pink, concealed, healthy-seeming tissue, after some months—*voilà*—the figure of the virile young man who had come back from the journey to the end of night. All the old habitués felt him almost like a Christ figure around the drugstore. Who else these days is a savior except one who seems to have saved himself?

As Ben was to think many times later, if only Lura and the make-do Magi who came to visit her at the counter to talk about the Child could have left it at that, not forever, but for as long as it takes a miracle to adjust itself to the common light of day—if only Ronnie could have accepted the image of renascence as a pro-pitiatory step in a world where the pretended often passes into the real—these moratoria and suppositions might have stretched more than a gangplank into the future.

But as Ronnie seemed to heal, Lura's ambition recovered, and the pressures mounted. The old uneasy picture of Ronnie as a dropout and wastrel returned to the minds of Maisie, Bill, and even ever-compassionate Ben. Ronnie, they feared, was going to let them down again. Was there no longer an image that kept even an ersatz sanctity?

That summer Ben came into the drugstore one muggy, soul-muffling day to hear yells and screams coming out from the drug department as if Lura and Ronnie were using each other as assistants to a knife-thrower who meant the flesh this time. Whoever managed to peel away from the wall would leave his image outlined in knives. Ben, who had just lost his publisher, wearily reflected—Throw every phony stage setting in the world away, and you still have this drama.

Going back to the drug department, he found Ronnie's face lit up into a human torch and Lura scowling like the one who had found the gasoline can but did not believe the flames were real. The actual, the fictive, match that had set fire to the genuine, the spurious, victim had been a quarrel over the fact that Ronnie, with whisky on his breath, had come in at four o'clock from a date with the sympathetic reporter to whom Lura had taken a profound dislike. Now her discontent was letting itself down the ladder into the bottomless darkness that was Ronnie.

"What do you mean charging all that stuff to me at Judd's over in Shaftsbury?" Lura continued, taking no notice of Ben.

"Mother, I needed it. You don't want me to go around like a hippie, do you?" Ronnie shot an appealing glance toward the poet who for once felt unequal to the occasion. He decided, though, that he might as well stay on as a silent referee, ready to throw his moral support to the loser.

"I sometimes think you haven't got the guts to be a hippie." Lura measured out some Fedrazil tablets she supposed Ben had come for.

"I sometimes think you haven't got the guts to let me be one."

"Don't mock me, Ronald. Just remember you're not too big to slap. Maybe you're not big at all." Lura pulled out a chair from her desk and motioned to Ben.

"And is this such a big deal?" Ronnie looked around the drug department as if the vials and drawers contained anodynes of the American dream.

"I don't want to hear anymore about *that*." Lura slammed a cabinet shut. "What I want to hear about is: When are you going to come up with something anywhere near as good as this which you scorn so much. Or, to put it more simply, when are you going to get a job?"

Ronnie's pink anger had drained back into some hidden lake of fire where figures of self-immolation sit in a circle, biding their time, ready to surface in the only laurel wreath with which they mean to adorn the brow of their time. He just looked at his mother.

"Who are you? What are you? That's what I'd like to know. From where I stand you are nothing but a good-looking bum."

"Do not try to understand me too quickly, Mother."

"Where did you get that from?"

"A writer named André Gide."

"I know who he is. I've read all his books." Lura knew how to lie quickly and confidently when the going was rough.

"He's a great man."

"Yes. And a great queer too. You would quote someone like that just when I'm telling you it's time for you to grow up. Let me tell you, my greatly misunderstood son, whom I can see through like a pane of glass, from this moment on, you're on your own."

A week later Ronnie left for New York, and Lura would not talk to anybody about it. Maisie prodded, Bill indulged in paradoxes, and Ben mourned, but she had locked the safe now that nothing was in it. Maybe too many cooks *had* spoiled the broth. These days, Maisie seemed fatuous, Bill hypocritical, and Ben sentimental—what was she running anyway? A mental health clinic where amateurs could ply their trade as physicians who ought to be told: Physician, heal thyself?

Every time a good-looking, clean-cut young man came into the drugstore, she pulled a blank. What was going on in *his* mind? Was there a single boy or girl left in America who could look into the future as if it were a sunlit painting? For all it meant to anybody these days, she might as well take down a reproduction of Eakins's "The Swimming Hole" which hung on the wall of the drugstore. Was the fine figure of a man about her age swimming in the middle of all those shining, beautiful boys some kind of boob or pervert? Did he pollute the waters just by moving around in them, or had he let them be poisoned by streams of thought and feeling which should have been condemned years ago? Had her generation scraped all the last honey out of the hive, and, knowing nothing was left, gone in for permissiveness and do-what-you-like as if "freedom" could compensate for the fact that there was nothing lucid and sweet left in the world? Was there nothing remaining for people like herself, the ones who were supposed to have let it all happen, except getting drunk, putting on a stack of records, and looking backward in a dream?

But, skeptical as she had become of relying on the silver cord, Lura kept in touch by the grapevine. She heard that Ronnie had gotten a job among the squarest of the squares, selling Fuller brushes, and was living in a bohemian boarding house in the Village. That figured. That was her son all right, split down the middle to the very end. Ben Grafton looked him up and said it was true—he cozened nice old ladies out of their money during the day and made the scene at night.

Christmas came unusually hard that year, for Lura had never spent one alone, but she made an extra effort anyway on the off chance that Ronnie might slip up for a day or two at the last minute. In addition to the tired old artificial trees and tawdry ornaments she always put in the drugstore windows, she matted the doors with bright red foil. It was kind of camp, but kind of cheery too, and she went through the whole rigamarole at the house as well—"Never say die, say damn"—that was the only spirit that would carry her through this latest little Happy Birthday for Jesus.

After she threw the switch on the tree to see how it looked, however, the whole thing seemed impossible and she went over to Hartford to spend the week before Christmas with her sister, leaving the store in the hands of her clerks. She didn't particularly care for her sister, but they had maintained a sense of family, partaking of the philosophy inherent in Robert Frost's observation that "home is the place where, when you have to go there, they have to take you in." Surviving on liquid cheer, Lura returned to Meadowmount Christmas Eve to find, nestled among the Christmas cards, as welcome as the babe in the manger, a letter from Ronnie mailed the day before she left. He sounded depressed, unduly repentant, very much the child who used to respond with regrets and promises when she scolded him for misbehaving.

Lura went straight to the phone and called his landlady, Mrs. Rubin. Could she speak to Mr. Lewis. No, she didn't think Mr. Lewis was in—at least she hadn't seen him in several days. She had knocked on the door several times to deliver the mail, but the door was locked. There was nothing unusual about this. Mr. Lewis often went away for several days at a time, and he always left his door locked. Could Mrs. Rubin unlock the door and go in to check? No, she couldn't do that. Her boarding house was not a two-key sort of place. Besides, her boarders liked their privacy. Couldn't she make an exception this time since it was his mother who was calling? No, she didn't think she could. Not unless the police were there or some member of the family. She had had trouble about this before. He'd probably turn up soon. He always did. Well, Merry Christmas anyway.

Lura called Ben Grafton, he said they'd better get down there, and they were on the road within an hour. About half way down the Merritt Parkway, Ben stopped at a gas station and called the police in the precinct, explained the circumstances, and asked them to have a man meet them there. When they got to the suburbs, he warned Lura to brace herself—Ronnie didn't live in the Ritz Towers—but Lura who washed her images as best she could every night when she went to bed was not prepared for the squalid building or Mrs. Rubin with dyed hair and purple face who looked as though she took something wilder than booze. It seemed to Lura the greatest travesty of all that Ronnie had to settle for her as a mother-figure.

The sergeant, a big Irishman who might have been weaned on the blood of the Mithraic bull, knocked in the door and said, "He's in here all right."

Lura asked Ben to go in first, and Ben wondered why it seemed to be his lot to be the father of poems and people who failed. The shades were drawn and Ronnie was stretched out naked on his bed, surrounded by the clutter in his room. Ben snapped on the overhead light, but it seemed unduly surgical, and he put on the lamp instead. On the table there was the empty bottle of sleeping pills which was becoming one of the little monuments of the modern experience. Ben was struck by the utter starkness, the paucity of gesture, of what must have been the last hours of a luxuriant human being. Ronnie, the American youth for whom Ben had wished the role of "Eros, builder of cities," had been dead for a week. He had already turned black—Anti-Eros, the brother of us all.

This is what Ben would have liked to have concluded, but a simpler, perhaps more pertinent, image occurred to him. It was all so dubious, even the enormous sense of failed possibilities. Like Wordsworth's Michael, Ben could have wept "and never lifted up a single stone."

He tried to persuade Lura not to go in, but Lura, dear Lura, who still had the clear eyes of a pioneer, went in to look at her son who might have been entombed for a thousand years. One did not need ruins whose gods had not lasted or piles of random stones as covenant to suggest the overpowering pressures that can close and fall around a single human being. One needed only a mono-lithic sense of the present. Lura looked at Ben, remembering a poem he had read to her at the counter in Meadowmount where they had discussed the prices, the procedures, the possibilities of life, and said, "How do you like your blue-eyed boy Mister Death." Ben would remember, and always wonder at the powerful con-trasts in the nature of his beloved Flora, when she said in the next breath, "Let's get him home, Ben."

Meadowmount did all it could for Ronnie. It literally "chaired him through the town." He had been such an obstruction and now he must move clearly, lucidly through. Nothing cleanses the spirit more these days than the recognition that American heroes may all be dead heroes. One did not need to have known Ronnie too well to recognize that he was someone more suited for the native pantheon than for life. Collective guilt knew what to do with boys like him, having the talent of a stonemason for making all figures look solid-seeming yet abstractly spiritual, substantial but vague, directing its appeal to anyone and everyone, pertinent to time as a whole. One wants something emphatically ambiguous at the end of the road.

But Lura wanted a little something more of the sort of thing

Ronnie would have remembered. The day after the funeral, she had a small private service at her house—Maisie, Bill, Ben, a few of the old regulars at the drugstore. Ben thought it was appropriate, but wondered how any of them could take it. He rarely got drunk now because of his ulcer, but he stayed up all night drinking and turned up at the service looking like Orpheus who had been beating at the gates.

They all realized that they had never before been inside Lura's house which was simple, plain, without fuss—a tribute to Meadowmount. Flora, who had kept the world going for them, had her own underworld which was as neat as this. But they missed the counter where all the myths were accepted, devalued or canonized, and returned to their owners. They missed being able to go away in better guise than when they entered. They regretted the generosity of the drugstore, which seemed to have been able to accommodate all but one. But, more than anything else, they wondered if Flora would become unregenerative, cynical or cyclical in mood, might not turn out to be Persephone after all.

When she could roll away the stone of her ego, Maisie had a heart, naturally twice as large as anyone in town, the true omphalos, and Ronnie's death had sent her back to the English poets like the source of some of her better feelings. She felt as wistful as the virgins at the end of Milton's *Samson Agonistes,* and, in an excess of good faith, promised to do a portrait from memory. Bill Byron, in time, would write a Faulknerian short story. But Ben Grafton had not been able to wait. He had worked all night trying to do a little poem since he knew Lura would need something for now. In an unguarded moment she had told him about her dream of Ronnie, and he tried to use that as the theme. It was just a fragment, but at the last moment he decided that might be appropriate after all.

When his time came to say a few words, he got up and read the two stanzas which he had entitled "The Faun":

> Whatever happened to the faun?—
> Is he the rioter in the street,
> Some tangled, hairy youth we meet
> Like a stylite among things long since gone?
>
> Whatever happened to the barefoot boy?
> Who was it who caused him to desist?—
> Some thwarted American impressionist
> Who taught him that the flowery meadows cloy?

Lura was too moved to do anything but close the service after that and, when they had gone, she sat down by the fire in the Christmas room. Ronnie had always loved the holidays so, and she would never forgive herself for not having been there to receive the letter which he had sent when he knew she would be remembering the old days.

Her eye caught an old battered reindeer, about a foot tall, a childhood toy, which they had always put under the tree no matter what. Everyone had given something to Ronnie except her. Lura picked up the deer and placed it in the fire. The delicate antlers melted first, and the body stood there alone, shorn, and infinitely appealing, like a faun in a glowing paradisal meadow. It seemed to be, as Ben Grafton's favorite poet had said, "standing in God's holy fire." But, of course, it might also have been someone else's notion of hell.

Rooster on the Roof

I do not know what it is in me that attracts the eccentric, even the grotesque, but if there is an oddball anywhere near where I live, sooner or later he will be drawn to me as if by a magnet. Even in a town the size of Meadowmount there are always more than one, and within a few years of my arrival they seemed to have clustered around me like filings of scattered ego.

We had come to Connecticut with one unfinished novel and a collection of radiant dreams for the future supported by what my wife Laura describes to our friends as "Jason's self-confidence." I was absolutely sure that I would be a successful novelist, that it would one day all work out, that I was in this sense a child of destiny. This sort of ebullience is like honey to other rich dreamers who have their feet stuck in the dark gum of doubt.

I am a good-looking man, tall, blond, with a faint, vigorous glow of red in my hair, muscular, big-boned, turned out, it would seem, by the best genes in America, and my self-assurance may be rooted in nothing more than this. I look like a Wasp without a sting—good background, good schools, enough money to live on modestly without working. Having been loved and expecting to be loved all my life allows me to work in a mobile spotlight which attracts all sorts of strangers from the dark.

The only suspicious thing about me is that I am a writer, and I suppose it was this deviation from the Ivy League type that let the oddballs in. I did not look or act like one of them, and yet I was, so they instinctively selected me as their liaison man rather in the way Communists are more than usually delighted to find a fellow traveler among the rich.

Being an oddball in America is about the most difficult work I know, and when I first met Adrian Clarkson, I knew I was looking at a man condemned to hard labor. Those of us in Connecticut who don't belong to the Establishment seem to meet all of our friends in the crowded corners of cocktail parties. But if you have to bloom in a corner, Meadowmount is as tolerant a place as any, perhaps because it so clearly belongs to those who run the world, and, of course, it was especially easy for me since I have this ability to pop up vividly anywhere like paper flowers from a magician's hat.

That Adrian had heard of me did not come as a surprise since even members of the Establishment were not above using the likes of Jason Warren as *their* liaison man into the peculiar world of art, and, no doubt, would have mentioned my name during an awkward conversation with the strange little composer. Alluding to some of these big shots when we met at the Ryersons, Adrian went on quickly to the names of several other oddballs around town like passwords into a secret fraternity. My magnet began to draw even more strongly then, and I clapped him to me once and for all. Even for me, however, it was an unusually close and tight fit, as though he were possessed of some unsuspected magic glue that would bind us together even if the force of my attraction experienced a willing power failure.

Adrian (born Albert) came from an impoverished chicken farm in Maryland, but that was only the beginning of the disaster. One wonders if there is not some merit in the old wives' tale about traumatic influences on the pregnant mother, for Adrian at birth must have looked like an enlarged biddy. That beak, that scrawniness, the prominent Adam's apple suggesting a repressed desire to crow, must have had an early start to produce this rooster of a man. If his trousers were pulled up, one felt, there would be spurs instead of garters. But all grotesques are impure representations, and what Adrian lacked was brilliance. Instead of being gold and burnished, he was dark and sallow, a rooster dipped in the acid of doubt and despair.

One intense, staring, lidless-seeming eye was perfectly in character, made for the cock of the walk, but the other, crossed, hung in a milky bag of tension, belonged to the human animal. If the good eye was electric, the defective one had blown a fuse. It was looking for another connection, and fell on me as subject to symbiosis. Together we would have made a Chaunticleer.

On the way home, Laura, who, like me, passes for normal but is also "one of us," said, "Well, you really hit the jackpot this time."

Tall, dark, big-boned, built for the rough traffic of life, Laura is a perfect compliment to me, sardonic where I am too sentimental, guarded instead of open, an artist's wife who suspects that the bright road long ago ran out of rainbows. But secretly indulgent, she loves the way I make conquests, welcomes every nut I bring home for her to crack.

"You'll be hearing from him," she said in her mock-ominous

voice as we went into our little saltbox, which was set in a tangled garden on the edge of town.

"Don't you hope I will?" I asked, reflecting that her prophecies nearly always came true. Since we had agreed that Adrian looked like a bedraggled rooster, I gave her a friendly pat on the rump and said, "Aren't you one of us chickens?"

"Watch your fowl language," she shot back, and gave me a punch in the ribs.

"Seriously," I said. "What did you think of Adrian?"

"He's like bath oil," she said. "A lot more clings than you think. Don't overdo it."

The next morning, not long after breakfast, the phone rang, shrilly, insistently, and Laura said, "Cockle-doodle-doo!"

It was Adrian, all right, with an invitation to dinner the next evening at his house in Woodbridge, which was only a few miles from Meadowmount. I was pleasant with him, even jolly, scattering some golden grains of complaisance which that hungry beak snapped up, and went back to my novel feeling like a big, warm, ruddy brother of the world. I consider the motives of my characters minutely, but do not necessarily analyze my own, and I suspect this keeps the gliding effect of my life from slowing down.

Adrian, who thought out everything, had his world set up blatantly as that of an artist. He, too, rented an old, small house opening into a tiny living room which had the atmosphere of a womb. Crammed with the huge black fetus of a grand piano, it was too parturient for comfort, dismally suggesting mammoth, stillborn, musical failures. We were to discover that whenever we went there we would always sit around the piano, caught in the nutritive caul, waiting for Adrian's masterpiece to be born.

Men like me get all the good wives, it seems, so Adrian had Janie, a modest, vague, unassuming Pertelote who was apparently not aware, if she was aware of anything, of the bleakness of his plumage or the solipsistic hunger of his eyes. The house was always a mess, and Janie moved around like a visitation, tall, ash-blonde, wide-eyed in a bewildering world of efficient people. A college graduate and reputed to have been a good student, she simply could not communicate. I could make the most casual remark to her, and she would stare at me as if I had sent a message to a star and it would take light years to be received. The two children, equally vague, looked not yet quite born—pale, spiritual, insufficiently imaged for the rough purposes of this world. Except for Adrian it was a house of ectoplasmic figures, of expectancy that waited for the brilliant, vocal child of musical success.

It was clear from the beginning that Adrian thought I had everything and that he was free to extract what he could from me. Inspiring the Robin Hood syndrome of robbing the rich to help the poor is, I suppose, one of the penalties of projecting a strong, confident image. Even Laura, who truly loves and admires me, likes to take me down a peg or two now and then when I seem more than usually effulgent. One might say that it is a universal impulse toward the leveling, the democratization of images.

This conception of my personality has put me, even more than I would like, in a paternal position. I find myself constantly listening to the troubles of others as if I could kiss them and make them well. I am forever being called upon to give advice even when the matter at hand is clearly beyond my comprehension and competence or when I do not altogether feel generous enough to extend the calming hand.

And so it was with Adrian that first evening. While Janie's tenuous but pervasive dream of muddled domesticity enclosed us like the mist of their inner lives with the scent of dinner cooking, two ghostly children draped limply in Dali-esque shapes over chairs and sofas, we talked about Adrian first, last, and foremost. Few people can give so much of themselves all in a piece. He was like a man too nervous to lie on a couch who sat talking with his psychiatrist while Laura served as the assistant, rather too clipped in expression, too jocular for Adrian's taste, I could see.

A minor problem is often a way of getting into the heart of things, and Adrian was shrewd enough to do just this. He taught music at Carlton Hall in Woodbridge, and was finding it suffocating, though in his telling of it I could not see why. Wilhelmina Barnes, the headmistress, known affectionately to the students as "Billy," had taken quite a shine to me, and I had spoken to the creative writing classes several times, finding her to be anything but a tyrant—a short, fat Tweedledum of a woman who loved her cigarettes and martinis and was, I thought, a little too loose in discipline and inclined to see the activities of the girls through a gauze of sentimentality.

"You know, she makes me play the organ at chapel, and I have to practice for the damn thing several hours a week," Adrian said. "The woman simply has no idea how that cuts into the time of an artist. Then when we have a speaker from the outside one evening every other week, I have to do special music. Billy puts on quite a show, and the girls come dressed in white like little angels. It's too awful."

Laura, who also rather liked Billy, asked, "Would you rather they came dressed in black?"

Adrian ignored her, as he was to do many times, and waited for me to say, "Too much Renoir no doubt, at the end of a day conceived by Goya."

Janie hovered in conveniently, and, like a deaf mute talking with her hands, waved us on to dinner—a roast beef ending with pears amandine. It was implausibly good, and, as Laura said later, must have been cooked by a genie. Adrian ate voraciously, beaking his food as if it were the first real thing he had done that day, but it was a hurried, hysterical appetite that staunched only momentarily a more powerful one.

Right after dinner we got down to business again. The subject of Adrian's music surrounded us like a thick sulphurous incense. You tried to change the subject, but found yourself so under the influence that you merely expelled what you had already breathed.

What little success Adrian had had came from riding on the backs of others. He had set a number of poems to music, and they had been sung here and there, but seldom published. He knew I had written and published a few poems as a sideline, and the idea of "setting" me was given a passing caress. But his big idea was that we should do an opera together. I am confident, but I am not altogether delusive, and I knew in a moment it would not work. It was Adrian's way of making one artist out of two, of getting outside himself into another. He thought that at last he had found, as the psychiatrists say, his "magic helper." I knew also that if the work were ever completed, he would expect me with my superior contacts to get it published and produced.

"That was quite a dose," I said to Laura on the way home.

"You're telling me," she agreed. "You're always too nice. You give too much. You'd better watch out. One day there may be nothing left for yourself."

"Don't worry," I said and smiled. "There will always be enough left for you." I hadn't meant to be cynical, but, on second thought, I wonder if I had not been a little. Did I, somewhere deep in me, think that even Laura was a trifle grasping? So many of my relationships have this ambivalence, and, if I have a complex, it is the fear of being used and drained.

Perhaps it was just the fatigue of a long evening, but Adrian's admiration of me seemed particularly onerous and exhausting, and I could not help reflecting how much people are capable of idealizing others for their own benefit. By the same token, they are just as prone to degrading and denigrating others unduly. Was the world, for good and for ill, held together only by images? Looking around us, we collaborate on a construction stuck together by illusions. Looking in a mirror, we see, in part, a metaphor. Was the real difference between Adrian and myself simply that for presenting a picture the world would accept I was born with better ingredients, and was this fatality in the metaphorical process built irrevocably into life? The question stands like a menacing little beak at the end of all of our proud statements about ourselves.

Nevertheless, there is a nerve, an instinct, in us that seeks both the "truth" and its possibilities, and in the weeks that followed, Adrian pressed against me as if to discover if my truth and my adornment were one, and to see if this synthesis, if it existed, could be put at his disposal. I was reminded, though in our case more often than not farcically, of the forceful, ardent, probing friendship that Melville wished to exist between himself and Hawthorne, and of Hawthorne's withdrawal, abetted by Sophia, not wishing, and perhaps with good cause, to yield the secrets of his cool, marmoreal image.

So I listened to Adrian, I counseled him, I bore with him, but, in the end, I wanted to keep my distance. He had started with a negative and I with a positive, and I could foresee the danger of his canceling both of us out. We exchanged many visits, but, in the long run, not much else. I heard him by the hour, drunk and sober, pour out his heart and I found myself feeling less rather than more sorry for him. But, strangely, in regard to the music itself, he was reclusive and diffident. The manuscripts strewn around the living room, the huge piano, and all of the externals of total dedication, were very much in evidence. But I never heard him play one of his compositions, and, of course, he knew it was safe to have his scores around since I did not read music.

How we recognize the vulnerable in each other, scenting it like a hidden sore! I extracted from Adrian the fact that he himself had never heard most of the music which he had composed though he had sent the scores in a barrage to the leading conductors of the time. I finally ferreted out the more merciless fact that he did have a tape of his First Symphony played by a student orchestra at Juilliard as a class exercise, and one night when he was drunk, I persuaded him to play it for us.

Laura asked for another brandy and gave me a look as if to say you'll be sorry, and Janie, even more cringing than ever, shot an agonizing glance at the tape as if the thin, depleted entrails of their life were now to be drawn into the light to be inspected by a haruspex. Adrian stood up all the time it was being played, weaving about unsteadily, and I could have sworn he would have liked to conduct that tape with all the flourish of a Stokowski.

The recorder was old and the tape itself in bad condition, skipping here and there where it had been broken and spliced, and one wondered how many times Janie had been subjected, like conditioning for psychosis, to this music. Also there must have been many a guest who knew nothing about music and whom Adrian did not respect who had been forced to listen as a form of obeisance. It was a tortuous method of assembling an audience one by one, and as Adrian stood over us, the veins bulging on his temples, one felt that he was imagining their combined presence.

In contrast to the superbly projected music of his intense desire, the symphony itself clucked along in a modern, discordant way, full of atonal cliché, and I suspected that beginning nowhere it would not get very far. But every now and then, the music straightened up, turned upon itself, and uttered a lyrical cry of liberation. It was like a rooster crowing in a waste of sound. One was awakened as from out of the morass of inattention into which one had slipped by the mystical cry, full of pink, amethyst mornings, lonely, remote, yet vibrant with the need to arise to possible beginnings and paradisal renewals. Possessed momentarily of what the Spanish call *duende*, it was music forced up through the notes by the daemon. It lit on the roof of the world and called us ineluctably to stand on tiptoe and expel the most vital sound of which we were capable. But it lasted no longer than a quick, bright flapping of wings, and we were back in the dull, essentially frivolous, carpentry of sound.

When it was over, Janie, Laura, and myself were quiet as birds on a roost. What was there to say? The morning had not come after all. We were still bedded darkly in sleep, waiting. The symphony was more like Adrian's dream of music he would like to write and perhaps would have written, I could imagine his saying to himself, if things had not been so against him.

Laura spares only those she thinks are motivated by love and even them not fully. "Very interesting," she said.

Adrian, who at least knew how uninteresting it is to be only interesting, turned morosely to me.

I tried to remember the iridescent passages, but now they did not seem to have existed in this music which was so modish, so obviously tailored for a "modern" success. It was as though I had dreamed them for Adrian; it was as though I had uttered them myself.

"I'm still thinking about it," I said, only half-lying since I was indeed thinking about it though not in the way I implied. "I hate snap judgments. Will you give me a little time? I want to relate certain passages to others."

Janie looked undyingly grateful, as if I had withheld a blow, and, for that evening at least, it seemed to be enough for Adrian, though if he had listened to my last sentence he might have had an inkling of what I had in mind. He nestled down on the sofa beside me as though to share my warmth and proceeded to get comatosely drunk, opening his good, staring eye from time to time to see if I were still there. Janie quietly put the tape recorder away like someone trying to bury the evidence, and Laura and I went home.

The next time they came to our house for dinner, Adrian suggested that he bring along the tape recorder, but Laura cleverly managed the evening so that we did not have to hear the First Symphony again. She had decided that our little drama was receiving the wrong emphasis; it was a comedy which was trying to take the direction of tragedy. From then on she superbly stage-managed our occasions together so that Adrian was able to impose very little of the burden of his career on me.

I shall never know whether it was this alone or whether those secret evaluations of each other which we secrete like the musk of life had begun to thicken our ambiance and were sensed even by Adrian, who protected his ego with a perpetual air freshener, but his attitude toward me dramatically changed. The eye that called for my compassion and pity was given no more, but the dynamic eye watched me constantly. Whenever he could, he sat obliquely, with his good profile toward me, and, when this was not possible, he had a maddening trick of being able to close his bad eye right in the middle of a conversation and of keeping it shut as if he were taking in only what he wished to hear. Somehow it seemed pathetically contemporary to be talking to a profile, and I had the feeling that the side I could not see was doing all of the hidden, subversive work of an increasingly uneasy relationship.

It became apparent that Adrian wanted a showdown with me, and, despite Laura's expert and emphatic management, one finally occurred on a beautiful June afternoon when we were having drinks at their house. We sat in the garden, which was messy and unweeded like ours but rich with someone else's planting, and twittering with glossy birds. I remembered that Janie had managed to convey that Adrian tended his birdfeeders religiously all winter.

The girls wore sunback dresses, and we were in sport shirts and shorts. I seem never to lose my suntan, and I suppose I presented a fairly rugged image with my ruddy complexion and golden-reddish down on my arms and legs. By contrast, Adrian looked mainly carved out of sickly white bone stretched with skin which incongruously had been able to sprout coarse black hair copiously. Always a natty dresser, he wore navy blue shorts and a blood red shirt.

I had sweated all winter on my novel and finally "killed the monster," as Winston Churchill used to say. Laura had conceded that "it would do," which is as near as she ever comes to letting me know she thinks I have done my best. So, stretched out in the sun, with a drink in hand, I was feeling pretty good. The urge to make and master had temporarily left me in peace, and I was in a state of eudaemonia, a perilous frame of mind if those around you would like to scratch your eyes out.

I never talk about my work in Meadowmount, and that, no doubt, is why I am tolerated. I let people live on the edge of me, protecting the center. But I was off guard that afternoon, supposedly among friends, and I said apropos of nothing in particular, "Well, it's off my back. I've finished the novel."

Adrian, who had never once asked me about its progress, looked as if an electric prodder had been applied to his genitals.

"I suppose you are going to sell it to the *Reader's Digest*," he said.

"No," I demurred with a tolerant smile. "I've already done the digesting myself."

"Not that you didn't have colic plenty of times in the process," Laura said, for she scented danger.

Adrian turned his good eye on her and beaked forward into her face. "You seem to know a good deal about the artistic process. Jason is very lucky."

Laura did not bat an eye, but I flashed with anger, "I am indeed," I said. "I can always depend on Laura to tell the truth."

I shouldn't have said it with Janie sitting there as if her mouth had been sewn together, but, without knowing it perhaps, I was filled with the loose, dangerous, unpredictable electricity of a writer who has just finished a book.

"Can your friends, then, depend on *you* to tell the truth?" Adrian demanded, rising, looking down on me as if the shock treatment I had begun to administer were working to his advantage. Something happened to his face. The distorted half seemed to turn like a revolving door until the bad eye swung into focus with the other. That simple mechanical correction gave him another personality. He still looked thin, depleted, but now like a forceful young man who had been through a lot. He even gleamed a little with the metallic mood of men ready to attack.

"What do you mean by that?" I asked, trying to keep the irritation out of my voice.

"I mean that you sit there like the cock of the walk, as if you owned the world. As if you could make anyone do anything just because you are you."

Since so few do, I am always amazed when anyone finally speaks his mind. I can see the pictorial fabric of the world tearing around me, and what steps forward, though brutal, is absolute.

"So you want me to tell you, do you?" I asked. "You want to know what I think of you?"

Of dropping of representations, once it has begun, there is no end, and Adrian, addicted to thinking of himself as a figure kept inflated and alive by the air fed through a hose I controlled, seemed rapidly to lose energy.

"If you wish," he managed, but his moment of insurgence was over, and it was his bad eye now that pled with me while the good one, nervously flickering, seemed on the point of guttering out. His head looked too heavy for his thin neck, one shoulder sagged underneath the red shirt, and I knew that unless I released my grip on the air hose, he would sink into himself like a punctured rubber toy.

I thought how allusive and, then, elusive, life is in its emphases. Just a moment before, we stood like gamecocks together. We were equals on the basis of a live, open, unrehearsed situation. Anyone coming in at that moment might have bet on the one or the other. It looked as if we had been dealt with equally by fate because something in Adrian made him think, just for a moment, that it was so.

Then in a technique, almost too cinematographic, the moment passed, the realities of things as we had been taught to see them reasserted themselves. The pit was there, but there was not going to be a cockfight after all. The torn fabric was hastily tacked back together by Adrian's conception of me, which served as a glittering brooch.

"Adrian," I said, feeding whatever life-giving sympathy I could muster slowly toward him. "Why can't we just remember that we are friends?"

Connecticut, so full of birds and flowers, seemed that afternoon more than usually theatrical. Something in me would have welcomed a sanguine and conclusive encounter, but something else told me that I did not have a right to push things that far. The challenge would have had to come from Adrian. One cannot imagine another's life for him.

After that fulsome afternoon, and I use the adjective in all of its ambiguous shadings since there had been less than a cathartic effect on any of us, Laura and I saw very little of Adrian and Janie, though we began to hear a great deal. Meadowmount and its environs are so tightly sewn together in their representation of quiet, orderly, New England life that any tear in the integument transmits a ripping sound to all concerned. It seems that Adrian's little scene of manqué rebelliousness with me was only a warm-up for a general upheaval in his emotions. We soon heard that he was involved with his wife's first cousin, Sara Evans, whose husband was a banker and trustee of Carlton Hall.

Sara, a tall, imposing blonde with some of the talents of Billy Rose, took it upon herself to act as Adrian's impressario and indeed arranged for him to conduct his music at several schools in Connecticut. She also enlisted the interest of Alba Canfield, who was as near as Meadowmount came to having a *diva*. Together they persuaded Billy Barnes that the school itself ought to do something for Adrian. Billy agreed, and it was arranged that Alba would give a concert of Adrian's songs at one of Carlton Hall's "evenings" with the trustees and selected guests from the surrounding towns in attendance.

Everyone had let the matter of the affair ride for a while, grateful that it took up the slack in Meadowmount's psyche. But gradually it became the chief subject of conversation at cocktail parties. The cousinship provided a hint of incest. Adrian was acting like a genius, so, after all, might he just possibly be one? Those more intimately affected searched their feelings for protocol. If Adrian was really somebody, how do you act toward the woman who has let him down and the one who might play George Sand to his Chopin? Hot morality is so much better than cold. Meadowmount, in trying to decide how to handle the case of Sara and Adrian, had the smell of life upon its fingers.

Billy Barnes looked the other way as long as she could, and since the invitations were out, the show had to go on, but the girls were already twittering about the musical comedy in their midst. I shall never forget, however, the way Billy managed to carry on at the same time that she subtly withdrew her approval from the participants in the occasion, particularly after she had the situation visibly brought home to her when she saw Sara, resplendent in pink chiffon and diamonds, sitting on the front row, and Janie, further back, a pathetic, noumenal figure in gray. As she presented Adrian to the audience, I remembered William Howard Taft's quip that "he could take care of his traducers, but it was his introducers who were hard to bear," and I am afraid that even "the girls in white" got the point as the introduction vaguely meandered on to the subject of the many fine artists who had visited the school.

When Adrian rose to accept the applause, white as a narcissus which had bloomed from the deviant, black stem of his evening clothes, his face an agonized abstraction of conflicting planes and angles, he was so pathetically not the dashing roué who might have titillated the repressed desires of his proper audience. A red carnation in his buttonhole looked like a floret of his life's blood, and it seemed to stick him up into the air with a congealed artificial brilliance. As he played his songs, the notes flew out of the piano like knives, never spreading into that soft graceful fan the audience wished to have waved in its face. Alba did her best, and she had a voice as powerful as a jet of blood, but her efforts to put a beautiful screen around the songs only left tatters where the shrill music kept flashing through.

Worse than angering his conservative audience, Adrian also bored it, and after that evening he became a lascivious joke around town. Among the more cynical, doubts were cast on the possibility of such extracurricular prowess in a physically unimposing man, but Madame Grandpré, the worldly old French teacher, was reputed to have come up with an answer, *"Le bon coq est maigre."*

None of this fazed Adrian. He began to flaunt his public appearances with Sara, but, as with his music, one wondered what his love life would amount to in the end.

A great deal depended on how long Sara and her friends would continue to believe that he was important. Is there something about the failed artist, the near-genius, that arouses the manipulative touch, the complimentary creative response? I suspected that Sara wouldn't have given Adrian a second glance if she had not felt that she was doing something worthwhile by going to bed with him.

Billy Barnes, always wary of the power-combine to which Sara belonged, was slow to move, but it began to be common knowledge that it was only a matter of time before her plump hand let the guillotine fall. Janie, expecting another child, went to stay with her mother. Rodney Evans, scenting which way the social winds were blowing, began to make menacing sounds, and Adrian suddenly realized the jig was up. He began running around like a chicken with its head cut off seeking support everywhere. But the fun and games were over, and everyone turned him down. The thick, stunning figure he wished to embroider on the sturdy gray silk of New England emotions rapidly unraveled and was about to drop like a scarlet thread into the rag bag of the unaccommodated.

For the last time, as far as Adrian was concerned, I began to sense the magnet in me quiver. I was the only one left; there was no other direction in which the weathervane could turn. I felt vaguely responsible; I even supposed I had been cruelly kind rather than vice versa just to sustain the buoyance of our relationship.

Nevertheless, I was determined to be inflexible when he knocked on our door one night at three o'clock, smelling heavily of drink, his bloodshot eyes the only touch of color in his face.

"I suppose you've heard Billy Barnes is going to sack me," he began, as I took him into my study.

"As a matter of fact I had," I said.

"She always hated me, you know."

"No, I didn't. I rather thought it was the other way around."

"She's jealous of all artists." He fidgeted in his chair as if he might hop out of it like a decapitated bird.

"Perhaps," I said. "But I wonder if you are not a little jealous of her, of what she stands for."

"I didn't come here to be lectured," he snapped.

"No, Adrian. I know you didn't. You came here to be loved."

"You should talk." He got up and poured himself a stiff drink.

"Why do you say that?" I asked. "I am only a sum of misunderstandings."

He turned as though he would like to throw the drink in my face.

"Then you won't stand up for me with Billy Barnes?"

"No, Adrian, I won't. I want you to stand up for yourself. Look," I continued, "life is a fatality. Must we always be indentured?" Having started that sententiously, I suddenly felt it was useless to persist. But I suppose I was as compelled in my way as

Adrian was in his. How could I make him see that we were prisoners together?

In any event, it was no go. Though I had not really pulled the picture apart, I suppose I had jarred some focus that wished to be implacably maintained. Adrian tugged at his bright tie like a stretched red tongue, ran his hand through the ruffle of his hair, rubbed his throat, pressed and nudged himself as if to feel if anything were hidden there. But the quake of images seemed to leave him weak for the undisturbed surface of things. Tears came into his eyes and dropped, strangely pallid, out of his bad eye in its tender-looking net of red veins.

We talked on almost until dawn, and Adrian managed to establish some semblance of our old camaraderie, extracting this hope, that blandishment, and I began to grow less and less confident of the efficacy, or even the truth, of what I had tried to convey. The light began to flow through the windows, pink, amethyst, mystical, and we seemed to be turning in our conversation as in sleep, waiting for some thrilling cry to come up out of fatality into its brilliant, burnished, proper shape. Somewhere, indeed, there must be morning.

Connecticut Cowboy

"A butcher, a baker, a candlestick maker." Ben Grafton could almost hear them rhyming their list when he heard the Graysons were giving one of their neighborhood parties. If Althea Sloane didn't make out too well with the plumber, Joan Phipps, the town hairdresser, would turn up at Lura Lewis's drugstore the next day, starry-eyed at having talked with the congressman of the district.

People like the Graysons needed to spend only a few years in the satellite towns around Shaftsbury before Jack got one of the biggest jobs in Connecticut, the presidency of Beth Lomax Clock. Quickly setting themselves up at High Hill, a large two-hundred-year-old house on a farm near Meadowmount, they couldn't help impressing even those who resented them. Ben Grafton liked to say that they belonged to the scattered gods of our time, but then Ben could be dismissed as the town poet by almost everyone. Except the Graysons—they spread their net wide and fine.

Carla, named Charlotte by her Boston family, was tall, slender as a model, with meticulously kept red hair which looked as if it had been worked by Fabergé. A rangy, dark, handsome six-footer who had made the long road from Montana to Chicago to Connecticut as though traveling the frontier in reverse, Jack enjoyed the intense satisfaction of the man from the wide open spaces who conquers the East. Even geographically, Carla and Jack had the tips of the nation in their hands.

But Jack was not quite so much all of a piece as Carla. He raised Black Angus, wore a large silver buckle on his belt, a leather string tie, and a ranchman's hat when it suited his mood. No one was ever to think that he worked in an area tight as the nickel where the buffalo was caged. Those who admired and hated him in the same breath began to call him the "Connecticut Cowboy."

Ben Grafton thought this quite the most interesting thing about him. It was all so oblique, so ironical, that it posed itself as no more than a snapshot that he might have had taken of himself at a dude ranch. But it left the wispy weight of an enigma on the inquisitive mind like the smoke from the cigarette of the Marlboro Man.

With her determined sense of the *real* neighborhood, Althea

Sloane finally decided it was time to give a party of her own and sound out the ambivalent.

When the guests settled down with drinks in hand, Althea, glancing around the room as if sweeping it with radar, picked out Gloriana Vreeland whose husband Matt was the retired head of Beth Lomax.

"I'm so glad you could come, darling. I didn't know you were back until I called Carla Grayson this morning," she said so that everyone in the room could hear.

"Really. I always thought Carla hardly knew I existed."

"Oh, Carla knows everything." Althea could not resist letting her wicked blue eyes rest longer than they should on Gloriana's freshly tinted hair, which looked as if it might have been dipped in a mash of nasturtiums.

"Anymore parties at High Hill while we were gone?" Gloriana asked as though she hoped by generalizing to change the subject from herself.

"Yes, indeed. Another one of *those*," Althea drawled.

"I know. They're awful, aren't they? But we always go."

"Only to see who's there, I assure you. Such an absurd conglomeration."

"I pick and choose."

"And suppose you're stuck with the clerk from the hardware store? Carla sweeps by and Jack looks the other way."

"I know," Matt Vreeland interrupted. "When I drop in at the office, Jack's always busy. He doesn't want to think anybody ever sat in his chair before."

Althea turned to Ben Grafton as if he were her philosopher. "But what are we going to do about them? What *can* we do?"

"Just watch them. Look at them. See how they grow."

"And what would that accomplish I'd like to know?" Gloriana twisted her pearls as if she could hang herself with boredom.

Ben ruffled long, bony hands through his black hair and straightened his bow tie. "You might learn something about America. How it's done. How it is being done to us. We're here to be processed, handled."

"Well, I'm *not* a Beth Lomax product," said Maisie Freemantle who was wearing a skirt her compatriot Augustus John might have painted on a gipsy.

Ben took a large slice of paté on a cracker, noting that, as usual, he and Maisie were eating more than anyone else. They hadn't had to learn to live on an artist's income for nothing.

"No one would ever accuse you of that, Maisie," he said. "All the same, didn't Jack buy your painting of a covered bridge for his office?"

As if she had not heard, Maisie held out her empty glass to Stuart Sloane and turned to the Wade Hills.

A striking brunette with a glow like a garnet, Mary came from an old New York family and thought herself above social climbers like the Graysons. "Carla had the nerve to say she did not like our Picasso," she said, jangling her charm bracelet. "I just looked at her as if she were a child. Which, of course, she is as far as painting is concerned. Have you ever seen the calendar art hanging on her walls?"

Wade was deceptively bland as he smiled at Maisie and gave her the benefit of his healthy pink and silver glow. "When she couldn't get a rise out of Mary," he said, "she tackled me, and I told her the painting was worth $300,000. That shut her up in a hurry. One doesn't usually say that sort of thing. But deep down, Carla is so brutal."

Maisie looked pained at the mention of so much money and might have gotten around momentarily to defending the Graysons, but Althea rushed on. Was Carla, who seeemed on the surface even colder than Jack, the power behind the throne? Or did she function merely as the company wife who would not be allowed to let him down? Nothing could be decided, each theory had its partisans. Even Althea's little groups of nonadmirers, *au fond,* were divided. Meadowmount had its androgynous Janus-figure—Jack and Carla, back to back, controlling both doors of the world.

As Ben Grafton was leaving, he whispered to Maisie, "That was quite a séance," and Maisie, who wished she had thought of it first, said, "Yes, they *were* here in spirit all the time, weren't they? This is what we get for living in—I won't say off—the small minds of others."

When Jack got home from the office that afternoon, Carla was already out on the terrace fixing a scotch for him and a diet cola for herself. Having driven by the Sloanes's and taken note of the gathering of the Meadowmount Mafia, she was not in the mood for his usual hermetic silences at the end of the day.

"This town's insufferable," she said irritably.

"What's wrong now?" asked Jack. He had changed into jeans and a red shirt and was standing up practicing his rope tricks between sips of his drink.

"Well, Althea Sloane for one thing. She had the nerve to call up this morning and ask if the Vreelands were back from Europe. She knew that I'd know she was giving a party."

"Small fry," Jack said, giving himself time to assess her mood.

"That's what you say. She's thick as thieves with the Hills. And I can just feel her working against us."

"Don't worry, honey. I'll buy you the Sloanes. And throw in the Hills if you want them."

"Oh, I can manage *them* alone, thank you. I know how to stick the needle in there. All I have to do is tell Wade I don't like one of his paintings and he blows a gasket. It's the Sloanes I can't stand. They have nothing, so how can you get at them?"

"There are ways." Jack sat down and looked at his Black Angus grazing in the far field. "Sloane used to be the company doctor, you know. I looked up his file. Some of Althea's friends might like to know why we let him go."

"Oh, you wouldn't, Daddy!" Their daughter Colleen had been standing in the door listening. She was almost fifteen years old, but Carla still kept her in braids. "I *like* Dr. Sloane."

"You would, darling. You have infallible taste for the inferior. By the way, is that my lipstick you've got on? And *my* beads?"

"Oh, Mother," Colleen said and went over and poured herself a Fresca. She was a beautiful girl who promised to be almost a replica of her mother, but her sullen expression destroyed the effect. Carla programmed her every day as the appealing child who was not to look old enough to make her look comparably older, and just as regularly Colleen returned the information garbled, the wrong report.

"And another thing," Carla said. "I don't want you seeing that Lindsay girl anymore. She looks like a tramp."

"She's the brightest girl in our class." Colleen kept holding up her face to her mother like a mirror that distorted.

"No, dear, you're the brightest girl in your class. Your bad report is only a little love letter to your father and myself."

"Do you ever read it?"

"Jack, you'd better answer that one," Carla said as he got up to go into his act again. "And do stop twirling that foolish rope. It's getting on my nerves."

Jack detested these scenes between his heifers. He was let off the hook by his son Jimmy who trotted out in his cowboy suit. With his dark hair and fine pale face, he could have been the Infante of Spain in masquerade, introducing the only fragile, poetic note in the Grayson ménage. He went over and leaned his head against his father's arm, a petal on a bough, and big, dark Jack stroked his hair protectively.

Althea Sloane would have loved to wander around in one of Jack Grayson's blue moods, but she would never be permitted that intrusion. He had taken the thread from Carla long ago, and he must kill the Minotaur and return to her, all well out of public view. Some days he would just as soon have let the hunted go free, emerge onto the surface of the American dream, harmless and peaceful as the cattle which grazed on his farm, but Carla wanted the ears *and* the tail of the mythical monster. Sometimes he felt like the dark, brooding beast himself, and Theseus seemed to be the most superficial of fellows.

Ben Grafton dreamed this dream for him, reminding himself that the trouble with dreams in America was that you could never tell whether they had any such content. There was this blandness everywhere, at least on the surface, and, whereas Althea Sloane would have thumped on the walls of the labyrinth beneath High Hill and called them false, he would have given a lot to have found them real. Jack Grayson, to save us all, just had to be more than he seemed.

Beth Lomax under its new management prospered beyond anything anyone could have expected, and the directors curled back in acquiescence. Jack pushed through town zoning, Carla organized the first Junior League independent of the Shaftsbury branch, Jack was the leading force in the celebration of the three hundredth anniversary of the town. Even old timers agreed, what could Meadowmount have done without the Graysons?

To put a special touch on their share of the tricentennial as well as to illustrate to people like Althea Sloane that they had reached the top, Jack and Carla gave a garden party for four hundred people. But Carla had not managed to cope with the Brahmins for nothing—she knew how to do a big affair. The August afternoon was clear, sweet, dry as the best champagne, and an enormous pink marquee set up on the lawn introduced a magical note of youth and childhood longing. Driving up to the house, one regretted all the circuses that did not turn out to be as glamorous as expected, unquestioning as a child as to why it promised to turn out differently this time and how it had all been done.

Carla and Jack were perfect ringmasters as well as star performers in any ring which needed a dazzling display of technique, and the guests were like charming animals who were willing to jump through hoops, even fire, to please the Graysons. At a late hour when he felt he could relinquish his hold on the party, Jack provided an extra attraction by swooping around the dance floor with Claire McConnell, a wealthy divorcee who bent to his powerful lead like an aerialist hung by her teeth.

The next morning, Ben Grafton struggled over for his weekly lesson with Colleen. He hadn't had such a rich chunk of the American dream for a long time, but if it had only been a dream, what was this huge toadstool still doing on the lawn? He looked inside and saw that it had been stripped of all signs of the party, balloon-fragile, too thin and overextended an integument for the passions of the Graysons. Ben's own private little pink elephant, which seemed to have escaped the efficient entrainment of the night before, was enough to make him realize that no one did anything more than one night stands at Carla and Jack's. It was always on with the show.

He found Colleen waiting in the study. Supposedly she had developed a fancy for the writing of poetry, and supposedly he was to teach her the rudiments of the craft, and how could he refuse at five dollars an hour. But after reading some of her doggerel, he decided she only wanted to talk to someone she could trust.

Mother was not yet up, so she had unbraided her long hair and was passing a comb through it like a downward swooping wing. Wearing lipstick, she had a compact set out stagily on the table, and with notebook on her knees, she might have been a young sibyl ready to read the implacable leaves.

"Well, Mr. Grafton, what did you think of the party?" she asked.

Perversely, an exquisite arrangement of roses loomed from the bookcase like a living Fantin-Latour, a lingering reminder of what a superior production Carla had achieved. Ben had to admit the damn woman had talent.

"Beautiful, beautiful. . . ." he ruminated while he collected his thoughts, wondering why America had to have so many bright, penetrating, disgruntled children these days.

"Really?" Colleen opened the compact and looked at her face. Was she, Ben wondered, trying to flirt with him?

"What do you want me to say, Colleen? I was the guest of your father and mother."

"Oh?" Colleen got up, walked around the room, managing to pause in front of the flowers.

"Yes, I think so, anyway." Ben was forced to look up at her. She was as mythical as her mother, but it was too early in the morning to be stalked by Diana. Why did these females always remind him of some uningratiating deity?

"Really?" she said again. "Mother and Father never entertained anyone in their lives."

"Well, they certainly fooled a lot of people last night." Ben smiled, gave her his "good," sweet, gray-eyed look.

"You, too, apparently. I thought it was horrible, every minute of it. I told Mother so, and she slapped me."

"What did you expect her to do? Smother you with kisses?"

"No. But I didn't expect you to lie to me."

"Wait a minute, Colleen. Not so fast. Again, I ask you, what do you want me to say?"

"Something more than, beautiful, beautiful. . . ." She mimicked his way of talking and then laughed, her natural self playing as fleetingly over her features as a delicate facial change by Marcel Marceau.

"Okay, skip it. But at least you'll grant it *was* interesting as long as you could forget the essential horror of the occasion." His brain was soft as an oyster, and he simply paraphrased a remark made by Eliot.

"Yes, I know. T. S. Eliot said that."

"Is there anything you *don't* know, Colleen?"

"Yes, I thought I knew, but now I'm not sure, whose side you're on."

"Oh, for God's sake, Colleen. There you go insisting on absolute choices. Can't we just for once be Negatively Capable, as Keats used to say, and let the parade pass through?" With a hangover as determined as the Seven Sins, it was too much to be faced with the Conscience of the Graysons. Colleen could be a maddening child, as uncompromising and oblivious of the shades of meanings and values as an allegorical figure. He quickly opened his folder, took out a miserable sonnet the girl had mailed to him and vivisected it with the moral earnestness she hoped he would apply to her parents.

A further development of the party was that the Hills were finally invited to one of the small, select dinners at the Graysons. The Vreelands had also been asked, Gloriana hardly able to conceal the fact that having capitulated, she meant to go all the way. The presence of Larry Caulfield, the art critic, and his wife Rachel had been used as the bait of the occasion.

But Wade did not like Larry, a dark, aggressive, little man, at the moment busily promoting Ad Reinhardt whom Wade loathed, and Mary had met too many important artists to be impressed with Barry Sax, a Western painter á la Frederic Remington. Nevertheless, she decided to be amused by him, and that, Carla saw with relief, was something.

Claire McConnell, whom Carla figured she might as well have around as often as possible to see if *that* needed looking into, simply plied her trade among all the men, tall, blonde, glamorous as the Lady of the Lake in white chiffon. Passing hors d'oeuvres, replenishing drinks, Wayne Thornton, a young vassal from Beth Lomax, sweated profusely in his armpits, and glowed with the wonder of it all.

But it might have held together if Carla, annoyed by Wade's patronizing manner with her celebrity, hadn't decided to take him on again.

"By the way, Wade, I've been discussing your Picasso with Larry who saw it in a show. He agrees with me." Carla looked as lavish and unbending as a gladiolus in her long orange-yellow gown.

Wade had had three drinks by then and was absolutely in no mood for her. It was too bad it had to be done in her house, but this was her evening to be disposed of once and for all. He looked down his long patrician nose as if she had disturbed him in the private gallery of his choicest thoughts.

"Really?"

"He doesn't like all those heavy black lines in the picture." Carla's mahogany eyes, Wade thought, revealed her true nature. They were as primitive as anything in Gauguin.

"Ah, so that's it. I suppose, dear girl, you don't realize that the whole definition of the painting depends upon those heavy black lines, as you call them." He was aware that there was always something faintly sexual about their encounters. She meant to seduce him or subdue him yet.

"Larry was wondering too if the picture had been authenticated," Carla said with her most innocent smile. It was taking longer than she had expected, but this ought to hit something vital.

"He would." Wade acknowledged her connoisseur at last. "Critics nowadays are so phony themselves they think everything is suspect. Well, you might tell Mr. Caulfield that Mary and I have met Picasso several times, and we bought the painting from him. It is inscribed to us on the back."

"I still don't like those black lines." It was all under water but Carla had the satisfaction of feeling her remarks cutting like crocodile teeth. Too bad that Wade wasn't more of an obvious bleeder.

"Well that's your privilege. You're wrong, of course. I don't know why you bother, Carla, darling. Everyone doesn't have to know about art."

Carla's knuckles whitened around her highball glass, and she opened her mouth to let him have a lethal surface charge from her high-voltage good looks, but he unplugged her as if she were a tall handsome lamp standing beside him. "Don't let me keep you, dear, from your other guests."

At the dinner table, even Carla felt like cringing at some of Larry's cheap humor and New York talk, and his dark little wife tasted the food as if she wondered if it were kosher. How different they had seemed when she had met them at the governor's house in Albany. Still, the Vreelands upheld their allegiance. Wayne never flagged, Claire kept her eyes off Jack, and Carla might have been able to close in on the Hills busily tantalizing Barry Sax with the hope of a sale. But the September evening had grown cool, and someone—was it Claire?—asked if the fire in the dining room could be lighted. But the maid forgot to open the flue, and in a few moments the room smoked like a barbecue pit. Hastily opened windows chilled the bare arms of the ladies, and one could have written finis to the evening with the mascara running down their cheeks.

But Carla did not buckle. Keeping her guests in their seats, she simply force-fed them their dinner, glaring at Wade as if she would brand him with a poker if he said one word. Suddenly Jack, who didn't plan to lose this one either, rose and drank a toast to his wife, complimenting her for "her courage under fire." Wade bit his tongue, but joined the others in lifting his glass to the Princess.

Jack took over after that, taking the men into the study for brandy and cigars as if he were leading a director's meeting. But there was still a smell of recalcitrant animal in the air. Wade stood outside the circle, refusing to enter the corral. Carla had complained privately about his behavior before dinner, and Jack decided to expose the son of a bitch to his *pièce de resistance*.

Wade, who meant never to be looked down on by anyone if he could help it, was offered a seat in front of a handsome, highly polished saddle rest which was as out of place as a coach in a throne room, but had been accepted as one of the "effects." Conveniently discovering that there was no other chair, Jack mounted the saddle rest and began to bear down. Every remark was like a cattle prod, every retaliatory gesture on the part of Wade received the whip of irony. Jack chased him around the range of his thoughts on art, politics, life in general, with the quickest lasso in Connecticut, and when Mary came in to get him, he had been thrown and tied. No one, but no one, was going to mess up Jack Grayson's rodeo.

When Wade told him about the dinner party the following week, Ben Grafton wondered how Meadowmount could mix so many myths at once. Jack was the Marlboro Man, but he was Theseus too. And Wade was the Minotaur of the evening. Wade was the only person in town who had ever dared tell either of the Graysons the truth, so he had to be gotten. Yet, he could suppose that, deep down, Jack might have a savage respect for Wade, might even subconsciously identify with him. Ben wouldn't bet the whole ranch, but half the ranch, that there was something in Jack that wanted to be as sure of himself and yet as free from convention as Wade Hill could be when it suited his purposes.

Of course, he kept reminding himself, the cowboy pose, the taurine implications, might be as superficial as a Zodiac charm of Taurus on a lady's arm. It might be there for nothing but show. The hardest thing of all was to know whether another human being contained any depth, if not a labyrinth, even so much as a maze on the surface of things.

But—and nothing so far had been able to entirely dissuade him—there just had to be. All of this powerful shining energy and grasp, this frightful, complacent skill and arrogance would blind God himself if it were not rifted inwardly. There had to be a darkness and something moving in that dark. Otherwise it had a kind of unreal science-fiction monster horror and heartlessness about it. Unless, at the very moment he threw his opponent, Jack knew that Wade Hill might very well rise from his knees to haunt him again, all was lost.

About a year later, it was learned that Wade had been quietly buying up Beth Lomax stock, and had aligned a number of directors on his side. Wade, who had not expected things to fall into place so easily, had the satisfaction of knowing that old money still counted. Profits at Beth Lomax began to drop at about the same time, labor trouble broke out, and the fast horse between Jack's legs began to look like a bucking bronco.

But Jack reacted, as he had always done to any setback, with increased aggressiveness. He persuaded Matt Vreeland and others to help him fight the takeover, but they had not counted on the fact that Wade Hill could be as implacable as Javert.

Then the plant was struck for three months, and, shortly before, Jack had fired the man who could have been his ablest negotiator. Wade had a nose for all of this disintegration of morale and direction, and, as he told Ben Grafton, he intended to keep Jack Grayson for quite a while under "reality's shower bath." Since it was an old-fashioned one and he had loaded the tank, and held the chain, there was simply nothing Grayson could do but come clean.

Nevertheless, Jack held on, but he became increasingly irritable and high-handed with his junior assistants, and there was a mounting atmosphere of crumbling hopes and last days around the office. Wayne Thornton began to look like a man who was ready to sprinkle gasoline on his boss and fly out from the beleaguered bunker. Vreeland, always willing to change his bet on a horse in the middle of a race, was seen to be dining at the Hills.

It was Carla, everyone said, the girl of spun copper, who kept Jack going. Carla personally got control of a large block of Beth Lomax through her family connections, and nothing, Ben Grafton said, but a deathwish could have prompted Jack to alienate her. But he was increasingly seen driving around town in his Cadillac with Claire McConnell, and even Althea Stone found herself tentatively bonding with the others. All except Colleen. She had decided to take her father's side. People claimed to have seen the three of them together, Claire was reputed to have given Colleen her first drink and her first package of cigarettes, and Althea managed to convey this information to Carla.

Not long after, Ben Grafton, who always seemed to be on hand for crises and denouements, had finished his lesson with Colleen, and they had gone out to the stables to look at a new horse Jack had given her for her birthday. Colleen had changed into jeans, a wild-looking blouse a flower-child boyfriend had given her, and was full of herself that morning, reminding Ben of Carla's blood-confidence, her ability to dominate those around her with her particular mood.

Yellow-shirted, her jodhpured hips like a perfectly shaped brown heart, Carla was in the paddock preparing to give "Gift of the Gods" his morning workout. "Gifty" was a beautiful but unmanageable chestnut who responded mystically to Carla's touch. He would not let Jack or Colleen come near him, and it was a joke around the house that they did not have the right odor.

Colleen was explaining this to Ben in as negative a way as possible when Carla cantered over. She looked unusually tough and resilient as though her veins were running with liquid ore.

"Where do you think you're going looking like *that?*" she asked without so much as a good morning to Ben.

"Like what?" Colleen wiped one hand on her jeans as if it had broken out in sweat.

"You know perfectly well what I mean. With your hair hanging down around your shoulders and wearing that revolting-looking blouse. I've told you a hundred times I won't have you going around like a hippie."

"Daddy said I could wear whatever I wanted to. I'm sixteen now."

"Don't daddy me. And while you're about it, put out that cigarette."

Colleen took a puff in silence, blew it through her nose like a hardnosed little idol. Some of the smoke drifted toward "Gifty's" nostrils, which twitched nervously.

"Where did you get them anyway?" Carla cleared the air with her hand.

"Claire gave them to me." Colleen shared a meaningful leer with Ben.

"I won't have it, Colleen. I won't have it." Carla was preparing to dismount when Colleen rushed at her, riding crop raised, and gave "Gift of the Gods" a quick lash across his face.

The horse reared as if he had had enough of human beings and meant to go back to his celestial donor, and Carla fell from the saddle, a bronze figure transformed into flesh in the downward chute. Even so, Colleen kept beating the horse, dancing out of reach like an avenging fury, darting back and forth, screaming hysterically until a groom ran out and caught him just as he came down on Carla with his front legs. To Ben the whole scene had about it a kind of violent, destructive, historical feeling of equestrian statues falling in the square, and though he phoned the doctor, called Jack, and saw to Colleen, he did not feel equal to rising to the occasion like a dictator who might sweep in at a moment of disorder and deliver a quietus.

Carla broke several ribs and her right hip, and was in the hospital for three months. But the hip did not heal properly and she was finally sent home in a wheelchair. Everyone suspected paralysis, but Carla kept implacably silent, pushing herself around in what she called her "little chariot." Jack did not respond to this latest blow with good grace—all he needed was to have a sick wife on his hands—and, though more discreetly, he was still seen around town with Claire. One felt that the portals of the Grayson world were not being well protected with one half of the Janus-figure no longer at its post.

Almost, it seemed, from a plan she had in her desk, Colleen took over the management of the house. Ben Grafton thought it had an Ethan Frome touch about it, and he found his heart going out to Carla. What was Carla grounded after all but just another beautiful girl who had accepted America at face value? Carla succeeding was monstrous, but Carla failed was like a nearly fatal pause in the romantic heartbeat of the country. Ben loved beauty no matter how thinly molded and empty, and Carla who sat so straight and determined in her wheelchair was like a golden figure bent in the middle, desperately trying to regain erect stature, her poor legs sodden with betrayal. Why did we produce such women if we did not want them? What expensive delusions of spirit required these Golden Girls of the West? Ben wished with all his heart he had the Midas touch and could apply it to Carla's legs.

But perhaps Ben had been too poetical, too soon, for Jack was still abroad. The labor trouble had been settled, there was a chance he might regain control of his company, the men at least were taking a milder view of Claire McConnell. Jack remained Theseus though hooked by the man-bull and holding a hand over his groin. Capable of many roles in any myth, Wade Hill, like Minos, still fed the beast on a diet of Jack's problems. But the thread was in other hands, and Jack might still put the ambivalent monster to the sword. Or did he now only want to set him free?

Althea Stone for the first time began to try to understand the Graysons, and she found to her surprise that she did not entirely dislike them. If they were not where they were, someone else would be. With the help of Ben, who thought the Minotaur mythology too misty for her practical nature, she began to see Jack as something mineral and necessary—a geode around which our glittering dreams accreted. Perhaps it was not wise, after all, to crack open the rich encrustation, as Wade Hill was trying to do, and release nothing but a faceless emptiness.

"Philosophies" began to abound, but, as they had always done, people miscalculated the imponderables. They would not have realized that it was crippled Carla who was still abroad. People born with the sacred glow of complete confidence are indeed a priestlike cult. If they go down, they go slowly like burning figures sinking in the sand. They mean for the last light of the world to come from them.

Meadowmount, which wished essentially to be sweet at least around its rim, disguising its blemishes as best it could, was only superficially acquainted with its own gods. What might go on in the mind of Carla, faced with a hopeless situation, was alien to most of its modest citizens. Ben Grafton might come up with some such phrase as "the nobility of violence," but few would have said that she was sane and clear-eyed when she shot Jack while he was practicing his rope tricks near the paddock.

She had come down the ramp specially constructed for her and surprised him with his back turned. Jack had taught her to be an expert, and Carla had not meant only to wound. The police said he bled like a bull and that, when they arrived, Carla was sitting beside him, dry-eyed, almost as if he were the prize he had promised and never delivered. She might be a glowing stump in the earth now, but not one policeman wanted to be the one to drive that light into the ground forever. Who would have thought that such a beautiful woman would do a thing like that?

But Ben Grafton would. He could understand that someone could belong to a community in the nation that might soon solve its racial problems, eradicate poverty, land a man on the moon, beat the Russians to the next planet, be one of the dispensers of this power and finesse, and still shoot her husband on a beautiful June afternoon. It was not simply that it was too much for one person to be a part of, and then lose, this spectacular dominance, but that Carla had decided to withdraw her support, and she had done it as an act of vision.

If it were not self-love, it might even conceivably have been a late, last act of love for Jack. The sacred fire burned out so much around it, left so much blankness. One could never be entirely sure what it had meant.

Skunk in the Skimmer

When Nan phoned to say that John Kramer had at last agreed to pry himself away from New York and would be coming with her to Houghton Bridge, Elizabeth wondered what her niece had in mind this time. Was it a peace offering, an overture of sorts, or just another attempt to show that her kind of life could produce a man like Kramer?

But why Kramer especially, unless she were still making it with him and had some political reason for wanting to show him what she had come from? Of course, and Elizabeth had to admit the unappetizing thought, Nan would not have counted among his disadvantages the fact that Kramer had reviewed about every other poet in sight except her Uncle Rutherford. Nan always enjoyed something negative stuck in the situation somewhere.

Well, Nan would have to get up earlier than she normally did to think out all the angles. Any day of the week a seasoned campaigner like herself could put down the pins more firmly and cannily. For her niece, with all of her rigid devotion to mod styles of living, was persistently vague. She flashed an aggressive enough image, approaching, as it were, legs first in her miniskirt, thereafter trading on her large myopic blue eyes, hair streaming down to her shoulders as if someone had poured a bucket of gold on her head. Until recently a kindergarten teacher in a ghetto school, when the going got rough she accepted the monthly check from her father and started a series of methodical, essentially asexual affairs, including "a pleasant three months' physical relationship with John Kramer," as she blandly described it to her aunt. Curiously ungiving, a narcissist who clouded every pool into which she looked, she was addicted to passive moods or was tactless in the extreme, as when she said to Elizabeth when they were having tea during her last visit to Fieldrock that it reminded her of a scene from Pinter.

Let her flap the generation gap as much as she pleased, the real competition was Kramer. But, considering the fact that he had taken up with Nan, what would he be like? Elizabeth in a sense "knew" and admired him, but at a distance, through his reviews of

drama, films, paintings, what have you. And the "distance" was a
good part of the problem. Rudd's career had never succeeded
enough for them to know many writers on equal terms. Consequently, Kramer was like someone she had talked to on the telephone and built up an attractive and interesting image, only
perhaps to find that it would actually pour itself into an entirely
different mold.

Moreover, with all of her confidence in this sphere, she had to
admit that an ironic difference of modern life was its slowness and
laboriousness if one attempted to produce such an occasion as she
had in mind. Her own mother had been borne through life as
though her feet, and her hands as well, were bound like those of
the ladies of the Chinese court. But there was simply not any help
to be had in the country, except once a week the uncertain assistance of black Mamie who compensated for being the size of
three by allowing each of them to rest separately. Suggesting a
crisis, Elizabeth wheedled an extra day out of her, and they went
through the house cleaning and polishing each item as if presenting it for auction.

But when Rudd drove to Meadowmount, which was the bus
stop for Houghton Bridge, he had the feeling that they had
overdone and might not have as much to give to the occasion itself
as Elizabeth had hoped. He was half an hour late, and, though it
was Nan who had confused the schedules, they looked at him
distantly as he drove up in the station wagon he had washed the
day before. How would this pair fit into the drama Elizabeth had
in mind? Nan in black miniskirt, panty hose, and leather jacket,
with her long hair for some reason done up tightly, resembled a
refugee from an Apache dance, and Kramer, though conventionally dressed, appeared to be smelling something bad. He
looked ten years older than the picture he used in his publicity,
though still a good-looking man of perhaps forty-five, tall, dark,
large-headed, with curiously small, undeveloped hands, but his
expression was his main characteristic—somewhere not far off,
the universe had quite recently defecated.

Perhaps it was a little insane to think so, but Rudd's impression
that these two would be leading with the nose was reinforced
when he suddenly remembered that he had had to haul a tweed
jacket and slacks out of winter storage because of the coolness of
the late September morning.

"Mmmm. Mothballs," Nan said as she took the seat between him
and Kramer, and Rudd felt as if he had B. O.

During the drive to Fieldrock, Meadowmount and then

Houghton Bridge had never looked more unappealing, proud as he was of the little white towns. They could have been made of molded cream cheese, bland and even uninteresting of odor, as far as this pair was concerned. They were after something gamier—that was it—they meant to root. What was the scent of a man who was trying to give them such a pleasant picture of Connecticut?

Elizabeth was waiting by the pool, and Rudd felt the balance immediately shifting the other way. She had never looked more stunning in her white wool suit, as if she had clairvoyantly planned to give them light in contrast to Nan, opening the visual cloture with a powerful hand. Elizabeth, Rudd thought, had enormous projective power, despite her dark coloring managing always to seem warmly luminous, exuding the most enigmatic confidence this side of the Mona Lisa. If anyone could pry them open with a wedge of her world, she could. She had been right to meet in the garden. With the blue pool, the pink canvas chairs, the giant clamshell on the flagstones, she was leading with beauty, and yet it was meant to be open and accommodating—if they had anything to offer, it could breathe here. There was nothing to smell but the flowers.

Nevertheless, Kramer looked at the pool and observed, "Kidney shaped," as if it actually reminded him of viscera.

"Oh, yes," Elizabeth said pleasantly. "We thought the flowing line would enclose our terrace better. We are not as square as we seem."

"Isn't it a lot of trouble to keep up?" he continued, and Nan looked pleased that he was taking that line.

"No more than it's worth," Elizabeth quickly countered. "Rudd's gotten some of his best poems out of that pool."

Kramer still looked at the water as if it were tinted urine, and Rudd was embarrassed at Elizabeth's remark, for it had not been a simple matter of pool equals poem. He diverted Kramer's attention, explaining how the filter worked, how the skimmer removed the surface scum leaving the depths limpid, the amount of chlorine put in daily, and the weekly ablution with algaecide.

"Then it is a lot of trouble," Kramer said. Nan giggled, and Rudd wondered if they would not have been happier with a muddy wading pool that stank of little boys who relieved themselves.

But Elizabeth still looked as cool as a queen in Africa. No one would ever need an Airwick within a hundred feet of her. She offered Kramer a drink or a glass of sherry, but he declined even that in favor of a Fresca and proceeded to concentrate on the hors d'oeuvres.

She gave him a literary cue and waited to see if he were not Pavlovian in that respect at least. He answered then, talking through a mouthful of cheese dreams, but apparently he would not "give" until he had made it sufficiently clear in what direction he meant things to go. His personality could rise and drop through any setting like the mercury in a thermometer, registering hot or cold without regard to anything around him. Even Nan gave him her Woman's Liberation look, but he made it clear that the only voyage he meant to share with her was on that ship between her thighs.

Any piece of the puzzle which was picked up and offered did not quite fit the picture. Rudd tried the modern poets and then relaxed chronology and went back and forth. Milton? Rudd might as well have said *merde,* and it did not matter that Eliot *had* finally said we were now to be permitted to read him again. Yeats? Well, yes, but then there were his fascist politics and the screwy Madame Blavatsky stuff. Melville? Leslie Fiedler had proved why *that* book had been written.

Elizabeth tried a different tack, offering a few negatives of her own, and Kramer quickly yielded the seat of the scornful. Dickey? The best contemporary poet, better by far than Robert Lowell. Jorge Luis Borges? A minor eccentric? No, indeed, second only to Nabokov among contemporary writers.

She recognized the switch and doubled back upon herself just to see what he would say. "I don't care for much of Dickey's poetry. But, of course, there's the criticism."

"Drivel. The worst kind of slop. He thinks Roethke is the greatest American poet."

"What about *Deliverance?* I thought it was sort of groovy in parts," Nan said, and smiled placatingly at both of them.

Elizabeth let an ambiguous look pass over her face, and Kramer cackled, "An outhouse novel. Written on the Sears Roebuck catalogue. Strictly sub-sub-Hemingway southern!"

The day had warmed to an apricot glow, and Elizabeth invited Kramer to take off his jacket. He took off his tie as well. The bastard would like to strip to his shorts, Rudd thought, and was amazed at how vehemently he had begun to dislike a man he thought he admired. But then he had never seen his ideas spread out in patchwork before. He and Elizabeth read him intermittently in the newspapers and journals and liked the way he could impale a phony. But it was clear now that they had liked him for his dislikes, always supposing that these were the bright bitter links of larger enthusiasms.

When Elizabeth led the way into the summer dining room, Kramer's priorities descended abruptly. Nothing more was said about literature while he ate voraciously without complimenting Elizabeth on a single dish.

But Nan saw her chance and came to life. Though eating like a bird herself, she had decided to make a human thing of food. She asked Elizabeth about recipes and culinary techniques and discussed how she might adapt them to her own use.

"I figure the best thing I can do for a man is to give him a good meal," she said. It was nice really, and Elizabeth would have responded warmly, but Nan managed to cloud the gesture, smiling with complicity at Kramer as if it were time to draw out dear old Aunt Elizabeth now that she had taken such a beating around the pool.

"The second best, honey. The second best," Kramer said, winking at her.

He finished off his lunch with another slice of Elizabeth's speciality, peach pie, and was ready to engage in a diatribe against Italian opera after he discovered that she liked it. Elizabeth lit a cigarette, wondering if it were only that she was getting touchy, or did she see him wave his hand in front of his face as the smoke drifted his way? It was becoming almost mystical how mismatched they were, passing the hemlock round and round as if it might become so bitter it would be sweet. Why did they sit in such uneasy conscience with each other? Let them start talking, and their values dispersed like billiard balls.

Elizabeth went into the kitchen and returned with a pot of coffee. Apparently, she and Rudd, and she had every reason to believe anyone of their sort, produced an automatism of antithesis, a revulsion against the compatible, in a man like Kramer. Why did people hunt each other down these days as though the scope of life, supposedly so broad and free, were curiously narrowed? It did not seem to be a question that could be answered around a luncheon table. Perhaps it needed some grave Last Supper grotesquely overlooking the disordered streets, a cold banquet table on the moon, or squatting figures eating around the fire in a cave.

They went out onto the porch and slumped in their chairs, all except Elizabeth. Her interior monologue notwithstanding, she still gave every appearance of having at her disposal some broader grasp of things which was also somehow finer, as if, no matter how much went in or how coarse it was, she sat in a handsomely filtered place.

About three o'clock Rudd suggested a swim. Kramer was non-combative; one could sense he thought he had a terrific build, and Nan liked anything undressed. Rudd changed, found them in the kitchen, that center of profound interest, spoiling the occasion for Kramer with his swimmer's physique and deep tan.

Nan saw this at a glance, and as Rudd passed her she leaned forward, widening her nostrils. "Oh, Lubriderm. It's great, isn't it?" she said. The nasal approach, the nose treatment again. She had borrowed one of Elizabeth's best-looking bathing suits, which showed off her legs, and Rudd supposed she had come up out of a slump in mood to knock off a male chauvinist. He had never been able to "uncle" her, and their relationship had always been ambivalent. She sexed him when Aunt Elizabeth wasn't looking, but drew a blank whenever he tried to act like anything but a possible penis. He had tried to read her some of his poetry once. One that had some bearing on civil rights went over since she transformed it mentally into a placard for a street demonstration. The rest, with their ambiguities and attempts to see both sides of a question, came out like bad breath.

And yet he had wanted to like Nan without in any way pater-nalizing her. He knew that her mother and father, for different reasons, had been a lot to take. But Nan with all her Esalen theories was really an untouchable. She looked like a swinger and had done a lot of casual laying about, but Rudd would bet that, in fact, she had a cold fish between her thighs.

Left alone with them, Rudd felt rather lost without Elizabeth, who had other things to do in the house. He did not have her power to stand like a column under any sinking occasion, and the situation became architecturally unsound the moment she left. He contented himself with a physical gesture, diving into the pool and flashing back and forth in the sun like a great firebird. It was a hostile demonstration—he wanted to arouse Nan sexually and subdue Kramer acrobatically. This was the sort of breakdown which could occur these days. A poet made his pitch on the level of a rejected child and had the sickening feeling that it was the only time he had communicated.

He went up to the house, leaving Nan and Kramer whispering and nuzzling by the pool. They wanted to breathe their own air. So let them. The Critic and the Concubine. He could not get over the feeling that they clung together out of unacknowledged ter-ror. It was a power group based on Nothingness, so what could have been more unsettling than this encounter with two who were apparently True Believers. Talking away, they were like radios left in a garden to scare off the animals.

That was one side of the picture, the half more flattering to himself perhaps. But flip the image—as he went back to the house, he might be seen as someone they could easily discount. Places like Fieldrock these days were little more than cages in disguise. If they had roamed uncertainly beyond their urban world, they meant to toss in poisoned meat if they could.

He left them alone for an hour, but it made him nervous as if there were indeed strange creatures wandering around the sound of their voices. He went down to the pool tentatively, and the little radios seemed to blare a little louder.

"Anyone like a drive?" he asked casually as though he had set out a bowl of milk for an indifferent animal.

Kramer thought he would not. He had this sound going now, and it seemed to be doing its work. Even the sun glowed like a captive audience; it did not belong to Rutherford and Elizabeth Graves anymore. But Nan, for some reason of her own, said, "Sure. Just give me a moment to change."

She sounded softer now. By all odds she should have been the pussycat in the setup. She was strokable, visually supple. If she had only recently acknowledged the relationship, she still belonged subterraneously to Elizabeth's world. Kramer trusted her as much as he could trust anyone. She should have been the one to say to the three of them, in Colette's phrase, "We are all one flesh." But would she ever realize, Rudd wondered, that her generation had had enough of a revenge on his?

Kramer, however, would not budge, impassive as a large solipsistic stone animal Rudd was once more trying to feed. "Let's go, Jack," she insisted. "Have you forgotten that you're a guest?" She looked uneasy, though, stepping back into Elizabeth's world of manners. It threatened the image to ever commit an anachronism.

"That, love," he said, getting to his feet, "I could never do," and he glanced at Rudd as if he were Clyde Beatty holding a chair.

As he got them into the station wagon, he and Kramer in front, Nan insisted on sitting in back—could it still be, he wondered, because of his scent? No, that would not do. That was viciously baiting his own mind. He would mesmerize them somehow, put them into an agreeable trance, at least give Elizabeth that harmonious gift for all her trouble. Moreover, it would not be too difficult. It was such a lovely afternoon to show them the little

white towns surrounded by this superbly leonine autumn landscape. He could relieve his own tensions with an indulgent metaphor—they were on safari through hills that ranged golden, chro-
matically all of a piece, or smeared with blood. Each beautiful tree
would be a trophy to the one who spotted it.

But they were hardly on their way before Kramer relegated him
to the role of White Hunter when he said, "Tell us if we are
missing anything, Mr. Graves. It's been so long since we've been in
the country, I'm not sure we know how to react."

Rudd had been gracious enough to call Kramer unobtrusively
by his first name, but he was the Sahib, and that was that. "Just
look out of the window," he said with a smile. "You'll see what you
want to see."

How could he share his metaphor with them even whimsically?
It would have been fun to think the three of them could play at
anything. But, under any circumstances, could he even chame-
leonize with Kramer. If one persisted, judged in advance that a
certain attitude would be green and rested on it harmoniously,
wouldn't he always resist the accommodation by changing *his* color
immediately, disrupting all prospect of tonal rapport?

Not until Rudd gave up and acted as if he had drawn blinds
over the windows of the car did Kramer settle down comfortably
into himself. Perhaps, after all, he was not quite as wary of a poet
as he was of Elizabeth. Perhaps he was willing to concede that
Rudd, without his Connecticut setting, might be one of them, for
he began to talk about his plans for the future. It seems he had
appeared on the Mike Douglas show with Gwendolyn Mouzon,
author of *Love for All Seasons,* and had given her a bad time, which
the audience found uproarious. Letters poured into the network,
and they were considering giving him a talk show of his own. It
was to be strictly a quality thing, of course—he would have complete control from the format to the guests who were to be invited.

So this was what it was. All of that furious attack on everything
had this pathetic little vapor at its heart. No jewel in the secret
casket. Just this mephitic little desire to succeed. It was so American that Rudd wanted to vomit. Gwendolyn Mouzon was only
John Kramer in drag. All of his fulminations were sad little farts
of repressed ambition. The Nose was just another bad smell.

But could he honestly say that he was happy about his conclusion? Perhaps more secretly, certainly more silently, than Elizabeth, he needed to believe that Kramer had an iridescent center.
Jewels seemed to have disappeared for good into the pockets of
some general, indeterminate, thieving circumstance.

While Rudd listened, Kramer became almost genial, content in the enclosure that contained his own attar, while Nan sat back as if narcotized. When he got out at the house, he even thanked Rudd for "a good trip," and Rudd wondered if he were aware of the irony.

Kramer did not, however, know how powerfully Elizabeth had regrouped her forces. She had been irresistibly drawn to peep into his room while they were gone, and had found his suitcase open. Would it be the only chance she was going to have to see what was inside of John Kramer? A first, ambiguous feeling of someone she was not reaching came to her as she leafed through a folder of clippings of his reviews. If not Rudd and herself, whom had he meant to read them? It had its affinity with the bread box where Melville's *Billy Budd* was found.

She would try again. Changing into a green dress that looked made up from the music of "La Mer," she took them down into the bar for drinks. Kramer had said that England was the only civilized country in the world—well, it just so happened she had tucked away in the basement of her house an exact replica of an English pub right down to the dart board on the wall.

Kramer went directly to the board and hurled darts until it fell to the floor and he was forced to sit down.

"You specialize in surprises, don't you, Mrs. Graves?" he said, acknowledging his surroundings at last.

"Oh," Elizabeth demurred, "we've lived here for a long time. The bar was added only a few years ago. It seemed right for the house."

Nan did not like material allusions, believing, as she affected to do, that as long as there was one child left in a ghetto, no one had any right to be happy. "Wow," she said. "It must have cost a lot."

"No, actually it did not. After Father died it was a gift from my mother, who was a teetotaler. When it arrived on the van it looked like a pile of junk. Rudd and I reassembled it and did part of the installation ourselves."

"You are determined to have the world the way you want it, aren't you, Mrs. Graves?" Kramer spoke as if he were informing, not asking, her.

"Aren't you? As a matter of fact, I believe in going as far as you reasonably can. I don't believe in the age of reduction."

Kramer looked as if he would like to squirt her in the face like a squid.

"Speaking of worlds," Rudd broke in. "Mr. Kramer was telling me he is planning a talk show on television this fall."

Kramer colored. "Oh, I'll probably be canceled before I begin. No one wants to hear the truth these days."

What a lot of patience a man with a folder of clippings required! Emanations from the bread box were beginning to smell moldy, but Elizabeth felt that she had some penance to do for having looked into it at all. No wonder Kramer had set himself up as Nan's Philosopher. And yet the truth of it was that he had nothing to give her but verbal display. The only symposium at his disposal was a talk show, and he was willing to try even that. She could bet that if the show materialized, it would not last long. Kramer had become too organic, too physical in anger. The words would spout out in orgasm. He could find no proper embrace anywhere, his thoughts accumulated in a seminal sack, and then bang again! But, poor man, he was locked into the notion that he never really made contact—it was like Onan spilling his seed on the ground.

Perhaps, and Elizabeth went to the bottom of her thoughts to admit this to herself, Kramer had chosen her as an antagonist because he might have had a good deal in common with her under different circumstances. He had his sheaf of clippings, and she had her collection of disappointments, but kept, of course, in a considerably more capacious box, as Kramer would have been the first to point out. Could no one these days recover from such a circumstance? Her whole mystique of the weekend had been built on the hope that one could. She and Kramer were like siblings who had not inherited equally. But how much longer could intelligent people use this excuse as if it were more important than the fact that what they really wanted was for someone to open the box?

Still, Elizabeth felt, her hand had lingered on the lid long enough. Without telling him that she had glanced inside, how could she point out how much their rage should burn in common? There was a difference, of course. She believed with Isak Dinesen that anything can be borne if you put it into a tale, but he was convinced that it was no longer possible to fictionalize the situation. He still claimed to believe in sex, like Norman Mailer and all the rest, but he did not really. He cohabited with a skeleton which had just enough flesh around the pubic parts for consummation.

All of this came out clearly when she brought him around to his main interest, films. He did not like any of the logical, linear, pre-McLuhan films. None were viewable except the very modern sort and only those that were rated X. Nothing was left but this explosive nervous experience. What passed for reality was only a sequence of vivid images irrationally grouping themselves for dispersal. The world, like people, was either in climax or building toward it. Of course, there was form of a sort, but it was only the place where the bomb was planted.

In contradistinction, Elizabeth led the way into the dining room and gave Kramer the best dinner he had had in a long time. How ironical, Rudd reflected, that it was she in fact, rather than Nan, who would always give a man a good meal. Nothing was said about the dinner from shrimp creole to chocolate mousse, but Kramer took two large helpings of everything and emptied his wine glass frequently. Couldn't he see that Elizabeth had produced this as if it were a final cultural exhibit? He must have seen at least intellectually, but to acknowledge it he would have had to stand for a while in her place among the pots and pans in the kitchen. He could not forgive her for being the only one he knew who had survived.

Elizabeth looked tired after dinner, but she meant to give Kramer one more chance. When he had eaten his last mouthful, he thought he had seen it all and expanded with the confidence that now she could be dismissed as a woman who lived well but uninterestingly.

"I've been wondering all day of whom you remind me, Mrs. Graves," he said, and went on to describe a woman he professed to admire, a managerial type who might have been married to a Washington bureaucrat.

"Then you knew me before we met, didn't you, Mr. Kramer?" Elizabeth asked. "Shall we go into the living room for coffee?"

His last insinuation had done it. She no longer cared if he would be able to look back on the weekend as a calculated progression. Let him think what he liked from this point on. As she turned on the light over *The Girl in the Blue Room*, she let Milton Avery, if he could, convey that he was not to be canceled out by social animosity. Rudd lighted up the six remaining pictures, two more Averys, Charles Burchfield, Philip Evergood, William Thon, and a small Georgia O'Keefe. Would it matter to Kramer if he knew they had bought Avery before he became famous, Burchfield before he died and the prices went up, and William Thon when he was totally unknown? Could one never free even works of art from "the politics of experience"?

Kramer, she was sure, would not have heard about the pictures, for Nan had taken no interest at all, merely asking when she saw them for the first time, "Which one would you save if there were a fire?" as if that were all anyone should be allowed to have. Among their reasons for enthusiasm in inviting Kramer was a favorable review about Avery when everyone else was saying that he was second-rate Matisse.

But Kramer acted as if she had ushered him into Hermann Goering's secret cache. He evinced no interest in Avery now that everyone had acknowledged his importance. To Thon, who had not made it all that big yet, he made a passing bow, and asked Elizabeth if she had read a review he had done for the *Times*.

"Oh, yes. It was one of the things that made us want to meet you. You sounded like such a sensible man," she said, wondering how he would react if he knew she had seen a copy in his suitcase.

Rudd could see that she had had it. He took Kramer off her hands for the rest of the evening, which she spent with Nan, who alternately repulsed and embraced her as Mrs. Graves of Fieldrock and Aunt Elizabeth who unaccountably was somewhat better than her mother.

Rudd sat on the sofa with Kramer, who wanted to talk about poetry again, bubbling over like a sulfur spring. But if his energy flagged and he were not miasmal and mineral as he now seemed, would he surround his listener with the subliminal afterglow of what had been lost, as if there were finally something starlike and long delayed in his antipathies? Rudd decided he preferred to let the spring bubble. Every poet in the country was either a fag or a lesbian, and Kramer was preparing a lengthy study which would be a general exposé of them all. He singled out for admiration several obscure names; otherwise everyone was just a perverted sex life, each man his own little Genet. Kramer's nostrils flared, and he looked as though he could smell in the air nothing but ejaculations that were not his own.

Suddenly he sneezed violently, and tears began rolling down his cheeks. He gripped his throat as if he would force from it some great final bubble of drool and fling its obliterating slime into the corners of the room. Rudd expressed concern, but he looked enormously offended—was this display of weakness all he could show the goddamned Graves outfit when they had rolled out all their power and glory?

"It's the dog," he spluttered as Elizabeth and Nan came over. "I'm allergic to dog hair."

"I don't see how that could be," Elizabeth said. "You haven't come within a hundred feet of Tannhauser, and he isn't shedding." They had been careful to keep the Doberman at a distance, concluding he was not a dog person, but Tanny had given a blast or two from the screened-in porch and the hostility registered.

"It could have been the ragweed," Rudd volunteered.

"It was the dog. I know it was," he repeated, and looked at Rudd and Elizabeth as if they were shedding spiritually if not in fact.

Nan evaporated as she always did when anything difficult arose. Elizabeth gave Kramer an antihistamine, a sleeping pill, and a large box of Kleenex, and left him in the study where he was to bed down on a rollaway she and Rudd had laboriously lugged up from the garage. Let him spit it all out, was her feeling as they went upstairs. She did resent the reference to poor Tanny, though—lovely, shining, black and tan creature that he was. He at least should have been left clean.

About three o'clock Rudd was awakened by the sound of Nan's voice calling, "Aunt Elizabeth, Aunt Elizabeth!" When he went down, he found her at the foot of the stairs in a filmy chiffon mini-nightgown that looked scarcely longer than a brassiere that had gone to seed. Her legs glistened like the curious double stalk of a gaudy Siamese flower. She seemed disconcerted to see him instead of Elizabeth, lifting her hand in a funny little finger wave when she said, "Hi."

Kramer came out as if the master of the house might be raping his girl friend; Elizabeth, tired goddess in a machine, let herself down on some final wire of suspended strength.

"What on earth is the matter, Nan?"

"There's someone in the garden."

"There couldn't be. I sleep very lightly, and I would have heard. You must have been having a bad dream." Elizabeth in her quilted robe felt like a grandmother.

Kramer smiled and seemed to be enjoying himself. Here was everybody piled out, rumpled, uneasy, a disarray of human images. Just shake things up a bit, and you always had Marat-Sade. He looked poised and self-assured, but he did not offer to go outside.

"I'll take a look around," Rudd said, and he considered releasing Tanny, kenneled in the bar because of Kramer and now belting up his powerful bark from the depths.

As he expected, there was absolutely nothing wrong, just Nan, no doubt, with a subconscious desire to be seen in her provocative nightdress. What a fury of nerves a house in Connecticut could contain when it was on the verge of not wanting to contain them at all.

Why? Why? Why? Rudd came back to the question which had been implicitly raised at the luncheon table. Twenty-five years ago a weekend like this would have been a resounding success. It had everything going for it. Even Kramer must have had some sub-merged hope for something better than this armed impasse. Had human beings simply been left in the world too long? Was the youth cult only an admission of what useless antiques we were? Where was the subtle glue that used to keep things together? Was the air too dry or too moist, too thick or too thin? Old things remonstrated and then yielded; the Eames chair soon fell apart, confessing its antiquity well in advance. Nan in many ways was older than himself, who must on the surface look a little period. Moreover, she would soon be hungrily passé in the way of those who have never had their youth, and Kramer was as old as the original stone bench someone had tried to blend into the cave.

The day, the night, the glorious global stretch—they had almost been given up for loss too. The Eternal Charwoman was tired, the slops ran everywhere. Each man huddled under his own little replica of the pollution umbrella. A walk by the sea was like a visit to a cancer patient; the oil slick spread its sliding melanoma. One came home to the cocktail party, dreaming of glow and glamor, to find a group of frenetic people invalidating each other's experi-ence. The human voice itself seemed to be approaching intoler-able decibels. Was the delaying action he and Elizabeth were engaged in only mildly therapeutic at best?

Just to be sure, as he and Elizabeth had been telling themselves for so long they must try to be about everything, he switched on the lights in the pool. "Kramer's Kidney" opened like the eye of the Blue God, absolutely clear and unwavering, curved under the brow of darkness. Though suggesting a vast recumbent figure, one eye heavily lidded in doubt, it also implied, if you had a trace of healthy imagination left, that the powerful struggle for unitary vision was not yet over. In the morning, of course, it would do its basic duty again for those who wished to think of it in urinary terms. Rudd turned off the light as if to give that great observer some restful coup de grâce.

Kramer, Nan, and Elizabeth sat in the kitchen like figured chairs carved by Marisol. They had some milk and cookies and then went back to bed, Nan with a sleeping pill and even Elizabeth with a double-strength one which would give her a chemically induced hangover tomorrow. Rudd took a distraught Tanny up to their room where he pawed the floor and whimpered as if he smelt the enemy below.

Breakfast the next morning was a sore and stiff affair. Eliza-beth, who had slept only intermittently, looked five years older but forged ahead with a "good" breakfast. Nan acted like the little girl who wet the bed but had not been able to empty her bladder luxuriously enough. Kramer's assurance seemed gone—he perhaps had emptied himself too much. His hands shook when he lifted his coffee cup, and he could not look anyone in the eyes. Rudd said very little, but he did not free Kramer from his gaze very often. After Rudd and Elizabeth had complimented her on it, Kramer roused himself sufficiently to say that Nan's dress, which did share some of its colors, reminded him of Mrs. Graves's bathing suit. But it was a tired effort at disparagement, and he soon motioned to Rudd that he would like to speak to him out in the garden.

It was a blindingly clear day, flashing in Kramer's eyes with the retributory vengeance of the Blue God. Apparently he had not been able to sleep and had taken down Rudd's last book from the shelf.

"I've been reading your poetry," he said, and then strained spastically as if he were making an excruciating effort to say something gracious.

"Thanks for letting me know," Rudd helped him. "I shall always remember that John Kramer read my poetry in the middle of the night when he could not sleep and had an attack of asthma."

Kramer looked relieved. He had not had to go on. "Oh, it wasn't that," he flashed acerbically. "Not asthma. It was the dog."

"Yes, I forgot. Poor Tanny—he should have been a Mexican hairless."

But this disconcerted Kramer once more. "You must think me an awful mess," he blurted out. "You'll be glad to know you're not alone. No one likes me in New York either. When I enter a room, they all scatter."

"You don't need to tell me this, Kramer."

"But I want to. Just say it's the gift I didn't bring as a houseguest."

"We're not so different. People in Houghton Bridge only think they like me. I am just a little better disguised." Rudd would almost have preferred to trade blows with Kramer. Penitence suited him worse than the direct attack.

But Kramer meant to have his diffusion. The only thing that kept him together was to be known as the meanest man in town. The phonies clustered around him, and he gave them a blast. It was a reflex action now. Even the halfway decent got the same treatment. People who might have helped him were immediately knocked down. Women were the only anodyne, but the dose had to be constantly increased, and he was running out of supplies.

Even Nan did not really like him—she thought he was important. On and on—Rudd glanced at the pool, and it looked like a ruptured kidney.

Elizabeth had been expecting them to stay for lunch, but there had been telepathic communication between Kramer and Nan all along, and apparently at some point he had taken her aside and insisted that they leave on the eleven o'clock bus, protesting a need to prepare for the opening of a film festival on Monday. Elizabeth demurred but only as much as her own code absolutely demanded, and she was glad that she had not done more when several weeks later Nan wrote one of her vague, pinched little letters from which all but a very few traces of gratitude had been carefully strained. She did say that Kramer had felt better when they reached New York, "glad to be back on his own terf" (sic). Not a word, not a card at Christmas from Kramer himself. Even the briefest thank-you note, Elizabeth said to herself, would have been like a page from some new book, but, then, Kramer did not believe in books anymore. Perhaps it was just as well, filling out the experience, having a curious negative perfection of its own.

The leave-taking itself somehow longed to be tentative, but did not quite make that either. There was a good deal of shuffling around and temporizing until Nan began rather hysterically to take candid shots of "Aunt Elizabeth" and "Uncle Rudd," tired and defeated, which she would send along with her letter, having uncannily managed to get enough of Francis Bacon into her camera to suggest corruptions of which they were not aware. Nan had her own moment, then, hectic, cramped, and small, hastily snatched from discomfiture, but still, at least hers. She had been brought up among scenes like this. It smelled of home, and any acrid human scent was better than none. It meant that she had been so right all along. Fade out, Fieldrock—it had not disappointed her in its disappointments after all.

When Rudd drove the station wagon up to the house, Kramer mumbled something which Elizabeth wished she could believe was "Beautiful, beautiful . . . ," but it came out blurred and would always echo as something like "Terrible, terrible. . . ." Just as well, she concluded later—anything more and language would have begun to hemorrhage.

Rudd could be surgically swift when necessary, and he rushed them to the bus stop as if he were driving an ambulance. He never told Elizabeth exactly what, if anything, was said en route, but, knowing Rudd, she could suppose that he would have held out hope even as he drove them almost forcibly to their own doctor.

When he returned, they sat down in the patio amid what seemed the shreds of a hallucination and had the cup of tea they usually had at midmorning.

Elizabeth, kicking off her shoes, said as she lifted her cup to Rudd, "Never, never again. . . ."

Like an echo, a sharp metallic sound came from the direction of the pool. It continued, the tapping of some very heavy blind man with a thickly shod cane who was circling the pool as an obstacle on the way to the house.

Rudd went down and stood in the sun, massively tired, the gold man within him almost ready for the smelter. At this point one did not need a chimera, or a phantom, he thought, and Elizabeth, the indefatigable exorciser, was more exhausted than he. It was so still everywhere, and yet one might have expected an explosion. It was one of those modern moments when one's fabric is so fatigued and sleazily stretched that there is room for anything.

Another sharp sound, and Rudd saw the lid of the skimmer quake. He went over, thinking it must be one of the frogs that sometimes got in the pool, drowning in the basket, little cadavers the peaceful country thought it should at least propose. But no, a frog could never lift the heavy lid. He got a rake, raised the metal disc which flashed and sent a pain into his head like a beam from a flattened Cyclopean eye, and he caught the first whiff of an odor coming to him like smoke through a water pipe. A skunk, looking as if he had been soaked in the blue pool a concentratedly long time, buried his face in the water again. Rudd gave him the handle of the rake which he refused at first, and then, as if he were aware of his options, clung on, allowed himself to be lifted onto the flagstones. He shook his pelt free of water, took his time crossing the lawn, pausing to gaze at Rudd complacently, the age-old ineradicable sense of his rejective powers undamaged. He did not spray, and then Rudd saw why.

At the bottom of the pool there was a methodically frantic circle of excrement in sections the length of a half-smoked cigarette, too heavy to float and be carried away into the skimmer. Rudd remembered that the spray was a secretion of the anal glands and the foolish animal, following his instincts, had tried all night to rout the invisible enemy. When Elizabeth, too tired to get up, called out to ask what it was, he said, "Nothing to worry about," but as he tried to dip out the filth with the leaf basket, it disintegrated on the way up, dissolving into the solution it had meant to be.

Rudd went quickly back to the house, letting Elizabeth, who

would never come near the creatures, think it was a frog with large ambitions. But he had a feeling she knew, for she would not swim that week though he dosed the pool heavily with chemicals, and remarked, when she finally came down, on how unusually lucid the water was. She seemed a little ghostly though, lovely as Venus returning to the enfabled water with some determined, chastened knowledge of its synthetic blue.

The Lady in the Lavender House

The life of a bachelor in Connecticut is rather like that of an uncommitted delegate in a perpetual primary. The wooing and blandishment never cease. As invitations roll in from one end of the social spectrum to the other, the happy few are almost as titillated with a sense of power as the happy warrior himself.

Moreover, I am a stockbroker, which gives me another hold on human convention. Connecticut is filled with intellectuals who believe they are motivated by their own special brand of idealism alone, but I have never known one, once he has begun to make it, who does not look to his investment counselor for a vote of confidence.

Consequently, I am constantly being offered incentives even to come by for a drink, and no one is more adept at this game than my client, Larry Gant, a Yale psychoanalyst. More often than not, it is one of his more luscious patients whom he has no qualms about offering therapeutically to me. This, of course, has been the basis of an ambivalent attitude, for I have steadfastly refused to return the compliment by being analyzed, preferring to give him tips on the market when he would suggest traumas.

Since I had not responded favorably to his overtures for a while, perhaps he thought he had gone too far in his last offering of a blonde with paranoid tendencies. In any case, I was intrigued when he persisted and invited me for a drink, proposing this time as bait a man, none other than Crawford Arnley himself.

I knew, of course, that Arnley and his wife Jennifer lived further down the road from him in a red barn made over into a studio house. Considering himself an artist on the basis of his wood carving and a little painting, Larry had made a great play for Arnley without ever sharing his friendship with me. It had been no doubt another source of irritation that, though I had been proselytized none too subtly, I would not buy, or accept for free, any of his work but owned an Arnley oil and watercolor, both studies of Jennifer.

So I was not surprised when he could not resist clouding the invitation with suggestions of an Arnley temperament and a wife who had a thing about New England that expressed itself in an allergy to white houses—a surface neurosis which probably tunneled back into the desire to undermine her husband to whom they were as alluring as canvases primed and drying in the sun. Since I live in an old white house myself, I suspect some of this was supposed to rub off on me in a subtle nuance of Larry's penchant for mixing the pleasure principle with a little pain, particularly as I had confessed, in an unguarded moment, a voyeur's attraction to the subject of the paintings.

Larry's house is a large, turreted, stone folly which he had built partly with his own hands and liked to think would still be there when white houses meet their final leukemia. It was late November, and I was glad that we could not be out on the terrace with the uneven stones which stubbed my sandaled toes in warm weather. Though the same bumpy masonry continued inside, it was covered with thick Persian carpets of inferior grade suggesting that the house was afflicted with lymphatic swelling. Vaulted Gothic ceilings, lofts and balconies which featured Larry's woodcarving completed the effect of what a man, born in the backwoods of Canada, would think of as a castle in Connecticut, though some might have seen it as a fortress built on the unhappiness of others.

When I arrived, Larry and his wife Flossie were cherishing the Arnleys. Crawford, particularly, could not have been framed except in the reference of the free-ranging imagination which advances an image and contradicts it with another. He looked like an English schoolboy who had started pubcrawling at an early age— short, stout, a Toby jug up to his face, which had somehow kept the delicate complexion of youth. When you expected an Eton collar, he gave you a turtleneck.

But, strangely enough for a painter, he was, in the end, less pictorial than aural. As I was to learn later, his pervasive and engulfing voice could be deployed even on the telephone as if, thinking you were in New York, he meant to get through anyhow, and one learned to hold the receiver at arm's length.

When Larry introduced me, he said, "Ah, yes, the collector," dropping the hood of a new face over my head. "*The Spanish Shawl* and *The Addict.*"

"Hardly, except for the Arnleys," I said, fighting for airholes. "I have all of twenty-five paintings, few of any distinction."

Larry tittered but looked discomfited, for he had hoped to pass me off as a kind of local Duveen, small, but not too small-time. He thrust his Freudian head between us, the gray beard sigmoid and saffron-streaked, and said, "Come on, Ned. Don't be so modest. You have a Burchfield, don't you?"

Flossie, white-haired, pink-cheeked as a milkmaid, who felt the lumps beneath her rugs as familiar as the clods in her native Tennessee fields, put a large stuffed mushroom in my hand which I promptly squeezed too hard, leaving large greasy spots on the ties of the Master and the Mentor.

"Bull's-eye!" Jennifer's small, hoarse voice sounded far off, buried in a ventriloquist's box, and I loved her from that moment.

She took me off to the sofa, a little strand of secluded beach away from the booming waves of Arnley's voice, and we looked at each other drily.

"Don't mind Crawfie," she said. "He was simply waiting for you to tell him how much you like his work. He doesn't see people, he sees paintings. Of course, Larry should never have told him you have a Burchfield. But Larry's a shitass."

She scratched the unexpected word across my face, but when I reacted as if the cat's claws had been pulled, she continued blandly, "But then you have two Arnleys. Just remind him of that one way or another every time you talk to him. If necessary, get a button to hang on your lapel: I own two Crawford Arnleys."

"You're very kind," I said, trying to decide whether this little woman were Sacred or Profane.

"No, not kind. Not kind at all. Just a survivor." She glanced at Arnley as if he sat in a lifeboat built for one.

"Oh?" I continued simply to look at her. I was having trouble with her face, but the nervous, entwining fingers of her long, slender hands played a nude scene in her lap, promiscuous and desperate.

"Don't feel sorry for me. I'm a goddamned bitch too. Just ask Crawfie. You won't even need to ask him. He'll give you the lowdown. You don't even have to wait for that. Just look at the paintings."

"I have. I like them both, but I can't decide which is you."

"*The Spanish Shawl* and *The Addict*? Oh, Crawfie must have done me a thousand times. He's not through with me yet. That's my secret weapon. That's how I survive."

Neither Arnley or Larry, nor Flossie for that matter, would leave us alone in our cove, but, like cannibals, we had already tasted the flesh of illicit friendship, and meant to have more. What the "missionaries" of Meadowmount were saying about her—that she threw tantrums until Crawford was not above man-handling her a bit—did not disturb me.

It was she, I could see, who would let me in. Genius has as many mysterious archways of entrance as a De Chirico painting, and in all probability Crawford would go out one door as I was going in the other. Jennie might not seem to control the traffic in the plaza, but I had the feeling she could snarl it when she wanted to, and that all the alleys belonged to her. I particularly like people with reservations about the world we live in, so her New England syndrome enchanted me. Most of us protest some tired, faded childhood source for our quirks, but Jennie had Crawford. And what did he have?

Refreshing my memory by turning on the lights over both pictures when I got home, I looked at the flamboyant beauty in a Spanish shawl, more shawl than beauty, for he had gotten carried away in the thick impasto of the work by the fantastic interlocking curlicues of color which could have been lifted from the canvas as a stunning abstract. It was a bravura piece, it now seemed to me, not too brave about the implications of personality. In the water-color, which must have been done right after one of their terrible fights, the shawl of color seemed to have sickened and deliquesced into a purple haze around the body, and I suppose the title of *The Addict* was meant to refer to some obsession or spiritual delinquency of which only he was aware. It seemed, however, the truer rendering, though the other was more "beautiful," and I went to bed thinking what an ambiguous showman Arnley was.

Before our next meeting, I began to gather versions of the Arnleys around town. Far from living exclusively in Connecticut, Jennifer, a ballet dancer of modest talent before he made her his mistress, had come up only on weekends, maintaining an apartment in New York where she pretended to teach, but, in fact, kept a young dancer rather as a pet. A series of Pomeranians the women in his paintings often held were a sardonic reference to this lapdog. At the time, Arnley had no redress, for following Benjamin Franklin's advice, he was comforting himself with a grateful older woman. Once that was over, he cut off the funds, and she came to Meadowmount permanently, prepared to fight with him for the rest of her life.

A few days before Christmas Eve, Jennie called and said in her whisky-stained voice as if she had known me for years, "Honey, how about coming by for a drink. I think I've got Crawfie quieted down for the moment."

I went over with a bottle of brandy for the house and a fruitcake for Jennie only to find the same poisonous, pentatonic group.

Didn't the Arnleys have any other friends, or had Larry broken down and bought a new version of Jennie?

The red barn except for the insulated walls remained pretty much as it was constructed—one large room open to the rafters, a loft where Arnley painted, a small, partitioned-off bedroom, and tiny kitchen. The main room was stacked with canvases, and there had been little effort to conceal the fact that this was where one life moved around and did its thing.

Christmas was obviously not one of Jennie's good times, and she had compensated by overdressing in a long, démodé, lavender chiffon. Did the mascara and the unusually heavy makeup conceal the trace of a black eye? It was clear that they were several drinks along the way except Flossie who never drank. I made a quick decision to alienate Crawford in order to clear a place for Jennifer and myself as rapidly as possible.

"Don't you think you've gone a little too far or not far enough?" I asked as I looked at the generous décolletage in a new canvas brought down from the loft.

"I think you've missed the point," he said to me, but glanced at us all as if we lived in the slums of the imagination. "It's the constriction of the voluptuous I am after this time. Of course, if it shocks you, I am afraid I can't help that. To borrow from Diderot, there's a hint of testicle in everything I do."

"What do you mean, hint, Crawfie. It's the whole ball game." Jennie smiled at him like a *gamine* who had learned to play stick ball with turds.

Anything to do with testicles alerted the analyst. "I like your Diderot quote, Crawford."

"You have my permission to use it with your patients," Arnley said rather ponderously, but he glowered at me.

"Crawfie's all heart tonight, Larry," Jennie purred, and I thought she rubbed her cheek tenderly. "Why don't you show him one of *your* paintings? The one you left at the door when you came in."

"Oh, that," Larry simpered. "A little present. Just put the finishing touches on it this afternoon."

Crawford still looked ready to throw his drink in my face, but Jennifer's hand lingered lovingly on a battered glass ashtray, and I gathered it was one of the little shooting stars she sometimes tossed at his head.

I was struck, as I had been at our first meeting, with a childlike quality in their relationship. Particularly Crawford seemed formed, and yet unformed. A restlessness quivered about him, an ignis fatuus which could light up in the most unexpected places as if the realm of the ego were a modulated, adaptive fairy tale where Tinkerbell was here, there, back into the woods, or just one step ahead. Since wandering lights can provoke mayhem as well as magic, I suspected that this occasion was somehow pinched for both of them, and my remark had not helped. It was not the time when Tinkerbell would light upon the tree.

So Larry and Crawford got drunk in one corner, and we got drunk in another, serviced back and forth by Flossie who did not seem quite sure which udder she should relieve of its bad humor.

"So now you know," Jennie said as we settled down on a love seat much the worse for wear. "That's the man I trusted with my life. Don't ever do it. Don't ever trust anyone with your whole life."

I temporized to give myself time to think that one over while I placed an old Fola rug over our knees. Her dress, thus shortened, had the effect of a tutu, pinkish, silvery, lilac-tinted, just as she had first presented herself to him. I thought, what a moment for an autobiography, and she gave it to me like a Christmas present.

The idea had been that they were going to pursue two arts, but then Arnley couldn't afford a model, and, in fact, could not manage another life in the house. To be fair to him, of course, and Jennie's emotions, so strident in address, breathed in and out like an accordion, all sorts of terrible things had happened. He had set himself on fire when he went to sleep smoking, and soon thereafter fought a difficult battle with cancer. She had matched him combat for combat, having suffered various fractures, once when he pushed her down the stairs, and undergone an abortion which had left her unable to have children.

But, most of all, they had endured together what she called the Long Watch when no one would buy a single one of his paintings. It was like waiting around for the world to change its ways, a new cultural epoch to emerge. Every critic who looked at an Arnley needed an eye transplant. All of his pictures were blue babies which had to be drained of their poisonous fluid and given the blood of the artist. He had to get his transfusions somewhere, so there was Jennifer with her pint a day.

"And you know, I could never do enough for him. I always disappointed him. He always felt I was holding something back," she said.

"And were you?"

"Not at first. And then just a little, a little more, and then, so he thought, a great deal, though, putting it all together, it doesn't amount to much."

I went home asking myself if anyone should ever fully trust another human being. Did more than a trace of the predatory remain in the most civilized of alliances? In everything one wished to accomplish, overhanging it, shadowing it, subtly trying to re-shape it was the qualification of what someone else wanted us to do. One wonders just how many can savor life without being reminded that our self-appointed custodians, and who is without them—father, mother, lover, friend—would have us bite and chew this bit differently, would, in fact, be the tongue to probe the texture and the teeth to grind our exaltations, affirmations, even our sorrows, more exceedingly fine. One of the major pilgrimages must surely be a search for "guests on mild evenings" who do not meddle or impose.

Jennie had given me quite a Christmas gift!

Someone who liked Crawford better, and there were certainly those, could relate that he had a recurrence of cancer which he engaged like the master of life he was, and stood up to his easel in six months. A little later, he set fire to himself again and to his studio, this time with a glass in hand, and a year's work on the female nude was committed to suttee. Moreover, an unscrupulous dealer had some years before, when Arnley needed money, gar-nisheed in advance a certain number of paintings each year at cut-rate prices, and he overworked himself constantly to meet the demands of his "little extra income tax."

Nevertheless, it is one of the laws of life that we promote and demote those around us in order to serve our own emotional needs, and I cannot be caressive of Jennifer without being some-what callous to Crawford. Even among our best friends we con-stantly upgrade and downgrade as though we were repricing stock according to current psychological values. But for a while all I could do was just watch the graph of the ascending black line as Arnley received one award after another and was given a major retrospective at the Whitney. Even his proletarian pictures found buyers—violent and acid scenes of strikes and demonstrations with which he "balanced" his art, in my view tipping it pre-cariously the wrong way for him. The compleat Arnley was in vogue.

After his election to the Institute of Arts and Letters, he quickly cleared out of the red barn into one of the handsomest colonial houses in Meadowmount. It had a red barn in the back, though,

like a remembrance of things past, and that was where Jennifer
established her Arnley School of the Dance in a last gambit against
white Connecticut.

Crawford complained that she had rounded up every fairy in
town—did he mean to include me as treasurer, I wondered?
Nevertheless, he outdid Degas, interrupting the classes with his
demands for this or that pose until, after a few months, Jennifer
closed the place down except for one student, Dabney Dorr, a
combination he must have gotten off a marquee. If Fonteyn could
change her name, why not Dabney, who would have settled for
Margot if the community would have gone along.

When they were practicing a *pas de deux* one morning, Crawford
came into the barn, heavy as Friar Tuck against the light. "Get that
little fruit off the place, or I'll can him myself," he said, and kicked
a stool across the floor in the direction of Dabney who grabbed his
pants and fled.

"I won't, Crawford. I won't, I won't," Jennie screamed and
picked up the stool.

"Now, let's don't get physical," Arnley drawled as he sought a
way to temper his approach. He simply stared, waited, as if with
her arm thrown up, she was incredible and there for him to paint.
In slow motion she put down the stool, stood in a trance, unable to
resist some secret life that blossomed between them, as he said,
"That's it. That's what I want," and led her like a sleepwalker back
to the studio.

But the moment the black line fell and went nearly off the
board, I saw my chance. Crawford's cancer returned, this time
inoperably, and, though he would not admit it, he would never
paint again. But Jennifer admitted it, not to him but to herself,
and the woman I had been looking for stepped forward.

Could one even *see* her more clearly at last? A Spanish blonde
with dark brown eyes—Crawford had been that much right about
her in the title of his painting—the effect of the eyes went in
deeper to a kind of concentrated seriousness of personality.
Under the heavy makeup which she began to wear less and less
was a trim determined little woman who had known from the start
what she had on her hands. Of course, the ballet dancer was there,
the woman with the pampered pets, but were they there except as
a distraction while she dealt with Crawford?

When they had settled down to a routine of nurse and patient,
not without some shooting stars at first, for planetary kings, even
in diminuendo, still attract meteoric showers, I went over to see
them. It was an afternoon in October, and the mood of nature

and narrator was "Ripeness is all." A woman bending over a man constantly and attentively is one of those reverses, one of those changes of role which, sending the man back to the mother, are curiously, curatively, archetypal, and I was attuned to the possibilities of the juxtaposition.

I had heard about the new Mexican maid, Carlota (Shades of the Hapsburgs!), who did not speak a word of English, but I was not prepared for an acculturative fantasy of Mexico and America. Montezuma would have envied her load of "Aztec" jewelry if it had been real. Her sagging skirt simulated lamé, and the final touch was superb—a pair of gold ballet slippers, perhaps as a sop to Jennifer, fitted over thick worsted stockings, indicated she did know where she was after all and that the snows were coming.

If only Crawford could have struggled to the easel, how he would have enjoyed letting go! With nods, bows, and gold-toothed smiles, so unctuous and subservient that I felt like stout Cortez, I was ushered through the house, littered with loaded ashtrays, unwashed glasses, stacked with paintings, altogether reminiscent of the red barn.

Jennifer met me in the hall, drink in hand, and I thought, is this going to be a costume party to conceal from the convalescent the fact that he will not convalesce. She was wearing a voluptuously cut, frilly, pinkish-violet dress of which she seemed to have so many variants, and wore her "stage" makeup again. Arnley had so often painted her as a ballet dancer, and I suppose she simply meant to give him a living picture—a golden feather between the thighs of the dying king.

If we were mummers all, Reality sat in a chair. On a decree of his own, they had gotten Crawford out of bed at the last minute, and there had been no time to dress the principal actor. He had been lying in shirt and drawers which had a tear in a pertinent place, and his penis hung limply down, disavowing the boast he shared with Renoir that this was the brush that had done it all.

Where were all his subjects now? Had they gone into exile at the first signs of deposition, leaving him, perhaps more than most, with a feeling of expulsion and separation. But what can one do but trust, for as long as one can, the sway of the imagination, that ceremony of images which should last forever? My mind to me a kingdom is—poor Crawford, *semper fidelis*, was left with a traitor on his hands.

"Hello, Ned," he said. "It was good of you to come." Incredibly, his voice still boomed, gripped me by both ears, and I recovered and suited him in the form of an English schoolboy who would lay all the maidens come spring.

He had a glass in one hand, a cigarette in the other—the old arsonist would never give up—and there were burns all around the floor like the tracks of some monstrous bird who haunted the possibilities of his ashes.

I don't remember now what I said to the women, with Jennifer bending over him, crooning, "Baby, don't you want another drink?" and Carlota peeping in, her bedizened head like a Mexican sunburst, a little tipsy herself now. I must have made the right impression, however, for Jennifer beamed at me as if a ticker tape recording a rise in Arnley stock flowed out of my mouth, and Carlota was ready to hang a collar of gold around my neck.

But the surprise was Reality itself.

"I suppose you think I never liked you, Hinshaw," Arnley said. That steady way he looked at people and things was now set in his face as if it could not be sustained without rigid concentration.

"I suppose I didn't, Crawford, but then you were in such vast company. How could I complain?"

"Well, you were right, and you were wrong."

"That sounds par for the course. Go on."

"Why didn't you go all the way with Jennie? Why didn't you have the courage of your concupiscence?"—this when Jennifer and Carlota went out for refills in case one fell by the wayside.

"Don't ask me. Ask Jennifer, Crawford. I was just the guy in the middle."

He proceeded as if in fact he were talking to himself. "Artists like me make lousy lovers. You see, there is just not that much time for that much involvement. When you are tired, just a quick trip to the nice old lady down the street."

"You are unique in every respect, Crawford," I said with a laugh. "I have never had a husband to belabor my lassitude in adultery.'

"Don't give me that shit, Hinshaw. We weren't poured out of a piss bottle. You and I know where we came from. The difference was that you had the time. You muffed it."

"And you wouldn't have cared?"

"No, why should I? Jennie didn't just love the paintbrush." He patted his penis. "She loved the paintings."

"So I should have dipped in where angels fear to dip?"

"Yes, God damn it. We should have made it together. A troika with Art holding the reins and shouting do any fucking thing you please, but get it done!"

"Keep the faith, baby?"

"Yes. And keep your mouth shut too!"

I almost added, "Keep the baby, Faith," but I doubt if that would have amused him. Jennie heard the last words as she came in with a tray of drinks, thinking we had quarreled, and I wondered if any man had ever been subjected to a more curious peace plan for the contestants in a romantic triangle.

Among the ins and outs, the hoverings and hints, the mugging faces of the two refugees from the Master's imagination, I had another little session with Arnley.

"I am glad you have *The Addict* and *The Spanish Shawl*. You weren't poured out of a piss bottle," he said, and I did not wonder at his fondness for the liquid metaphor as full as his own bladder must have been. "You know my work. You have seen what I have tried to do. Something sad and something happy. Something bitter and something sweet. Can any man do more?"

And then, "Jennifer will keep the show on the road as long as she can. Take care of her, Ned."

The audience was over, but I turned in the hall to see him, now grappling, in fact, with a urinal, shaking his wilted paintbrush as if a whole sea of color had been left untouched.

But out in the wings the actors had not spoken all their lines.

"You're a livin' doll, Ned. I haven't heard Crawfie talk that much in a month," Jennifer said, and she had an ecstatic, world-of-her-own look on her face.

"He thinks we're in love, or should be," I ventured.

"I know. He always did," she said, and I knew that any important lines I had left were over before they had begun. "He never did understand how much I loved him."

I was not, however, to get off even that easily. Having allowed love its fictive turn on points, Reality relinquished the field to that instrusive sister Fantasy who sauntered over from a guesthouse on a pair of monstrous cork platform shoes. The heavy clop must have drawn my eyes to the floor before she entered, and, like gas rising in a balloon figure, I filled out a travesty of Jennifer. Jackie, her twin sister, stood there to show me the way to go home.

I hate the notion of twins, particularly when they are identical. Fate should never double its odds against us by suggesting how common and repetitive our clay can be. I had never met Jackie, always kept in the background of my Arnley friendship, but the family situation produced her like an understudy.

The surrogate, however, had taken things into her own hands, a gipsy fortune teller who predicted a very bad end for Jennifer and then dressed up to enact the part. Her eyelashes were so thick with mascara that they seemed to need the hydraulic action of her rheumy eyes for elevation. She wore a gold scarf around her head, a treasure of trinkets—borrowed from Carlota, my sister, the Sun?—and a long beaded brown dress. She, too, was a "Spanish" blonde all right, but poured, to use Arnley's scatological verb, from a bottle made by Clairol.

"Hi, honey," she said in Jennifer's voice an octave lower. "What's your hurry. Stay on a while. Live a little. Pull up a chair."

I got out of the house as fast as I could, wondering what in the hell was playing havoc with my images.

Arnley died a month later while I was in England. Jackie had called me on the phone every day until I left, and I felt it was only a matter of time before she would appear on my doorstep. Was this the part of the Arnley ménage which was left to me? I had indeed been too long at the fair.

Jennifer cabled me when Crawford died, and I promptly decided to stay on another month. I didn't call her the day I got back to Meadowmount either. She heard I was in town, however, and rang me up, saying that Crawford had left me a legacy that concerned us both. Would I come over? She said also, to prepare me, that she had not been well, and not to take it too hard. Since she spoke of herself so casually, I am afraid it was the first message that struck home.

With the manner of a sentinel, Carlota opened the door like the entrance of a tomb. She looked as though she had fought to the end for the life of Arnley. The brocaded dress was streaked with the dried blood of ketchup, and the heavy heap of jewelry, greenish with what might have been the tarnish of dungeons, needed a trip back to the alchemist.

Nothing in the grand design of baroque litter had been altered except by increment and addition, and I smelled the old familiar Arnley blend of cigarette smoke, whisky, and paint. Carlota took me down the dark corridor, which glimmered now for me, like the caves of Altamira, with luminescent memories of aboriginal encounters. Had I been one of the elect after all to whom Crawford had tried to introduce the mysteries, the arcana of creation now to be archaeologically buried forever?

Having delivered me like a hostage, Carlota stood guard while I looked past the throne of the former king and saw a woman sitting in a wheelchair. Jackie? For a moment I nearly buckled with anger and surprise. But no, it was Jennifer, the heavy makeup and mascara fitted back over like a burial mask, the pink and white dress once more cut off at the knees by the Fola rug. It must have been the arthritis which had troubled her for years—or was it something worse? She had held the prongs of her body wide open by main force until Arnley died, and then simply folded up like a safety pin.

"Long time no see," she said. The fingers still made love in her lap, even more restively now as if the love story might have a shorter run than expected.

"Yes, Jennie. Long time no see." I kissed her, bending over with empathy for the arc which had bound her and Crawford together.

"Well, let's not be too mournful about it, Ned. Have a drink." She pushed me away gently as if that rainbow were folded into the ground for good.

So we had a drink and another and another, which Carlota brought in, each time more tipsily, hitting me in the face at one point with one of her swinging necklaces as if I deserved that much of a slap for having left the Master to die alone.

But the drinks were what was needed to take us back to the red barn and the days before Connecticut had quite won what appeared to be the final round.

"Do you remember," she asked, after we had remembered so much, "how I said that I had trusted Crawfie with my life? Well, I was wrong. He trusted me with his."

"And then?"

"There isn't anything more. Just that. He trusted me with his *whole* life."

"I didn't know, Jennifer. Or, let's say, I didn't want to know. I suppose I didn't think anyone could."

"It wasn't your fault, Ned," she said ruefully, and for a moment she did release an inch or two of buried iridescence. "How could you know it was a closed corporation?"

"But, oh, the dividends!"

"Yes, the dividends. And Crawfie didn't forget. He thought you were our biggest shareholder." She motioned to Carlota who turned a canvas which had been facing the wall.

It was the last painting Crawford had done, a study of a young ballet dancer á la Jennifer sitting for her portrait in pink and violet tutu. It seemed unusually poignant to me, a final extension of the extended risk Crawford had been taking all his life. He had brought this dominant image forward so long in the face of the merely innovative who would consider the subject old hat without recognizing the triumph passion and commitment can sometimes produce. It suggested a way of turning the stigma, of piercing the critical integument and transferring the debased image to the eye, sinking the tattoo into the heart. I had seldom seen a recent painting that aroused so elliptical a sense of past-present, of the man with the brush who had not insulated or encapsulated himself anywhere in time. Though modern in this very longing for kaleidoscopic feeling, it was done rather in the style of the Madonnas with a landscape in the background—in this case white Connecticut. But in that green valley, with its winding river, among those pristine buildings, stood a lavender house. This was my legacy.

I was appalled at how I had "understood" the Arnleys. Everything that I had seen was, of course, incontrovertibly there, but I had not realized how static and unimportant it all was, the screen around a mobility, a constant, kinetic rendezvous of which I had only superficial knowledge. Nothing mattered but that they should meet, and meet again, in a place where he stood at the easel and she assumed whatever pose he required.

It was curious, though, this lucid space, uncharacteristic of any enclave carried around by others, having a kind of undying resilience. Crawford and Jennifer were continually breaking camp and moving on in search of it, the place itself like a collapsible fitted puzzle with changing contours. I remembered the mystical look on her face as she followed him into the studio after their quarrel over Dabney. She heard the call to congruence, and had attached the missing piece. Nothing, I could see, was more thrilling than this secret basis of their life. When Crawford raised his brush and Jennifer lifted her arm, they performed with elemental certainty, a cessation of metaphysical anxiety. Was there anything like it in this world or the next?

I left Jennifer definitely in the mood of the long fête over. About a week later, the first selectman called and said, "Ned, you'd better do something about your friend, that Arnley woman. You know what she wants to do—paint her house lavender. That lovely old white house. I've argued and argued with her. Told her the town wouldn't stand for it. But she won't listen. Ned, you know as well as I do that people would just as soon see a lady walk down Main Street in purple drawers."

I told the selectman if he didn't mind his own business, I had a good notion to do the same. But after I had slammed down the phone, I laughed until I cried. This cut-and-dried, carefully selected selectman could not understand that he was dealing with a scattered puzzle. The congruence was gone, and, belonging to incongruity, Jennifer had chosen this way of showing it. All of the subtle responses to Crawford's needs and feelings were still there waiting to be called upon, the mating dance of the Model and the Master still yearned for its ineluctable place. What could she do but grasp some startling something which had transpired there and bring it up starkly, brutally, into the light of common day—a substitute to be sure, a form that needed to be surrounded by missing pieces, but something, something.

Poor Jennifer, her mind, I knew, must be like a carousel of colored slides turning in a projector, all of those pinkish, silvery, lilac gestures Crawford had made toward her person. It would come round to her that he had always thought of her as the Lady in the Lavender House, and that the best she could do was "tell it to the world." If Crawford had really meant her to live there with me, well, she would do anything but that. I had, and I could believe that it was the sweetest second best she could allow me, the conciliatory, the consoling, but not the congruent touch.

The workmen were promised overtime, and before the Town Planning Board could assemble or anyone fabricate a reason to get out an injunction, Jennifer selected the right shade of silvery, pinkish lavender and carried out the implications of Crawford's will by fiat.

Having brought the house into the foreground with the sure touch of a painter, she suggested to the town at large that she did not mean to live in tableau, that she might make it into a center for youth with a lilac touch. But her grand gesture did not last long, for the selectman got to Jackie, next in line to inherit, who clomped back on the scene, not wanting any trouble with a Reality she already knew too much about.

Kindly but firmly, since in an eerie sense she might have been doing it to herself, she bundled Jennifer off to Arizona for her health and briskly set about the business of selling purple dreams to people who had never had one. Jennie did not live much longer. As she wrote me, the desert was "not her bag"—no white houses on which to cast a lilac glow. But I could see that it didn't matter anymore.

The new owners of the house called in the painters and restored to its virginal state one more white canvas for dreamers. If it were possible, I think Crawford with his great implacable voice would have boomed up out of his coffin, "My kind of town," in some last ambiguous gesture of the circular and inclusive.

And what about Jennifer lying among the Gila monsters of Arizona? The one who is left with a dream resorts to particulars as

if extending in the face of the absurd a missing piece. I suppose
you could say I was the only one remaining to see the gesture or
care about its erasure or abstraction. Still, painful as it is to return
to the generalized, which controls the world, I have, you might
say, hanging on my walls the model of a particular house for
people who trust their lives to each other. It looks lilac, then white,
lilac, as one searches for its secret place.

The Secret of Aaron Blood

Aaron Blood opened the door of his study just enough to hear Webb and Daniel having a discussion about wiretapping. Webb thought it was an invasion of privacy. Daniel was not sure. They sounded like a television debate—the fallout perhaps from some public affairs program they had heard the night before.

He and the boys were not often on the same wavelength, but oddly enough they seemed now to be providing a marginal gloss to some of his own thoughts. He had been trying to put together a sermon on the banality of modern life—the term applied in somewhat the same sense in which Hannah Arendt used it in her discussion of Eichmann.

As he sat down at his desk and began to collect his notes, he winced at his own desuetude. The morning had wandered off into another stretch of brooding on such matters as how commonplace it had become to shove a microphone in the face of a tearful woman whose husband had just died in a mine accident, bring the wounded bleeding into the living room, give every "crisis" the saturation treatment. It was all in the day's work—nothing should be held back. Even a minister, certainly one of the low men on the totem pole as far as public interest was concerned, was not allowed to have secrets any longer. He was expected to be a pane of glass through which one could see the bland features of God.

Wondering if he could ever make a sermon of such thoughts, and if he did whether he would have the courage to give it, he heard Evelyn coming toward the study as if to say, No, he could not. It was twelve o'clock and lunch was ready. Evelyn had not been a social worker for nothing. Was it unkind to think she had merely transferred her talent for organization from losers to someone she could count on to win? Social causes were ultimately so murky. He was a good man—indeed, a pane of glass where nothing lurked.

The boys, still arguing as he came down the hall, clammed up when they saw him. Webb, the elder, was so handsome, having Aaron's dark coloring, his well-shaped head haloed in short

curls—a vigorous young bull of a boy, yet somehow restive-look-
ing beneath the air of the confident panelist he had deployed
against his brother. Daniel was sandy-haired, wore glasses like his
mother, looked more fragile, but he had Evelyn's reclusive manner, and one wondered if he were not less vulnerable.

Aaron said grace, and they ate their good, nourishing meal in
silence with the knowledge that Daddy had been working and
might still be thinking things over. Did any of it, however, mean
anything; was he at all interesting to them? Was he, as a matter of
fact, really "interesting" to Evelyn? She would find the question
absurd. They kept nothing from each other—shouldn't he know
then that she admired him enormously?

"Aaron, you won't forget you have an appointment with Bennett Jones at four?" Evelyn was cleaning around him, leaving an
exact circle where he could finish his coffee. "And you will remember not to let him upset you?" Her gray eyes in their horn-
rimmed glasses had a penetrating, telescopic quality as if he must
be seen clearly, but at a distance.

"Don't worry." He went over and brushed her cheek lightly. It
was a long time since he had kissed her on the mouth. Was it
several years ago when she stopped wearing lipstick?

As he reached the door of his study, she called down the hall,
"I'll have tea made. Bennett always likes a cup."

Speaking out of their monumental routine, she had cued him
into his expected reflex, and that was all she would say for two
hours while he was shut up in his "tomb," as he jocularly spoke of
the study, "doing his thing." As he looked back down the long,
dark hall, he saw his reflection in the mirror. Well, he looked the
part anyway—tall, slender, lacking all opulent physicality, his eyes
the color of blackheart cherries, his hair almost the same shade,
tinged with red. When he was a young man, people who knew he
was going into the ministry had said he looked Christ-like, and he
resented this since the calendar-art Savior was always presented as
so effeminate, long-locked and pale.

But no doubt he would never have gotten the job at Saint
Mark's if it had been otherwise. He *did* look saintly, he *did* look
spiritual, though he would have characterized his expression
more ambiguously as yearning. A son of Whistler's mother to his
congregation. But to himself? Perhaps Soutine's *Little Priest*.

Down in the green which he could see from his window was his
part of the Connecticut summer, well trimmed and weeded, but
some deviant, perhaps an Italian gardener, had insisted on encircling the war monuments and the fountain with blood-red gera-

niums. Heating up the scene, it was the only thing that related to the down-and-outs lolling around on the benches, the ones the purists had never been able to do anything about. The lumpish, the sodden, the venereal, was not what Saint Mark's was after. It was a kind of filter-church, appropriately situated there at the end of the green. Whatever the city streets had to offer, it meant to have only the crystals left in the sieve.

Strangely though—Aaron could just see it in the corner of his window, breasting the tide of traffic, pseudo-Gothic, heavily smogged—it did not look pure. An enormous clinker, accreted with something or other in spite of itself, it suggested some untoward amalgam. No wonder they tried to keep the green so spotless, so Mondrian-neat. Bennett Jones would certainly have had a hand in that. Bennett had handpicked him for Saint Mark's as he might have expertly selected one of the antique bottles which he displayed on shelves in the windows of his house. Aaron Blood was a quality container, a reliable receptacle, which did not hold anything one could not identify.

Dreading to see Bennett, he could not get on with his sermon. It was going to be a pedestrian affair again, not daring to touch on anything ambiguous or complex. Most of his congregation wanted him to be merely correct. They were, of course, good, upright people, but they often seemed to him as inert and ghostly as the plaster casts in the Environments of George Segal.

One had this church "environment," and all around were the dark, satanic mills of Shaftsbury. It was essentially a company town—brass, copper, thread, clocks, and watches—and in the old days the rich and the powerful had lived on the surrounding hills at least in sight of the industrial sore which suppurated from their wholesomeness and efficiency. But they had moved out into Meadowmount and Woodbridge, the "pure" New England villages which served as well-kept museums for their values. The Italians, the Poles, the Negroes, were like the Body from which the Brain now disassociated itself, though members of the establishment kept coming back to church Sunday after Sunday as if they subconsciously felt too noumenal.

Bennett Jones arrived, like one of Mussolini's trains, just on time. Aaron, who came from West Virginia and, in a sense, felt he belonged nowhere, would never get over how "New England" Jones was, a shrewd-faced portrait by John Singleton Copley in modern dress. He took in everything at a glance and passed on. Having clarified an aspect of the world, however, he expected it to stay put as in gelatin.

Aaron Blood required his attention as something that needed molding after all. You couldn't quite get him into the jar. He had verve and brilliance—everyone said that about his sermons—but he was like fruit juice that would not jell. You thought you had brought him around to the right consistency, but when you tested the mixture for ropiness, the promised viscosity, it was always back into the pan. If he came around at all, it would be as one of those dark, tough, overcooked jellies no one could hold up to the light for the neighbors to admire.

"You're looking well, Bennett," Aaron said gropingly, for all salutations seemed just that to him, awkward attempts to latch on.

"I don't know why I shouldn't." In the immaculate dark suit and the tie of lighter shade, Bennett's compact person might have just been sent back from the cleaners. "You, on the other hand, Aaron, look as if you have been working too hard. You should take up golf."

"'Here was a decent godless people: Their only monument the asphalt road and a thousand lost golf balls'—T.S. Eliot," he added. It was part of his compulsion to annoy to quote authorities to Bennett.

"Nonsense. The man was sick. Everyone knows that. Confused anyway. Maybe that's what happens to a man who comes to New England via St. Louis. No wonder he thought the world was a waste land."

"I came via West Virginia."

"True, Aaron, true. Give it some thought." Aaron poured him a cup of the tea Evelyn had laid out. "A slice of lemon, no sugar."

He watched with impatience as Aaron dropped into his own cup two cubes and a dollop of heavy cream which addled through the liquid like a cortex expanding.

"Now to get to the point. I've read over your plans for the Social Center, and the committee has asked me to speak to you about them. You have some good ideas. One might say you have more than enough. It will be a good large year if you find time to get it all done. I see you plan to put on Eliot's *Murder in the Cathedral* first thing in the fall. It *is* a religious play, isn't it?"

"Yes, in a way."

"Well, is it or isn't it?" He did not wait for an answer. "Samuel Beckett's *Waiting for Godot* is another matter. I haven't read the man, but someone on the committee said he has his characters speaking from ashcans. Not exactly relevant to the church, eh?"

"That depends. Some think he is writing modern morality

plays." Aaron wondered how much longer he would have to submit to this ignorant bullying.

"Some people think a lot of things. Think it over, Aaron. That's what I ask you to do." He put down his cup firmly as if it would leave a seal. "One more thing."

Aaron knew that Bennett, working from the comparatively trivial to the important, was getting near the heart of the matter. It meant a demand for consensus was in the offing.

"I see you recommend William McBroom as the director of the Social Center. I've read over all the applications. I noticed there were several well-qualified candidates."

"I thought McBroom was the best of the lot."

"Did you really think that, Aaron, or was it because he is black?" Bennett looked at him as if he had found a soft spot on a fruit.

"I thought it had been decided long ago ours was an open church."

"It is, Aaron, it's wide open. But let's not sell the white race down the river either. As long as there are two qualified candidates, there's no reason why we shouldn't in all good conscience select the one who would be congenial to the most people."

"I may as well tell you, Bennett. I'm sticking to my guns." Aaron felt as if he were sitting down in front of a tank.

"You're making trouble for yourself, Aaron. Unnecessary trouble." Bennett gave him his glassiest look, the sort that made Aaron feel his own eyes looked red and sore, like day-old tarts in a bakery. "The truth is I don't think you know your own mind. Your report on your second choice, Barbara Couch, sounds as though you would really rather have her."

Aaron wondered if he blushed, which he did so easily, and if Bennett would notice. "Mrs. Couch is well qualified, of course. But since she's a member of the church and our community, I thought some new blood—"

"Particularly if it's dark blood," Bennett interrupted, watching Aaron's Indian color deepen.

"Remember you're speaking to your minister, Bennett." Even as he said it, Aaron thought it sounded sanctimonious, superficial. He would like to have used some gutter language. It was truly absurd that half of the expressiveness of the world was considered to be off limits to him.

"I shouldn't have said that," Bennett quickly put in, but he did not sound the least contrite. "Where's your sense of humor, Aaron? You take things too much to heart. It's as simple as this.

You make your recommendations to the committee, and I'll make mine. May the best man win." Bennett rose from his chair as though propelled by a well-oiled spring.

"One more thing," he said as he turned at the study door, this time in diminuendo as if he always saved something non-controversial for last. "You worry too much, Aaron. Let God take the strain. That's what He's there for. I'll let myself out. Tell Evelyn she makes the best cup of tea in Connecticut."

Truly, Aaron reflected, much redounded to a man who believed so confidently in Peace, Power, and Plenty. Bennett's God was waiting right outside the door, the Great Weight Lifter who had the thrust of a slow rocket. Even Aaron had to admit that He worked better than His Own. Bennett was an ineluctable sort. He had weight and clarity like a jewel. Density for him was other people's neuroses.

William McBroom got the job, and Barbara Couch was appointed his assistant. Aaron, turgid with what seemed in some ways, even to him, merely a desire to put down Bennett Jones, used the hint of resignation, and Saint Mark's was not quite ready to go that far. But Aaron felt it was not really a whole-hearted concession, merely more of a drawing him out into the open where they could see him better. It was as though they had made him roll up one sleeve to reveal a large tattoo on a man they had thought totally untapestried.

What made the appointment more palatable at first, even to Bennett Jones, was that Aaron, once he had done his duty by McBroom, seemed to let Mrs. Couch run the show at the Center. If it was a kind of ethical window dressing, that was all right. One could understand that these days. Moreover, Bennett could not think of any reason why Barbara Couch, under his guiding hand, would not be dependable. Thinking in terms of twenty years ago, he and his friends could have counted on the fact that her sort would be, since she came from one of the "hill families" who had moved out to Meadowmount. But long after she should have been married, she was experimenting with a number of different life-styles. She worked at the U.N. in New York, returned to Shafts-bury to do newspaper work, and finally, on the wrong side of thirty, married Will Couch, the vice-president of Shaftsbury Brass, a neat, dark, unaggressive little man who was one of the secret coils in Bennett Jones's mainspring.

Everyone was pleased—Will made Bobbie finally look totally reliable. No one realized at first that he was simply an appendage, an arm, a leg, a means of grasp. But marriage by prosthesis did not satisfy Bobbie, and by the time she met Aaron it was like one luminous cloud meeting another, hoping for an exchange of deities. Both of them were filled with Yeats's "Asiatic vague immensities," bringing the aroma of incense into the church. The gods, however, might turn up in the avatars of the moment, wearing fright wigs and belting out soul music.

But momentarily the two clouds seemed to clarify each other. Barbara ran the Social Center as if it were the church, and William McBroom, safe in the cradle of the white power structure, did not appear to mind. The infection of Saint Mark's congregation by the most modern sensibilities was the prevailing objective—Beckett, Genet, Pinter, and finally Le Roi Jones, which doubled back and took in McBroom, who appreciated the culmination. The play was the thing wherein to catch the conscience of the king—Bennett Jones and his surrogates.

Bobbie resorted to the old orthodoxies of flattery and cajolement and made it all right with Bennett. "It brought the young people in off the streets." Or, "It was keeping up with the times," which she made sound like a good investment. That the potency which went into his agreement was the secret coloring of sex, Bennett would never have admitted. Bobbie, highstrung, not quite totally committed in her just less-than-mini skirt, her Modigliani combination of tortured modern face, all disordered substance, on a classically voluptuous body which was all ambiguous form, led the masculine mind in a variety of directions. For a while Bennett indulged her like a child. He let her play with his ponderous old church, knowing that the Weight Lifter would in time let them down easily on the old foundations.

The conservatives who followed Jones wherever he led them also let things slide. The young people began to think of Aaron as the next best thing to a guru. Psychedelia listened at the door. Folk Rock began tuning its guitar. The Drug Culture rolled its joints and filled its needles. The figures of a New Allegory were waiting on the green. The Weight Lifter, the ironic parodist Bennett Jones never dreamed him to be, was ready to release pastel balloons to the tune of "Up, Up, and Away."

It was Estelle Jones, on whom Bennett's leniency with Barbara had not been lost, who started the first grounding motion at Saint Mark's. Estelle, coming from Vermont, indulged in rather the same view of Connecticut that North Italians take of Naples. It needed goading, managing, it was waiting to be told what to do. She, too, looked like a Copley portrait and could have passed for Bennett's twin. They drank out of the same cup, never in gulps, but sipping for quality like wine tasters, and what Bennett could not look after around Shaftsbury and Meadowmount, Estelle added to her list of civic activities.

She liked theater and, determined to get to the bottom of the Blood-Couch variety, poked around during rehearsals. Coming in unexpectedly one afternoon, she went down to the basement where some of the younger members of the cast were supposed to be making scenery for Ionesco's *Rhinoceros*, found no one, tried a closed door nearby, and discovered several sons and daughters of her friends smoking marijuana. They were not exactly stoned, but Estelle smelled all the illusions of the modern world pouring out of that room. The boys and girls were expelled from the cast immediately, the affair was hushed up, and ostensibly it was left to the parents to do the right thing about the delinquents.

But Estelle did not really leave it at that. Something had to be done about the Center as long as it could be approached indirectly, obliquely, for the sake of the scandal it might cause in the church. She devised the means of giving a dinner party at The Manor, gathering together the Bloods, the Couches, the Hills, because Wade was treasurer of the Center, and, of course, McBroom. Marjorie Wilson, who went to the Congregational Church in Meadowmount, would be invited for camouflage.

If an invitation to The Manor was frequently another move on the chessboard, it meant many other things to Aaron Blood. He loved the old, white-columned house which had been in Bennett's family for more than two hundred years. If only one could have lived in it even fifty years ago, he sometimes thought ruefully, when it would not have seemed so immoral.

The Hills were there when he and Evelyn arrived—had they been asked a few minutes earlier to emphasize the right tone? Wade, taller than Bennett, considerably younger but almost as gray, "gave" Aaron his hand to be shaken. The memory of that dead fish would startle later when he began to clean up Aaron's ideas as briskly as a fishmonger. Mary, wearing a vintage Mainbocher, presented an absolute counter to Evelyn who managed as usual to look so Salvation Army.

Barbara Couch, in short evening dress and panty hose, was all legs, enticing as Circe and as metamorphically loaded. Her small, pinched-back face kept threatening to be superseded by another which would bloom upward, in its full nature, from the tubers of her breasts. Though the most modern note there, McBroom, uneasy in a rented tuxedo, looked like a visitation. One expected him to disappear and return, more solid-seeming, from an older reality, with a tray of drinks or a silent butler for cigarette ashes.

In The Manor, one simply could not with any degree of verisimilitude adjust to the latter half of the twentieth century.

Nevertheless, Barbara did her best. She smoked too many cigarettes, drank too many drinks, crossed and uncrossed her legs. But Estelle and Mary patronized and went around her, and she went in to dinner on spiritual stumps, needing all the prosthetic assistance Will could lend.

Pouring the wine, Bennett gave Barbara less than the others, but took a glissading peep down her breasts. Marjorie managed to remind McBroom that he did not need to pass the tall heirloom salt shakers up and down since there were several. But Estelle kept tight control of her handsome table—she never scalped anyone until she had fed him royally first; Will Couch got the eye from her to put the damper on Bobbie, and he responded almost electronically.

This, Aaron granted, was only one, perhaps a hallucinatory, way of looking at the occasion. It was a beautiful, civilized performance, and all that the evening really lacked was proper stand-ins for himself and Barbara—a "good" minister and a "nice" woman, and you would have an arrested effect of life at The Manor as it had always been. It was just such outsiders as Bobbie and himself, rowing in troubled ideological waters like modern prototypes of savages, that made the mansion seem ready for barbarous attack.

Bennett and Estelle were the only people in Meadowmount who could divide the sexes after dinner and still make it seem right. Estelle led the way into the large drawing room, followed by Marjorie, Mary, then Evelyn like the tail of the human condition, and Barbara its unsettling rattle.

In the library, sitting under the portrait of Bennett's grandfather, Aaron allowed himself a Courvoisier. He spoke fluently from the pulpit, but felt vulnerable with three or four.

Wade stood at the fireplace like an ambassador, and it was not long before he got around to the subject of the Social Center. "Aaron, I've been thinking," he said. "Barbara Couch is such a vivid, interesting person. But I wonder if temperamentally she was quite the right choice for the Center. Bennett didn't want any of us to discuss anything behind anyone's back. That's why he asked Mr. McBroom to come over too."

That was white of you, Bennett, Aaron wanted to say, but even he must remember that with William there black was beautiful. Instead he temporized. "I don't think I quite know what you mean, Wade."

"Well, for one thing there was the marijuana incident. There is a rumor, repeat, just rumor, that Barbara joined the group from time to time."

"I don't think there is a word of truth in that."

"Nevertheless, the *word* is there. We just can't have such suppositions around the church."

Bennett, curiously, said nothing, and Aaron turned to William and simply asked, "McBroom?"

Called back out of reverie as the director of the Social Center, McBroom looked a shade lighter than when he arrived. "I just don't know, Aaron," he said evasively. "I've heard the rumor too."

Aaron could hardly believe his ears. Did McBroom secretly hate Barbara, or was it simply an old, old question of a power struggle that had no color?

Wade, a master at presenting a stone and then throwing it into the pool, smoothly rippled the conversation into the more comfortable problem of the role of the church in a changing society. Since Aaron stood for the church, the evening, he decided, was more subtly about the problem of Aaron Blood.

Joining the women, he sensed that Estelle, receiving some telepathic communication from Bennett, would be glad to bring the evening to a close. When they got back to the rectory, Evelyn went to see if the boys were all right, and he had another brandy in his study, wanting to blur himself a bit after exposure to a quintet of definite personalities. They were all such distilled people. If not Marjorie, the other four at least were learning that they might have to let through some of the impurities, even some of the lumps. The times were curdling round. They were being looked in on through the decorative cages and compounds to which they had been reduced—the rara avis of whitest feather, reminding one of lost graces and virtuosities of motion.

But was he simply sentimentalizing his own guilt for having feelings of animosity toward them? There was no doubt that he had made the church a more difficult place, and what had he offered them in return but the troubling mystery of what it is to be a person like Aaron Blood? He was in a sense a dead body coming to the surface of their lives. Some weight had finally not kept him down. One thing he was sure of now—they would look for something that would. And it was his dilemma that he did not know whether he fully blamed them.

The only person who made him think otherwise was Barbara Couch. She clung to him as if he were a buoy. She thought all the others were submerged, trying to drag him down. Bennett, Estelle, Wade, Mary—all were archetypes of those who had been down under, living in lost Atlantis for years. But they could never be hauled up out of their own depths like dripping stone figures. They had to be attacked in the places they had not really guarded as carefully as they thought—the churches and the college campuses. They were the places where every tenet of modern life should be tested. Let everything flood in and by its own weight give new foundations.

Armed with her theories, or so he thought, Aaron let Barbara stay on at the Social Center. Then Will Couch went away on a hunting trip with some of his friends at the brass company, and, as one of the local wits said, left Aaron Blood with a Body on his hands. Soon after Will took off, Barbara asked him to come over and discuss some of the problems of the Center. How it happened, except with Bobbie anything could happen, Aaron did not know, but, instead, he found himself discussing the problems of her love life with Will.

"I can't go on, Aaron," she said in her extravagant way. "I can't make love with someone who thinks Bennett Jones should be the Man of the Year. I try, but nothing happens. I thought I had found a man, but I married a valet."

Aaron, watching her stretch out her long, elegant, lubricious legs, felt sickish, and wondered if he were supposed to answer her as a minister. "Will's always seemed like a good sort to me," he said lamely, marveling at how women could make a dance of life just by uncrossing their legs.

"Oh, Aaron. That's just the point. He's so good he stinks. I swear he even smells too clean." Bobbie got up with a motion that reminded him of someone lifting a whole basket of ripe fruit. "Do you think I'm a barbarian?"

"No, you're the most frighteningly civilized person I know."

"You mean I'm too verbal?"

"Yes, and the exact opposite as well. . . . You're an antinomy."

"Oh, for God's sake, Aaron. Whatever that means I doubt if it applies to me. I'm just another disappointed woman." A trace of contempt flickered across her face.

"Perhaps. I only wonder—whoever meets you at one side, will he always find you at the other?" Aaron picked up his glass for a refill and watched Barbara wander out to the kitchen as if she would dip his drink from a Red Sea no one had ever been able to part for her.

But after a few more drinks he found himself talking about Evelyn, and in no time at all they were having a dime novel discussion about sex and marriage. Alike as they were in some ways, they were totally different in this—she had made Will try everything, while he and Evelyn had tried nothing. If they all did a sex film together, their techniques would be an illustration of too much too soon, and too little too late.

Nothing happened that first evening, but Aaron found he was hooked on the very kind of vulgar confessionalism he had always loathed in others. By the end of the week, sleeping with Bobbie was the steadiest thing he could do. It was like driving a pike into a quivering mass of uncertainties. He would not sleep in Will's bed with her, but his shadow was everywhere. Even in the moments of the greatest ecstasy he had ever known, he wished Will would come home unexpectedly and discover them, walk over their flesh in his hunting boots, and then expose them to the public. For, having told Barbara "everything," he knew that this was the one thing he could never tell anyone.

Nevertheless, every night while Will was gone he was at their house. It seemed the only real thing he had ever done. Barbara's theories meant nothing to him now. This was nonverbal; there was the salt of all beginnings in its tang. He felt physically eloquent for the first time—his body was packed with all the love stories that had never been openly, fearlessly written. And Bobbie was the most stimulating of lovers; sleeping with her was like rolling in a bed of spice. It was what he had wanted all along. It sheared him of modern life; it was simply and ultimately Aaron Blood. The only secret worth keeping, it would have to be torn from him by others.

But still another impulse induced him to park his car boldly in front of the house. Wade Hill saw it at a very late hour, passed the word on to Bennett who reacted like Cotton Mather, spending an entire afternoon at the rectory trying to persuade Aaron that his actions were taking him on a disastrous course. He raged, stormed, threatened like a jealous lover. Aaron admitted nothing. For the first time in his life, he felt his heart give off the rich light of a ruby, and for a while he wanted it that way. Let Bennett have all the diamonds in the world; things incarnadine belonged to Aaron Blood.

So Bennett let the cat out of the bag. He went to Evelyn first, who treated Aaron thereafter as if she had been hiding Satan in her house. The boys were told nothing, but Daniel, sensing something was wrong, became protective of his mother, while Webb's confidence and poise seemed to drop from him like a slick integument. It was as though the picture of his life, which was moving fluently before him, had jammed in the projector. He would not look his father in the eye any longer, and Aaron sometimes found him loitering in the dark hall outside his study as if he had been getting up nerve to come in to see him.

Someone, Aaron bitterly reflected, would fill him in on the specifics. He could tell from the chilliness with which some of his congregation treated him that Bennett and Estelle had not been idle, and the parents, of course, would subvert the children. By the time Will Couch returned, the rich rumor had spread like a drop of blood on a pane of glass, and Aaron began to know the full import of what it was to have a secret nobody wanted him to have.

By hints, by parables contrived feverishly in his study, he tried to infect his sermons with just enough suggestiveness to arouse an empathy in others. But he felt he was received two-dimensionally like a figure of stained glass. Whatever light came down to them through such bold color was still diffused by Bennett Jones: a minister should have nothing to hide. Would there never be an end of polarities that excluded him? Many of their children believed the exact opposite: no one should ever hide anything.

Aaron finally allowed them their static illumination and gloried privately in his ecstasy and torment. After the cold winter, Connecticut, moving into June, responded ritually. The red rose seemed to him the true rose. A woman in flamboyant dress wished to tell him something. Lips had never seemed so inviting, so ideographically haunting. As he walked around Shaftsbury at night, people seemed luminous to him underneath their clothes. If they walked naked in the street, they would shine in the darkness, lettered with fluorescence, as though trying to spell out some strange forgotten language that had not yet come into being.

Sometimes, perhaps in an unconscious desire to bless his affair with some kind of morality, he felt it had arisen from the same source as his desire to change the world. If his love for Barbara was anarchic, it was perhaps just such a pommeling of passion that Shaftsbury needed to awaken it from its own spiritual death. Two people standing naked and free in the eyes of others could be like a challenge to a greater honesty and spontaneity. A naked man, a truly naked man, could hardly be a segregationist; a church which harbored Aaron Blood could never be as smugly conservative again.

But one night when he returned from an encounter with Barbara, Evelyn, like Reality in her frowzy bathrobe, met him at the door. She was weeping hysterically and glared at Aaron like a crazed animal. Only minutes before, as if he knew when his father would be coming home, Webb, who would have been fifteen on his next birthday, had shot himself with a rifle he had secretly borrowed from Will Couch, explaining that his father "needed to get rid of some rats in the basement." He had left on his table a note which said: "I don't like people."

Stoical Evelyn succumbed totally, refusing to be comforted; she would not talk to Aaron and cringed from his touch. Daniel had nothing to say to his father when they ate alone, and this leukemia of silence left Aaron feeling terminal and yet still rabid and heart-hungry. Only Barbara kept him going, though there was some-thing frantic in her attentions as if she were filling an old sock full of holes with the pulp of her life.

What had this boy, whom "people" so much liked, really meant? Read *my father* in place of *people*, Aaron had bitterly to conclude, and you had Webb's "message to the world." One day he would think it all through to its implacable conclusion. At this point it was simply too much. Was it Louis XIV who said that two things cannot be looked at for any length of time—the sun and death?

Nevertheless, Webb's succinct, terribly desolate sentence, as ex-treme in its way as his own passion, had a final, releasing effect. Aaron resigned even before he was forced to, asked Evelyn for a divorce, informed Will Couch that he wished to marry Barbara. And he did all of these things with a lucidity and dispatch Bennett Jones would have brought to the conduct of business. Somewhere in his soul Aaron was part New Englander. For the first time, he felt like an ordinary member of his congregation.

The parting with Evelyn was the hardest to bear. Evelyn was right in the middle of the world which had been divided between himself and Bennett Jones. All he had come up with at the end was what any corny wife-beater might have said. "Forgive me."

"Try to forgive yourself, Aaron," she said, but did not sound as if she believed it possible.

He thought of trying to get another church, but he knew that his record without any extenuating circumstances would follow him wherever he went. Lacking other possibilities, he and Bar-bara went to Washington and found positions in Evelyn's old profession, social work. It seemed ironically fitting that her for-mer world promised to claim them for the rest of their lives.

He did not like "government" Washington, which he found too blandly beautiful. It was all so heavy, inert, symbolically white. He missed the dark, satanic mills of Shaftsbury, the nitty-gritty, the rough and tumble of an industrial city. Sometimes it seemed that

Bennett, Estelle, Wade, Mary, large showy white dahlias that they were, had been more soot-laden than he had imagined. How had they managed to exert their purifying influence in such an environment? Were they more subtle than he had ever dreamed? Had they clarified their situation with an utterly sophisticated, and yet not more than normally heartless, knowledge of the tenuous, tentative, ultimately expendable design men could make of their experience? He would miss the enigma of their lucidity.

But, most of all, he missed the existential fever of being Aaron Blood. The upheaval of his life was like a sea-change that left him anything but more rich and strange. Were the expectations of every modern individual, white or black, doomed to disappointment? Now that we "knew everything," was any decisive action enfeebled by the knowledge of all that it excluded? Living in a cloud which issued like steam from the confinement of his clerical clothes, he had felt the latent poetry in him promise to exude some night-blooming cereus, a handsome shadow-flower to the daylight world of dahlias. It was the emotional stuff from which some sort of prophet might have been expected to bloom once in a hundred years.

There had been a time, something deeper than his finest hour, when he had stood in the pulpit at Saint Mark's full of the story of Aaron Blood, and had had the thrilling feeling of being willing to suffer for the surface actions of his life without letting anyone extract its essence. Was the real horror of the times a kind of universal arrogance which thought it could understand everyone at a glance, and so discount him?

Barbara, too, poor child, missed Shaftsbury and Meadowmount. At the end of their hard, practical days, she lay beside him, plump and passive as a fruit he was supposed to enjoy. All the windfall of sex had left the garden strangely quiet and toneless. She did not care about her clothes and frequently went without lipstick, echoing Evelyn in little ways that made him wonder if guilt could ever stop experimenting with roles among its chosen. Did he, in his vaporous longing, finally affect his women this way? He had heard by the grapevine that Evelyn had moved to New Haven and gotten a job at Yale, wore contact lenses and pants suits, and was active in Women's Lib. Would all of her "causes" now be cues of some mod "Alice" proselytizing on the talk shows from a looking glass of disillusionment?

"The dimension of depth"—Paul Tillitch would have yielded theology, all of the requirements and dualities of religion, for this. Modern life was aglow with vivid scenes, but did it have any more sense of depth than a color film or, even in its pauses, than a brilliant billboard? One simply did not know. Who was a witness to the future? Himself or Bennett Jones? One simply could not be sure. Each man might be someone else's Antichrist. Yeats's Beast had slouched forward, leaving not so much progeny as a condition around which reeled the white forms, the black shadows, of "indignant desert birds." Who, what, could be the catalyst? In all of its temptations, let the indignation persist. If Aaron Blood had any secret, this was it.

The Naked Swimmer

The swimming pool occupies these days a mobile place in the American psyche. Elaine Morrison could remember the time when it was a possession of the rich, then the well-to-do, and would always be grateful she had lived long enough for it to become just a tempting reach away for a person like herself. It could hang there for years, a radiant peach far out on the bough, but with the lengthening material arms of most Americans it might yield to one of balletic spirit who could stand on points, give that extra little push upward, grasp and catch it at the same time so that it would come down unblemished, only a little déclassé as a notion of the glamorous life.

Best of all, she had been the dancer beneath the tree, not Gus who had shaken down into her lap nearly everything else she owned. He had a good law practice, and she was, she supposed, a good keeper of the hearth, but only after some years of marriage had they been able to position themselves near the shadow of the tree. Starting out with no capital, they had lived in an apartment in Shaftsbury, then acquired a place in the country near Meadowmount, a New England paradigm of old filial white houses and red barns. A little later, it had been necessary to buy some more land to fight the developers, like so many boll weevils amid this architectural cotton. At the same time, the girls were growing up, and there was education, education, education, a word that seemed to have buried in it a pruning saw which was determined to keep the Morrison orchard barren of any special, shining fruit.

Then an aunt, who had lived on and on, encrusted in illness and expensive care like an Ivan Le Lorraine Albright figure sitting up in a baroque bed, died and left her a legacy, dwindled it was true from fifty to ten thousand, but who could quibble if it gave an unexpected lengthening power of reach? By this time, the steady providers, the right, ruthless topiarists of the tree, were on their way to becoming male chauvinists, and Elaine was not without a sense of triumph at presenting Gus with the thing both of them had secretly wanted for so many years.

On the swimming team at Yale, Gus had a superb physique

which he managed to keep in trim by working out three times a week at the Y in Shaftsbury. But she had married him for his muscles anyway, he used to say, and he had somehow to keep solvent in the love department. Maybe she had, she sometimes thought. Would she have married him if he had not been the sort of man who would one day look good in a pool, with his black hair, eyes the color of the alluring water of the future, and his muscles like golden harpstrings, the music of a man in motion?

So, with his rather stagy indulgence, she had decided to blow the bundle on the best pool of a certain size Connecticut could provide—kidney-shaped with ample flagstone terrace, tile trim, nine and a half feet deep at the diving end, covered with a spotless marbleized coating—specifications which would make of that delved and flattened globe of her imagination something blue and paradisal as an enormous split passion fruit.

The Magnum Company had come that very spring Aunt Edith had capitulated, and she would never forget the mythical characters she suddenly had working for her as if it were very special money which had lured them out of books. They were beautiful-bodied young men with names like Gaetano, Guido, and Antonio, who treated her as if she were a siren each time she came down in her housecoat to coax and croon. The girls were away at school, and, for the time being, she was the only woman in the world anyway, the only woman, that is, who was being excavated, eviscerated, if you will, the only woman who was willing to submit to any degree of open surgery to prove she had a heart like a pool.

She would never forget feeling she was finally exposed (or was it proposed?) to the world as she wanted to be when it was finished and filled. Gus came home from the office early, a man of forty-five who looked ten years younger standing on the diving board in a regal new pair of trunks that looked cut out of Joseph's coat of many colors, waving a bottle of champagne over the water.

Addressing her, as he always did when he felt best, like a boy with high school memories of Tennyson, as "Elaine the Fair," he acknowledged that she had somehow, on her own, achieved a romance.

"Sir Lancelot," she said, lifting blue water cupped in her hand, congratulating herself, in a mixture of myths, on having a Narcissus who looked down and found *her*. Oh, there were not enough myths. Certainly not in America. One had to borrow them everywhere.

They got a little drunk that night and made love in a way they had not done since their first couplings. All Gus would say was,

"Elaine, Elaine, Elaine," as in those early inarticulate times, before he had learned to direct and correct her, but it was the essential word, almost itself too much for the omniscient body which recognized her dream.

That first spring and summer of the pool was the best. It was so absolutely and thrillingly clean and pure, as pristine as a primary, tender organ of herself. When Jan and Ellie came home, even they were intruders though she loved them dearly, and she savagely complained if they asked too many of their friends over too often, or flew into a tantrum when they forgot to knock the grass off their feet.

If the hyperbole proved too much to sustain, she began to conceptualize in nonsensual terms.

"It's another world. It's a spiritual thing, really," she would say.

And Gus would agree, "You're right, honey," diving in exuberantly, treating it as if it were very much of this world as well.

When she was too fastidious, too persnickety, he laughed and called her "the Puritan of the Pool," and let it go at that.

If she insisted defensively, "It's the only thing I ever had that is not material at all," he would surface close to her, pinch her on the bottom, and say, "Maybe it's all that good, clean, old maid's money that went into it."

But that made her feel too much like an heiress-come-lately, a fairly frigid, acidulous one at that, rather than an odalisque lounging in their common dream, and she didn't particularly like that either. Aesthetically, she had no doubts, but, morally, she could never quite make up her mind. Putting it to herself in human terms, she observed that the pool had loads of personality, but did it have any character?

The pool, however, as things conceptualized too exclusively are likely to do, took its own little revenges. The winters began to wear the coping stones ever so slightly, the snow abrading some looser, more sensual notion of things, leaving its little heaps of moraine on the bottom as a natural admonition that the mills of the gods grind slowly but not all that slowly. Scars, streaks, chipped places appeared on the blue tiles like hieroglyphics of some emergent, primitive, antipathetic language, and the acceleration of industrial pollution from Shaftsbury let down its invisible monster to loll, bathe, and leave his bathtub ring. If one could try to control the summers with a constant cosmetic hand, the winters had a glacial indifference to the dreams of suburban women.

But in her heyday, Elaine had a collapsed, elliptical sense of destiny, and held to her expectations, a tireless ideologue, deter-

mined to present to Gus when he came home a flawless tympanum for his thrilling percussive touch.

Most poignant of all, with her built-in sensor, she had awakened
one night to hear an enormous thrashing and coughing coming
from the direction of the pool. Leaving Gus blissfully snoring on
the other side of the bed, she put on her robe and went down to
find a large, dark form rising and falling between dreadful, rack-
ing gasps. Nothing could have been more unnerving than the
pronounced, though not clearly defined, motion, accompanied by
this râle. The pool, her pool, had taken its final vengeance—it had
killed someone.

She turned on the lights and saw a large, black German shepherd circling desperately around, passing right by the steps which
domed up like a little temple of redemption, caught in the obsession of struggling in a circular unknown sea. He was beyond
endearment or reason, turning in his own death-wish, beyond any
intelligent effort to extricate himself. Elaine knelt down and with
all her force grabbed him by the legs and shoulders, almost as if
he were a man, and hauled him out, smelling of overheated
viscera and debased fur, casting a quick hallucinatory montage
from a bestiary where men had turned into animals and were
trying, without success, to revert. His head nuzzled her breasts
curiously, amatively, a moment until he freed himself from the
good witch of the water, but still a witch, and disappeared gasping
into the bushes. Elaine had a chill from the huge, drenching stain,
and the whole episode seemed like a bad omen.

Nevertheless, she would always say that the pool gave her the
best ten years of her life. It saw her through Ellie's early elopement and Jan's somewhat later union with an older man. It helped
her survive an extended menopause, soothing, cooling her hot
flashes with its own subtle form of cryonics as if it were quietly
trying to help her put away youth for safekeeping and future
regeneration.

At what point do ambiguities that have held us together fall
apart? In what unhappy hour do inner conflicts that have, in fact,
sustained us announce their fatal separation? We make up our
dedications, our cohesions, as best we can, and one day there is
not enough staying power, not enough glue in the world to keep
us stuck to the cast and accoutrements of our lives. Making sense
in little ways that once seemed big no longer serves. An overwhelming awareness of other combinations, other constructions,
besets the mind with the odious, limited particularity of the place
one ineluctably occupies. There is a vague, vaunted thing called

Life all around one, and you have caught it, now forever lifeless, in some kind of absurd little Have-a-Heart trap of self-indulgent egoism. A husband, a house, a picture, a pool goes absolutely dead, and the difficulty is, taking these four as random possibilities, one is never quite sure who, what, is hiding the magic. Ambiguity, which was impacted and immersed, the thick medium in which one moved, separates, sets out the pieces of life as in a shell game. All density of motive is lost in the invisible labyrinth of motion: Keep your eye on the piece that moves.

Elaine thought she was doing just that when she announced on her fifty-second birthday after the cake she had herself baked proved to be a frosted nonentity and the odious little gifts, turned over, were found to be empty, "I want to redo the pool."

"What do you mean, hon. It's set. Set for life." Gus leaned back, bracing his stomach as if she were going to land on it from a seventh-story window.

"No, it isn't." Elaine who had an eye for animal movements decided the tension in her husband would hold. "I only wish it *were* set. It's going downhill. It's in a deplorable state. Chipped tiles. Worn coping. Take a look at the way the paint is peeling."

"Oh, if that's all. Perhaps we can manage that. Next year. Or the next."

"That won't do it." Elaine aggressively pushed forward her brown-eyed, sun-tanned face with its fringe of blonde hair. The fact that she had begun to look like a sunflower, weary of time, didn't exactly make her husband the Sun King.

"What do you mean?" Gus, who loved champagne, looked at his glass as if it contained a urine specimen.

"It's too small. Two strokes for me, one for you, and we're on the other side."

Gus, having learned to go through a gamut of roles in these sessions, took his final stand as cost accountant. "I give up, Elaine. You haven't any idea what it would involve. You don't enlarge kidney-shaped pools that easily. The contractor, the designer, would have to be called in. The bulldozer would have to come back. If you wanted a larger pool, you should have thought of it ten years ago. Not that Aunt Edith's money would have gone that far. Do you realize what the Magnum Company would want for this sort of job these days?"

"As I was saying," Elaine interrupted, realizing that this had been one of her favorite phrases for some time now. "Something has to be done. Why repair when you can improve?"

"We've been through all this before, El. As a matter of fact, last year, as I remember, on *my* birthday. Only then it was just repairs. Be reasonable. You know I'm trying to save something for our retirement."

So this is the shell that hides the substance, she almost said aloud, but Gus was in no mood to continue the games people play. He put the cork back in the bottle, went into the house, got a towel, and—something he had not done at night all summer— went down for a swim.

Had she really been talking to this man? Who was he? She looked at the pool throwing up a glow like something which had been confined beneath a shell, powerful, exhaled, a moulded radiance. And suddenly the substance was there. It was the top of a spaceship, all mysterious light tinted with aquamarine which would dome up like a giant toadstool, rise and take them God knows where. But in a moment, when Gus hit the water, she recovered into overwhelming confusion. Was she sliding? Where, where, indeed, was her mind attached?

What brought her back to "daylight" and simple, single-minded disaster was that all Gus would allow her was one quick par- simonious peep beneath the shell. He swam two laps—no gasping German shepherd he—turned off the lights, and went upstairs to the room across the hall he had been occupying to relieve her, so he said, from his snoring.

That last picture of him, standing by the pool, nude, like a new word without syntax, before he turned off the lights and evapo- rated in a shower of gold had done it! What right had he to portion out a little instant Jove to her diffuse, insatiable Danae? No doubt, he was upstairs marbleizing himself in the white steam of a shower. He could take hot or cold indifferently. It was she who was left with *coitus interruptus*—worse than that—no contact at all—an abandonment of ambiguity.

No wonder she had to have the hard, bitchy light of day, the succession of scenes lined up on one side of an argument. All that remained was a grudging intimacy of tone, but not of content. Gus was a master of evasive connectives. He could listen without listening, talk without talking, putting in the deceptive responsive phrase just to keep things moving.

By God, did all she have to hang on to come down to a series of fierce, intrusive sentences beginning "As I was saying . . ."? This, of course, was grossly unfair, but she had wanted to be unfair for ages and ages. She could not, no matter how she badgered and battered, get him, paradoxically, to combine, and say, "It's split. There's nothing one can do. It's finished forever."

What a birthday! She went to bed hating the pool for all she was worth, and the next morning gave Gus a heavier than usual dose of "As I was saying. . . ." He was hardly out of the house when she decided violently to throw over her housework and go down *nude* to what she had decided was the source of her disturbance. Never had the hard, bitchy light seemed more ruthlessly focused on a blonde who now got her color out of a bottle. The pool was an implacable worn mirror which nevertheless specialized in remembering caricatures. Only yesterday hadn't she come down in her long, flowery, yellow robe and seen herself depicted there as a late, late American geisha who thought of herself as a girasol? Now, brown and buttery with oil, she cooked in the sun—Apple Pan Dowdy with accent on the last word. The coldest emotion she had ever felt seemed to close over her like a carapace, and she went back to the house with a vertiginous sense of encased pieces of life moving maddeningly, menacingly, around her.

Not long after her birthday, there was a period of disregarding the pool altogether, of, in fact, disowning it. If Larry, their gardener and general factotum moonlighting from the night shift at Shaftsbury Brass, did a sloppy job of vacuuming, she didn't bother to jack him up. Then, of course, incongruously, Gus did, and the pool lay there with all its scars, circulating purely, but now somebody else's transplant. As soon as she stopped swimming, he resumed, early in the morning and again in the afternoon, as if someone's living touch must never leave it. She cagily recommenced for a day or two, and he developed another bad case of late hours at the office.

How does one figure out one's relation to anything? Gus, a linear Lancelot if there ever was one, never seemed to have any trouble. With him it was this, and then that, with, so it seemed, never even the slightest tinge of ironic bitterness. If her state of mind was a crisis, was there something peculiarly American, or just modern, about it? Was America more than any other country in history the place where affirmatives had a way of turning into negatives? Was it, in fact, as Gertrude Stein observed, the oldest country in the world because it had lived most of its history in the recent, accelerated past, heavily freighted with terminal logical conclusions? There was Gus beside her still spinning out the reel of the old-line movie, but by rote, not as they had seen it the first time together, and here she was with the end of the affair—The Woman and the Pool in constantly widening Cinemascope.

A few days of on again, off again, and Gus's afternoon sickness spread into the evening, and sometimes he didn't return until after midnight. Though this had happened before, when she intimated that he must be catting around, he brought home a fat satchel of legal stuff and worked in his room until he had established his case. If she were going crazy, was he simply going to let her do it on her own time?

Later, she would conclude, American life—and she was unwilling to admit, except in hypothesis, any other country could harbor a woman quite like herself—resorted to the only kind of shock treatment of which it was capable—capricious surprise. It came about this way, she would say to herself when she felt a "spell" coming on, as if she were splicing herself back onto the main-line film—locking the doors securely since Gus had his own key, she had gone to bed at nine o'clock, finding the night the only dome comprehensive enough to hold her body in place for more than a few moments. She wanted to believe that she was lying there wide awake when it happened, but the version of herself Gus expected her to believe would have to admit that she had perhaps fallen briefly asleep—No matter. In either of these versions it was incontrovertible that she had heard like a tearing of silk someone cutting through the pool—an expert swimmer, a cool, lovely, alluring sound. There would be a pause, a dive into the yielding trampoline of her nerves, and then the parting of the fabric, the incision into the water—an absolutely delicious male voice laughing, followed by a lyric snatch of song.

Looking out of the window but seeing a motion no more defined than that of the German shepherd, she was enchanted and then overwhelmed with fear—hoodlums had taken over a place down the hill some weeks earlier when the owners were on the Cape.

She banged on the screen and called out, "This is private property. Will you please leave at once!" A watery chortle. Then silence.

Gus would only have laughed at her, so she said nothing in the morning and found herself compensating with some agreeable breakfast chat. As if the gesture had aroused a telepathy, he stayed home after dinner, comfortingly, but not a little provokingly too. The next night she gave in to the fact that she felt an enormous sense of relief when he had left the house and, the food put away and the dishes done, she could stretch out on her bed, this time nude as a mermaid, taking an amphetamine just to dare American home life to put her to sleep. She waited, she extended her feelings like an adventuress, her empathy for the pool a regrooved artery. Again the musical laughter, the powerful plunge, the master of moiré moving in the water, the darkness. Less muted now, more provocative, as if to suggest her complicity.

Gus would simply have gone down, turned on the lights, exposed the shady character or chimera. The only thing to do was to tell him. He pooh-poohed her version, but stayed home, and Meadowmount had no prowling swimmer that night. It was a town of white house, white church, white inn bedded in green, and one delusive woman who could not fit into the summer crèche.

"There's a gun in the closet," he said the following evening when he left. "You're overwrought, honey. That's all."

Like hell she was, not in the way he meant anyway. She was underwrought, or why couldn't she wait to lie in bed, clad, wishingly, only in the jewels with which Baudelaire adorned his nudes. One might as well be whimsical at a time like this—it provided some class. Moreover, the pool now had a country to itself, a lagoon on its own stretch of earth, blue in spirit, even in its basting of night, detached, absolute—an island with a single savage on call.

Later in the week, something gave her the courage not just to lie, but to lie in wait. When Gus, alternating regularly, stayed home, she called him just in time for a tantalizing trail of laughter, dripping water, a quicksilver fade-out, but he professed to have heard nothing, in the same breath shaking the screen furiously and bellowing like a bull. It was the first time he had been in her room in weeks, streaking the air with just a touch of sleepy animal musk, arousing her old baffled addictive sense of ambiguity. She was furious and yet would have hidden under the sheets if he had not said, "There's absolutely nothing out there, Elaine. You must be hearing things. Why don't you go to bed and get some sleep?"

Nevertheless, she made him do penance, insisting that he go outside with his gun, turn the lights on, beat the bushes. Men like Gus had to pay. By God, they somehow had to pay. But, naturally, the pool obeyed him perfectly—no savages, no susurrations.

Alone again the following night, Elaine decided to put the gun by the bed, thought better of it and laid out Gus's hunting torch, wishing for a switch that would turn on the pool lights by remote control just as she changed TV channels. With a sense of having arranged a *mise-en-scène* as far as she was able, she lay down, never having felt more existentially bloated. Of course, it would serve her right if Gus were wrong and she were right for the wrong reason. For example, suppose the swimmer were there, but only somebody like Larry, disgruntled, wanting a raise, goofing off with the "rich" people.

Thinking of Larry made her recall the odd exception to these nocturnal encounters. One night, not being able to calm down, she took two Seconals, finally dozing off and sleeping on long after Gus had gone to work. At eleven-thirty she woke feeling the whole house had fallen down on her, its tablets and entablatures, and went out groggily to water her flowers, which she usually did before the heat of the day. In one of her loveliest beds, packed like an English garden with a riot of bloom, she saw the swimmer lifting that tight arabesque of color into the air. His whole body looked tattooed with flowers, and there was a subtle, combined floral scent coming from his skin.

Too much Seconal, she thought, and was about to go into the house to get herself a cup of coffee when the flowers faded, as if consumed by her rejection, and only the outline of his body was there like a figure of bronze wire. A ghost at noon, a see-through man who gave an unearthly depth to her feelings. The pool beyond extended its color to make him a blue man rimmed with gold.

She must have fainted briefly for she woke, hot, wet, as if she had been in the arms of an ardent lover. When she stood up, she would have liked to pour plaster into the imprint of her body on the grass, and, recovering from her swoon in paradigmatic clarity, she realized that she wanted to surrender, that she did not want there to be any difference between night and day.

It released her even now to recall that vision in the sun and feeling receptive, she lay there, having spiritually gotten into something comfortable, namely, absolutely nothing. This time, nuder than nude, Elaine the Fair (Ambiguity's lily maiden)—an all-American body wanting to be able to sustain its two-way stretch. As far as the pool was concerned something told her this was the last move in the shell game. There had to be something under this hull of her experience or she was over the hill. Relax. Relax. The blue, the midnight blue, man was coming into anatomical focus.

So just for the full, beautiful play of the thing, she let the intruder dive, swim back and forth, laugh, do the whole bit. No strident voice at the window this time, no withdrawal either. Slipping quickly into her nightgown and robe, she went downstairs with the flashlight in her hand and out into the garden. Kneeling down in the grass, she groped around, cursing the fact that the Magnum Company had had the brilliant idea of attaching the switch to the bottom of the post and rail fence. The rambler rose had grown all around the metal box, and she got up, realizing the noise must have alerted the prowler. Quickly turning on the powerful beam of the torch, she found a naked swimmer climbing out of the pool. In one quick glance she at first took in only the legs, then, separately, the thighs, the torso, and it was the most beautiful male body she had ever seen, turned toward her now, standing full-length, encased in its own rectangle of night, propped up like a newly excavated golden statue from a Pharaoh's tomb—he was that still, frozen in surprise. Overcome by the equally powerful sense of shame and decency, she snapped off the flashlight, and then kept snapping it on and off uncontrollably.

The naked man, and now she could see he was young, oh, so unbelievably young, though his body was gloriously muscled and decorated with body-hair, kept standing, catatonic as a rabbit suddenly come upon. She directed the beam alternately, here, there, stigmatizing him like a Saint Sebastian receiving arrows of light. It was deliriously beautiful, yet too painful to bear, and the pulse of the light went slower. The swimmer still did not move, though she could hear him dripping as if he might be preparing to melt, and her hand seemed stuck to the flashlight. They were in some kind of impossible matrix together—nothing would come of it, but nothing need come of it but itself. It, quite simply, should last forever.

Common sense, of which she had had, through exposure, more than her share, and so must have more, would later have to admit that this stasis wedged in a staccato play of light could not have lasted more than seconds before she heard the sound of tires crunching on the gravel, the brakes slamming on half way up the drive. Having seen the startling semaphore in the garden, Gus came around the corner of the house, quickly enough, but by no means frantically. Must he for the rest of his life, Elaine had time to think, *always* come on like Jove?

"What on earth are you doing out here at this time of night, Elaine?" was all he bothered to ask before taking the flashlight as if she were a woman gone berserk with a dangerous weapon. Deftly plunging his hand into the thorns without even catching his sleeve, he turned on the lights like a stage setting. If for one burning moment Elaine—and what could an American do but live in everybody else's classical myths—reveled in a touch of Phèdre, Hippolytus across the pool was having none of it. He had just drawn a large white towel up to his chin, now trembling and rather exhausted-looking, a bronze charioteer in his makeshift chiton.

Elaine looked at the face of the swimmer, conscious now that she had seen it before but had not wanted to take it in, having stylized it to go with the body. A young man, a handsome, but ordinary, young man was acting as if he had been caught in a tabloid set-up. Tony Stephani and Elaine Morrison in flagrante delicto—was that how it was always said? He was, of course, the same Tony who sometimes vacuumed the pool when Larry was laid up with a bad back, and did a little hit-or-miss gardening. He had been a champion swimmer at the local high school, and was going out for the team at the University of Connecticut that fall. Gus had even given him some pointers from his own famous past. He might have been the son they had never had. It had an ironic Oedipal touch about it, a motif in reverse working itself up through layered abstraction.

Unbelievably, though he did it as if you could pay for a dream as easily as a case of beans, Gus reached into his pocket for his wallet, took out two tens and a five, and gave them to Tony who accepted them, almost dropping his drapery in one last fumbling act of slapstick striptease. Gus, looking like a direct descendant of the Father of his Country, was paying him off as if he were a male whore.

"Gee, thanks, Mr. Morrison," he said, darting a glance at Elaine, the obvious heavy of the piece. "I'm sorry it didn't work out though." The towel had a secure twist in it now, and he was just a high school lad who had come in from the showers. He turned for his valedictory to Elaine for he was, after all, a good American boy. "I hope you're not mad, Mrs. Morrison. I never thought you would come down like this. It was only a joke." Still a little stylish to the last, he walked out of range in his best athletic manner, buoyant on the balls of his feet, and disappeared into the bushes like the German shepherd.

Elaine turned to Gus. "You son of a bitch! Why did you do it?" she exploded, filled in part with molten anger and with, as yet, some curiously undefined feeling.

Gus began cautiously like a man who had been handling a hot woman much too long. "I'm not exactly sure I know. You were so hung up about the pool. I thought it was the right thing to do."

"Don't give me that. You're not the kind that doesn't exactly know. You have reasons for everything. So reason number one, number two, number three, if you please, and I may not stop counting until you get to the real reason if it takes all night."

"I thought it would cheer you up."

"That's not a reason. That's an emotional evasion. Let *me* take care of how I feel." But while casting about so angrily, so emphatically, she realized that her filmy chiffon robe blowing in the wind made her look like a bacchante, compromising her words absurdly.

"That's just it. I wasn't sure you could. I wanted to help."

Gus, on the other hand, was in no mood of the satyr. Now that he had paid off the illicit help, give him a bell and he could make the Salvation Army playing the provinces before Christmas. "Oh, come off of it. You wanted to make me look like a fool. You did it because you—" and she paused as though it were a word she had kept in solitary confinement for several years—"hate me."

He looked at her without acknowledgment. "I thought it had gone too far. Someone had to do something."

"Go on. I'm listening and not believing a word," she said, but even as she spoke, beset with a sense of diminuendo, aware that for all her resentment she had not been able to come up with even one "As I was saying. . . ." Was Gus beginning to interest her at last? Or, was it again?

This was costing him plenty. She could see that. Under that business suit, a wrestler was sweating, but indurated, isometric Gus was going to press one thing against another if it killed him.

"Look, Ellie," he said. "I don't know how to say this without sounding corny. But we have squared off for some time now. And it's got something to do with the goddamned pool—how we look at it—how I think of it, and I think it's fair to say, how you *feel* about it. But I'm a lawyer. I don't believe in insoluble problems."

"Oh, I know you don't. Oh, how I know you don't."

"Could we cut the sarcasm for a minute? You won't believe this, but Tony was sort of my idea of letting you feel the way you wanted to feel—at least for a while."

"Until you could knock some sense into me?"

"Not at all. I was worried. I thought you had lost something I was counting on you to keep for both of us."

"Namely, my mind?"

"No. A proposal, if you will, a proposition."

Even now, she thought, he couldn't help dropping into legalese. "You have strange ways of making a point."

"I can't help it if we articulate differently," he said. "There was a time when I thought we had reached an agreement. But then I was not sure. I hoped Tony would trigger the situation."

"*À la recherche du temps perdu?*"

"In a way."

"And you're the one who ate the *madeleine?*"

"In a manner of speaking," he said sheepishly, and turned away before her fluent imagination could make anything too Proustian of it.

She did not continue, but took off her robe, nightgown, everything, and plunged in, swimming back and forth as if she were gunning for the Olympics, back and forth, dragging one fragment after another of the heavy, heaped up collage she had been trying to mount from those shifting pieces assembled by main force from too many shells, maneuvering them into a manageable texture with the power of her body until she was moving in a seamless painting. Out of the corner of her eye, she saw Gus pulling off his clothes, leaving them in the most unlegal pile any blowzy romanticist could have desired. Why hadn't she noticed before he could still look like long-locked Tony shorn of his wig— the naked swimmer, taking his place beside her, stroke by stroke, hard as a bronze to her touch. This man was inlaid with blue, he was matted with flowers—it was he who was the source of hallucination. She would never again in all her life want to understand him completely. Leave that to women who had no lust for ambiguity. Leave it to the one who had not suffered a ghost at noon.

The question, nevertheless, remained: What is the power of a proposition? Elaine realized the issue would never have arisen and she would not have been able to ask it of herself if the naked swimmer had not come to her aid and provided the brilliant, enigmatic, pictorial occasion. It was built into her life now, that beam, that pulse of light uncontrollably turning off and on, the stigma, the stability, and, yes, the irrational surrender, the wandering floral specter—the stereoscopic glamor of images. If one could answer a question by asking another: What would we do without them?

The Leech in the Chinese Rain Hat

I have known Jonathan Barley now for thirty-five years. In fact, I am his oldest friend, and I do not think anything would induce him to give me up. He lives in England, I live in Connecticut, and we do not see each other much more than once a year, but there is a viscous quality in our relationship which has been able to stretch across time and place, and if it were released or broken now, I think it would snap and thrash around me like the thick coils of some subliminal creature.

The metaphor of our friendship was provided long ago by the students at the university. Good ruddy North Carolina country boys, with here and there a sprinkling of more sophisticated types, they were conformists all, and Jonathan Barley was just the sort to make them feel they were right about everything. His name amused them. His totally unathletic build, poor coordination, the way he rolled the blue eyes in his enormous head shaped like an inverted pear, his general sloppiness, the slightly fermented odor of his body, gave these lusty, centrally focused young men the eccentric which made their world safe and wonderful.

Moreover, far from being hostile, Barley seemed to welcome their jibes, any form of notice that came his way. He employed his peculiarities the way most people use their most attractive qualities—I have never known anyone more intent on making friends by any means whatever. It was as though friendship were the great unknown in his life. Somewhere someone would tolerate him long enough to teach him what it is.

He let it be known that he spoke Chinese, and indeed he did with much grunting and blowing from the nose so that one of the football players said he sounded like "an elephant farting through his trunk." It became a general indulgence to stop Barley on the campus for a session of China-baiting. He always responded with good humor, looking hungrily at his interlocutors, his loose mouth hanging open like a suction cup. It was the active submissiveness that finally earned him the nickname of "The Leech," and the country boys waded through him as if they did not have an extra drop of blood to spare.

I took several classes with Barley, and since my name happens to be Reed Rice, this in itself paired us together in the humor of the undergraduates. A fraternity man, a good athlete like myself, did not have to worry too much about his image. It did not bother me that the other fellows called us "the guys from the grainery," or sometimes, "the silo boys," and I began to think of it as a distinction to have Jonathan as a friend. After all, no one else liked me all *that* much, and youth easily settles into unequal relationships of admirer and admired.

As Jonathan became more obviously a protégé, I even encouraged his Chinese proclivities. He blossomed out on occasion in a coolie costume. But one spring day when it had been raining, I was not prepared for his emergence in a large, weird contraption which he had made himself and called a Chinese rain hat. It was lacquered a bright green on the outside and sat on his head like a parasol. If one had any imagination at all, it began to create a montage effect. Beneath it, Jonathan's large face seemed to swell in its proportions, more impressive than ever before, monolithic, like a carving under the eaves of a pagoda. This melted back, of course, when he bobbed his head too vigorously, and the hat slipped to one side, an enormous dripping saucer someone had crowned him with.

It began to rain again and when I joined him half-way underneath, I said, "You've done it this time, boy. You'll never get away with it."

"Why not?" he asked. "Much more practical than an umbrella. Leaves my hands free to carry my books."

"And to fight off the local gentry as well?"

"Now, Reed," he said, drawling heavily in a tone that always made me feel the need to substantiate what I was saying. "Who would want to do a thing like that?"

I ignored his question, looked up, and saw that the inside of the rain hat was painted a vivid blue. "All this and heaven too?"

"Yes," he said slyly. "It makes me feel the sun is shining even when it's raining."

Two heads under a bright bowl must have been too much for one of our professors who passed us, and he never seemed easy with us in class after that. The rain hat, of course, did not get accepted as such. Some called it the "Green Pee Pot"; the football players, who began to avoid me as well, referred to it as the "Fruit Bowl." To accept an invitation in under the rain hat for a steamy little session was as good as posing for a caricature in the college *Buccaneer.* Once when I returned to the dormitory after dinner, I found on my desk a dead white rat on a plate with a knife, fork, and folded paper napkin beside it, the gift, no doubt, of some science major.

My conservative parents disapproved of the association, my older brothers threatened to take me down to the barber shop and have my head shaved and plaited in pigtails, and I might have yielded to their pressure, except, even then, I found the world so boring. Consequently, those college years which might have passed uneventfully are staccato with images: Jonathan driving our gym instructor to distraction with his pratfalls, trotting through the campus with books swinging from either end of a bamboo pole, Jonathan entangling his Chinese kites in the trees of the arboretum, or staying after class in Victorian Lit to sit in the lotus position like a late, late Buddha on the desk of Dr. Hooker, arguing some minuscule point with the fastidious, high-collared professor—Jonathan pulling his long face and saying, "Now Reed . . ." when I became too coercive or autocratic.

Summer was hard for us both since I was required to go home to Charlotte and he to the little mill town where his father was postmaster. It was a test as to just how stretchable a relationship like ours could be. I grew irritable and felt bloated with idleness during the long hot days, feral with tiger lilies in July, hectic with crepe myrtle in August, when the obscure psychic buildup of late adolescence had no outlet. Jonathan wrote regularly long ornate letters that looked as though they had been done with a brush, while I condescended with postcards.

Then came the first of his fabulous maneuvers, worthy of the intrigue of the Chinese Court. He persuaded his neurotic mother to invite me for a visit to Batesville. I was to be handled like royalty, called for and delivered by Jonathan's father, and a whole list of activities and entertainments was projected. It was clear that no one had ever visited Jonathan before, and since the protocol of the situation had no precedent, everything was overdone: special food they couldn't afford, a constant watchfulness for any sign of tedium on my part, and an almost suffocating deference from every member of the family, including Tom, the younger brother, a wastrel and a hellion, but, nevertheless, much preferred by his mother since he appeared "normal."

My background has taught me to be a master of pretense, and Mrs. Barley who tried to take me into her confidence was constantly put off by my unwillingness to cooperate.

"I do wish you would speak to Jonathan about his clothes," she said when he was out of the room. "I can't do anything with him. His father and I are so worried."

"You should see how some of the other boys dress, Mrs. Barley. No socks, no ties. They're all a bunch of Sloppy Joes."

"I didn't mean that, Mr. Rice. I mean *how* he dresses."

Though the Barley-Rice exchange seemed too ludicrous for words, I kept a straight face and said, "Well, at least Jonathan isn't dull."

"Oh? Perhaps not, perhaps not. I suppose college boys always have a whimsical turn of mind," she said unhappily. "I just don't know what will become of him in the long run."

Though I had my doubts myself, I was not going along and have her turn into a leech of another sort, one that fed on tears. I said more sententiously than I should, "Let the long run take care of itself, Mrs. Barley. Life is made up of a lot of little short runs that succeed, and your son hasn't been sent home from the university yet, has he?"

Jonathan, who as far as I could discover resented no one, did not even seem to dislike his mother. He treated her many moods with boisterous, irrelevant laughter or Chinese solemnity, staring at her as if he were trying to understand what on earth she was talking about. Only if her petulance was exceptional would his face grow pink, his loose mouth pucker up like that of a child about to cry, and there was something suctorial about his subjection as if, after all these years, there should be something more in her to extract than this.

Looking back now, it seems that the country boys and the football players were not as hard on Jonathan as they might have been, and I was perhaps closer to what he desired of me than I was ever to be thereafter. College boys, or so it could have been said of my generation at least, had no real power and tended to extrovert their latent cruelties in jokes and pranks. Jonathan did not have to be disposed of because he did not get in the way of anybody's vested social interests or encrusted view of life. Even in my case, he was mainly a diversion. I did not have to fit him into any permanent scheme of things. Jonathan in the sustained camaraderie and leisure of the campus was one thing, in the world, another, and I can see now that this was what his pathetic mother foresaw.

After we graduated there was a long interval in which Jonathan receded, becoming more or less spectral to me like a Chinese lantern bobbing in the dark haze of forgotten college friendships. I went to one graduate school, he to another where the Oriental studies were particularly good. Marriage and career loomed ahead—I must put away childish things, and Jonathan seemed of the most infantile I could recall, belonging to a time when self-love is able to avoid any contact that might sting or deplete it like a bee. Jonathan had flitted about me, bright, lacquered, zany and amusing, but I had kept most of the nectar as balm for future wounds.

But this was my idea, not his. Since a car was beyond his means, he bought a motorcycle and came roaring into Cambridge, crash helmet and all, usually around exam week or some equally inopportune time. His enormous head stuffed in the oversized helmet looked as weird, and a good deal less amusing, than in the rain hat, and, like many a hard-pressed graduate student, I suppose I had begun to lose my sense of humor.

Moreover, it became clearer and clearer that the modern world was too much for the dreamer from Batesville. On a rocking horse he might have been a winner, on a motorcycle he could one day be easily catapulted out of control. As he became mobile, he seemed more disturbing and irrational, and one wondered how much longer he would be able to land on his feet. His motorcycle broke down, he got lost constantly, and was stopped by cops for various infractions of the law. His leather jacket and baggy pants were packed with innumerable schedules, directions, and memoranda to himself, and, hanging on a long chain which ran from his belt to his pants pocket was a collection of keys that could have belonged to the warden of the unknown. The ecology of the rain hat was now as diffuse and vast as the sky itself.

It was about this time, I suppose, that I tried to construct another persona for Jonathan, or so I thought then, but now I wonder if he did not lure me into being a kind of paternal constructivist. Since I did not have too much time to devote to him, I thought in my ambitious graduate student way that we should make it count. Anybody studying *Beowulf* for three hours a day has had enough of monsters, and my approach to Jonathan became briskly clinical. He always brought me a large platter of problems and difficulties, and I cut them up for him as if I were feeding a child.

But then just as I was completing my graduate studies, the war came along and tossed up greater chunks of the unexpected and irrational than even my bright engine could handle. My dreams of pushing on were exploded overnight, and what homilies and exhortations still held water were sorely needed for application to myself. An eye injury in childhood put me in Naval Intelligence and kept me in the United States. Jonathan, however, was immediately drafted and shunted around the country as unreliably, I thought, as any explosive in our arsenal.

It turned out, however, ironically enough, that we managed the war about equally well at first. I took it seriously, whereas his approach was unintentionally comic. I recognized another kind of Establishment, adapted myself to it, but Jonathan, I am told, one day "sounded off" in Chinese. His habit of leaving his trousers unzipped earned the new nickname of "One Hung Low," and his sergeant found him one morning in the lotus position meditating by his cot. Long before the war was over, he was cashiered out with a pension as a psychological casualty. For the first time in our relationship, I was jealous of Jonathan. He had succeeded by failing.

Since we could not really meet and I would not write, he evolved what he called his "Continental Communication Service." He would compose letters to himself filled with blanks, and all I had to do was check alternatives, interpose missing words, and return the letters to him. It was surprising how clever he was at reproducing my tone, and I sometimes had the eerie feeling that more of my civilian life was in his keeping than in my own. I found this system of communication not only undemanding but curiously calming: the great fatigue of being Reed Rice was being handled by my former consultant. Somewhere sleeping in every man is the desire to be a leech.

But if war toyed with our relative positions, the armistice belonged to me. I had finished my Ph.D., married, got a good job at the University of Kansas in furious reassertion and reaction. There was nothing for Jonathan to do but reattach himself to the source of energy which was going to run the postwar world after all, and he came to me wanting a blueprint for peace.

Since I had always counseled persistence, concentration, and order, we talked things over and he decided to study Library Science at the University of North Carolina as something that would force him into methodical discipline. It took a load off my mind since Jonathan wanted me to "place" him, and I had put him somewhere comparatively safe for the next few years.

Meanwhile, Carolyn and I quickened our pace as young American couples are likely to do. It was the next bit of progress, the new acquisition, the next deal or plan that made us feel, at least kinetically, movers in our time, but there among his card catalogues, I could feel Jonathan growing heavier, lagging farther behind. Whenever I was feeling low, some memory of him would wriggle reductively past like a worm I had divided once too often. Again, in more resigned moods, I could sense him, always surrounding me, far off, vaguely comforting, like the serpent swallowing his tail.

But since American education adores the underachiever, Jonathan got his degree, or this was my judgment on the matter at the time. Recommended by me and the university he even got a job as head librarian at a little teacher's college in New England. That year very few letters with blanks to be filled in came from Jonathan, and those that did were Kafkaesque in their mystification. No one was mentioned by name, but there were hints of a plot to undermine him. Even at so great a distance, one could sense the tension growing in his large head as if a cistern had been called upon to handle the resources of a dam.

The following August when he turned up in Charlotte where Carolyn and I were vacationing with my parents, he looked like a figure of edema. Sitting with us under the raw sensuality of the crepe myrtles, his cheeks were hectically moist, there was sweat under his eyes, and he smelled of cancerous defeat.

Since it was clear he had come to be drained, I got right to the point. "How do you like New England? How's the work going?"

"Well, Reed . . ." he said and paused, staring at me like a doll whose eyes were stuck.

"You always wanted to live in New England," I prompted.

"Yes, I did." He shifted one large haunch and a squeak of gas suggested a slight puncture had been made somewhere.

"Must have been a good place for winter sports," dear Carolyn put in as she searched wildly for an entrée.

A blush started somewhere in Jonathan's shoes and flowered furiously as if his face were chameleonic beneath the crepe myrtles. "Yes, Carolyn, it was," he drawled and waited helplessly for her to proceed with the development of her gaffe.

The silence became engorged, empurpled, as they both looked to me as the only one who could lance it.

"When do you have to go back?" I asked, and Jonathan, with obvious relief, began to suppurate. "You are going back?" I plunged the scalpel into the heart of festering matter.

"Well, Reed . . ." Jonathan began again, and then mumbled his story like a patient under anaesthesia who could drift off in the calm belief that I would deal with him surgically.

He had had two assistants at the college, and this in itself presented a labyrinth of human relations since he had never in his life had to tell anyone to do anything. In his effort to initiate reform, he had gotten hopelessly entangled in trying to transfer the collection from the old-fashioned methods of his predecessor to the Dewey decimal system. By spring no one knew where anything was, and the library was totally inoperative. At the end of the term, the president had fired him in an excess of rage with the parting shot that "people like him ought to be locked up," and that "he had done twenty thousand dollars worth of damage to the library."

When the story was finished, stretched out like a new lake of sorrow on the New England landscape, I wasted no time reading the riot act to Jonathan. I explained his errors and misunderstandings to him, and, I suppose, explained them away. I sutured him with reproof, reproach, and advice for the future, and he got up from my ministrations like Lazarus. I still cared, I was still interested. That was enough for Jonathan. When he left, he had tightened up and actually looked ten pounds lighter, but I felt the heavy increment left with me. Had I any right to encourage him? Was I releasing into the world a victim or victimizer?

After that, Jonathan went back to the safer sphere of arts and crafts. He attempted pottery, but his hand had a quirk in it which produced little hernias of irregular modeling on all his pieces. He tried making tiles since he had heard they would sell, but insisted on decorating them with inlays of silver and priced himself out of the market. These failures were deposited in my lap, and I was called upon to tell him what to do next. Having been handed chunks of misadventure so often with no instructions except my own as to how to rebuild the person Jonathan wanted to be, I felt that I put back together a somewhat smaller person each time and would one day end up like a wicked sorcerer with a toadish little mannikin at my feet.

Finally, however, since I had no ready answer for the first time in our long acquaintance, I forced myself to think about Jonathan rather than the next move I might suggest. Had he ever progressed in my imagination beyond that picturesque collegiate image of the kookie boy in the rain hat? Pushing ourselves and our possessions along in the world, we frequently let our friends accompany us as little more than counters of their former selves, but imagination saved only for oneself as we make the painful solipsistic thrust into the future is blind at least in one eye. What did I really have on my hands in the person of Jonathan?

I came to the conclusion that I did not know him and probably never had. What was he really like apart from our brief, pictorial encounters? He stank of loneliness but only like sulphur on a passing breeze. What was his experience of living entirely in its fetor? There is a time in youth when loneliness can be like a fresh lover in your bed, but it grows flatulent and flaccid with age, the slut who has pretended to you all your life that things will be better.

I had to admit that the flesh of our relationship was literally scythed with unanswered questions. What did Jonathan do for a sex life? Had he ever touched a woman? Did he have fantasies that filled the underworld with such passionate force he was aware in every social encounter that all of the meat of life was underfoot? Did Rimbaud's *la nuit seule* sometimes really give him the day on fire so that at least he had a hectic sense of existential extremes? Or were all of his powers consumed merely in the mechanics of living? Moreover, did he perhaps *prefer* to live like a figure of allegory? Were there, in fact, many people like him in the world who were nothing but pictured forms in the minds of others?

But it would not, I knew, do any good to go too far down the unused road of sentiment. I had been giving directions too long when I really did not know the way for Jonathan. No one can release another from the allegorical prison. Not once had he ever challenged me, shaken me up, forced me to think of him in any other fashion, demanded that I give him room to grow in my developing imagination. If one thought about him too hard, one could grow slightly sadistic about his passivity. He imposed a presence, but he did not want to inject himself with full vitality into the three-dimensional human scene. If Jonathan had meant all along to infect my life with guilt and obliquely turn the tables on his teacher, I did not need, no matter how picaresquely presented, a long, sustained instruction in how visible life can be flattened into a form of Loneliness.

So, after this latest series of fiascoes, I took a new tack. I did not try to change Jonathan. I did not advise him unless he absolutely forced the issue. When he came to see us, I listened without raising any objections to his latest proposals and ventures no matter how impractical they were. I simply blessed him and let him go. I pointed out the difficulties of my own life, pockmarked the idol as much as I could, let him know in many subtle ways I was not the person he seemed to think I was. It was a red-letter day for Jonathan if he could successfully attach his siphon and get the old warm flow of homily and solicitude which could make his future seem a matter of importance.

But, curiously enough, all this accomplished was to age our relationship in a manner I had not counted on. I was enjoying an extended physical youth—no gray hair, no paunch, few, if any, lines in my face, and I am fastidious in the extreme. So it was disconcerting that as I began to push Jonathan away emotionally, he became more physical with me. His fat, moist fingers lingered longer when we shook hands, he sat closer, got in my way, it seemed, so that I jostled against him. And, all the while, he dressed more sloppily, grew more obese, grayer, and could hardly sit still for an hour without farting like a man stuffed with stink bombs. Sitting before me like the portrait of Dorian Gray, he seemed to draw from me all the physical poisons my system refused to absorb. The old compulsive guilt and concern for his welfare mounted, and on one of his visits, I jacked him up about his appearance. He thanked me for my "long-playing advice" and went away like a man who had not had a good fix in a long time, leaving me with needle in hand and a criminal feeling about life in general.

I have spoken of the imagination as the propulsive force in life, and, up to a point, indeed it is. Think, plan, dream something, and, in part, it begins to exist until one reaches the wall of one's own future. We can dream for a long time, and this in itself provides enough kinetic thrust to give us the feeling that we are moving toward a goal. But at some point in the forties, except in very rare individuals, the imagination begins to weaken, and the wall of the future seems to come in closer, to jut toward us rather than stretch back before the momentum of our approach. One is not going to be president, become a millionaire, one is not, as in my case, going to be a Kittredge or a John Livingston Lowes.

It is then that people like Jonathan may begin to have their first illusion of catching up. They have survived too, and, ironically, with one-tenth of the effort of persistent dreamers. They have had their dreams as well, but have simply let them float along. Forced to come to terms with reality only occasionally, as Jonathan did in the New England library, they have learned the pure art of fantasy which bumps into walls but only as mists do.

This moratorium between stress and fantasy came later to us than it does to some, but there were a few years when my full professorship did not materialize and none of my critical books won the National Book Award that the distance between myself and Jonathan seemed largely chimerical. Carolyn and I began to accept him simply for what he was—avuncular in friendship, the ancestor of all my acquaintances, poignant in the long, drawn-out ceremony of sequential devotion. He had the grotesque glamor of one who had traveled all over the world in search of friendship. Carolyn even overcame some of her feelings of physical repugnance and began to speak of him wryly as our "Senior Eccentric."

It might have ended there—all of us waiting at the wall, subdued and patient, with Jonathan now having perhaps a slight edge on things, nice and goofy as an old Chinese genie whose flesh could turn to smoke when it struck against stone. He enjoyed those years like none since we were two boys standing under the rain hat.

But the wall suddenly shook itself free of the stalled imagination and took a giant step forward on its own. My father died, leaving me an ample income, and Carolyn, the children, and I moved to Connecticut where I could pursue my critical studies unhampered by departmental politics and the jealousy of colleagues. Imagination began to strain forward again, lean and leathery as its neck now might be, scanning that wall with the hardened, practical vision of the fifties. Not long after, Jonathan's bitch of a mother died and left him a considerably more modest income, but, combined with his pension, enough for him to don for good whatever kind of hat he chose to wear.

It put us back on the old footing immediately. What were we going to do about it all? If I were to proceed as before, but now with caution, where was he to live? What could a man of many parts not very conventionally put together do but circulate? After several sessions and proposals, he decided, with my blessing, to live in England since he had a distant cousin in Wales. There was also a London friend who was something of a Sinologue, others in Paris, Majorca, whom he had met on his travels, and one or two acquaintances more distantly placed. No doubt he exercised a certain canniness in choosing England, which has had a long and honorable tradition of offbeat characters.

In any case, he settled down to cultivate his garden on a far-flung, world-wide scale in such a manner as would have amazed and perhaps amused Voltaire who originated the phrase on more intimist terms. Making his plans months in advance, he would go half-way across the world to have lunch with someone in Hong Kong or dinner with Carolyn and myself in Meadowmount. Perhaps the preparations, the logistics, the effort of the journey itself, made him feel that he was actually spending longer with his friends than he was. He always arrived heavily encumbered with baggage, cameras, equipment, as if for a lengthy stay, and invariably showed photographs, colored slides, and memorabilia of places where this or that person who still tolerated him lived. He was like a landscape architect who had to carry with him the evidence of all his constructions and plans. So many beautiful scenes, and here and there the shadow of a human being. It produced in the viewer the eerie feeling that there were perhaps only two or three people left in the entire voluptuously beautiful world and that Jonathan worked tirelessly at keeping them alive. One paused in the midst of furious activity to admit him like some mysterious doctor burdened with nostalgia over the imminent death of human contact. With his exquisite sense of place, attendant on "the world's body," he nevertheless diffused an anxiety of vacuity. Hopping from island to island, treading softly from one place to another in search of those who would agree to discount the abysses that lay around them, he seemed to be warily drawing together the rich contingency of nature and human nature that was stretched out of all proportion, limp, and full of holes like an old net of meaning of which too much had been demanded. It gave us a rarified feeling of figures in a rotted sieve.

It seemed curious that this mood should have come over us when the world, in fact, was becoming dangerously filled with people in the extremes of confrontation. But, most depressing of all, Jonathan pointed up the fact that the huge, meaty world had no spiritual center anymore. When so many were "freaking out," there was no way in which one could be gently and picturesquely off-center. Where any form of behavior was readily accepted and soon became conventional, Jonathan seemed now oddly old-fashioned—solicitous, even gallant, in his peculiarities. Compared with a bearded young man who strolled on stage nude or a girl who walked down the street in a black cape and hip boots like a spider with patent-leather legs, Jonathan had lost all status as an eccentric except in the eyes of a few of us—reliquary, shadowy, fragile figures who must somehow be kept alive.

The last time he came, loaded with the impedimenta of a call he had made most recently on Jorge in Majorca, he looked more heavily encrusted than ever before, like an Ivan Le Lorraine Albright "There Came Into The World A Soul Named Jonathan." His old dark blue suit was decorated with the squama of soup he had spilled, things he had sat in, paint and ink stains here and there—a patina of persistence, the ontogeny of his faithful journey.

When he shook my hand, he lingered even longer than usual, as if he were taking my pulse.

"You're looking well," he said, and I wondered if I really were.

He embraced Carolyn as one might kiss a spoiled little girl who might not recover from some illness of which only you were aware. He gave her a package which contained a small, perky bird of blue crystal, exquisitely done, and then sat down heavily at the apex of our triangle so that he could keep us both clearly in view.

"I need your advice," he said, and I marveled at the way in which he reached for that persona as if it were still as delicate and lithe as a figure in a Chinese print.

Nevertheless, I brightened immediately like a man who had been given a benzedrine. Carolyn giggled and said quickly before I had time to come out with anything serious and ponderous, "Oh, Jonathan. You are priceless. You never give up, do you? How can we advise you about anything?"

Jonathan looked uneasy as if his visit had not taken effect, and I knew it was time to roll up my sleeve and extend the arm for puncture. "Let the man talk, Carolyn," I said.

"I am thinking of making a change," he plodded on. "I've stayed rather long enough in England. I'm looking around for another place to locate myself. What would you think of my settling down somewhere in Connecticut?"

If he had said Meadowmount, I think both Carolyn and I would have felt that we were in the hands of Svengali.

"I don't know about that, Jonathan," I temporized. "Would it be as convenient, I wonder, as a base of operations? We would love to have you closer by, of course, but you might find it rather slow after London."

"Then what would you advise?" he asked amiably, even, I thought, with relief.

"Connecticut looks greener than it is," I said as I gained momentum. "There are nematodes in every soil. I don't know whether you would like it here."

"Well, Reed . . . ," he said with an old tired smile of gratitude. "You're always right. I can count on that." He turned to Carolyn expansively. "You know, there's nothing like having a friend you can turn to."

"And you are my oldest friend, Jonathan. You are indeed."

For a moment, the old tone was there. I had relieved us of the world as it threatened to be. The terror had been in the complex shifting around us of possibilities which had taken place lately. If I had yielded, if I had said, Come to Connecticut, I think Jonathan would have given up all hope. But he had to test us, reaffirm the fact that, as he experienced the term, we were still among the living. The trick lay in refusing to acknowledge the overpowering patchiness of things, in manipulating topography to defeat the desert. So far, so good. There were green spots in the great stretched view which a man of many parts could quilt together. The enchanted, shadowy garden had survived.

When he left that evening, noticing that it was raining lightly, I asked as I handed him his battered fedora, stained, empurpled with age, rococo in the associations it summoned up, "Whatever happened to the rain hat?"

Jonathan grunted, wriggled boisterously with laughter like an old fat snake dancing on his tail. "Now, Reed . . . ," he said. "Can't you see? I'm still wearing it."

So Jonathan was still with us, stuck, it would seem, not so much in our flesh as on the surface of the past as if for no other reason than to show us that the stony-seeming body still ran blood. In a very real sense he would not let the spirit of our youth calcify. He had the greatest gift for the vicarious of anyone I have ever known, capturing us long ago in a conclusive field of feeling— "Forever wilt thou love, and she be fair"—and I suppose our greatest failure had been in not seeing that he was the poet of our experience. We have always wished to conclude, to terminate, to arrive, but neither Meadowmount nor my father's money has prevailed against the modern world. If Carolyn and I have learned anything, it is how inconclusive life is when it does not carry with it its own radiant atmosphere of contained devotion. It has been heartbreaking to at least conclude that all along our methods may have been our motives. The trip was the treasure. Linear types like us may not necessarily get any further than those who visit in meandering fashion the corners of a sickened garden.

At this point we reach a conclusion of a sort, and I wish I could leave it at that. Plateaus, even with misty views around them, are more pleasant than always climbing or going down. One might say that we have gone as far with meaning as most of us would like to go, but plot has a way of wanting to drive in deeper as if to see if we have really hit the quick of the matter. So there is a postscript. Jonathan did come to Connecticut after all.

On a lovely afternoon last summer, Carolyn and I were sitting in our garden cherishing ourselves for having lived another day when a telegram arrived from Jorge in Majorca saying that Jonathan had died of a heart attack. The news overwhelmed us, for more than I think we realized we had counted on Jonathan as an unobtrusive fixture of the years ahead. It was as though we sat on a beautiful but flimsy piece of material which had suddenly become unstitched from everything around it. For the moment we had the feeling of floating in absolutely nothing. The point of the needle that patched things together, searching quietly through the further reaches of plot, had broken off in the hard flesh of time.

But the next day even these images were not left to us, for we came down from our detachment onto parts of the world which we had been persuaded were not there at least as far as Jonathan was concerned. A lawyer in North Carolina telephoned us to say that he had also received a wire from Majorca and had been instructed, in this event, to inform us of the contents of Mr. Barley's will. All of his material possessions were to go to Jorge in Majorca, but Mr. Barley had willed us his body.

No one else would have thought of this way of making a permanent visit. Even in our stunned condition we had to grant the wit, the originality of invention. No excuses, no evasions were possible now. We were going to have him on our hands for good. In one master stroke he had made himself into a real person.

So Jonathan is buried in our little cemetery in Meadowmount. We never opened the coffin when it arrived. We simply did not have the courage for that. But we have finally stopped resenting this final touch of black humor. It seems the right thing for him to have done. Jonathan saw that perhaps he had been too subtle, and we had missed the point. We temporize for the sake of the things we love. We use the powers of levitation to moor a magic carpet here and there, make every connective gesture at our disposal, will an idea or an obsession for as long as we can. But one cannot conclude by leaving the world suspended in a dream.